PACK

PACK

MIKE BOCKOVEN

Talos Press

Skyhorse Publishing books may be purchased in bulk at special discounts for sales promotion, corporate gifts, fund-raising, or educational purposes. Special editions can also be created to specifications. For details, contact the Special Sales Department, Skyhorse Publishing, 307 West 36th Street, 11th Floor, New York, NY 10018 or info@ skyhorsepublishing.com.

Talos Press® is a registered trademark of Skyhorse Publishing, Inc.®, a Delaware corporation.

Visit our website at www.skyhorsepublishing.com.

10 9 8 7 6 5 4 3 2 1

Library of Congress Cataloging-in-Publication Data is available on file.

Cover design by Rain Saukas
Cover Art by Keith Negley

Print ISBN: 978-1-9458-6325-7
Ebook ISBN: 978-1-9458-6326-4

Printed in the United States of America

For a good dad and a strong mom.

PART 1 - TWO IN THE GROUND

It took a lot for Byron Matzen to admit he had made a mistake, but as his best friends in the world came from his blood, Byron had to admit they might have a point.

Seconds before he had given them absolution, at least as much as he could muster given the circumstances. When they first came to him, armed with the truth, he had cried and he had yelled, he had blamed anyone and everyone in ear shot. He had blamed the devil and his minions, his own damnable weak will and, before the end, he had blamed his friends, telling them they just didn't get it. They didn't know. A town like this couldn't hold a person like him, he was destined for more, for better and he was going to get it, even if it meant . . .

He didn't finish because, by then, he knew. He could see it in their eyes, a potent mix of disappointment and rage. To put it bluntly, he'd done fucked up and there was no fixing it, no unscrewing this pooch. He had betrayed his friends and he had meant to turn them over to those who would hurt them, maybe kill them and now, brother, the bill was due. And it was steep.

As if outside his body, Byron understood what was going to happen and what his part in it was, and in an act of rare selflessness, he gave it to them.

"Guys," he said, running his hand through his black hair which came away wet with sweat. "Guys, I . . . um . . . there's more."

No one prompted him. He had the floor.

"I killed Sandra, like, half an hour ago. Tore her up and left her behind the bar."

There was a gasp and the silence that followed him was deep as he struggled hard for the next series of words and the sweat from his scalp had slid down his minor sideburns and down his cheek.

"I did it because she was going to sell you out. She was going to take all my money and leave me and I don't blame her. I'm a piece of shit. I wouldn't want to run away with me, either. I thought, you know, a young thing like her next to me, money in my pocket, this town in my rear view . . ."

One of his friends, who had cornered him in his house outside of town, sniffled a bit. It was the closest he got to sympathy that night.

"I just want you to know I'm sorry. I did it all and I'm sorry and I know what you gotta do just . . ."

The wicked, barbed knot in his throat he had suppressed finally got the better of him and he choked on his own spit and tears, breaking down completely. He cried, bitterly, occasionally getting out a phrase like "we grew up together," and "I love you." It wasn't until he said "where's Josie" that he felt a fist slam into his right eye, driving him hard into a puddle of his own tears and snot that had collected on the concrete floor of the garage where he had been led.

"Please," Byron said. "I know I fucked up. I know you gotta do this but . . ."

"But what?" The leader of the group said, his voice already changing into something else.

"Please, remember me."

"Oh Byron," the voice said, getting deeper and deeper as it went. "I don't think we're ever going to forget you."

The next hit wasn't with a fist, but with sharp claws that widened into thick talons once inside his skin, as if fed and grown by his blood. The tearing started and the pain increased as his friends descended. Byron

2

screamed and bled and just before one of them took to his neck with their teeth and the end was in sight he tried, one last time, to make it right.

"I'm sorry," he said, half screaming, blood in his throat already threatening to drown him. "I'm so sorry."

The last thing Byron Matzen ever saw was his friend, whom he had wronged, spreading his massive jaws and plunging his top teeth straight into Byron's eyeballs as the bottom teeth did their bloody work piercing the underside of his jaw.

•••

As Byron was meeting his end, there was a full-on party happening a few blocks away.

From the splintering wooden motif on the outside to the inside full of barstools where the padding had worn down to the metal underneath, the lack of amenities at the bar at the end of the road was obvious. But, if those clues didn't do it for you, the name of the place certainly would. It was just called "Bar."

"Bar" was owned by Chuck Nesbit, who had graduated from high school in Cherry, Nebraska, in the late seventies. Chuck joined the Army, he traveled a bit, but when the juice you get with being young and dumb ran out he wandered back home. It was like that for a lot of folks in Cherry. Situated near the middle of the state, Cherry was near the highway, one of those towns people saw when they were going from place to place, but not anywhere they stopped. There was a gas station/grocery store. There were two churches, one Methodist and one E-Free. There were a few businesses along Main Street, an insurance storefront, an antique shop, a Subway. Then, there was "Bar", far away from Main Street, at the end of 3rd Street, half a block of nothing on two sides and trees and dirt on the other two.

Chuck had inherited the place from his dad, Jim. Since the sign that said "Jim's Bar" had lost the "Jim" part due to one particularly stormy spring, Chuck has not replaced it. Why would he? The sign said all it needed to say.

Usually, "Bar" did a fine business in the late afternoons, and always had someone hanging around in the summer, mainly because Chuck had bought a big-screen TV and a subscription to the MLB network. There were a few regulars who kept the place afloat, but Chuck never had anyone waiting to get in when he opened up around 11:00. There were no hours of operation on the door. There was a fish fry on Fridays and the occasional special food item. It kept the doors open. But, on the night of October 3rd, Chuck had gotten a wild hair up his ass and booked a band. He wasn't sure why he did it but it was easy-peasy. Two guys and one pretty red-haired girl formed a nice, solid trio and on the night of October 3rd, the dive bar had transformed into a moderately decent honky-tonk.

The band had started out with a few upbeat numbers, a few modern tunes like you'd hear on Country 96, one of only a few stations in the largely rural area Chuck deemed worth listening to, and then had slowed things down. The guy who sang and played guitar did a respectable "I Love This Bar," and, when the crowd of seventy or so seemed receptive to slow it down, the redhead belted out a "Stand By Your Man" that had beer mugs above heads, swaying in unison. Then, they hit the first few chords of "Friends in Low Places" and Chuck had never seen his bar quite so lively.

Everyone sang the country standard like they were singing from the Gospels, the melody giving way to atonal shouts as everyone strained to hear their own voices over the rest. Then the band took a break. That was when he first clocked Sandra at the jukebox, nestled smack between two halves of the long wooden bar along one side of the establishment. The chattering had died down when the first strains of a song Chuck didn't recognize started filling in the void, and Sandra Riedel, a local girl who did IT and other odd jobs at one of the elevators in town, started shaking her ample hips. The song had a solid, 4/4 time, and her hips hit on 2 and 4 with such precision that Chuck couldn't take his eyes off her. He had thirty years on the girl, easy, but that didn't stop him from looking. Other guys had noticed as well. In the absence of the band, Sandra's hips were, by a wide margin, the most interesting thing in the bar.

It was Byron Matzen who went up to her first, and given the situation, it was a gutsy move. Everyone knew Byron's situation, and they knew the last thing he needed to be doing was hitting on recent divorcees shaking their asses in a small-town bar, but up he went, like it was nothing. He grabbed her from behind and she slung her arm around his neck, looking up at him with her sad blue eyes and by the time the band was back, they were together, nuzzled up in one of Bar's three shabby booths. If it wasn't for the band, this would be big news. If it wasn't for the band, someone probably would have checked in on them. But dammit if that band wasn't really killing it tonight, Chuck thought. Besides, it wasn't his place to get involved. This sort of thing had a way of sorting itself out.

It was during the band's well-received rendition of "Red Solo Cup" that Chuck first noticed Sandra and Byron were gone. And it was a few songs later when they had ventured into rock with "More Than A Feeling" that he got more than a bad feeling. He went out to have a look around a few times, but the parking lot was full and it wasn't hard to see there was nothing going on. The party was inside and the party went and went and went until 12:30 when the band finally packed it up. Chuck paid them, gave them a little extra and hung around until 1:30, blowing another twelve-pack of beer on the band that had brought the folks in, just like they said they would. Then they left, everyone else cleared out and, before heading back to the trailer, he decided to have a good look around.

The parking lot was clear; the font had some vomit on it, but nothing major. The rain or the sun would take care of that, no problem. Chuck slowly strolled the perimeter, going over the night in his head. The image of Sandra's hips had lodged itself in his head as he rounded the corner and came upon the volleyball court. Years ago, a girl he was dating convinced him to put a volleyball court in the back. It had been used a grand total of six times, and cost him eight parking spaces, not that parking was an issue. Even on a busy night like this, the cars lined the streets and no one complained about walking half a block. But it required upkeep and that was something Chuck was not willing to provide, the practical result of which was a giant weed pile on the west side of his property.

That more-than-a-bad feeling started working its way from his stomach to his head and, on instinct, he went back in the bar and grabbed his Maglite. Once back at the volleyball court, it didn't take him long to find what he figured was there.

The weeds were up five feet high, and the blood had spattered all the way to the top of a patch of crabgrass. Chuck stood on the border of the court for a second and listened. He wasn't afraid. He likely knew what was in there and what he would find, plus, if old Byron was still in there and meant to do him harm, Chuck's options consisted of "standing there and taking it" and that was about it. But Byron wasn't in there, Chuck knew. He was long gone. The whole town knew he wasn't sticking around a lot longer, one way or another. Instead of any movement, all he heard was the wind and, for the first time in the season, he saw his breath. Thanks to the miracle of alcohol, Chuck hadn't noticed how cold it was, but it made sense. This was just the sort of night that Byron and his "friends" would love.

Chuck heaved a sigh and waded into the court. Sandra's body wasn't far. One of her arms was gone, torn off at the bicep leaving long strips of flesh, and her head was at an unnatural angle. She had a large gash in the side of her face that was visible, the other half pushed hard into the dirt. Chuck couldn't tell if her eyes were open or not because of all the dirt. He had heard guys in the Army talk about dead bodies, how the eyes haunted you, so Chuck didn't look too high up. He had enough trouble sleeping as it was, due to acid reflux and the likely need for a CPAP machine. He panned his flashlight down past her stomach and the lower half was worse. There was massive tearing below her navel and her thighs and hips and everything in between was torn down to the bone. A few of the gashes were big, but he could tell they had devolved into lots and lots of smaller scratches. The swell of her stomach was perfect, white and inviting but everything below that was bloody and bad. She'd suffered and not a little bit, Chuck thought. Enough of the ground was covered in blood to suggest there had been some thrashing involved. Between the wind hitting the weeds, Chuck heard himself give out a small "oh, Sandra" in his gravelly voice, then he reached into his pocket and pulled out his phone.

Josie picked up on the third ring. She sounded rough.

"Josie? This is Chuck down at the bar."

"Chuck?"

"Yeah. Listen, I've got a mess over here."

There was some rustling on the other end. She must have been asleep.

6

Chuck briefly pictured her pulling back the sheets of her bed revealing white panties, but banished the thought.

"What are you talking about?"

"Sandra Riedel's body is all torn to shreds outside my bar is what I'm talking about."

More silence. No thoughts of pretty girls in underwear this time.

"Is it obvious what happened? Could she of . . ."

Josie trailed off. She still sounded scratchy but it was clear to Chuck she had a hold of the situation with both hands.

"It's obvious what happened, girl. I figure you'd best get the boys in because I'm going to have to call the cops on this."

"Can you give me some time?"

"How much time you thinking you need?"

"Hour and a half maybe?"

Chuck exhaled a deep lungful of cold, bracing air.

"Look, I don't want to be a hard-ass here, but it's been a long night and I want to go to bed and . . ."

"Then call them in the morning, Chuck. Jesus. If you're tired go to bed and tell the cops you saw the body in the morning."

Chuck didn't like being talked down to, but Josie had a point. He was a bit embarrassed he hadn't come up with the solution on his own.

"Yeah, that sounds all right."

"Where'd you find her?"

"In the volleyball court."

"The what?"

"Jesus, girl, the volleyball court. The one Courtney put in a few years back."

"Chuck, that lot full of weeds was a volleyball court for about an hour and a half."

"Call it whatever you want, there's a dead girl in it and I hate dealing with this kind of shit. Good night."

"I'll tell the boys hi for you."

"See that you do."

Annoyed and tired in equal measure, Chuck finished closing up and

7

took the long walk up the flight of stairs to his apartment above "Bar." The apartment was actually rather nice. It used to be Jim's apartment before his heart attack, and Chuck was glad to take it over. It was roomy there was some good furniture had come with it and best of all he hadn't paid rent in over fifteen years. He inherited it free and clear and even made a few modifications. Since he was far away from any streetlights, he had installed two floodlights at great expense and had rewired them to turn off from his apartment. He had bumped his shins and shoulders too many times stumbling around in the dark to not do something about it.

Just before he turned off the light, he snuck one last glance toward the volleyball court. She was out there. He could tell from up here. He couldn't see any body parts, but he could see red stains here and there. Anyone passing by was going to get an eyeful. He would have to get up early, he thought. Then, he thought better of it.

"She's wrong. You can totally tell it's a volleyball court," he said, before the floodlights made a loud, whooshing noise and the dark flooded everything.

• • •

It was the morning of October 4th when police found Sandra, and the morning of October 5th when they found Byron and it wasn't pretty. He was in much the same state, only moved around a bit, and they found him in the woods near the Beaver Creek, next to the town's only historic marker, a big piece of granite set deep into the earth. It was quite a production after they found him. Law enforcement, coroners, and other folks had to come from three counties away and they noted there was a lot more slashing on the chest, neck, and head than the girl, but the wounds looked very similar. They were deep and frequent and the victim never stood a chance. He had died quick, but he had suffered. They all agreed on that.

The folks who had to drive across the expanse of highway to reach the small town of Cherry all looked to Grey Allen to lead the investigation. He had no interest in doing anything of the sort. He was pushing seventy, slight and, well, gray and he had worn the same mustache for over thirty years, every single one of them spent in uniform. In some smaller communities, people say things like "he knows everybody" when, in actuality, there are hundreds of people who had never met hundreds of other people. In Cherry and the surrounding county, Grey Allen knew everybody. Barter County had 458 residents and encompassed 134 square miles of land. That's more than a quarter of a mile for every man, woman and child in the county. Grey Allen had driven every mile on every road and knocked on every door. Grey Allen, literally, knew everyone.

Sheriff Allen, who had never campaigned a day in his life and kept the job because no one else wanted it, arrived after everyone else, despite living a few miles away. He was in no hurry, but he was immediately inundated with requests, which did not make him happy. After ten minutes of some State Patrol asshole yelling at him about needing to be "lead on the scene" to the coroner needing him to sign something to trying to answer questions from all the damn people who had gathered, Grey Allen did something he hadn't done while in uniform in years.

He raised his voice.

"Enough of this shit!"

The guy from the State Patrol looked like he was going to start up again, but he saw that the scene and the pressure was giving Grey Allen all the stress he could handle, maybe a bit more, so he backed off. After adjusting his hat and breathing deeply like he had been told to do, Grey Allen finally arrived at the scene of the crime.

"No good, that," he said.

At this point, the guy from the State Patrol could hold his tongue no longer.

"Sheriff Allen . . ."

"Grey."

"Grey . . ."

"Grey Allen."

The man looked dumbstruck.

"Sheriff Grey Allen, your most exalted majesty, that's all you've got? That this is 'no good'?"

Grey Allen took a deep breath.

"Well, what else you want?"

"Do you know who he is?"

"Yep."

The man from the Nebraska State Patrol could contain himself no longer. He walked behind Grey Allen and spoke softly, yet quickly into his ear.

"You are half an hour behind the ME and we had to pick up crowd control, we had to set up tape, we had to secure the scene and we had to do all that without a word from you or your department. This is the second body in your county in two days. As a professional courtesy to all these people who are here doing your job for you, would you please knock off the country bumpkin crap and tell us what you know so we can move forward. Please."

"Since you said please."

Grey Allan spit and turned around to face the young man in the slightly rumpled uniform.

"This, here, is Byron Matzen. He's got some land, not too far back off Rural Road 77, over there. Raises cows, plants the odd crop, but not much of a farmer. Big drinker. Never the brightest bulb, but he wasn't likely to hurt nobody."

"You know that for sure?" the State Patrolman asked.

"I know that for sure," Grey Allan said. "I also know he was single. I know he drives a blue Dodge Durango but I'm not sure what year. I know he liked to speed on occasion but a warning would usually take care of it. I know he was at Bar a few nights back and, if I were a betting man, I'd bet he's the guy who killed Sandra Riedel."

"What makes you say that?" the Patrolman said, listening very closely.

"Makes sense. Don't it?"

The Patrolman kept his voice down as to not tip anything to the crowd gathered in the parking lot of the Sinclair station.

"Not really."

"What don't make sense about it?"

"Well, Grey Allen . . ."

"Sheriff Grey Allen."

"God damn it, Sheriff Grey Allen, you have two dead bodies in three days killed in the same way. Torn to shreds. Doesn't it make sense that someone killed the first victim and then killed a second victim in the same way?"

"Nope."

"I . . . what?" the Patrolman stumbled. "I . . . I don't even know what to say to that."

"Looks like this guy killed Sandra and then some animal got at him. I don't know. A bobcat maybe."

"A bobcat? You're not serious?"

"We get bobcats around here."

The Patrolman left Grey Allen to talk to someone with a better disposition. He ranted and raved to the assembled group of investigators, this time not taking the step of lowering his voice. Those gathered in the parking lot of the Sinclair station would report hearing words like "fucking idiot" "mind bending-ly stupid" and "Alzheimer's Disease" thrown about. Grey Allen ignored it all, keeping his eyes on Byron's body. They had really done a number on him. He thought he had this under control and now that it was clear he didn't, there was only one thing left to do.

Grey Allen pulled his old frame up on top of his dusty patrol car. He stood on the hood and immediately felt a rush of shame. What a stupid thing for an old man to do. It didn't take long until all eyes were on him.

"Everyone. I would like to take this opportunity to announce my retirement from Law Enforcement. If you'd all like to send a card, just drop it by the post office and I'll make sure to stop by and pick them up."

A SELECTIVE HISTORY OF BARTER COUNTY, PART 1

Way before Grey Allen, one of the men who cracked the code of effective law enforcement in Barter County was a lawman by the name of Norbert Farber, a first generation German immigrant who served as Sheriff from 1913 – 1939. Before him, no lawman had lasted longer than a year in the area, though, to be fair, some had joined the military and others had no intention of staying in such a rural area. But others were, to put it kindly, run off.

Immediately upon landing the job, Sheriff Farber decided to track down all those who had left and ask them if they had any advice, insight or could offer any help at all. When no one replied to his repeated letters seeking counsel, he took it upon himself to really dig into his community. He knocked on doors and introduced himself. He asked about concerns. He made his services available. By all accounts, he was the sheriff of a rural but perfectly lawful patch of land but he never stopped looking over his shoulder.

Sheriff Farber's first piece of trouble came in the form of dead animals, often dismembered and scattered, turning up in public places. None of the contacts he had made knew what was happening and any whispers that took place behind the scenes were too quiet for him to make out. Then Alan Caspersen's dog wound up disemboweled but still tied to a leash in the blacksmith's front yard. Mr. Caspersen, not one to stay quiet about any issue on his mind, made the issue the talk of the town and surrounding area. The Caspersen dog would not go unavenged.

One night, out of frustration, Sheriff Farber visited the town bar and found blacksmith Caspersen drowning the memory of his deceased canine. The two got to talking and it wasn't long into conversation when talk turned to devils and demons, men possessed and devoid of the Grace of God, men who ran with the devil, literally, according to Caspersen. Men who had no regard for holiness, charity, or other people's animals.

It didn't matter whether or not the sheriff believed the stories. What mattered was he found the men, had a nice talk with them, and before long order had been restored. Blacksmith Caspersen never forgot the death of his dog, but before long the town moved on, the animal slaughter stopped, and time marched on. Twenty-six years later the sheriff died of a massive heart attack while on the job. In his last will and testament he instructed his wife Millicent to hand deliver to his replacement a set of letters he had written with strict instructions to not read the contents for herself. True to her word, Millicent resisted temptation and delivered the letters to newly minted Sheriff Bradley M. Godfrey who read the letters, took them to heart, and served in the position for eighteen years.

PART 2 - THE RULES OF THE SCRATCH

A week or so had passed between the two bloody nights in Cherry and between the crickets and the birds that don't know what damn time it is and the distant wail of train horns, the country can be a noisy place to try to get some sleep. Add a girl screaming and running out of your house at two in the morning and Dave Rhodes Sr. was in desperate need of coffee. Plus, he had to have a word with the boy.

Dave Jr., who everyone had called Dilly in a nickname whose origin was lost to the ages, wasn't up yet. Josie was up, though. Dave had felt her toss and turn after they heard the girl scream, run out of their house, start up her car and drive away. Both of them were pretty sure what had happened, as it was something they had dealt with in the past. Dave's mind never really calmed down and the night's sleep was restless, the clock on his bedside table particularly bright in the darkness. He woke up thoroughly unrested as he joined his wife in their kitchen.

"Should we get him up? We need to talk to him," Josie said. She had this conversation planned out, Dave could tell. If that woman had a chance to play things out in her head beforehand, she was hard to beat.

"Let's let him sleep for a bit."

"That girl may be hurt, Dave. She might have told her parents about it, they might be on their way over here right now."

"Adam and Charlotte? Not likely. He works at the John Deere, I've met him. He's a levelheaded guy."

"But if she's hurt . . ."

"Then chances are Dilly would have made sure she's OK. He's a good kid. He's not a monster."

"No, he's a teenage boy and they are hardwired to make bad decisions. Besides, we don't know what happened for sure. Go get him up, please."

They sat in silence for several heavy seconds. Dave took a sip of coffee and stood up.

"Let's get this over with."

Looking at his wife as the morning light beat through the window, Dave felt a pang of nostalgia. She really didn't look all that different from when he met her in high school. She was still beautiful, still unwilling to deal with any of his bullshit. He often had thoughts that, left to his own devices, there was no way he could have carved out the life he had, no way he could have balanced it, without her hand in his life. He walked over and leaned down to kiss her, hoping the coffee would mask his morning breath.

"It's not going to be like you and me," he said. "For one thing, we don't have Willie to worry about. We're going to do this solid."

"We couldn't do much worse than Willie did," she said pulling away and blushing.

"No, we could not."

He wandered down the hall, taking a second to look at the family photos. There was the photo from Disney when Dilly was ten; there was the one with the cutouts that showed his photo from every grade, there was one of Dilly in his baseball uniform. The paint was uneven from where they did some patch work a few years ago, but didn't get the exact right color. Dave paused for a second outside of his son's door, listened and heard the heavy rise and fall of a teenager dead to the world. At least the boy had gotten some sleep. That was a positive.

Dave walked into the room and started to slap Dilly's feet.

"Up," he said. "I know you were up late, but we've got miles to go before we sleep."

"Miles to go before we sleep" was something Dave's dad, Willie, had said to him every morning during his childhood. It wasn't until Dave's brief stint in college that he had learned it was a Robert Frost poem. Dave still had never read the entire thing but it rolled off his tongue every morning, just the same. Dilly let out a long groan, the kind Dave always hoped he would outgrow, but hadn't yet.

"Seriously, kid. Up. Your mom and I need to talk to you."

A couple minutes later, Dave D. Rhodes Jr., all 6'1 and 165 pounds of him, stumbled out of his room in a plain brown T-shirt, blue boxers and socks. He always wore socks. Dave the Senior was convinced he wore them in the shower. He took a hard right into their kitchen from the hall, and took his sweet time pouring coffee, then creamer from the fridge, then sugar, then stirring the mixture and sitting down, all while his parents clocked his every move. It was hard for Dave and Josie to figure why he was taking his time like that. He wasn't the type for a power play. If pinned down, the adjectives his parents would use to describe Dilly would include "tall," "straight forward," "humble," and, if pushed, "shy." He was a boy without an aggressive bone in his body until you put him on the basketball court, then he was an entirely different animal. He had made varsity as a freshman and now, in his junior year, was one of the best players on the team.

Dilly plopped down in his seat and took a sip of his coffee.

"What's up?" Dilly asked. His parents stared, saying nothing.

"She's OK," he said after a long breath. "I mean, I suppose you heard a scream last night."

Josie looked at Dave, telling him to take the lead.

"OK. First off, we like Allie. She's a . . ." he paused, and looked at Josie who, most definitely, did not like Allie. "She's a sweet girl. But this isn't about her. It's about you and what's happening to you."

Dilly rolled his eyes, but stopped halfway through. They had talked about this and he was showing effort at not rolling his eyes, which meant his mother would not bring it up.

"Is this 'the talk'?" Dilly asked.

"Not exactly," Dave said.

"Then what?"

"How'd you hurt her, Dilly?" Josie asked.

The teenager took a long drink of his coffee, realizing he was cornered.

"I'm not sure you'd get it."

Dave sighed. He had prepared for this. His son wasn't much of a conversationalist, but there were a few issues they connected on: football, movies, fitness. Josie and Dilly liked to garden, but there was a sturdy wall between the two of them that largely went unacknowledged. But Josie wasn't the only one who could game out a conversation.

"It started with your hands, didn't it?

Dilly stared.

"I know because I've been there. Your hands start to tingle at the palms and then spread real quick to your fingers. It goes from tingling to fire until it's all you can think about. You can be kissing the prettiest girl in the world, but your hands are on fire and when you sneak a look at them, they're longer than they were. There are curves in weird places, hair where there wasn't hair before. Then the fire spreads. Am I on base with any of this, Dilly?"

There was a silence only teenagers and parents could understand. Then a faint "yeah, that's how it started."

"You probably wanted to stop," Dave continued. "But maybe things were . . . heated. Maybe you were in a position where stopping would have been difficult, so you didn't. Then the fire spread from your arms into some place deeper. And when it hit that deeper place, that's when you hurt her, wasn't it?"

Dilly nodded.

"Yeah," he said. "Yeah, but, no. Not really."

"How was it different?" Dave asked.

"I . . . damn, this is embarrassing. Could I just talk to Dad about it, or . . ."

"Hon, this is a family thing," Josie said. "I'm sorry it's embarrassing but we've got a lot to go over and the quicker we get past the embarrassing stuff the better."

16

She reached out and grabbed Dilly's hand and held it and stared at him until, after a few seconds, he met her gaze.

"This is important," she said.

Dilly exhaled deeply and took a drink of coffee.

"Allie and I were kissing and everything was fine. Nothing was . . . unusual, I guess. Even though I don't know what usual is in this situation. She's the first girl I've ever done anything like this with."

"We figured," Dave said.

"Thanks for the vote of confidence, Dad."

"That's not what I meant. Any girl would be lucky to have you. Now quit ducking and let's get this over with."

"She . . . she went down on me. I didn't ask her to, but that's when it happened. That's when the fire thing started but it wasn't in my hands. It didn't start there, I mean. It was from the chest and it spread out and, and, this is going to sound like I'm holding something back, but I'm not, I don't even remember hurting her. My hands were, like, on her head and then she's screaming and jumping up and when I . . . came to, I guess, there were holes in the back of her shirt and blood. Not a lot, but you could see it."

"OK," Dave said. "Is that when she ran out?"

"No, not right away. I apologized right away and I didn't know what to say so I told her she really got me excited and I lost control for a second and that's when she felt the blood."

Dilly took a big drink of his coffee, his job almost done.

"I offered to help her and I was all 'I'm sorry, I'm sorry, I didn't mean to,' and she saw the blood and saw her ripped shirt and that's when she screamed a little bit and said she was going home and I couldn't stop her."

"That sounds about right," Dave said, tapping Josie with his foot under the table.

"You did OK," Josie said. "But here's the important part, Dilly. Did you feel yourself change? Is it time for us to start exploring that?"

"A little," Dilly said. "You guys know the transforming part really scares me."

"I know," Dave said. "It scared me too the first time."

"Do you think she noticed?" Josie asked, finally getting to the heart of the thing.

"If she did, she was too polite to say anything," Dilly said, running his hand through his sandy blond hair. "She was hurt and mad when she left but I don't think she was freaked out or anything."

Suddenly, the boy's face changed as did his posture. He sat up straighter and leaned forward in a way that suggested a shift from defense to offense.

"Did you guys know this was going to happen?"

The smile across Dave's face was wide. The boy had never been a genius, but he could figure things out. People, too. He was disarming but kind and that combination made people want to talk to him, made him attractive. That was only going to help as he learned to live with this thing that their family was carrying.

"The answer is kind of," Dave said. "You want me to tell you about when I wolfed out on your mom, where she was and what she was doing?"

"God, no!" Dilly said. Back on defense.

"I'm not going to lie. Kenny Kirk, Ron and maybe Carl, that's how they first started with the process. When they were with girls like that. I don't know, kid, it brings something out in us guys. But it's different for everyone so we didn't know for sure."

Dilly opened his mouth but Dave cut him off.

"I know it seems like a risk, but it was a pretty good bet you weren't going to hurt anyone too bad, Dilly. You're not that kind of kid."

His coffee cup empty, Dilly traced the rim of the cup with his index finger.

"I wish you'd have warned me," he said. "I could have been on the lookout. Maybe not ruined Allie's shirt."

"Allie's mom can fix the shirt and scratches heal, hon," Josie said. "But here's the big thing you need to be thinking about. Do you think it's time to go out with the boys?"

All of a sudden, a rush of nostalgia hit Dave so hard it threatened to consume him. He remembered the sheer, heart-pounding terror of walking out to the woods and seeing his dad and all his friends. He remembered how they greeted him, how they embraced and welcomed him to the fold, prompting Willie to say "this ain't so special. Leave him be." He remembered how odd the men looked when they took off their shirts. Then their pants. How all these old men and their old wrinkled bodies weren't that scary, and how it actually calmed him down. Then it started and it wasn't as bad as he'd built it up to be and before he knew it, he was flying through the woods, the fastest among the pack, navigating trees and foliage faster and faster.

The rest of it, the first scent, the first trail, the first blood, the first kill, the noise that came out of his chest like fire and into the cold Nebraska air on a clear Nebraska night where the sky stretched out for eternity. The high he would never capture again. The high his son was now on the path toward. The realization that he would protect this life, that he would work for this life and all the abstractions that came with it all piled into his head so fast he couldn't stop it.

Dave stood up. He needed some air.

"It doesn't need to be this time. Come when you're ready," he told his son. "We're not going anywhere."

Dilly and Josie sat at the table and talked for an hour, carefully avoiding land mines like torn shirts and oral sex. Dilly got all the information fresh, even though he had known of his special situation since he was eight years old. Dave left them, mother and son, with something to talk about. He loaded up some old tires into the back of his pickup as an excuse and headed into town.

• • •

"Town," such as it was, consisted of a bar, a church, a small business district with a grocery store, a hardware store, and a repair shop among a few streets dotted with houses in various states of upkeep. One house, damaged by a tornado several years ago, had never been repaired and was now so much a part of the landscape folks were surprised when out-of-towners brought it up. It's not hard to ignore something peculiar when you see it every day.

The shop, known as "Rathman Repair and Service," was owned by

Kenneth Rathman, who made a fairly good living because he knew how to repair most tractors. He had grown from "tractor repairman" to general repair of all sorts and now had three men working at the shop full time. There were a few men in town with that much business acumen or his particular skill set, but Kenny Kirk to his friends was easily the fastest, the fairest, and the best in a fifty-mile radius, which is why he got away with being the way he was.

"Where you at, dickface?" Kenny half sang as Dave got out of his truck.

"I was at twenty percent this morning, but it's gotten significantly higher since then. You?"

"Man, I'll tell you, I've been itchy," Kenny said. "A rabbit was in my yard this morning and I swear to God I started at that thing for ten minutes, munching on dandelions, wanting to get at it. Without thinkin' to I had taken my pants off. Gave JoAnn a little bit of a treat."

"So where you at?"

"Let's call it seventy," Kenny said. "I know Ron's up there too, so maybe we start putting it together."

"It's going to be the first time since we had to do that thing."

They both kicked at the dirt, careful not to look at each other.

"Doesn't change nothing," Kenny Kirk said, kicking a rock hard enough to where it flew into the street next to his shop. "And have some decorum, man. Don't just bust that out there. Ask how I'm doing or if JoAnn's OK or about that travesty in Lincoln last week. Don't just jump to that thing. Besides, it's over. Doesn't change a damn thing about how we conduct ourselves."

"I don't think that's right," Dave sighed, mostly to himself.

"That's cause you think too goddamn much, man," Kenny said. "You put it all in, like, this historical context when that ain't what you should be doing. This is a clear-cut case of forward, not back. It's like we all agreed on. It had to happen and it happened. You'd have more luck teaching Josie to barbecue than you would changing what's already been done."

"She made a brisket once. Wasn't too bad."

"Yeah, I'll believe that when I taste it. Last time we let her near the grill half of that chicken she made was burnt to shit and the other half was raw enough to complain about it."

The two men stood in silence, which was exactly what Dave had hoped to avoid. Normally Kenny's mouth was a constant source of focus as he was the kind who talked just to talk. He could be belligerent, he was often crass, he could sometimes come up with a cutting insight but one thing the man was not was quiet. If there was a silence more than a couple of seconds it meant something was wrong.

Dave decided to see if he'd go for ten seconds, counting silently in his head. When he got to twelve, he finally took the bait.

"Something on your mind, Ken?"

"Yeah . . . um . . . look, I was talking before about how you overthink things and that is the truth, you ain't changing my mind on that, but maybe you want to call Dilly off for another few weeks, man."

Etiquette was again breached as the silence returned. Dave only gave it five seconds this time.

"You gonna make me guess why you'd say something like that?"

"Well, no, I'm not. But you clearly ain't heard."

"Heard what?"

"Look, I hate to be the guy to tell you, what with Byron and your kid . . . I mean, those are both more than enough to get that brain of yours working and then there's that thing at your school that's causing all the ruckus . . ."

Dan furrowed his brow and bugged his eyes at Kenny, who promptly remembered the law he had put down a few nights before.

"Tell me what's going on, Kenny."

"Grey Allen's retiring."

"Wait . . . the sheriff is stepping down?"

The news out and the hard part done, Kenny's mouth started running again.

"Yeah, man, he did it right there on the scene where they all found Byron in front of the State Patrol and investigators and shit. He stood up on his car, of all the stupid things, and was like 'I'm done. Grey Allen out.' So they're looking for a new guy and they're looking quick."

This was bad on several fronts, but for some reason Dave had started doing math in his head. How long had Grey Allen been the sheriff? How long had he been old? Grey was one of those guys who "has been old forever," as his mother used to say, and picturing Grey Allen as a young man was an endeavor sure to end in laughs if done in a group of friends. But he was a bedrock, a gentleman and, ultimately, a trusted force when trust is in short supply. Plus, his absence complicated things enormously.

"Why the hell didn't I hear about this?"

"Well, we're all dealing in our own way, man. It's not like I'm going to come over to your house and have a beer after Byron. I wanted to be by myself and since this is the first time we've talked since then, I'm guessing you did too. We all kind of . . . I don't know, went back into our houses and tried to do our own things, I guess. You forget sometimes, man, you're the only one of the boys with a kid to worry about and that means you've got a few distractions that we don't have."

"So because I don't go to the Bar all the damn time I'm out of touch," Dave shot back.

"That's not what I'm saying," Kenny said, drawing the words out for emphasis and maximum redneck drawl. "What I'm saying is we've all got our own shit to deal with and that means your ear ain't as close to the ground as mine or Ron's or Carl's or even Willie's. You get what I'm saying?"

"Yeah, I get what you're saying," Dave said. "Anything else I need to know since my ear is so high up in the air?"

"Don't be like that, you asshole," Kenny said. "And quit taking all this shit personal. Yeah, we're in kind of a tight spot right now but it's not like we're looking at a change in leadership. Carl would piss himself and Willie would run us all off a cliff, man, if he could make it that far. Figured you'd find out sooner or later. Now you know."

Dave had to catch himself from falling into another memory, this one involving his father, specifically his face, twisted and angry. All of a sudden the smells of lunch came wafting from the house down from Kenny's shop—the sandwiches were turkey, the chips sour cream and onion. The wind had kicked up as well, the sound it made through the trees suddenly almost deafening.

"You all right?" Kenny asked.

"Yeah, yeah. I'm at seven or eight now. Let's get the boys together. It's already been too long."

"That sounds about right," Kenny said. "We meeting at your place?"

"Nope," Dave said, sidling up to his truck. "By the creek, please. And tell everyone I'm bringing the meat, the rest of y'all can bring side dishes or chips or something."

"I'm bringing shots."

"If you still need 'em."

"Not for me," Kenny said. "Your boy might need a nip before."

"Let me handle my boy," Dave said, starting the car and kicking up dust that colored the air.

"You're the boss," Kenny muttered.

• • •

That night, a black town car pulled up outside of Rathman Repair and Service. The occupant, a tall, lean man dressed for the fall weather in northern Nebraska dress pants and a long-sleeved dress shirt covered by a light windbreaker, saw the windows were dark, got out of the car, and knocked anyway. Then he knocked harder. The man was not accustomed to these sorts of sparsely populated towns, where a long road might have a business, a few houses and nothing else, familiar enough that when a second round of knocking produced nothing, he started pounding.

Before long, a light came on in the yellow house next door. The man continued pounding. The yellow house's owner, Mr. Sidney Layton, retired, came out tying his flannel robe around his gaunt waist.

"Hey, hey, nobody's in there."

The old man made his way down his front steps in a way that was both hurried due to circumstance and slow due to age. The tall man pounded a few more times and turned to face the man he had disturbed.

"Kenny Kirk closes up at six or so," Sidney said. "You're making a racket for no reason."

The man was considerably taller that Mr. Sidney, so much so that he could see the top of his head. When he spoke, the man's voice was calm, deep and smooth, a stark contrast to the old man's.

"Will Mr. Kirk be in tomorrow?"

Sidney took a second, marveling at the way the man drew the last word into the lower register of his voice. It was very slick and not something he was used to.

"Nah, his last name ain't Kirk, it's Rathman. We just call him Kenny Kirk because when he was a kid he . . ."

"Sir," the man interrupted. "Will this store be open tomorrow?"

"No, it won't," Sidney said. "You need a tow or something?"

"I don't need a tow, thank you," the man said. "What I need to do is speak with the owner. Can you tell me where I can find him?"

Sidney didn't betray anything to the stranger, but he now acutely felt the power shift. At first, he was the disturbed one, ready to help but also to shame this guy for making all the noise. Between the demeanor of the man and the questions he was asking, the justified anger had evaporated.

"Nah," Sidney said. "I don't think Kenny's interested in having visitors tonight. They may open in the morning but they . . . they don't do a lot of business on the weekends. Not before noon anyways."

The man said nothing.

"If I was you, I'd try maybe after lunch. Kenny'll be in at some point tomorrow."

"Tell me," the man said. "I noticed a good number of storage structures on my way into town, the ones with the white roofs on them, when you're coming in off Highway 21. Do those belong to Mr. Rathman?"

"Yeah, yeah. He's got a few cars in there and a few parts of cars. That sort of thing."

The man reached into his pocket and peeled a fresh, unworn $20 bill from a roll held in place by a rubber band. With a big hand that possessed surprising strength, he grabbed the old man's hand and pressed the bill into it.

"Thank you for your help," the man said in a calm voice.

"I . . . I don't need your money, mister," Sidney said. The bill was so new he could feel the subtle texture of the bill on his weathered hands.

"You've given me information I need," the man said, not breaking gaze with Sidney. The man's eyes were dark as was his hair. "That's worth paying for. Now, if you were to give me more information, like where Mr. Kirk might be tonight, that would also be worth paying for."

"I . . . I don't . . ." Sidney stuttered. He had not anticipated having his scruples questioned while standing outside in his bathrobe.

"I understand," the man said. "That's a bridge too far."

The man turned to get back in his car.

"Mister," Sidney yelled. "If I see Kenny Kir . . . Mr. Rathman before then, who should I tell was banging on his door?"

"Tell him Mr. Stander came by," the man yelled back. "Tell him to be in his shop. I'll be along."

The tail lights of the town car were very bright, almost fluorescent, Sidney thought. Extremely bright. They stayed bright all the way down the street and the old man clocked them two blocks north after he made the turn that would take him to the highway. After tossing the $20 on the table his wife used for keys and such, he dialed Kenny's cell phone and got his voicemail.

"This is Kenny. If you've got my voicemail I'm probably shit faced somewhere so I'll get to yer call when I sober up."

The voicemail ended with a huge belch, then the beep.

"Kenny, this is Sidney, down by your shop. Look, I know you and the boys are probably out somewhere but you need to give me a call when you get this. There's a weird guy looking for you and I'm thinking you're really going to want to get in front of this. He was asking all sorts of weird stuff about your shop and . . . give me call, would ya?"

He hung up, went back over and held up the $20.

"Where the hell do you get money like that?" he said, putting the bill up under his bushy grey mustache. "Even smells new."

Sidney did not sleep well that night between his thoughts and the howls off in the distance.

···

By now, they all knew how this worked. Step one. You break bread.

Most of the time, the boys alternated between backyards and cooked up a giant mess of ribs, burgers, or Nebraska-raised steaks, but this time they'd loaded up Dave's portable grill and gone out to a spot not far from the Beaver Creek that was particularly good for fishing. There were also picnic tables there. No one was sure where they had come from or who they belonged to, but they were frequently used, with paint peeling and grooves carved and by sunset, the smoke was rolling off the grill, like usual.

One time Ron Smith, the guy in the group who had adopted the "biker" look but had a heart of gold, had brought a deer in the back of his truck that he had shot earlier that day and they took turns butchering and grilling. Grilled deer might seem odd but the wood smoke of the grill often overtook the gaminess of the meat, making for a perfectly acceptable meal that left everyone leaning back in their chairs and picking their teeth.

This was also the step where you messed around and joked, but under no circumstances did you raise hackles. If there were sore spots, you didn't apply pressure. If there were land mines, you steered as clear as you could and this evening, there were land mines. Bunches of them. But there would be time for that after, and . . . well, at this point they knew how this worked. This tradition had been passed down for generations in great detail and with great purpose.

"Did you marinate these at all, Josie? Not that they taste bad . . ." Carl Eakes asked Josie, who was pulling out plates from the back of the truck while her husband slung the spatula not far away. Carl wasn't much of a talker and was also the youngest of the group, so Josie made sure to answer him. It hit her Carl was the youngest of the group until tonight. Then he would graduate to second youngest.

"Yeah, we used this brown sugar recipe of my mom's," Josie said. "It's got brown sugar, soy sauce, ketchup and a bunch of other stuff."

"Smells good," Carl said and let that sit.

Aside from Dave and Josie, Kenny brought his girlfriend JoAnn with them. Ron's wife, Karen, was on call at the local hospital and couldn't make it out, though there were whisperings that she was avoiding this particular scratch for emotional reasons, which was strictly against the rules. While the group could have easily been mistaken for a group of weekend campers, what was happening was a ritual hundreds of years old. For the people gathered in the clearing, this was church.

Dilly had spent the first part of the evening, while the "men folk" worked on the food, sitting on top of one of the picnic tables staring out into the seemingly endless field of grass and weeds that exist only in rural areas, where you can see for miles and track the wind as it rushes across the flat plains toward a tree line. Josie desperately wanted to go to him. She went to Dave instead.

"You should go say something," she said.

"We will. This is the worst part. Trust me."

"Then go tell him that. He's suffering over there."

The boy had sheepishly told his dad that he wanted to "go out with the boys" the afternoon after they had had their uncomfortable talk. He had tried hard not to seem overly enthusiastic but Dave knew his boy and knew there would be little to no holding him back for much longer. After a short conversation, Josie had given up as well, so here he was.

Dave was about to tell her that Dilly's behavior was perfectly normal, but before he had the chance a blue truck that could have easily been mistaken as missing a muffler pulled up. The stink the truck brought with it, that acrid bouquet topped with a chemical sweetness, lingered as it always did. Willie was late. Willie was usually late. Everyone was OK with Willie being late. As Carl politely observed after one particularly spirited evening, a little bit of Willie went a long way.

William "Willie" Rhodes, all 6'4 of him, seldom did anything quiet. Any subject needing an opinion, Willie would let his be known first, loudest and most often least informed, which, given he had very little by way of a social filter in his old age, often made for uncomfortable moments. Among the boys, the pause in the conversation that frequently accompanied something loud and obnoxious out of Willie's mouth had become known as a "Willie Pause."

Willie and Josie got along like oil and more oil lit on fire and poured onto a pile of gasoline-soaked rags. Things had been particularly rough lately and Dave was hoping his father would suck it up for his grandson. Dave tried to give Josie a smile, but it was too thin and they both knew it.

"Where's Lacy?" Dave asked.

Willie dismissed his son with a wave and laser-focused on Dilly.

"What the hell you mopin' over there for, boy?" Willie said. "Get over here and hug your grandpa."

Dilly obliged as the two had always had a soft spot for each other and were soon embroiled in a conversation about this year's basketball team. Before any tension could manifest, low and behold, the food finished cooking and everyone jammed some in their mouths. Beers were cracked and before long a nice, easy mood settled over the camp as the conversation turned to the most important topic in the world.

"You know what I say," Willie started after wolfing down his trout. "If you gotta get rid of a coach, they couldn't have done it any better. And if that new guy who used to play quarterback knows what's good for him he'll start kicking ass early and often. I remember what that "N" on the side of our helmets used to mean something."

"You gotta give him some time," Dave said. "Let's see what type of team he can put together. Talk to me after in a few years when it's all his guys."

"Actually," Carl jumped in. "He brought over some coaches and recruits so some of them are his guys. Not that you don't have a point, plus he had a great recruiting class."

"He better have a good recruiting class!" Kenny said. "Goddamn Michigan's got that pro coach, the damn . . . what are they . . . Ohio State, their guy is the best recruiter in the damn game. We're screwed worse than a . . ."

Josie shot him a look.

"Worse than a one-legged man in a butt-kicking contest," Kenny said, making a grand gesture of toning it down.

"He's supposed to be a defensive genius," Ron said, throwing his bulk back against the chair. "If he's a defensive genius I'm Jabba the Hutt."

"Jabba the . . . what the hell are you talking about?" Willie said.

"He's from *Star Wars*, Grandpa. He's a giant slug thing," Dilly said.

"Fine, if he's a defensive genius I'm Marilyn Monroe. That more up your alley, Willie?" Ron said to a few chuckles. Tipping the scales at 240, Ron had played football in college but his physique was now more biker than athlete, with the long beard to match.

"I'm gonna stick my foot up your alley if you're not careful," Willie said, followed by a Willie Pause.

The talk continued, drifting from football to gossip to business then back to football and before anyone had time to really get going about anything. The occasion called for camaraderie so no one talked politics. The occasion called for good feelings so no one got up on horses, high or otherwise. The sun had gotten low and it was time. They had gotten to this point without talking about Byron or any of the unprecedented, bloody business of the past few weeks. There was time for that later. The moment felt right and it would be wrong to waste it.

By now, they all knew how this worked. Step two. You go back to nature.

Dave put his arm around Dilly as they walked from the clearing into the woods with the rest of the men. The boy was hot and was trembling slightly. Before they got too far out, he snuck a look back at his mother. She was standing, her hands folded palm to palm in a nervous stance. She didn't make any motion but was wearing her anxiety like an ugly hat.

"Don't worry quite yet," Dave said. "This part isn't anything scary. You're going to lay in the grass, you're going to clear your head and just, listen."

"You've told me what I'm supposed to be listening for but I don't know that I get it," Dilly said. "There's nothing out here."

"That isn't true at all," Dave said. "It's so noisy you almost hear too much. You'll hear when we get there. You're not listening for any one thing, kid. What you're doing is taking in all the sounds and once you get the sounds, then you'll start taking in what makes the sounds and the smells and how everything feels."

"Yeah, but what happens if I don't?" Dilly said.

"Then don't freak out. Relax, breathe and everything will make sense once we're out there. Then it will be time."

They walked far out into the field until the women and the food and the cars and trucks parked along the way were dots on the huge sky horizon. They kept walking into a thick growth of trees until Dave moved to the front of the group, and said "here."

First Willie, then Ron, then Carl, then Kenny Kirk stretched out on the forest floor. Dilly looked at his father hesitantly, but the time for words passed. Dave nodded, which he hoped conveyed to his son that all was well, and Dilly took his spot, stretched out his long frame and folded his hands. Finally, Dave laid down to the loud crunching of grass and leaves.

Once your head is near the dirt, the sounds of the forest become magnified. The wind is as loud as a train, the scuttling of bugs and small animals immediately apparent. As Dilly lay on the cold ground, his dad's prediction came true and suddenly the scent of the Earth underneath him was as strong as coffee in the morning, the prickly feel of the dead leaves under his arms now a persistent poke. The waning sunlight through the trees was getting less and less but somehow seemed more and more and before long, Dilly's head was buzzing with dirt and wind and scents and moss and bark and sweat.

Dilly was also acutely aware of the others as well, particularly their breathing and their scents. His father's scent he knew from home and his grandfather's from when he used to sleep over when he was a kid, but the smells of the other men—oil for Kenny, musk for Ron, a sickly sweet for Carl—suddenly filled his nostrils. The question "what do I smell like?" floated through his head, temporarily dethroning the anxiety that had set up shop there a few weeks earlier.

Then, he caught another scent all together. It was a softer scent, but also a grittier one. It evoked fur and sweet grass tinged with something else. Something that had really grabbed Dilly's attention. He noticed Carl was standing up and soon Willie joined him.

The second Dilly got to his feet, Dave was behind him.

"Don't turn around," he said in a lower voice than normal. "Keep that scent in your head. Feel it, then add to it."

Dilly knew what Dave meant. They had spoken at length about how the transition works and what thoughts and feelings he could use to get there. He knew the thought had to be his own and that he shouldn't share it. Dave had told him sometimes it takes a while to find the one that does it, but once you know what your trigger is, it becomes your best friend and your worst enemy. Dilly had three thoughts to pick from that he had chosen after careful consideration—a time when he was a seven-year-old and got lost at the mall down in Grand Island, the first time he took an elbow to the face during a basketball game and then Allie, that feeling of moist pressure from her mouth on his as they kissed. He had no stronger memories in his entire head than those three and his anxiety rose again, hoping they would do the trick. If they didn't, he was in serious trouble.

The other men had started taking off their clothes, starting with their shirts, their torsos a variety of the rural Caucasian experience. Willie's expansive belly was huge and covered in fine white hair the color of his beard, Kenny Kirk was stick thin with a bit of a sink in his chest. Their smells became much stronger once they lost their clothes and Dilly registered they were all facing the same direction, into the woods. The men were naked in a short period of time, all of them in front of Dilly facing the thick overgrowth except his father, who was behind him.

By now, they all knew how this worked. Step three. You scratched.

Dilly's brain was swimming with smells and sensations, but he was still lucid enough to remember, vividly, that Ron was the one who jerked forward first, as if he had been hit hard in the small of the back. His stomach pitched forward, his face jerking upward, then his body jerked the opposite direction as Kenny Kirk started flailing as well. Carl's arms flew around his body as though unconnected. Willie stood there and it was on his grandfather that Dilly kept his fleeting focus.

Willie was growing hair. He was a hairy dude to start with but his hair was elongating, growing noticeably thicker and shaggier, taking on a different consistency. As Carl, Ron, and Kenny Kirk flailed and jerked around him, Willie stood, his feet planted as his hair, and then his body, began to grow.

At that moment Dilly heard his father's voice, lower than he had ever heard it, whisper and growl.

"Breathe deep. Use your thought. Do it now."

The deep breath in brought all the smells of the men, the forest, the camp and the strange new one which he somehow knew was blood all flooding into his head, each fighting for space, battling to be the predominant scent. As he exhaled, the substantial anxiety Dilly had been carrying for years flooded out of his nostrils and in its place was desire to howl and to run and to get into the fucking forest already. There was only one thing stopping him and he was still conscious enough to know it. He had to use his thought.

He tried thinking of the fear of being alone and helpless. Nothing happened. He jumped around and thought of Allie and her softness, her smells and moans as their tongues intertwined. Nothing happened.

Well, this must be the one, Dilly thought to himself.

The moment was as vivid as any memory he possessed. He was in the middle of a junior varsity game and a player on the Castleville Coyotes had been on his ass from the opening whistle. They had locked horns on a couple of defensive plays and Dilly had still managed to use his height and his arm length to get around the guy and score. He had 12 points and hadn't seen halftime yet when the elbow came, fast and hard and square in the soft part of his nose. If it had been to the side or gotten some of his eye in the shot, Dilly could have been persuaded that it was an accident, but the elbow was square and sharp and Dilly knew, even before he opened his eyes, that there would be blood all down his face.

When Dilly was able to look and shake out the stars that filled his vision, he was the Coyote with a shit-eating grin. *I hit you* the grin said. *And you ain't doing shit about it.*

That night, Dilly had done something about it. He had scored 35 more points for a school record. He had played his heart out and his teammates, sensing the energy, had fed him the ball and every time Dilly had it, he took it straight to the Coyote, knocking him down, drawing foul after foul, and winning the game almost singlehandedly. His mother had said she'd never been so proud. His father had said he'd never seen such guts. Dilly knew better. He knew he wanted blood and in this case, blood was humiliating your opponent. Dilly knew who he was that night. He was the guy who got up after you knocked him down while serving you a nice big shitburger in the process. He was a soldier that way. He was merciless. He could bleed and he could make you bleed.

The memory was so fierce that Dilly tasted blood and smelled the leather on the ball and then the first spasm hit. It hurt. Dilly felt his spine shift in ways it never had before, not even close, and the pain that came with it was white hot and unrelenting, only subsiding when pain in his arms and legs took its place. It felt like his back was twisting and pulling muscle and cartilage with it in a sick, unnatural dance. He tried to scream but couldn't as his throat had taken an odd shape and the taste of blood, once in his head, was now very real and tangy as it flowed down his throat. He squeezed tears out of his eyes as his conscious mind shut down and his thoughts and memories left him, his last alert sensation being a strange stretching and tearing sensation accompanied by terrible popping sounds.

Dilly's body continued to spasm and pull and stretch and break. If the boy had been conscious, he would have had to witness his back arch and seemingly gain mass and sprout hair, his nose pull away from his face, his teeth sharpen to razors, his nails grow to claws. The other men around him underwent the same transformation, scratching at the dirt with all their strength, leaving fresh, damp grooves in the floor of the forest but none of them made sounds like the boy, his screams a reflex, his considerable blood loss, a product of his first transformation. By the time the screaming stopped and it was done, steam poured from small pools of blood around where the boy had been.

The Young Wolf emerged from the dirt. Not a wolf, exactly, but long and hairy and lean and hungry, covered in hair and drooling, a creature unfamiliar by man but thousands of years old. The Young Wolf was big yet slightly fragile in his coiled and aggressive stance. Had the wolf stood on its hind legs it would be seven feet of children's nightmare, drooling and snarling and dripping blood.

The new wolf opened its eyes which were yellow and sharp, and scanned the ground for the thing he needed.

Pack. My pack.

From their spots in the grass, the other wolves emerged. One white and big, one thin and fast, one small and straight, one large and ready. The new creature turned around and saw his father, the biggest of the pack. His chest between his front paws was large and heaving, his eyes sharp and his teeth bared. Bigger than any wolf in the wild, or any man, the Lead Wolf, the new wolf's father, reared up his head and started to howl. The other wolves followed and the new wolf heard a sound escape his throat that was perfect and right and carried with it one uncompromising message from the pack.

We are here.

By now, they all knew how this worked. Step four. You run.

The Lead Wolf took off with a speed and dexterity that shocked the Young Wolf. The others followed, fast and hard and soon the new wolf was running as fast as his new body would allow and was having trouble keeping up. He dug in and soon passed the White Wolf and the Thin Wolf and was in line with the Large Wolf when the new smell hit his nose and penetrated all the way down to his heart.

Blood. That way.

This is what they were chasing, why they were here and the Young Wolf suddenly had a purpose. At breakneck speed, he made a long circle, turning to his left and losing ground to the Large Wolf, whose turn was sharp and direct. He almost lost his balance but his back legs were strong and the dirt was thick and supported him. The forest seemed to help as he found a root under his paw that helped him push his weight in a new direction and two trees leading to a clearing seemed to lead him exactly where he wanted to go. The smell was pungent and thick and an unparalleled desire grabbed the new wolf and shook him. He had to have this smell. He was merciless. He could make you bleed.

The Lead Wolf had slowed and was moving in a manner that was curious to the new wolf, not using his unnaturally long, curved nails to dig into the dirt, but pulling them up and using his pads, changing the way his hulking frame moved. The White Wolf, who had snuck up on him, rammed the length of his body into the new wolf, prompting him.

Shhhhhh

Understanding, the Young Wolf began slowing, eventually moving to a crawl with the others. The scent was farther away now, harder to find. His long snout searched the air as did the others, but the Lead Wolf snorted at them and they all fell silent. They had come upon a small clearing and a stream, swollen with water from a late, muddy early fall. The creature giving off the scent, whatever it was, had gone through the stream and the scent had intermingled with moss, very strong moss, and fishy scents and hearty buzzing flies and water. The Young Wolf fixed his new wolf eyes across the river, searching for any sign of movement. It was dark and there was none.

The rest of the pack had begun to turn around when the Young Wolf spotted it, far, far away. A low branch of a tree, with leaves starting to die and turn yellow and smelling sweet in their death, had a branch that was swinging opposite the wind. He saw this small, telltale sign of life and took off running. He was over the river in a second and to the tree branch with the pack behind him, howling in disapproval. He blew past the tree and the second he got to the other side, the scent returned and strengthened and the Young Wolf saw red around the edges of his vision whenever he breathed it in. He then heard the sound of hooves, frantically clopping and could hear the deer, darting around in fits of panic trying to milk every last second of speed from its coiled, tight muscles.

The Young Wolf was aware of his pack behind him when his eyes set upon the deer. She was young, two winters or so, and after running for just a moment the Young Wolf could make out her tail bobbing in between thick patches of leaves and bark. Zeroing in on the movement, focused on nothing else on the planet, he gained ground, plowing through underbrush and causing enough noise to alert every animal in the forest. The deer was already at top speed and losing ground. The Young Wolf was gaining with the pack close behind him when his back paw hit a patch of mud disguised as solid ground and he slipped. His large, long body pitched to one side and crashed into the trunk of a tree, and he let out a yelp as the thundering of the pack ran close by his head.

NO

Up off the ground and angry at the fall, the Young Wolf was now in the back of the pack, struggling, striving to make up any ground he could. The White Wolf was the slowest and was breathing heavily when the Young Wolf passed him without acknowledgment. The Large Wolf was next, and he received a snarl and a small, unconvincing snap as he passed. The Young Wolf was big, but the Large Wolf could have knocked him off course easily. He did not. Ahead of him was the Thin Wolf and his father. They showed no signs of giving ground if they could help it. The three wolves at the head of the pack ran without changing ground for a short time with the Young Wolf not losing steam, but starting to feel the pull of fatigue on his limbs.

The desire to stop became stronger and stronger and just as the Young Wolf was surrendering and slowing down, the scent of blood filled his nostrils again, this time accompanied with a faint sound of the deer's heart as it thumped faster and faster, desperately trying to lose the hunters that were so close on its trail. The sound of the heartbeat locked the Young Wolf's brain like a vice and he pushed himself harder and harder, making his strides longer and growling with genuine aggression as he passed the Thin Wolf, who made a slight bow with his head and dropped back. The fatigue gave way to the hunt and all the rest of the smells and sounds battling their way into the wolves' heightened senses gave way to the hoofbeat of their prey.

The Lead Wolf and the Young Wolf were even now, with the deer just feet away, pumping its legs in fluid motions and gliding over obstacles the forest had placed in its path. The wolves smashed through them, wood splintering, dirt flying off the back of their paws. The deer ran down a slight ravine and kept going, which gave the hunters the opportunity they needed. They both leapt through the air, silhouetted by the sun, low and huge on the horizon, and landed on the deer, the Young Wolf near the head and the Lead Wolf by the haunches.

The Young Wolf was so frenzied that his teeth were in the deer's flesh before he realized he'd missed the neck and bitten into the face. He ripped the flesh away causing the deer to make a half scream but its eyes were still very sharp and focused when the young wolf found the neck and began to bite. Behind him, the Lead Wolf had tasted blood, but stopped to watch his son, his back to the pack, tear at the neck and shake with a ferocity the pack had forgotten. He bit and the deer bled and died, its sharp eyes rolling back and its pain ending, long dead by the time the entire pack had gathered around. The scent gave way to physical fluid as blood poured over the young wolf's face and down his throat, coating it with its viscous saltiness that wild hunters have known for as long as there has been a hunt.

With the wash of blood, the Young Wolf felt a wash of pleasure and accomplishment unlike any he had ever known. If he could have put the feeling into words, he would have said he never felt more at absolute harmony with his body or his soul or the Earth. He was doing exactly what he was supposed to do and he had the bloody snout and the flooded throat to prove it.

The howls began, softly at first, then louder as the circle of ancient and giant and experienced and new wolves screamed in their victory. The moon was barely visible through the light that was giving way to a darkening sky and the Lead Wolf joined the howl.

Smeared in blood, his senses sky high, every beat of his heart pumping royal blood through his mighty veins, the Young Wolf at last raised his head from the carcass and howled the loudest of them all, bellowing to the forest and the state and the world one united message.

Do not fuck with us.

They reveled for a moment then, one by one, ran farther into the woods. There was more to do. They dispersed, but each one was in touch with the pack, each knew not to go too far. After they had taken their own paths, the Lead Wolf took a moment to watch his child enjoy the kill. It was a moment he was envious of and when he finally approached the Young Wolf, still face down in gore, and nudged him on the hind quarters, his message was simple.

Miles to go before we sleep.

The Young Wolf understood and before long they were off, the sun was gone and the wolves of Cherry, Nebraska, ran through the woods, hunting in the thick trees as darkness covered the land.

•••

Depending on the range and atmospheric conditions, the howls could stretch well into Cherry proper. Most of the residents ignored them but no one was more deaf than Chuck Nesbit. He was hard of hearing anyway and, by trade, everything was his business and nothing was.

But the stranger at the bar, he sure as shit heard it.

"You got wolves around here, do you?"

Chuck was making a meal out of cleaning glasses because, as much as he didn't want to admit it, the dude in front of him was interesting. Not that he would let *him* know that.

The man was lithe and coiled, his leather jacket covering a frame that looked like it had a bit of muscle, but not much. He definitely wasn't from around here and it wasn't just his lack of denim or other fashion choices. He came at Chuck with an intensity he was not used to and had no idea what to do with.

"I didn't hear anything," Chuck said.

"Oh yeah, you did," the man continued. He had an Irish brogue but Chuck wasn't able to identify it primarily out of ignorance.

"Don't know what you're talking about."

"Yeah, you fuckin' do," the man said. "That loud howling sound everyone just heard. Coming from outside. From wolves. Aooooooo, that noise. You follow me?"

Chuck put down his cup, now thoroughly dry, and picked up another one.

"Can I get you anything else?"

"I've still got half a pint left, and don't change the subject. I asked if you had wolves around here."

"Wolves, deer, squirrels, all sorts of things," Chuck said, now actively avoiding the man's intense eye contact.

"I've never heard a wolf make a howl like that. That sounded like something else to me. Are you following?"

"I've got to go do some dishes."

Without breaking the intense eye contact, the man reached over and knocked his beer glass onto the bar, spilling the contents onto the laminated wood.

"Ah shit, sorry about that," the man said. "Could you grab a rag for me please? I'd hate to leave smelling of beer, am I right?"

Suddenly, Chuck didn't find this guy interesting anymore and wanted nothing more than to get in the back and away from his company. He grabbed a rag and quickly tried to mop up the mess. Without warning and with staggering quickness the man grabbed Chuck's arm and quickly applied pressure to his fingers. It wasn't painful particularly, but the promise of pain was there.

"Brother, listen to me. I know you're the stoic sort but I need to find some very special people in this town and I know you know who I'm talking about. It's the same people responsible for those bodies a week or so ago. The ones all ripped all to hell. Now I'm not going to hurt you but what you need to do is write a name on a piece of paper and give it to me. Do that and I'll never darken your door again."

"What happens if I don't?" Chuck said, suddenly defiant.

"Then I'm going to stay for a few more drinks and we'll see where the night takes us."

"Can I finish mopping up your mess first?"

"Please, allow me."

The man with the leather jacket and the Irish brogue snatched the rag out of Chuck's hand and went to work, leaving the barkeep dazed and more than a bit conflicted.

"Just one name," the man said. "I'm not here to hurt them, either."

"Bullshit," Chuck said.

"Your beer, your beer is the real bullshit. Watered down, light as fucking air. How you wash away your troubles without the benefit of a good, stout beer is beyond me."

He smiled and Chuck wrote the name "Kenny Rathman" on a napkin and nearly handed it to him.

"You promise? He's a pain in the ass but he's a friend. I don't mean to send him no trouble."

"My good man, trouble has already found him," the man said. "I'm trying to bail his ass out."

• • •

It was around 3:30 in the morning when the men started returning to camp, slowly and teetering from exhaustion, all of them breathing heavy. All except one.

Dilly had done his best to clean up. When he came to, or "got back on the reservation" as Kenny Kirk had put it, he was grotesque. His body was fine, as far as he could tell, and he wasn't all that achy from the transformation and every joint and bone seemed to be well back in place, but he was naked and covered with dirt and blood. There were some other substances as well that he didn't think too hard about, opting, instead, for a quick dip in a shallow, mossy stream that ran near the campsite.

Dilly was splashing water on his neck, doing his best to not freak out over what had just happened, when he realized his grandfather was in the creek as well.

"Hell of a thing, huh, kid," Willie said.

"Yeah," Dilly said, head down, knowing what he said was completely inadequate for the occasion.

"I've got about three memories left floating around in this noggin, and one of them is my first scratch," Willie said. "It was 1970, that or there about. Went down just about like this one. I was wobbly and shaky but I got the job done, believe me."

On the edges of the bank, Ron had found his footing and was walking upright, once again a slightly intimidating middle-aged man. Dilly tried hard not to look at his naked body, but caught a glimpse of Ron's penis which was floppy and surrounded by coarse-looking hair.

"You're awfully quiet," Willie prodded. "Hell of a thing that just happened to you. My first scratch, I couldn't stop talking about it."

"I bet you couldn't," Dilly said.

"Ahhh, don't give me that tone," Willie said. "I'll tell you this—I didn't take down no lily-ass deer. Got me a buck my first time out. Those antlers make a world of difference, boy, believe me."

"I believe you, Grandpa."

"A deer," Willie said, shaking his head, his white beard swaying. "Anyone can take down a deer. They're fast is all. Hell, I'd have been disappointed if you didn't kill a deer. I'd have been worried about having bringing you out with us."

"I'm starting to think the same thing about you."

Dave walked out from behind the bushes, chewing on one of his fingernails.

"You were puffing pretty hard out there."

"Bullshit," Willie said. "I was holding back because of the boy. We all were."

Physically, Dilly made no indication he'd heard. His posture changed just slightly enough for a father to recognize it. To degrade, belittle and generally be a giant asshole was Willie's modus operandi and had been for as long as Dave had been alive. Criticism was the man's life breath and ninety-nine percent of the time, easily dismissed. Dave had hoped against hope that he would tone it down for his son's first run but Willie had been Willie. Of course he had.

"So you're telling me I didn't just blow by you after I tripped on that root?"

Both men turned and looked at Dilly. The boy's head was still down, but Dave could see a little grin working its way around the corners of his mouth.

"You blew by me because I let you," Willie said. "And watch your tone."

"I was just worried about you, Grandpa," Dilly said. "It sounded like your heart was going to explode."

This elicited a snort from several trees away, giving away Ron's position.

"Quit eavesdropping, you asshole," Willie yelled.

Dilly didn't wait around to keep the argument going, laying down in the filthy stream and coming up rubbing his arms and doing his best to clean off. The cold was like a punch that pulled the breath from his body. Willie, clean enough, apparently, got out of the stream, muttering and saying a few choice words to Dave as they passed, but they didn't land. Instead, Dave knelt down by the water, deep shadows of the trees covering him.

"You all right?"

"Yeah, that's just Grandpa," Dilly said.

"That's not what I mean."

"I know."

The only sound was Dilly still trying to get some of the caked-on blood off his shoulders and chest. The water, full of all sorts of crap, was not up to the job.

"Willie was kind of a jerk just now, but he has a point. He said he doesn't remember much, but he remembers what you just did. I remember too. It's one of those things . . ."

Dilly had stopped washing and turned to look at Dave.

"Every time you go out there, every time we scratch, it's an amazing thing. It's primal and . . . well, you know now, don't ya. It's a rush. But it's never as much a rush as your first time and it's a high you can never really get back. I guess what I want to tell you is enjoy it. You're going to get older and things are going to be more set and you will have less and less of these moments that make memories like this."

"So . . . I did OK?"

Dave's eyes welled up at the innocence and sweetness of his kid. After undergoing this truly odd and extraordinary ritual that would change his life forever, all he wanted was his father's approval.

"Son, yes, yes. You did great. There's no real wrong way to do it but I'm proud of you. I'm proud of your bravery, how you were scared of the transformation but did it anyway. I'm proud of how you got back up after tripping. I'm especially proud of you giving Willie the business a couple of minutes ago."

They both chuckled in the deep moonlight. The rest of the pack had moved on.

"We should get back, but you did great. And you'll want to do it again."

"That's what I don't get," Dilly said, getting out of the water. They both headed for camp. "You say everyone gets this urge to scratch every so often and that the whole pack has to go out together. What's it feel like? What should I look out for?"

"It's hard to describe, but you'll know," Dave said. "It usually starts with the senses. You'll smell things you couldn't smell, sounds will really start to bother you. Sometimes it's tied to whatever your thought is. Your emotions go all haywire. It's got nothing to do with the moon like in all those movies and more to do with whatever you're going through at the time. This one time, Ron was going through a rough patch with his first wife and they would fight all the time and he would want to scratch every other night almost. He was really pissed off morning noon and night so we had to put some rules in place and get him some help. The point is he didn't go out alone. No one goes out alone."

Dilly's face was a mask of concern behind spatters of blood and dirt.

"It happens less the older you get. Just, be mindful, I guess. Really get to know yourself and how your brain works and you'll be fine."

"Fine?" Dilly said, taking a moment to let the word dangle and dissolve into the air. "Dad, I know you've been, like, getting me ready for this since I was seven but I just turned into a wolf and bit off a deer's face."

"You found the neck eventually."

"That's not the point!"

This time, Dilly's words did not dangle or dissolve, but pierce. Dave flashed back to watching his son throw temper tantrums as a toddler. His son had been an epic fit thrower, a destroyer of worlds until his face turned red then purple with the pure rage of a child. Then, magically, it stopped over the course of a month and he had been an even-tempered kid ever since. When he exploded, there was a reason.

"Look . . ." Dave started.

"No, Dad. Just . . ."

The two men stood, clothed only by the shadows.

"I understand what this costs."

"What do you mean?

"I mean you're right about the high. You're right that I've never felt any-thing like that. You're right that I want to do this. And you're right that I'm going to understand myself and you guys in a really profound way."

Dilly exhaled hard, his breath visible as the night turned frosty and bitter.

"I also know it means I can never go back."

"How do you mean? What is it you're worried about?"

"Dad, we live in the middle of nowhere. My graduating class is going to be twenty-nine kids. There's one restaurant within twenty miles of here and it's OK but it's the only restaurant for twenty miles. You didn't grow up online, Dad. I know kids from Ecuador and San Francisco and, hell, from Lincoln and Grand Island and they're going away to big schools and they're making big plans. They're going to visit places and meet people and they're going to eat in restaurants that serve amazing food and I'm going to be . . ."

Dave finished for him.

" . . . figuring this out."

"Yeah. I'm going to be figuring out how to be whatever it is we are."

Dilly immediately tried to soften the blow.

"I mean, I love you guys and I don't think for a second that I'm taking this for granted . . ."

The kid had a point. When Dave had learned the rules of the scratch it was presented to him as something like the weather or car maintenance. It was something you had to do and Willie, nurturing father that he was, didn't answer a lot of his son's questions, leaving Dave to figure it out for himself. At the end of the day it had been a good thing and taught the young wolf self-reliance, but on the other hand he didn't realize he would be stuck in Cherry until he was already stuck in Cherry.

"No, I get it," Dave said. "And I don't have an answer for you now because it's going to take a little while to figure things out. But maybe college isn't out of the question for you. Maybe trips and hot foreign girls aren't out of the question."

"Dad, don't be gross."

Dave's hand found Dilly's shoulder in the dark.

"The truth of the matter is we don't know what sort of wolf you're going to be yet, or what sort of man you're going to be. But we'll figure it out together, like we always do."

The sounds of camp, gentle as they were, filled their sensitive ears. Dave stopped them.

"Your mom and I knew this was coming. Don't worry that you're going to hurt our feelings."

Dilly hung his head a bit, exhausted.

"Come on. We've got miles to go."

"You say that too much."

"Yeah, well."

They found their clothes right where they had left them and started putting them on.

"Why doesn't Mom ever come out with us?"

"Because she doesn't have any fun. That's why."

•••

The unofficial "step 5" in the rules of the scratch is you crash hard for at least ten hours and then wake up and go over what went down the night before. By this point Josie and Kenny Kirk's girlfriend JoAnn were used to these sorts of mornings, and had cooked up pancakes and bacon, carbs, and protein. Karen, Ron's (second) wife had shown up after her shift ended and had helped on and off so when the boys started stirring around noon, breakfast was rolling.

The men had all thrown on pants, at the very least, before passing out the night before, and hurriedly went about finding their shirts and other clothing before presenting themselves, all except Willie, who honestly couldn't care less and wore his gut not with pride, exactly, but with something very close to it. He strode up to the women, throwing red

suspenders attached to his jeans over his hairy shoulders. For some reason, Josie felt he was giving off a Santa Claus–style vibe.

"Thanks," he grunted, barely audible.

"Rough night, gramps," Josie said.

"You cook these?"

"You know I did, Willie."

"You can't cook for shit."

"Then maybe you should invite Lacy out to cook for you."

Clearly bested and clearly hungry, Willie muttered something and
turned toward the picnic table. Lacy, Willie's long-standing, long-suffer-
ing girlfriend, did not know about Willie's woodland adventures and was
sincerely not bright enough to ask. It was a sore spot with Willie and the
group as they had been together for upwards of five years. She should
know, but Willie was not going to tell her and Willie was going to do what
Willie was going to do. Carl was next in line for late breakfast and was
remarkably clean and alert given what he had been up to.

"How about you, Carl Atkins? Rough night?"

"No ma'am, I feel great," Carl said. "That boy of yours sure is fast,
though. Drew first blood and everything."

Josie gave a knowing smile. She snuck a look at Dilly who was sitting
on top of one of the tables, his long legs pulled up to his chest, his back to
the camp. It was impossible to know where he was emotionally, but Josie
knew enough to let the boy sit. He'd come over when he got hungry.

"Don't let him threaten you," she said. "You've got experience on your
side."

"Oh no, it's not like that," Carl said. "It was nice to have someone who
was faster than me. Makes me try harder, right?"

"Suppose so," Josie said, spreading the bacon to the side of the pancakes.

"Thank you, Josie," he said.

Kenny Kirk had cut in line and was trying to wrap his arms around
JoAnn, who was fighting it. Not that anyone smelled great after a night
of camping and/or transforming into wolves and running through the
woods, but Kenny had found some brand-new nasty smell and had made
friends with it.

46

"Come on, baby, it's not that bad," he said as she spun out of his two-armed hug.

"You smell like a big shit took a little shit that grew up to be a bigger shit," JoAnn said. "Get off me you giant freak."

"You like the way I freak," Kenny said, moving closer to her.

"Take some pancakes, you smelly ass," JoAnn said, grabbing the plate Josie held at the ready. "Eat it down wind."

"I'll eat you up later and you'll love it," Kenny said, the lure of the food finally getting the better of him. He straddled one of the picnic table seats, put his food in front of him on the seat and dug in with his fingers.

"I don't know how you keep your hands off that," Josie said. "He's too much man for me."

Kenny shot both girls a quick middle finger, his mouth full.

Ron was shambling up, a little slower than the others. Usually when one of the boys hurt themselves as a wolf, they were able to shake it off when they changed back, but Ron was clearly limping, his broad shoulders drooped as he winced every time his thick left leg struck the ground.

"What's with your hitch, there?" Josie asked, handing him a plate.

"That kid of yours, he blew past me out there. Knocked me into a tree. I'm still feeling it."

To demonstrate, Ron shook his leg and rolled his ankle. He winced when the roll reached the top.

"I'll talk to him. Sorry about that."

"He'll hear from me," Ron said. "Newbie or not."

"Don't be like that."

"I'm already not like that. I'm calm as a fuckin' cucumber, Josie, but I can't let it stand without saying anything. If Willie had done it I'd still be knocking the teeth out of his idiot head. Point is, he'll hear from me and that will be that."

"That will be that," Josie repeated, squeezing syrup out of the bottle a little too vigorously. "He's a good kid and he doesn't know his own strength, Ron. Never has."

"Doesn't change nothin'," Ron said. "My leg still hurts. Besides, how else is he going to learn?"

Ron limped off and before long, Dave trudged up by himself to the table. Josie had always kind of loved the way Dave looked the morning after a scratch. His hair found ways of shooting off in different directions and his eyes were stubborn and refused to open all the way. After being married for twenty years she had seen her husband get up and out of bed literally thousands of times and in dozens of conditions—tired, rested, hung over, mad, thrilled, horny, sick—but he never looked the same way he did after a night out with the boys. It was a unique look for him and only she knew what it looked like.

It didn't hurt that Dave had aged remarkably well. He was an athlete in high school and never lost the habit of running and watching his diet, so even at the ripe old age of forty-two he was lean and toned. For some reason he disliked going without a shirt, something that no doubt tied back to living in a house with Willie for eighteen years, but when he did she still found herself tracing the veins from his arms to his shoulder, then following the hair down his chest to his navel and beyond.

"Morning, pretty girl," he said, using a line he'd used longer than he cared to admit. "Make mine to go, I've got a wife to get home to."

Josie ignored his good mood and got straight to it.

"Dilly bumped Ron last night and Ron's gunning for him."

"It's worse than that," Dave said. "Willie wants to bring up Byron. Wants to hash it all out over pancakes."

"But Dilly . . ."

"Yep."

"We have to . . ."

"Do what? What happens if we run him home now? Do you think Willie won't bring it up on the way to the car?"

"Dave, I don't want him to know that yet."

"I know."

"He's just gone through it for the first time. He's a beginner. He doesn't need to deal with this. Not yet."

"Try telling that to Willie."

"I just . . . I will."

"You'd get further trying to get that rock over there to buy you a beer."

He was right, of course. Once Willie's mind was made up, he would stick to his guns and would stick to them harder if you gave him a good reason why he was being a jackass. When Dilly was a boy, Willie decided he was too old to believe in Santa Claus and proudly told Dave he intended to relieve the boy of his childhood belief. Dave told Josie and the two of them caught Willie before he'd had the chance. What resulted was a knock down drag out fight where the phrases "you have no right," "this is not your job," and "we're his fucking parents" were all but screamed, eventually waking Dilly from his nap. All of these were excellent, rational points but, sure enough, Willie walked right into Dilly's room, sat on the corner of his grandson's bed, explained to him that Santa was "bullshit" and "a lie" and then asked what was for dinner as if the fight had never happened. This was not a matter of being cruel. It was a matter of Willie knowing better than anyone else on the planet.

After the Santa Incident, Dave and Josie kept him away from Willie for two months, a huge feat in a town the size of Cherry but, eventually, he showed up little by little and by March things were more or less back to normal. Willie never apologized. Now, Willie had made up his mind that it was time to air some of the family's dirty laundry, no matter how inappropriate, damaging or confusing this information might be and nothing short of the Voice of God was going to change his mind. Maybe not even that.

"Can you get to him before Willie brings it up?" Josie said, her eyes blazing.

"Maybe," Dave said between bites of pancake. "My guess is we have a little time. He wouldn't start some shit until everyone had a chance to eat, right?"

"All right, listen up!" Willie yelled loud enough for the camp to hear. "We need to hash this Byron thing out if things are going to get back to normal."

Cries of "aw Jesus," "we're still eating," and general groans met the old man, but he plowed on, undeterred.

"No, no, I get that this is touchy for all you ladies, but we did something serious a few days ago and we got to reckon for it."

The combination of words had broken through whatever haze Dilly was in and he turned around to join the group.

"Knock it off you old fart. I still got syrup on my fingers," Kenny Kirk shouted back.

"Then talk about this with sticky fingers," Willie said. "We got to get this out in the open."

"What part of this isn't out in the open?" Dave piped up. Josie was glad to hear it. When Willie got rolling it was easy to look for an escape hatch and let him rant and it wasn't unheard of for Dave to turn back into a little boy and cower before his father. But Dave was running at him head-on, not raising his voice but not backing down either.

"Byron made his choices and we made ours. We talked about it for a while and it weighed on all of us, Willie. Don't you remember all that talking we did?"

"I remember you running your damn mouth all night, I remember that."

"Fuck you," Dave said, escalating quickly. "If you don't remember that meeting where everyone said their piece . . ."

"Not everyone . . ." Willie stammered, shocked at being knocked back.

"Where EVERYONE said their piece, you included, if you don't remember that then you've come down with Alzheimer's or some shit because we did that together. We did that as a pack."

"That's how you remember it?"

"That's how it was, Willie."

"That's how it was," Willie repeated, chewing the words. "Cause I remember you going on and on about how he was 'threatening this whole thing' and how 'something had to be done.' I remember you pushing for it cause you never liked Byron. Not since you caught him and Josie . . ."

"You shut your fucking mouth old man," Dave said, moving fast toward Willie. "You shut your fu . . ."

Before he could get there, Ron had grabbed one arm and clamped down hard, pulling Dave back. Both father and son had cut loose now and were screaming at each other, producing a large garbled ball of hate. Ron gave one hard pull and Dave spun around, running his punching hand through his spiked hair.

"What's everyone talking about?"

Josie closed her eyes. If Dilly hadn't brought it up they could have gotten him home, gotten their version of events into his head first, told him the history he needed to know and left out the history he didn't. Now they had to do it in front of the camp with Willie barking behind them. Dilly had hopped off the table, still bare chested, walking to stand between Dave and Willie.

"Dad, don't say F-you to grandpa. What's going on?"

Willie shot Dave a look ten times worse than anything he could have said.

"He's my boy. I'll talk to him."

"He's in our pack. Tell him now," Willie said.

Dave plopped down on a bench and reckoned with the tightness in his chest and the low, deep hurt in the pit of his stomach.

"You all see it that way?" he asked.

"Of course they do, don't be an idiot," Willie barked.

Dave stood up and got very close to Willie.

"I will tell him but you will keep your fool mouth shut while I do. Anything you got to add, you do so when I'm done, is that clear?"

"What you gonna do if I don't," Willie asked. "You gonna yell more curse words at me?"

"I'll do more than that," Dave said, sitting back down.

"Dad, I feel really left out here," Dilly said, smiling awkwardly. He was trying to crack a joke to relieve the obvious tension in the camp, but hadn't bothered to say anything funny.

Dave snuck one more look at Josie, who was already choking back tears, and launched in.

"Well, Dilly, your Uncle Byron was not a very nice man."

A SELECTIVE HISTORY OF BARTER COUNTY, PART 2

Of course, the rumors of creatures in the woods exist through the history of Cherry township. Since the community was founded in 1873, the farmers and ranchers had whispered of strange sounds coming from the woods with the occasional sighting of a hairy blur here or a disemboweled animal there. But after a while, it faded into the background and became part of the scenery, something you knew about that made you a local, that gave your town some flavor.

The only officially recorded case of an "unusual sighting" came in the spring of 1922 by Mr. RJ Meyer and his family. They were on a nature hike, which was a popular activity for children of the time, and reported to the local weekly paper they had seen a "devilish creature" that was easily eight feet tall and was clearly of the devil. The Meyers implored the local churches of the area to organize a posse, to come to the woods and help rid the community of this demonic influence. The family even co-signed a Letter To The Editor of the *Barter County Buck* calling for righteous men to take up arms and protect their community. Nothing came of it.

It should be said the Meyers were not well respected in the community and after the community leaders paid them a kindly visit, they promptly dropped their alarmist calls. In particular, it was the influence of Mrs. Erma K. Rhodes, the wife of Pastor Kane F. Rhodes, that apparently changed the mind of the Meyer clan. Later, they recanted, saying their youngest, Samuel, had made up the story and was so convincing that the family had believed him. Plus, good Christians must be on the lookout for demonic influences, wherever they may appear.

To pour through the official history of Cherry, the Meyer incident, as it was known, was not only the only mention of "the W word" in the record, but was likely the most exciting thing to happen to Cherry in a hundred years. Yes, there was the tornado of 1981 that destroyed a grain silo and took the roof off several houses. Yes, there was a high-speed chase in 1992 that involved the Nebraska State Patrol and ended with the suspect running into a cornfield. And, yes, there was the time in 1997 when young Mr. Cronk bedded the new science teacher in town and the scandal lasted well past the school year. But you would be hard-pressed to find a quieter place to live in the whole of the United States.

Roswell had aliens. Loch Ness had Nessie. Boggy Creek had the mighty Sasquatch.

Cherry did not have werewolves.

That didn't, however, stop the Nebraska State Historical Society from putting up a historical marker just outside of town in the early 1960s commemorating the Meyers and their claim. The historical marker, made of granite and buried deep, gets the occasional traveler off the Interstate and into town but, like most historic markers, you've got to be looking for it if you want to see it at all.

Part 3 - Nice Work If You Can Get It

S tuart Dietz wasn't a broken man.

Sure, his girlfriend had left him a couple of months ago without as much as a raised voice or a shattered dish. Sure, he had been dismissed from the Detroit Police Department after all but being laughed off the force. Sure, as the subject of a viral video he had been both publicly and privately shamed and couldn't get a goddamn drink in a bar without having someone point and laugh or, worse, point and whisper. Sure, he had devolved from a man hanging on week to week, month to month, into a man who had procured the bitter stank of failure and desperation, a man whose very existence was an apology.

But Stuart Dietz wasn't a broken man. At this point, he wasn't much of anything.

After seven years on the Detroit Police Department, Stu had run into what fellow officers affectionately called a "very bad day." It started with a drug bust gone wrong where a suspected drugs dealer had removed the "suspected" part of his title by throwing his stash in the air after Stu had tried to arrest him. The stash became airborne and Stu, being a human who breathed, had started the day unexpectedly high, his gums numb and heart racing. His partner, a sensible spark plug of a woman named

Officer Regan Anson, but "Regs" to her friends, had tried to send him home but Stu was having none of it. He would power through. It was the sort of cop he was.

A domestic dispute later that morning ended with a drunk man vomiting on Stu, which ended up being a nice appetizer for the main course of his "very bad day." They rolled up on a grade-school-age child who was standing in the middle of the road with a very real gun, waving it around. The boy had screamed about his mother taking away his iPad, and Stu had done his best to calm him, which gave onlookers time to gather and fire up their smart phones. Footage of the incident existed from multiple angles and they all showed Stu trying to calm the kid down but failing as the kid continued to scream and gesture with the gun. By the time the kid shot himself in the chest, there were more than a dozen cameras trained on the boy and then on the cop who tried, desperately, to perform CPR and bring the boy back.

What Stu remembered, more than anything, was something the camera couldn't show. The moment after the gun went off the boy, pudgy and dirty, clearly a product of neglect, had widened his eyes and stared at Stu, every part of him screaming "I wish I could take this back." Memories of the boy's eyes had burrowed into Stu's psyche and stayed there, returning again and again, giving the cop no respite, hollowing him out emotionally. Then came the aftermath.

Of course, there was an official investigation that basically cleared him of wrongdoing, but it wasn't the official stuff that really twisted Stu's guts, it was the everyday stuff. It ruined his day when people yelled at him from passing cars on the street. It sucked in a big bad way when his Facebook profile was hacked and flooded with photos of the dead kid in the middle of the road. And he drank a little more the night his mother told him the ladies at the church were "talking." But, as he told his sister over the phone, it was happening to him but in some way it felt like it was really happening to somebody else.

"They're only clichés because they work," she had said. And she was right. Like always.

Since they were kids, Stu and his sister Dana had shared an odd relationship. She was two years older and while Stu had always been solid, if a little timid as a boy, it was clear from the time she was a toddler that Dana could track, kill, and eat her own food. She was the person you wanted on your side in a fight as long as you were absolutely sure that she was going to land on your side. One defining moment in their relationship centered around Stu getting in a scuffle at school in a hallway where bad things frequently happened. He was giving as good as he got in the way boys fight to maximize movement but minimize the possibility of someone actually getting hit. The fight was almost over and Stu was started to let up only to be jerked up by his hair, hard, by Dana and thrown into the corner. She was mad at him for making a scene and embarrassing her, so she decided to end it. The kid Stu was fighting had run off and dinner was a very awkward affair that night.

But they had been in good shape for a while. Dana had come out to her parents when she was twenty and seeing how she handled an awkward and potentially explosive situation had been something Stu remembered, even years later. Dana had laid out the facts in a reasonable manner—she was a girl and her romantic partners were going to be girls and she had known this was the way things were going to be for quite some time—and shut down all the stupid questions her mom and dad had thrown at her while answering the smart ones. Stu, who was seventeen at the time, was listening from down the hall and started to really admire the way Dana could deflect all the bullshit she must have known was coming her way.

"Maybe this is a phase" was met with "I don't believe that's the case and regardless, this is the way things are for now and you need to accept that."

"What about a family" was met with "I'm not interested in a family but if I was, adoption is a very good option, given the number of children who need stable homes."

"You're going against God's law," from their mother was met with "this conversation is done until you can accept me for who I am." And then she followed up, not speaking to her folks for two years, during which Stu was the go-between. It was during this time they established their rapport that carried them into adulthood. Stu had learned to accept that Dana, strong, confident Dana, was right about most things and the things she was wrong about sounded pretty decent and logical coming out of her mouth.

"Do you think your life is viable there anymore?" she had asked him about a week after the incident had made his life nearly intolerable. "Can you live this down and if you do, what are you left with?"

"I'm definitely not living it down," Stu said. "The thing that sucks most about it is, if you look at the rules, I'm in the clear. I didn't do anything wrong, you know?"

"That's good as far as it goes but I'm talking about you," Dana said, bringing it back. "What I'm talking about is making a clean start somewhere else. You don't have much tying you to Detroit anymore. Not Mom and Dad, that's for sure."

"I'm not moving to Florida," Stu said. "Speaking of clichés."

Their parents were exactly where retired people of moderate resources ended up—a Florida retirement community. Stu hadn't been down in a year and even then buoyed the chore by promising himself and his then girlfriend an afternoon at The Wizarding World of Harry Potter.

"I don't want to sound like the cranky lesbian Mom thinks I am, but here's what I see. I see my brother without a job he enjoys, without a girlfriend, and the frequent target for people who throw things from their car. Get outta there, Stu."

"And go where? You think this isn't going to follow me?"

"Sure it'll follow you," she said. "So you find something out of the way, you do that job for five years or so until this blows over, more or less, and then you're back doing what you want to do by the time you're forty."

Again, she sounded reasonable.

"I guess," Stu said. "But I don't know where to start."

"That's kind of what I called to talk to you about," Dana said, showing her first sign of hesitancy. "There's this job down here . . ."

"No. No. I am not moving to Nebraska. Nobody lives in Nebraska."

"That's the whole damn point, brother!"

"I am not living anywhere where I can't get a decent sandwich twenty-four hours."

"Don't be a snob."

"I'm not a snob. You know I don't have any money saved up."

"Being a snob isn't about money, you idiot. It's about your attitude. You think because you can see live music on a Tuesday or ride a bus or get a sandwich at four in the morning, which is awful for you by the way, that somehow makes you superior to people who live in the sticks? What an asshole thing to think. I can tell you a thousand good things about living here. First and foremost is that there are not a lot of people to bother you, which is something you need right now, and second, your big sister lives in the sticks and is more than happy to help you get back on your feet."

"I thought snob meant rich."

"Yeah, you're wrong on that."

Stu had ended the call in a good place but totally, unequivocally sure that he was not moving to Nebraska, much less rural Nebraska. He spent the next day online, avoiding news sites and looking for jobs in law enforcement. Then in law enforcement support. Then he widened his search and, by the time the next day rolled around, the little bomb his sister had implanted in his head had started to make little explosions in his brain. Maybe he needed a clean break. Maybe the sticks wouldn't be so bad. Maybe he could order the makings of a decent sandwich online or something. He held out another day and then called Dana back.

"Knew you'd call," she said, not bothering with any sort of greeting. "You held out longer than I thought."

"Yeah," he said. "You're always right."

• • •

The interview for Sheriff Grey Allen's position was an easy one being that there were not a lot of applicants and those who had applied were not the sort of folk you'd want mowing your lawn, much less wearing a badge. Two applicants had criminal records, one had a warrant out for his arrest ("it was only a speeding ticket"), one gentleman might have worked if not for his need to take harvest season off and then there was Stu. Tack on to that the need for someone on the job ASAFP, the fact that he had law enforcement training equivalent to what was needed in the job and was willing to relocate and the whole incident in Detroit was overlooked.

That's how it came to be that Stu found himself with his sister's arms around him being welcomed into her home just two months and a week after watching a boy die. Dana and her wife Robin had their own business roasting very specific sorts of coffee which they sold online. Apparently things had been going well because they had added on to their house which sat on about ten acres of land about a mile and a half off the highway.

"I'm glad you're here," she said, continuing the big hug born more out of sympathy than affection, Stu figured. She smelled like coffee in a very pleasant way.

"Good to be here, I guess," Stu said. "I wish it was under better circumstances. Hey, Robin!"

Robin had poked her head out from the house and waved. Short-haired, slim and always impeccably put together, Robin was one of the cutest women, in Stu's estimation, that had ever walked on two legs. She was overly friendly and a great cook, something Stu was hoping would come into play shortly. Before leaving Detroit he had tried to make a tour of his favorite eateries only to get variations of the "whisper and point" wherever he went. Apparently he was still big news. The bottom line was he had eaten Subway and its analogs for most of the past week and a half.

"Hey Stu!" Robin yelled back. "I'd come give you a hug, too, but I'm setting the table. Come eat."

Magic words. He did eat, a lovely spread starting with walnut and cranberry salad leading into a fantastic pasta dish with some sort of cream sauce and mushrooms and topped with strawberries on a biscuit. Stu was about ready to pop by the time Dana handed him a beer and told him to come out to the porch, an expansive affair that ran the length of the house. They settled onto chairs with metal lattice backs and Stu took a long swig of the beer.

"Lucky Bucket," Dana said. "Brewed about a hundred miles from here, give or take. You still a beer guy?"

"At this point I'm an 'anything I can drink' sort of guy."

"Don't be like that," she said. "If you turn into a drunk I'm going to beat the shit out of you and bury you neck deep in my garden until you come out of it. No rehab for you, my friend. It's the garden all the way and the snails and birds will be your only companions."

"Good to know someone's looking out for me, I suppose."

"So, do you want to address this 'woe is me thing' for a little longer or do you want me to tell you about the job you start on Monday?" Dana said. "Cause I can do either one. Or both, but I'm going to need more beer."

"I think I've got some 'woe is me' coming," he said. "Or didn't you watch the video."

Dana had never actually brought up the specifics of "the incident" other than to offer some much welcomed sympathy. The truth of the matter was Stu was feeling sorry for himself but he had three excellent reasons, to his mind, a pity party made all sorts of sense.

Reason one was the obvious. He had left his job, his girlfriend had left and he couldn't go out in public without significant negative attention from strangers. Reason two played into the fears he had always harbored about himself. Stu didn't have the highest self-esteem but being a cop was something he was good at and was one of the cornerstones he had built his identity on. Technically he was a cop again, but by all accounts a disgraced cop, a failed cop, a cop who took a risk during a precarious situation and paid a price for it.

It was the third reason that he hadn't reckoned with yet. Post-traumatic stress was something Stu had been tested for before he had unceremoniously left the Detroit Police Department and he wasn't sure what he was experiencing was covered by that particular diagnosis anyway. If he were to be dramatic about it he would say his experience was less "traumatic stress" and more "being haunted." Between six and twenty times a day, the face of the boy, his eyes extremely wide in surprise and pain, floated into his mind's eye.

I want to take this back. I want to take this back.

He had been living with the "haunting" for long enough to notice a few patterns. He would know by the time he plugged in his electric shaver in the morning whether it was going to be a good day or a bad day. On a good day, the kid's face would float and he would feel a familiar dropping sensation in his stomach just a few times and it wasn't enough to significantly affect his mood. On a bad day he would have to roll with it, play out scenarios in his head, letting the scene play out over and over throughout the day. He would think what he could have done differently and how it would have played out with a pain and anxiety that, after a time, got to be familiar. He even started actively thinking about his "haunting" while he worked out and the pain and drive it gave him, plus the extra time he had on his hands, had put Stu in the best shape of his life. He had thought of some of these scenarios so often that they almost seemed like a well-worn VHS tape he would play a dozen times when he was a kid and the pain was not friendly, exactly, but more safe.

While, outwardly, the "haunting" didn't change anything about his day-to-day routine, it was making him pretty damn miserable. The worst kind of pain, Stu figured, was the kind that made no mark and couldn't be shared with anyone else. Even his sister.

"Of course I watched the video," she said after a longer than usual silence for her. "It was awful, Stu."

For a moment, all that was audible was the wind in the trees, making a rustling that was loud when you stopped to listen to it. For the first time in a long time, Stu's mind was blank, then he realized the silence was going on for too long and something probably should be said.

"Thanks."

"For what?"

"For saying it was awful," Stu said. "No one does that. I get a lot of 'you did what you could's and a few 'you should've done that's but no 'that's awful.' Thanks."

Another couple of seconds, another big gust rattled a thousand leaves into a loud burst of sound. It wasn't unlike a scream, Stu thought.

"Are the trees always this loud?"

"Yeah," Dana said. "It was one of the first things I noticed when we moved out here. Nature is not a quiet lady."

"Neither are you," Stu said.

"Got that right, brother. I have a lot of friends back East and they all have opinions about living in Nebraska. I remember this one girl, Taylor Gainsberg, you remember her?"

Stu shook his head.

"She wasn't gay but was very touchy feely in high school . . . anyway, she had this loud nasal voice . . ."

"Wait, was she the 'Mr. Daaaaavidson' girl?" Stu suddenly recalled a birthday party where one of the guests had latched on to a funny vocal affectation and ran with it the entire night. In his memory the girls had made fun of a teacher named Mr. Davidson and one girl had drawn the name out so it took three or four seconds to say, all at a high, nasal pitch. It had become a family joke, briefly, until their mother had shut it down.

"Yeah, that was her. I remember running in to her last time I was back East and she asked where I was living and after I told her she said "Nebraaaaaskaaaa, nobody lives in Nebraaaaskaaa."

Stu smiled and leaned back on the warm metal of the lattice chair.

"I told her I live in Nebraaaaaskaaa. I said it just like that but in my normal tone of voice, and she kind of got pissy and left. You basically said the same thing on the phone a few weeks back."

Dana swigged her beer and Stu felt sufficiently sheepish.

"Point of the story is most folks can't fathom living out here. There are only a few restaurants in driving distance, only one grocery store worth going to, there are bugs and deer and you can get where you're going in five minutes. Truth of the matter is I've only been out here a few years and I can't imagine not living here."

"Really?" Stu asked.

"Really really," Dana said. "If I had to move back to Detroit . . . hell, if I had to move up to Sioux Falls, I think I'd be miserable real quick."

"Why? You can sit on a porch in a city. You can see a movie in the morning, you can see live music on a Tuesday night, you can . . ."

"All that shit is secondary, man," Dana said, waving his argument off with her beer bottle. "All that shit, that's just to feel important. People think that if they're surrounded by people doing interesting and important things they'll be interesting and important when the opposite is true.

You can waste your life in a city the way you could never, ever waste it out here. This . . ."

She paused for effect. The wind cooperated.

"This, you and me sitting out on a porch listening to the wind, this is just as important as any of that meaningless crap you just said. Out here you've got to reckon with yourself. Out here, you can figure out who you are. Or you can perfect it. Ahh, speaking of perfect . . ."

Robin had made her way out to the porch and had pulled up a chair. Dana scooched over and put her arm around her wife.

"I was just giving Stu the 'why we live in the country speech.'"

"Did you pause for effect?"

"Sure did."

"Do you think he bought it?" Robin said, her big brown eyes looking Stu up and down for what he would mistake as attraction if he didn't know better.

"Hard to see. He's stubborn."

"He's also about done with this beer," Stu said. "I would stipulate to all your points if I had another beer in my hand in the next five minutes."

•••

There's being full, and then there's what Stu would refer to in the future as being "Robin Full."

Regular full was having eaten until it was prudent to stop. "Robin Full" involved shoveling food hard and fast for an extended period of time because it was so fresh, so flavorful, so sweet, so perfect that stopping just didn't make sense. Then, after the food was gone, you regretted it.

In the following week, dinner had been at Dana and Robin's three times and Stu had eaten more than was socially acceptable ("are you kidding me with this guy?" Robin had asked) at each sitting. He was staying in a bed and breakfast, about fifteen miles away from Cherry in a town called Springview so it wasn't that much of a trek, although he couldn't drink more than a few beers before hitting the road. The owner of the

63

B&B had big dreams of something called "Sandhills Tourism." Stu found her friendly and strange.

There were very few apartments to speak of in the town of Cherry and during the interview for the Sheriff's position he had stopped at the local bar/diner, named "Bar," and asked around. The bartender, a gruff guy named Chuck, had served him a reasonable hamburger and given him three numbers of people who had space to rent. One number was disconnected, the second had seemed promising, and the third was answered by a gentleman who asked Stu if he was "a Jew." Stu had hung up without giving the man any information, ethnic or otherwise.

The second phone number belonged to Carol Cryer, a nice young woman with a two-year-old daughter named Cassidy who seemed permanently affixed to the top of her hip. Her husband was a soldier, off on deployment, and they had a guest house in the back that was bigger than any apartment Stu had ever lived in. It was dingy and slightly depressing but it was big—three rooms, a bathroom, a full kitchen—the kind of apartment that would go for several thousand a month in parts of Detroit.

Stu took the "guest house" and Carol expressed happiness at "having a man around, especially one with a gun."

"My Fred, he can shoot the wings off a fly at one hundred yards," she bragged. "He's still got thirteen months left on his deployment and we've gotten along, but it'll be nice to have someone close by."

"I'm not nearly that good a shot, but I'm glad it worked out, ma'am," Stu said. He almost never used the term "ma'am," considering it more of a little kid thing to say, but it felt appropriate. Carol smiled and bopped back into her house and Stu drove to pick up his stuff. A quick trip to the Shopman's Market in Springview for supplies and a six-pack of Lucky Bucket and he was something resembling settled. Stu had moved enough to know home didn't really feel like home until the TV was plugged in and the wifi was working.

Unfortunately, no one from the cable company would be out until mid-week (though he was surprised at how fast and cheap the available Internet connections were) so he was stuck with his meager DVD collection. On a whim he popped in *Robocop* and almost instantly regretted it as the connection of "ultraviolence" and "Detroit" brought his "haunting" around. He shut off the movie and dove into his six-pack. Beer dulled the feelings a bit but by the time he finally fell asleep the clock on his bedside was spinning and his last thought was "I hope I'm not hung over the morning I meet the guy I'm replacing."

No luck.

Grey Allen was ancient. In his ten years as a law enforcement officer, Stu had never seen quite so old a man still in uniform, which hung off Grey Allen like he was a hanger. To his credit, the old Sheriff immediately stood up, firmly shook Stu's hand and exchanged pleasantries before offering Stu a seat.

"Not much to it, I suppose," Grey Allen said. "The holding cell is over there. This key opens and locks the cell. There's a computer over there if you can figure out what the hell to do with it. I sure can't."

"So you don't have electronic files or access to any national databases or anything like that?" Stu asked, realizing how dire the situation was. "What if you have to file a warrant or something?"

"I call Lynda down in Basset off Highway 20, there. She does all that computer stuff for me. Let's see . . ."

Grey Allen stood up and Stu kept his breathing shallow for fear that a sharp breath might knock the old fart over.

"I'll issue you your weapon. That's important. Every now and again you . . . you get a call from the State Troopers and you gotta deal with that."

There was a long, long pause as Grey Allen scratched his head and tried to think about what else his job entailed.

"There's a lawnmower in the shed out back. You're responsible for that."

"I have to mow the lawn?" Stu asked.

"You have to mow the lawn, yes," Grey Allen said. "The toilet in the back is a bit sticky, too, you might want to look at that if you have any . . ."

He trailed off again. Stu stared at him expectantly.

" . . . any plumbing expertise," he finished.

Stu had been nervous meeting the sheriff whose job he would be taking over, but never in his life would he have come up with this scenario. This wasn't law enforcement as he knew it. As near as he could tell, it wasn't law enforcement as it had once been. There were no computers, very little paperwork that Grey Allen had deemed important enough to tell him about, and a lawn to mow. The theme song from *Gilligan's Island* popped into Stu's head—"no lights, no phones, no motorcars, not a single luxury."

"Like Robinson Crusoe . . ." Stu said under his breath.

"What about Robinson Crusoe?" Grey Allen asked, his hearing still sharp.

"Nothing, sir. I have a question for you and I'm trying to figure out how to say it as respectfully as I can."

"Just go," Grey Allen said. "No point pussy footing around."

Stu drew a breath and neither pussy nor footed.

"How do you spend most of your time?"

"What do you mean?"

"Well, when I was in Detroit I spent some time on patrol, some on paperwork for patrol, I did some investigating using online tools and databases, I spent some time training. I don't see anything like that here and I'm wondering . . ."

"What I do here?"

"Yes, sir," Stu said, careful to add the "sir" lest he seem disrespectful.

"I can tell you," Grey Allen said, pulling up a chair and slouching down low like an old-fashioned baseball manager. "I always figured a bad day out of the office was better than a good day in it so I spent most of my time out there in my truck. I logged over 350,000 miles on this job just driving around town, driving out to see folks I know, driving back. I know everyone in this county by sight, Mr. Dietz. Every single person is known to me and I'm known to them. That's how I get around all that paperwork bullshit, to be honest. People know who I am and I know them."

"I understand the concept but you've got to keep records, sir. You've got to have arrest records, traffic stop records, you've got to have warrants and paperwork for the courts. I don't see any of that."

"Nope," Grey Allen said.

"Nope? That's not a question you answer with 'nope.'"

Grey Allen smiled, stood and put a withered hand on Stu's shoulder.

"I'm sure you'll get us all up to speed, then," he said. "If you run into any problems, you seem smart. You can figure them out."

Grey Allen made for the door and his feet were hitting the dirt outside until Stu realized he meant to leave and, likely, never return.

"Wait!" Stu said, out of his chair so quick it threatened to tip over. "That can't be it. You . . . you're not going to help me any more than that?"

Grey Allen turned around and looked at Stu with tired eyes. The wrinkled bags seemed to almost glow in the hard light of the autumn afternoon.

"You're on your own, kid," he said. "Anything else I could tell you, you'd brush it off. Best figure it out on your own."

"You're not staying around town then?"

"Nope," Grey Allen said. "I promised myself a long vacation a while back. It's time to collect."

Grey Allen seemed to shrink as he got closer and closer to his truck and Stu, not sure what to do either in the situation or at the job in general, stood and watched him go. It took the old-timer almost a minute to open the door to his truck, push it, and climb in before he shot Stu a look and one pearl of wisdom.

"I'm getting out of here," he said. "This town's not cursed exactly . . . but . . . I don't know. Something isn't right."

The door creaked shut, his tires crunched on gravel, and Grey Allen drove away, never to be heard from again.

•••

It took a day or two for the word to get out that Grey Allen was gone, but once it was official Stu's phone did not stop ringing. First it was the County Attorney who had long ago given up the idea of working with the Barter County Sheriff's Department.

"That man," the Attorney, a nice man named Michael Gatliss with a fast mouth and a sharp tongue, said. "He was a son of a bitch, is what he was, if you'll pardon me. I tried to work with him and I tried to work with

67

him and I tried to work with him and he would never return my calls. How do you run a Sheriff's office if there's no office to speak of? How the hell do you do that?"

Stu had assured him he didn't know but he looked forward to working with Mr. Gatliss and that he would value any advice he could give him. The man calmed down and said he would send him over some documents.

"You could email them to me," Stu said.

"Email? Email? Are you playing with me?"

"No," Stu said surely, not sure how to take it.

"That's fantastic!" Mr. Gatliss almost yelled. "I will send you an email. Sweet baby Jesus, yes, I will send you an email."

"That's . . . that's great," Stu offered, not nearly as enthusiastic.

"It's a brand-new day," Gatliss said before hanging up.

This conversation, more or less, played out a dozen or so times in Stu's first few days of duty. Someone would call, feel Stu out, learn he wasn't a technological neophyte or someone hell-bent on obstruction, they would be thrilled and then they would hang up. In between time, Stu did a few patrols, answered a few service calls, though fewer than he had anticipated, and mowed the lawn. It was a small lawn and the mower was well taken care of.

He was on call, more or less, during the evening hours and he slept with his phone close to his bed. It hardly ever rang and if it did it was most likely Dana. In his fourth day he was called down to "Bar" over a dispute concerning a tab, but once he walked through the door all the yelling stopped and things got resolved pretty fast. In between he would visit his sister, who seemed to genuinely like having him around, he would exercise by running some of the flattest land he had ever run, and once cable and Internet got hooked up he spent time in the embrace of serialized television. Even Carol the landlady came by on occasion, once with homemade casserole with bits of Doritos mixed in it. No one bothered him much, no one asked too many questions and most importantly, he didn't have to deal with "the look" once. He had one bad day when his "curse" wouldn't leave him alone but beyond that he was getting the distinct feeling like this move *had* been good for him.

The only meeting of note came when a Mister Stander showed up, in person, at his office for no reason Stu could discern. The man, who was tall and thin but very polite, sharp in his light-colored suit and bow tie, said he was a visitor to Cherry, there on business, and wasn't having any luck tracking down some of the people he was trying to find. Stu had told him he was new and that he was still learning everyone's names and would be little to no help at the present time.

"I would put you on to the former Sheriff, but I got the impression he's left town for good," Stu said. "Seemed eager to put us in his rear view."

Since he started his life in Cherry, Stu had found himself slipping into colloquialisms with more and more frequency. Phrases like "in his rear view" had crept in there but he seemed to be delivering them well. If he sounded like a moron, no one had mentioned it.

"You're not the first one to say that," Mr. Stander said in a voice that was both gravel and silk at the same time. "Sheriff Grey Allen was well known but, as I understand it, he's not missed."

"No, I get that impression too," Stu said. "What are the names of the men you're looking for again?"

"Two men," Mr. Stander said. "A Mr. Kenny Rathman, known as Kenny Kirk, who owns the local garage and a Mr. Ron Smith, who works with the local grain elevator."

"Give me a month on the job and I bet I could help you, but I'm not part of the community just yet," Stu said. "You've driven by their houses, obviously."

"It seems I always just miss them," Mr. Stander said, his voice a fascinating combination of nasal and bass. He sounded like a radio announcer.

"Right," Stu said. "What's your business with these men?"

"There's no way to say this without sounding mysterious, but it's business between my employer and Mr. Rathman and Mr. Smith," Stander said. "It's nothing sinister, I assure you, but it's nothing that I want out in the community. I'm sure you understand. Keeping secrets in a small community is . . . extremely difficult."

"Yeah," Stu said, standing up. "I understand. If I meet these men I will make sure to mention you. Do you have a card or something I can give them?"

"No," Mr. Stander said. "Thank you for your help."

And, like that, he was out the door.

The conversation had sat with Stu all day and the more he thought about it the stranger and stranger it seemed. He had made a point to jot down Mr. Stander's Seattle license plate as he left and ran it the following day on the computer system he had spent half a day getting up and running. It was a personal car and Mr. Stander (first name William) had no outstanding warrants or traffic citations. Not only was he clean, he was cleaner than most.

Aside from that little mystery, things rolled along for a week, two weeks, then three. He met people, but didn't make any friends. He spent time on Facebook, he ran through all the seasons of *Game of Thrones* he had missed, he tried online dating but the nearest match was over fifty miles away. They had a date planned for later in the month and didn't have much in common.

But the longer he spent in basic isolation, the more he had come to the conclusion that Dana had been right. He was healing. He could feel it. The constant reminders of his curse were gone, his sleep patterns were returning, and he made a conscious effort to cut down on beer, though he and Dana had gotten rip-snorting drunk one night and Robin had tucked them into bed on the floor of the living room. Stu had brought up Mr. Stander to Dana and she had given him some good advice, but in the morning it was gone and replaced with headache, nausea and, eventually, vomiting.

If he had remembered his sister's advice, things would have gone a lot smoother in the long run.

"You've done your job," she told him between sips of a particularly stiff amaretto and cream. "What you shouldn't do is let it bug you. What you shouldn't do is let that whole thing set up shop in that head of yours. You should do your job and not get involved with strange men in bow ties."

•••

The reason Mr. Stander couldn't find Kenny was that he had left.

After the events following the scratch, it seemed like the right call. They had all watched Willie pick a fight, Dave take the bait, and things get really ugly, and that's saying something from a guy who had killed a rabbit with his teeth just a few hours earlier.

Part of being in the pack and living with the world-altering secret that you could turn into a wolf was controlling when you "scratched." When you have the ability to turn into a hulking creature capable of doing unspeakable things to small woodland creatures, not to mention human beings, it makes sense to keep that power in check. That's why they broke bread before heading out into the woods, that's why they checked with each other as to how badly they wanted to "go out," it's why they were absolutely honest with each other. Holding back, even with good intentions, could mean both an unwanted transformation and exposure to the outside. Fear of unintentionally killing and/or being found out was what kept them all in check, and honesty and camaraderie were the glue that made those checks possible.

Willie had twisted the system into an outcome no one felt good about. Dave had to confess to his son that he and the rest of them had killed Byron, a family friend that Dilly had known since he was old enough to know anyone. On top of that, Willie had forced Dave's hand and he had confessed that Byron and Josie were lovers in high school before he was born and that they had rekindled that relationship not that long ago. And that the decision to kill Byron was a group decision that had nothing to do with the affair and everything to do with something else, something darker, something that threatened to expose that secret and God knows what else.

Dilly didn't stick around to hear the "something else," opting to run into the woods in his human form to be alone after Dave told him the truth while Josie stifled tears. Afterward, Dave sat at one end of a picnic table, Josie at the other, both with their heads down, the damage done. The rest of the pack, save Willie, kicked at the dirt and tried to figure out a way to leave.

It was Kenny Kirk who figured it out first.

"To hell with this bullshit," he said. "JoAnn, come on."

"I think we've got business to discuss," Ron started.

"Ya heard me say 'to hell with this bullshit,' didn't you?" Kenny said back. "Nothing's getting solved today, not with everyone flipping the fuck out every five minutes. Nah, we're getting out of town."

"We are?" JoAnn asked. "Where we going?"

"We're going to the corner of the highway and we're turning left or right, I don't care which," Kenny said, almost over his shoulder as he headed to his car, JoAnn running to catch up. "I'm done with this soap opera bullshit."

Dave said nothing. Seconds later Kenny's late model Mustang fired up.

"You just gonna let him leave like that?" Willie asked. "I figured you had sack enough to deal with Kenny Kirk throwin' a hissy fit."

"No, he's right," Ron said. "We aren't solving anything today. Especially not you, Willie."

"Whaddya mean, especially not me? All I said was what we were all thinking. Dave's acting like a pussy over there . . ."

"If I were you I'd head on home before Carl and I shut your mouth for you," Ron said, cutting Willie off. Carl took his place next to Ron, who raised his eyebrow at his friend's assertiveness.

"That's how it is, then?"

"That's how it is," Ron said.

"It's amazing you all lasted this long," Willie said, heading to his truck. "Bunch of pussies, the whole lot of you."

Willie ranted and swore all the way to his blue and rust-colored truck, occasionally stopping to see if there was a way he hadn't thought of to get under Dave's skin. But Dave was already broken and Ron and Carl held firm on getting Willie out of there. Two minutes later, Willie was on the road headed back to town.

The minute the old man turned onto the road, Ron whispered something to Carl and they were off as well. There were sympathetic looks, but no words spoken between the group. Dave and Josie stayed in their positions at opposite ends of the picnic table for what seemed like a long time.

"One of us is going to have to go after him," Josie finally said in a soft voice.

"I'd like it to be you, if you don't mind," Dave said. "He's heard my side." Dave stood up and started walking.

"Home is six miles, Dave," Josie said. "Don't walk that far."

"Not going home," Dave said.

"Then what are you doing?" she asked, but Dave was already fifteen yards away, not turning around. He knew his house was six miles away, but "Bar" was only four and some change.

• • •

It was into the late lunch rush when Dave got to "Bar" and most of the regulars had cleared out. He was muddy and gross, he was deep inside his own head (the last two blocks had been tough with swatted-away dueling scenarios concerning his wife and Byron having sex and murdering Willie) but most of all, he was hungry. For a brief second he had panicked thinking his wallet was still at the campsite, but found where he had left it before the "scratch" the night before.

Chuck Nesbit was working the grill and his hearing wasn't so great. Dave had to yell to get his attention.

"CHUCK. Come on, man! I need some food."

Chuck, forever putting the customer first, wandered over about two minutes later.

"Burger?"

"Three of them. Plus fries and beer."

"Someone was out late," Chuck said. "Missed your breakfast, did you?"

"Shut up, asshole," Dave muttered as Chuck got back to the grill. Dave did whatever he could to distract his mind, which was producing new and original dark thoughts every couple of minutes. Unfortunately, "Bar" was not a place to go for distraction. There was a television playing college football, which helped, but Dave was beyond caring about the fate of any team from the SCC (much less two of them). That left the other patrons to look at, but there were fewer and fewer of those all the time as lunch was ending. That left staring at the bottles on the wall and vivid, vivid thoughts of sex, violence, and pain.

73

It was a relief when a new customer walked in wearing a uniform.

"Hey Chuck!" the man yelled. "The grill still going?"

"What's it look like?" Chuck yelled back from the grill, smoke rising over his wrinkly head.

"Looks like you're in a peachy mood," Stu said under his breath, then, much louder, "I'd like a burger and fries please."

"Yep," Chuck said. "Good thing, too. I'm almost out of patties thanks to Dave, there."

Dave looked up from the bar at the new sheriff, his hair flecked with mud, his clothes wrinkled. He was surely putting off a smell. None the less he stood up.

"How you doing, I'm Dave Rhodes. I'm not sure we've had a chance to meet yet."

"Stuart Dietz. I go by Stu. I took over for Grey Allen a couple of weeks ago."

They shook hands.

"You been camping, there, Dave?"

"Yeah," Dave said, running his hand through his brown hair. "I would have showered if I knew I was making a first impression today. That doesn't happen here too often."

"I get that," Stu said. "Mind if I sit?"

"No, go ahead," Dave said. "Glad for the company, to be honest."

Chuck plopped two plates in front of Dave, one with two burgers and one with the third burger and fries. They made the resounding, heavy clash of sturdy dish wear and Chuck went back to the kitchen without a word.

"That's . . . a good bit of food, there, Dave."

A sheepish "yeah" was all Dave could muster before diving in. Between bite two and three, when it was obvious the new sheriff wasn't just sitting there to be polite, but to get to know one of his constituents, Dave slowed down enough to talk.

"You liking town so far?"

"Yeah, it takes some adjustments, but I'm doing all right. It's a different pace than what I'm used to."

"I bet," Dave said. "I've always said this is a great place to live if you already know everybody and are into classic rock."

"I noticed that!" Stu said. "I was expecting everyone to be a country music fan out here but all I hear is that one station, what is it . . . "105.3 The Wolf?"

"That's right. I haven't heard so much Aerosmith in my life."

"That sounds about right. I heard you were from Detroit, right?"

"Worked there a while, yeah," Stu said, going into the spiel he had done several dozen times at this point. "It's been an adjustment, but I'm finding things pretty interesting around here. There's certainly a lot to do. Grey Allen wasn't . . . how do I put this . . . he didn't do things in a very modern way."

"I bet," Dave said, shoveling in fries three at a time.

"So I've been getting the computer up and running and I've been . . . I'm sorry. I don't know that I've ever seen anyone eat like that."

Dave had gotten the first burger and all the fries down and was working on the second. He wasn't usually a glutton, but there were times, especially after a night out in the woods, where his body absolutely demanded food. During those times, consuming calories was like coming up for air after several minutes underwater.

"I'm sorry," Dave said. I don't usually eat this fast."

Chuck took the opportunity to slam Dave's beer on the counter and return to the kitchen, again, without a word.

"I get it," Stu said. "Sometimes you just gotta get some food in you. Can I ask what you do around here, Dave?"

"Yeah, absolutely," Dave said, being much more conscious as to his food intake. "I'm a teacher and a coach at Cody-Kilgore High, about fifteen miles away. I coach volleyball and teach a little bit of everything, but math, mainly."

"Mild-mannered math teacher," Stu said. "And Barter County hamburger-eating champion."

For some reason, Dave found that particularly funny and a laugh bubbled out of his mouth before he could stop it. A chunk of bun went flying from Dave's mouth and both men decided to ignore it.

"Man," Dave said. "I needed that. I know about ten high schoolers who could eat me under the table, though. My kid is one of them."

"How many kids you have?"

"Just the one," Dave said. "Dave Junior."

"Cool," Stu said. "Hey, before I get my food, there's a question I'm asking a lot of the folks I run into and was wondering if I could ask you."

"Shoot."

"Well, Grey Allen was around here a long time and he told me the way he did things was to get involved. He said he knew everyone personally, right? That's going to take me some time to manage, so what I'm asking everyone to do is to give me some time to get to know you all and to kind of keep their eyes open in the meantime. If there's anything I need to know, give me a call or look me up. If there's anything Grey Allen did that I'm doing differently, tell me so I can see if it makes sense for me to do, too. Basically, this one guy did this job for a long time and now we all need to do this job for a little while until I get situated. Does that make sense?"

Stu's lunch clattered on the counter and Chuck went back to the kitchen.

"Yeah, that makes sense," Dave said. "I imagine there are all sorts of things that Grey Allen dealt with that aren't in any files anywhere."

"Exactly," Stu said. "I'm basically setting up from scratch. But don't tell anyone I said that."

"Mum's the word," Dave said, but with a mouthful of chewed food it came out as "mumbs da word."

Stu's food hit the table with the same clatter as before but this time Chuck didn't head back to the kitchen.

"What y'all talking about?" he asked.

"I'm introducing myself," Stu said. "Trying to get to know everybody. Isn't that what I'm supposed to be doing?"

"I figure," Chuck said, now eager for conversation. "I imagine you would have met Dave by now, unless it's that time of the month."

Dave's face was full of fries, which was good because had it not been stuffed he might have told Chuck to shut his face, making himself look more suspicious. Instead he drew in air and some fried potato into his throat and started coughing.

76

"That . . . uh, that wasn't exactly politically correct," Stu said, slapping Dave on the back. "Why would you say something like that, man?"

Over fits of coughing Dave shot Chuck a look that said "I'm not in the practice of killing people, but in your case . . ."

"I didn't mean nothing by it," Chuck said. "I've, uh . . . dishes."

As he beat his retreat, Dave cleared his throat a few times and smiled at Stu.

"Small towns, huh?"

"Yeah, I guess."

After sitting for a second, Stu started eating and Dave took a long draft of his beer and reverted to the only neutral territory available after making such a distinguished first impression.

"So," Dave said. "You a Cornhusker football fan?"

• • •

A few hours later after Stu had headed out on patrol and Dave had returned home to an empty house, Kenny Kirk and JoAnn were still on the road. Although he was financially comfortable and owned several businesses vital to the community, the house he and JoAnn shared was humble, old, and lived in. The staircase creaked whenever anyone got near it, the fuses blew with alarming regularity, and one of the bathrooms on the second floor had a noticeable sag in the middle, denoting structural decay. The consequence of the house's age was it groaned and squeaked anywhere you went and it was very hard to sneak up on someone.

This made it particularly surprising that Mr. Stander had been able to break into the house and sit in a chair without making so much as a peep or alerting any of the neighbors. Kenny and JoAnn were gone, of course, and would stay gone for a bit, much to Mr. Stander's increasing frustration.

He was a patient man, but even this was pushing it. After sitting in the house from the late afternoon until after sunset, the tall man in the bow tie let out a long sigh and pulled himself out of the (admittedly very comfortable) lounger in the living room.

"No wonder no one's found them yet," he said to the empty room. "Who in their right mind would want to spend time in such a dump?"

Stander made no effort to not set off the symphony high-pitched squeaks as he tread the floor out of the living room and out the back door.

AN EXCERPT FROM THE DIARY OF J.P. CODDINGTON BARTER COUNTY, 1876

June 22, 1867

I fear the loss of the Railroad will be the death of this town.

The county elders lobbied for the Railroad to come through, but there was resistance, particularly from Homer Rhodes and his group. There was ample discussion in the First Baptist Church over the weekend and much was discussed, but not decided. There was talk of what the Railroad would bring, both good and bad, and how we might grow prosperous with or without the tracks going just south of town, but I do not think the arguments against the train hold any water at all.

Homer Rhodes swears there is oil under the ground and that the right men with the right equipment might get at that oil quickly. Once the wells are built it would be a "short road to progress and prosperity" he said. Neither I, nor my friends have ever heard of oil being found here in this part of the country and his promises rang hollow in my ears. The Railroad is a known thing, proven to be a boost to the towns and counties they encounter. Why a man would push against such progress is a mystery to me.

I was going to say as much in the meeting, but Mr. Rhodes and his crew of men are a boorish lot. They silenced many a naysayer yelling such phrases as "we've been over this" and "next question" to the point where civilized discourse, even among the educated, was a fool's errand. I left frustrated to a point as did Mr. O'Conner, Mr. Smith and several others. We commiserated at the local bar a bit later, and I'm afraid I had too many drinks and am paying the toll for it today in a sour stomach, among other ailments.

To add misery to my condition, I also found the oddest pile of animal remains very near the doorstep of my home this morning. If I'm not mistaken, it was a deer at one time but whatever had taken after the pitiful creature left some doubt. The head was either gone or in such small pieces as to be unrecognizable. The hide had been torn open, as if all at once. I am at a loss to what force on heaven or Earth could do such a thing or how the doomed creature ended up on my doorstep, for all intents and purposes.

Needless to say the entire scene churned my stomach and I vomited on the mass. After a few shovelfuls of dirt I composed myself and was able to move the carcass to a more suitable location.

May my fortunes improve.

PART 4 - HOME OF THE WOLF

Carl Eakes was not much of a talker in the normal course of affairs, but he was one hell of a gardener.

As a vocation, he owned a small towing business that Kenny Kirk had helped him get started. He had a good-sized wrecker, bigger than any in the area, and the boy knew how to drive it. When he was in high school he had dreamed basic dreams—diesel mechanic, law enforcement, something with computers. While he had gone to school and was a diesel mechanic (one dream down!), he hadn't taken to working on the clock for a number of reasons. One was his garden.

He owned a modest home in "town" with a two-acre-wide backyard where he grew vegetables, flowers and had a very small orchard. When late March rolled around and the temperature was tolerable he lit outside and would check his compost piles, start tilling and fertilizing the soil and making ready. In the spring it was planting then constant watering, weeding, watering, separating, watering, pruning and watering. By July the harvests started. By September there were buckets and buckets of tomatoes and cucumbers, squash and potatoes, melons, carrots, onions, peppers and anything else you'd want from a garden.

Then there were the flowers. Peonies, mums, roses, lilies and so much more, rows and rows of fragrance and color that led to an entire insect infrastructure of bees and hummingbirds and yellow jackets and mantises and ants and spiders. Everywhere in Carl's garden was life and when the life started to fall away and peel back as the weather got cold again, Kenny ate fresh salsa and crunchy salads and cut sweet melons and put strawberries on his ice cream. He even fermented some of his apples into the best goddamn cider in a three-county area, but he didn't tell too many people about that. There might be laws and such.

His neighbors always knew he was in the garden because Carl was a loyal listener of 105.3, The Wolf, Central Nebraska's Classic Rock. The station was sometimes hard to get in Cherry, but Carl had rigged up a 25-foot antenna to his shed and was able to play The Wolf at a reasonable volume any time he wanted. His neighbors were cool with it, so his backyard was Carl's favorite place in the world. It was him, his plants, and AC/DC, Aerosmith, Lynyrd Skynyrd, Rush, Styx and even the occasional foray into Metallica. When James Hetfield would come through his speaker system, Carl swore the whole garden lit up.

It was mid-October when Dilly had his first "scratch" so his garden was producing a fermented smell that you get when plants die. Two days after they had run in the woods then fought at the campground, Ron was the first to come by and he specifically asked for some cider.

"Where you at?" Ron said.

"Not close. Maybe a three."

"Well I'm at a six and I need something to drink. Normally I don't," Ron said. "But I think this calls for it. Don't you?"

"Probably," Carl said. "It's been a good year for apples."

"That's not why I want to drink."

"I know."

"It's because we're cracking up."

"I know."

"It's because that's about as nasty and mean as I've ever seen Willie and I don't know if all of us are going to be together much longer. Something's bothering Willie and it ain't about Byron. We all agreed on that."

"Yeah, we did," Carl said. He stood up and headed into the kitchen, returning with a pint glass full of homemade hard cider. He handed it to Ron, who was off again. The big man didn't usually talk but when he did it came in torrents making it very hard for the much smaller Carl to get a word in edgewise.

"It was kind of brilliant what he did, really," Ron said, as if Carl was unaware. "He knew he had Dave by the balls, man. He knew he would have to tell Dilly everything in front of the pack. Willie knew he had him and he may have just destroyed that family tonight. Plus, I don't know if Dave will ever run with Willie again after what he did."

"I don't know," Carl said. "People fight all the time. They get over things."

"How the hell does a man get over that?" Ron said. "I couldn't promise I wouldn't have killed Willie where he stood if I was Dave."

"Yep," Carl said.

"Instead, there's a guy who's been cheated on and second-guessed and forced to kill one of his friends and his son has to hear about the two worst things in his life back to back. I couldn't get over that."

"So whatdya think will happen?"

Ron was now up wandering the garden, going full blast, his volume and hackles up. Carl had been friends with Ron for coming up on fifteen years but they were friends in the way that Marcie and Peppermint Patty were friends in the Peanuts cartoons. Not quite bad enough to be a motor-mouth like Kenny Kirk, Ron could get worked up and go for a while, and Carl knew it was best to let him go, kicking at decaying plants as he went.

"If Dave had just said 'I'm breaking the rules right now for obvious reasons' no one would have thrown up a fuss. They would have still had to talk to Dilly but they could have done it on their own terms, I guess. That's damn sure better than what happened. What do you put on these melons, Carl, they are fantastic?"

"It's about the soil," Carl said. "It's not what you put on them."

"Yeah I guess," Ron said, having talked himself out. "The cider is good. How much did you make?"

"More than I should've," Carl said. "You can take a jug home if you want."

"I'd appreciate that, man," Ron said. Having talked himself out and checked on his friend, Kenny was alone in his garden ten minutes later, a gallon growler of cider gone from his fridge. It wasn't half an hour later that Kenny Kirk showed up, leading with "That was a complete whirlwind of a train wreck of a shit show out there," before he had made it inside the door.

"Where you at?"

"Three, maybe."

"Well, I'm about with you but I'm worried we might not get another chance anytime soon. I know Willie used to run lead and I know Dave took it from him but goddammit, man, get over it. This isn't . . . God, it's not King Lear . . . what's the one where they all conspire to murder the king?"

"Macbeth, maybe? Shakespeare liked that storyline."

"Yeah, that might be it. Wasn't there one where the king had a bunch of kids and they were conspiring against him and he was really old? What you got to drink around here?"

"Got some cider in the fridge."

"Damn, Carl, you're a good dude. That's why I tell people that Carl Eakes is a good dude. You never let a man go thirsty."

"Where's JoAnn?"

"Dropped her off at the house. We've talked this to death. I need some fresh ears."

The same-sized growler disappeared from Carl's fridge, but this time it went straight down Kenny Kirk's throat. The two wandered in the garden, Kenny stopping every so often to wildly gesticulate. He spoke twice as much as Ron had and said just about the same amount.

"What do you think we should do?" Carl finally asked, when the dire nature of the situation had been suitably articulated.

"You asked me that when we were talking about Byron."

"I'm not good at hard decisions."

"Well, then you're lucky to have a friend like me to figure it all out. The way I figure, Willie and Dave are done. Done-sky. Caput. They're never running together again."

"I don't know . . ."

"Well I do know, goddammit, and you've gotta make up your mind on which pack you're going to run with. And what you're prepared to do to run with them."

"It's not going to come to that."

"Do you see Dave forgiving Willie? Do you see him going 'no biggie, you made me confess to murder and your mother's adultery to our kid after one of the seminal moments of his life? How about some pie?' You see that happening?"

"No," Carl said. "But . . . I don't know."

"Well, I do."

"Family does some crazy things," Carl said, measuring his words to not get immediately shot down by Kenny. "And that's without the weird part of turning into wolves and chasing deer through the woods."

"All I'm saying is get comfortable with two packs or one pack trying to kill the other pack or . . . shit I don't know. That was some great cider."

"Take some home."

"Thank you, I will. JoAnn needs to chill out on a few things and this might help."

"JoAnn is great. Don't talk like that."

"Yeah, you're right," Kenny said, stumbling toward the fridge. "I'll tell her you said so. Catch you later."

• • •

The sun was setting when there was a final knock on the door. Carl half expected Kenny Kirk to be back peddling another theory or begging for more cider, but got a deep, sinking feeling in his gut when he opened the door to find Dilly. The kid looked worn and defeated.

"Hi, Carl."

"Dilly."

"Can I come in?"

"Yeah. Come sit in the back."

The sickly sweet smell was always worse in the evening for some reason and Carl noticed it was worse than just an hour ago when he and

84

Kenny had been strolling. Dilly plopped in one of Carl's white, plastic chairs that wobbled under the size of a tall, gangly teen.

"Sorry I didn't call first."

"No problem," Carl said, easing into his own chair. "No one ever does."

"I . . . uh . . . it's been a rough couple of days."

"I figure."

"I've got a lot of new information I'm trying to figure out."

"Yes, you have."

A wind cut through the garden carrying away the scent of Carl's plants and bringing in grasses and dirt, trees and something that smelled dimly of fire. It reminded Carl, as new scents always did, that he was not a normal guy. He was a guy with responsibilities, a guy who had to be in control of himself and had to be part of a group that controlled each other. If they didn't do that, they risked hurting more than each other and if one of them went rogue, then it would be Byron all over again.

"So, where you at, Dilly?"

"Huh?"

His dad should have explained this by now, Carl thought, then felt weird about being critical of the guy running lead.

"All of us, we are always checking in about how bad we want to . . . go for a run."

"Oh," Dilly said.

"We usually use a one to ten scale so if I meet up with Kenny or Ron the first thing I always ask them is "where you at?" They give me a number and that helps us figure out how bad one of our brothers needs to run."

"How do you know how bad you need it?"

"Your dad should probably tell you that."

"My dad's not here," Dilly said with a sneer. His tone was, by far, the meanest Carl had ever heard from the boy.

"That doesn't mean it's my place."

"I'm asking you," Dilly said. "I'm asking you how you know because . . . because it was the greatest thing that had ever happened to me. I felt like I could face down a hurricane. I felt . . . I don't know how to put it . . ."

"You felt your ancestors in your blood. Felt like you were part of something that was ancient and powerful and badass."

"Yeah," Dilly said, not acknowledging Carl's uncharacteristic eloquence. "Nailed it."

"I don't know how it's going to work for you," Carl said. "It's different for everybody. For Willie, it comes on fast. You talk to him in the morning and he's a two, then he gets in a fight with Lacy and he's suddenly at a seven or an eight and you gotta change your plans. All I can tell you is figure out your rhythms and the way your brain works with this new thing and you'll be fine."

Dilly shifted in his seat.

"OK, this is a . . . this is a hard question, but, does it always feel this good? Is it always such a rush?"

"It's great every single time," Carl said. "You know Ron. He don't look it with his beard and his gut but he's a stone-cold genius. With computers, there ain't nothing he can't get them to do and he's working in a grain elevator. Kenny Kirk, with a mouth like that? He could be running something. I don't know what, but something."

Dilly laughed the laugh of a kid still trying to figure out what his laugh sounded like.

"Hell, Dilly, your dad, and I know you don't want to hear this right now, but your dad was a beast on the football field. He could have gone to college and played football and gone on to better things and your mom? Your mom studied chemistry for a semester, did you know that? She wanted to go be a pediatrician and she could have done it, too. JoAnn wanted to write for a newspaper. Karen could have been in the ballet, I swear. I could have left this town and found someone to be with. Why do you think all these people who could have gone on to better things in bigger places, why are they here? What's keeping them in podunk Cherry, Nebraska?"

Carl had intended to let his speech hang for a second and let the glory of it wash over the new recruit, but Dilly ruined it and started to cry. It started when he tilted his head at a strange angle, then sniffled a little too hard. By the time Carl turned his head, Dilly was full-on trying to stop crying. He wiped tears with the heel of his hand, and Carl gave him a long time to speak.

"Sorry," Dilly said. "It's too much."

"What's too much?"

"You're telling me this is it. This is my life? My mom and my dad and my grandpa and their friends and, oh yeah, by the way we might kill people you know from time to time and your mom's a whore and your dad is a fucking pussy and this's it? This and the woods, this is what I get?"

"Dilly, you gotta talk to your dad about this."

"FUCK HIM!" Dilly yelled, the veins standing out strong along his neck.

Carl stood up and walked inside, reemerging soon thereafter with two glasses of cider. He placed the glasses on the wrought iron table, flaking paint but sturdy, and spoke to his young guest in a serious, clipped tone he saved for special occasions.

"A couple things, Dilly," he said. "And if you tell your dad I told you any of this or that I gave you this cider I'm going to deny it and he's going to believe me. One, calling women 'whores' is a nasty habit and one you should break toot suite. It's ugly and sexist and nothing a man of substance does. Second, next time you see Willie, ask him how big a pussy your dad is. You don't get to run lead unless you earn it. Third, you don't know the whole story about Byron so I would strongly suggest you reserve judgment, as hard as that is, until you know all the facts. And most importantly this isn't all there is. You think we're trapped here? You think I couldn't move to Omaha or Kansas City or Nova Scotia or Germany or some place? I can leave any time I want. I choose to stay here because I'm part of something and being part of something, that ain't nothing."

Carl threw back his cider. Dilly watched him do it and then followed suit, shutting his eyes hard after it hit the back of his throat. He let out a couple of short coughs.

"What's the matter kid? Never drank before?"

"No," Dilly said. "As a matter of fact this was the first time."

"Well, now I've done it," Carl said, grabbing the glasses. Dilly followed him into the house and made for the door.

"I won't tell Dad I came here," he said.

"I'd appreciate it," Carl said. "I wish I had more advice for you, but it's different for all of us. What works for me, that ain't going to work for you."

Dilly nodded and made his way to the road. There was no car in the driveway, which put him a good mile from home on foot. He had plenty to think about, Carl figured.

In a rare act brought on by a rare time, Carl poured himself a second, much taller glass of cider and sat himself on his couch opposite the biggest window in the house. He had had enough of the smell outside for one day.

He played through everything again in his head—Ron's panic, Kenny Kirk's fatalism, Dilly's discovery, his own ability to give halfway decent advice. All in all, he concluded, things were bad, but things looked like they could get better. The train wasn't all the way off the tracks.

"But if Willie shows up tonight, he's not getting any cider," Carl said to the long, deep shadows that had taken residence in his living room.

•••

The night after the "scratch" that led to the blowup, Dilly had gone straight to his room and shut the door. With a kid not talking to her and a husband who was out somewhere for an indefinite amount of time, Josie found herself alone in the house. It wasn't an uncommon occurrence but the empty house that was sometimes her friend was certainly not in this instance. The silence was screaming and work or family was not there to distract her.

There were dishes to do. There was always laundry. She had three books in varying states of completion. At one point, she thought it would be fun to go punch something until her knuckles bled, that way there would at least be some sort of physical component to the soul-shaking pain she was going through, but there would be questions and blood to clean up. There was only one thing left to do.

Without a word to Dilly, she laced up her shoes, fired up her music player and was off, the fall air cutting into her lungs. Josie was a nurse by trade, a mother, a wife and a keeper of some very big secrets (fewer of late). These things would come and go. But the one thing she had been since she was thirteen years old was a runner.

There was a treadmill in their house and on certain days when the weather would freeze her to the bone or melt her into a puddle, it made sense to trek into the basement and spend some time on the bulky machine. But if it was at all possible, Josie wrestled with asphalt and gravel, traffic and road signs. She hadn't grown up in Cherry but Lincoln, an entirely different world by comparison. The first time she ran in Cherry, two very kind people stopped their cars and asked if she needed a ride someplace.

By now she was a fixture on the roads, usually in the early morning hours, but it was not uncommon to see her out after dinner. What was uncommon was the volume of the music in her ears, the pace she was pushing, and the distance she ran. The night and day flashed in her head and scenarios, conversations, what she would say to Dave when they finally talked, how they would deal with Dilly, how she might murder Willie and get away with it, all of it and much more flashed in her brain, blotting out everything but the road and blur of her feet underneath her until her run was over. Then she did it again. She ran ten miles and by the time she came back to the house, Dilly was watching TV, her iPod was drained of its battery and she felt better. Not good, but certainly not the wreck she had been a few hours earlier.

"Dilly," she yelled down the hall. "I'm getting in the shower and then we should talk. Don't go anywhere, please."

There was no response, so she made it to her room and stripped off her gear. Her left sock was bloody from the run with one toe and the heel of the foot shredded and sacrificed to the endorphin gods. The shower was long but not too long and when she got out, Dilly was there, like the good boy he was.

"Where's Dad?" he asked.

"I don't know. He walked off and I was hoping he'd be back by now."

"When's he going to be home?"

"You know as much as I do, Dilly."

In her mind's eye as she ran, Josie had pictured this going differently.

If Dave had been there, they could have put their own feelings aside for an hour or so for the sake of the boy, they could have made sure he understood what was happening, why it had happened and what happens from here, but Dave was out sulking God knows where and Josie made the decision right then and there that this talk could not wait.

"Do you understand what happened a few days ago?"

Dilly stared at her, not really grasping what she was getting at.

"Do you understand why we told you all that stuff? Do you understand we didn't have a choice because of how this thing of ours works?"

"I understand you slept with another man and Dad killed him."

"Then you don't get it at all," Josie said, wincing a bit. "You didn't even get the facts right, sweetie."

"I think I got the gist," Dilly said, turning back to the TV. She was losing him.

"There's a ton we have to sort through here, but right now there's one really, really important thing I need you to understand about our group. What Willie did . . ."

"Grandpa."

"What Willie did was use a bond that we all share to pick at your dad and me. He knew, better than anyone, that in order for all this to work we have to be one hundred percent honest with each other. We have to be rock solid. There cannot be secrets and there cannot be grudges because if either of those things happen when you boys are out in the woods there's going to be so much blood, Dilly. So much blood."

He had turned back around and was at least listening.

"This thing of ours, it goes back hundreds of years that we can figure out and some of the other packs, I guess you could call them, they would write down what worked for them and what didn't work for them, what their problems were and how they solved it. Stay here, just a sec."

Josie got up, the lactic acid in her legs already settled and inducing a decent amount of pain as she got to her feet. A couple of minutes later she was back from her scrapbooking area with a leather-bound book she kept in a drawer.

"This is a history of our group. It goes back all the way to 1870 when this guy, Homer Rhodes, started keeping a journal about his group."

"They ever kill anyone?" Dilly asked sharply.

"Yeah," Josie said. "Three of them. Turns out there was a big fight about the Railroad they couldn't get over so they sort of . . . had a wolf fight. It was a bad idea. They destroyed three buildings and were seen by half the town."

"Whoa," Dilly said.

"Homer Rhodes wrote in his diary that he had to use all his power to keep everyone quiet. Then it became a thing people accepted and then it sort of became part of the town. And here we are."

"Great history lesson, Mom. What's that have to do with anything?"

"Because Homer Rhodes wrote down the rules, you smart ass," Josie said. Her tone was playful but they both knew she was serious about not being pushed. "The rules of the scratch, he called them. And rule number one, and this has always been rule number one, is there are no secrets in the pack. No matter how much pain, no matter how many hurt feelings, the survival in society depends on everyone knowing what's going on. There are no secrets between any of us, and like it or not, kiddo, you're one of us now."

"OK," Dilly said. "You need me to be honest with you?"

"Dilly . . ."

"Honestly, I'm thinking I need to get out of the house for a bit. Maybe go for a run, like you did. That OK?"

"Yeah, that's fine, but we do need to talk."

"Let's wait for Dad."

Dilly was out of his seat before Josie could stop him, grabbing a jacket (he wasn't a stupid kid) and heading out the door.

Even though Josie got it, she understood, that didn't make the house any less empty or her head any less full. She hobbled over to the kitchen sink to start the water for dishes and then made her way to the bathroom to get some bandages for her swelling foot.

• • •

It's stupid, the thing that goes through a man's head when he feels sorry for himself. Can I start a new life in another town? Maybe I'll sleep tonight in some inexpensive hotel, that'll show her. Suicide, if done right, might not be so bad.

Truth of the matter is, Dave was in a stupor. He had spent the past few nights at "Bar" and had exhausted its limited pleasures. He was exhausted and wanted his own bed or, failing that, the couch. It was time to go home.

"Thanks for the place to crash, Chuck," Dave said, standing up.

"Yeah," Chuck grunted. "I don't mind your money, but it's probably better if we see less of each other."

"Rejected by my bartender," Dave said, tossing a few dollars on the bar. "New rock bottom."

Another fun thing about Cherry was since Dave and his crew didn't keep secrets from each other, the whole town basically knew when something was up. He knew what Chuck knew—Byron, who was his responsibility, had slaughtered a girl out back and ruined his evening. A graceful man would have said nothing. Chuck had brought it up at least three times that night alone. For some reason, the decreased dependability of his air conditioner was somehow tied to the incident. It was really time for Dave to go home.

Josie had the car, so Dave got set for a long walk back to the house. Cherry was not populous, but it was big, with houses running north to south for about a three-mile swath. Dave's house was somewhere in the middle so he had a fifteen-to-twenty-five-minute walk in front of him. Turned out it would be longer.

As Dave rounded the building and pointed himself toward home, a man in a light-colored suit and a bow tie was standing beside a black sedan. He waited for Dave, not giving a hint as to his intention, but simply watching the whole time. It was when the men were fifteen feet apart that the man spoke.

"Mr. Rhodes. Good evening."

Dave had not had much to drink, one beer after the one with dinner, which he had nursed as a football game finished up on Bar's shitty TV, but the combination of fatigue and emotional pain had left him a bit loopy.

Initially, the fact the stranger knew his name didn't register. Dave, being a polite fellow, stopped anyway.

"Lovely night," Dave said.

"If you mean the weather, then yes. It's quite temperate, Mr. David Rhodes."

It stuck this time, as did the man's formal tone and odd, deep voice.

"I . . . uh . . . are you a parent of a student of mine? I'm sorry, I don't recognize you."

"No, I'm not. My name is William Stander and I need to talk to you."

"What do you need to talk to me about?"

Before William Stander, the man in the light-colored suit and sharp bow tie could answer, another car whipped around the corner running parallel to "Bar" and onto the street. The car was low, sporty and coming very fast. Before Dave could get a bead on what was happening, the car had pulled into the narrow space between him and Mr. Stander, squealing tires. From inside, loud hip-hop was blaring and as the passenger side door flew open it clipped Dave in the lower torso. Inside was a thin man with wild, brown hair and an unmatched scraggly beard who Dave had never seen before.

"Get inside, you fucking idiot," the man yelled over the music. "Right now before he says another word."

Mr. Stander was already moving to the other side of the car, but his long legs proved more hindrance than help as he had a short distance to cover because of the car's sporty frame. Dave, not accustomed to being called an idiot, stood there dumbfounded.

"Fine," the man in the car said and, in one swift motion, reached over, grabbed Dave by the shirt and dragged him into the car. Mr. Stander was around the car at that point and had a hand on Dave's arm.

"I implore you, Mr. Rhodes, it is very important you hear what I have to say."

"Fuck off then fuck off some more you dandy!" the man in the car yelled over the thump of the music, pulling on Dave the whole time. After a few seconds, the man hit the gas and Dave, half in and half out of the car, had to make a choice—get in the car or bail.

"Come on, Dave!" the man yelled. "Make a good decision for once."

"I will make you richer than you can imagine," Mr. Stander yelled as Dave hopped in the sports car. They were half a block away from Mr. Stander when he finally shut the door. The second the door's locking mechanism clicked into place, the man tromped on the gas and they were gone into the Nebraska night, sputtering gravel behind them.

The man with the beard turned on the dome light, took one look at Dave and cranked the music louder. It was impossible for Dave to communicate with the man until he suddenly slammed on the brakes in the middle of a dirt road about a mile away, shut the car off and turned to Dave. The dirt roads surrounding the town always reminded him of his younger days when Dave and his dates would drive to the middle of nowhere and have at each other. On their anniversary a few years back, Josie had taken him out to the dirt roads far beyond the streetlights to that special sort of dark you could only get in the country and screwed his brains out. None of this came to mind tonight. "Oh my, Dave, you've made a fucking mess of it, haven't you?"

Now that the music had died down and it was just the man talking, Dave could make out the man's accent. It was Irish, he figured. The Irish flag tattoo the man sported on the back of his left hand confirmed his suspicions. In fact, the man had a few tattoos but in the low light, Dave was having a hard time making them out.

"Respond to me, please," the man said. "Or are you too fucking stupid to speak, because, to be honest, I kind of think you are."

"OK, hello, I'm Dave, why am I in your car?" Dave said, torn between wanting to be polite and his fatigue.

"Ahh, the leader finally speaks. Good for you. I've got a lot of work to do on account of your dumb ass, so if you'll sit and listen . . ."

"STOP!" Dave yelled as the rage he had been sucking on all day finally found an outlet. "Just . . . stop. I am going to need your name and I'm going to need to know what the hell we're doing here in the middle of nowhere. And how you know my name. And how you know where to find me! And how you're Irish . . . you're Irish. I've never met anyone from Ireland much less one that knows my name and pulls me into his car and drives me to the middle of nowhere."

The man in the beard raised his eyebrows but didn't budge.

"So what do you want?" the man asked.

"What the fuck just happened?" Dave said, breathing hard. "Give me something to hold on to because I feel like I'm falling right now."

Things got a lot brighter as the man opened the door and got out. The car was still running, though the music was mercifully turned off, and the man walked in front of the car so the headlights could hit him. The man began to twitch.

Dave's eyes got wider as the man started sprouting hair, hunching his posture and growing, or more accurately, stretching into a familiar form, but somehow different than the one Dave was used to. It took the stranger a mere ten seconds to go from man to wolf and once the transformation was complete, the Irish Wolf stood on his hind legs, walked over to Dave's car door, opened it and in a deep, devilish growl, spoke.

"Like I said," the Irish Wolf spat, *"you've made a big, fucking mess."*

• • •

Dave and the man spoke into the night and less than an hour later, he dropped Dave off at his house with strict instructions to not open the door for anyone other than his pack, and even then, beware. Things were about to get complicated, he said. He was right.

More than two miles away in his rented space, Stu was getting ready to plow through another Netflix original series when his cell phone rang.

"Hello, Sheriff. It's William Stander. We met several days ago."

"Yes, hello. You've caught me at home. How did you get this number?"

"If I had a tip for you about something very odd happening in your town, would you be interested?"

"Yes. Can we talk at the station tomorrow?"

"I'm not coming in to the station," Mr. Stander said. "What I will tell you is I believe I know the identity of the person who killed Sandra Riedel and Byron Matzen."

Stu scrambled to find his note pad and something to write with.

"That's . . . um, yeah. That's definitely something I'm interested in. Where are you?"

"I'm not at liberty to tell you that, I'm sorry," Mr. Stander said. "I know I'm being cryptic, but it's absolutely necessary, as is this. Do you have a pencil and paper?"

"Yes," Stu said.

"Would you meet me at the following address tomorrow evening at 7:15? I will be there in person and alone."

Mr. Stander gave the address which Stu didn't recognize (to be fair, he didn't know his own address well at this point), but wrote down.

"Mr. Stander, can you give me any more information? This all strikes me as odd and slightly alarming."

"Good," Mr. Stander said. "You are in the proper frame of mind. Until tomorrow night."

He hung up and Stu immediately put on his uniform, got into his car and drove to the address. When his GPS barked that he had "reached his destination," he double-checked to be sure. It was an old picnic area right off the highway with nothing but a few picnic tables and some debris from previous campers to make it stand out from the miles and miles of grassland surrounding it. Stu spent about twenty minutes walking around inspecting the area. He found nothing of interest, but did find a good hiding place in a tree stump about twenty-five feet into the wooded area. He could see the entire area, see who was approaching and even had the drop on them should they decide to run.

"Man," Stu said. "That guy is never going to see me coming."

A Selective History of Barter County, Part 3

Adam Rhodes was born in 1897 and grew into a strapping young boy. At twelve, he was both smart, winning the admiration of his teachers, and a fiercely physical boy, winning the respect of his coaches. He could keep up on the track with high schoolers, he could hit harder than any bully and he was popular with both boys and girls. As he entered his high school years he even managed to fit business into his busy schedule, working at Shreiner's Grocery and Goods in downtown Cherry. The Governor of Nebraska, Ashton C. Shallenberger, once visited Cherry and tipped young Adam a dime for taking care of his car.

When World War I rolled around, Adam, who was of prime military age, dutifully and proudly enlisted. His brother Kane was too young, but would eventually become a minister at the urging of his mother, who could not stand for her only children to both be overseas fighting a war. She was rumored to suffer from a condition of the nerves and Adam being overseas did nothing to improve her health.

As in all things before, Adam proved a smart, physical and adept soldier. While it was very uncommon for a "grunt" to rise through the ranks, Adam was able to do just that, moving from Private to Sergeant First Class by the time the war ended. To hear his men tell it, Sergeant Rhodes could outrun a bullet, he could inspire a coward, and he could tear a man apart with his hands. Only one of these things was hyperbole.

Sergeant First Class Rhodes came home to a hero's welcome straight out of American lore. He never paid for a meal and he raised the flag at sporting events for years to come. He married his high school sweetheart, a girl named Nellie Buxton, in 1919, a year to the day after he returned home from the war. Through it all, Adam never once showed any desire other than to stay in his town and make it strong. He purchased Shreiner's Grocery and Goods, the place he had worked as a boy, and turned it into the shopping destination for miles around by adding more variety and household items that old Mr. Shreiner had refused to stock. The result was a booming business, a young wife and, quickly, a child on the way.

When Adam's body was found in a ditch, torn apart by what appeared to be wild animals, it tore the town apart. Men wept, women wept, children wept and a malaise descended over the town, from which it never recovered. Nellie miscarried their child out of grief. At Adam's funeral, Kane gave the eulogy and opined that his brother's death "would leave a mark on this town that may never fully heal."

His words were prophetic. Shreiner's closed six months after Adam's death and other businesses followed suit. Even the happy occasion of Adam's son Bruce being born could not make a dent in the town's mood. Things continued, but growth all but stopped.

Some in the town looked to Kane for leadership and on a spiritual level, he provided. His church thrived during hard times and eight months after his brother's death he married Nellie Buxton Rhodes, his brother's widow. It was looked upon, by most in the community, as an act of charity in line with biblical teachings. They had two sons and a daughter, Adam, Thomas and Sarah. Thomas followed in his father's footsteps, becoming a pastor, marrying young and having two boys and a daughter, naming them Thomas Jr., William and Cynthia.

PART 5 – OUT OF YOUR SYSTEM

The man with the Irish accent was expected to speak in front of the assembled group in the "family room" of Dave and Josie's house, but he had not yet arrived. Ron and Carl were on one couch section, Dilly and Josie on the other. Kenny Kirk and JoAnn were hanging out by the television, Dave not far away. Willie was off by the laundry room. No one was having fun.

It was a rare day when Dave called everyone together for something other than a scratch but the socializing was part of the comfortable routine they had all fallen into during their time together. They would see each other socially, they would talk one on one or in small groups but the only time they were all in one place was when they scratched. It wasn't policy or for any particular purpose, so the gathering was an odd one. No one was talking and no one wasn't looking at the stranger in their midst.

"You should have made some food," Willie barked out of nowhere. "I'm hungry."

"You know, little smokies wouldn't have gone awry," Ron said.

"Yeah, shut up," Dave said. "This isn't a tailgate."

"What the hell is it then?" Willie said. "Are we gonna all get in touch with our feelings now? Is that what this is about?"

"I've told you the story, Willie. That's what I know."

"Your story has the whiff of bullshit if you ask me," Willie said.

Dave turned away from him and exhaled deeply, trying to regain his composure.

"Tell you what. It's 7:30 right now. If he's not here by 7:45, leave."

"Yeah, you'd like that, wouldn't you?" Willie said, and left it at that. He didn't have a firm hold of the thread and his mouth had gotten ahead of him.

But 7:45 came. Then 7:50 and at five before 8:00 there was finally a knock on the door. Dave went to open it and everyone peered from their seats to get a good look at the man. He was wearing a leather jacket over his thin T-shirt and whispered something to Dave, who whispered back. Even with their above-average hearing, no one in the room heard what was being said.

"OK, everyone," Dave said. "Conall Brennan, the man I was telling you about."

"The man who saved your ass from a businessman then turned into a wolf, right?" Willie said.

"I'm sure your son-in-law's ass would have been fine, but things would have been a lot more complicated," Conall said. "Can you save your questions until I get the intro out at least, or are you too much of a tough guy to sit and listen?"

Willie started to answer but couldn't come up with anything. Conall stared at the old man, raising his eyebrows and leaning forward, almost willing him to come to some sort of point. When he didn't, the newcomer made a big point of turning away before getting down to business.

"Yes, I'm like you in that I can transform into a wolf. I've been doing it since my early teen years, much like you, there, son," he said, nodding to Dilly. "You didn't think you were the only ones in the world, did you?"

"We never really got around to researching it," Ron said.

"Well, you fucking well should of, shouldn't ya?" Conall spit back. "I mean, it just makes sense that in a world of seven or eight billion people, you're not the most special group on the planet. Are you the least curious people on the planet or the dumbest?"

"Hey," Josie said, loud enough to startle the room. "No need for that in my house. You're a guest here and, to your point, things were going fine. We didn't need any help."

"I hate to say this, Josie, is it, but you need help now. You're all in shit up to your belly buttons and you're just now asking what that smell is."

"Why are we in trouble?" Dilly said.

"Because everyone, and I mean everyone knows where you are. Look, I've got to back up a bit and I can do without all the jabbering and interruptions."

"You're the one asking questions," Josie snarled. Dilly put his hand on his mom's shoulder and she let him.

"I'm sorry, you're right," Conall said, softening. "I'm in your home. I have a bit of temper and I will try to keep it in check. So please, Josie, may I get back to it?"

"That's what Byron said," Willie mumbled.

The room exploded with noise and everyone started moving at once. Dave lunged for his father trying to tackle him but Dilly, who had the height but not the weight advantage, tried to hold him back. By and large, he succeeded. Carl, ever the pragmatist, put himself in front of Willie while Ron yelled from the couch. Kenny Kirk unscrewed a flask, offered some to JoAnn, who demurred, then took a long dreg. It took a good fifteen seconds of yelling before anyone could make out anything resembling a word in English.

" . . . KING BEAT YOU TO FUCKING DEATH," Dave yelled.

"You ain't got the balls you pussy!" Willie yelled back, less convincingly.

"E FUCKING NOUGH!" Conall yelled over the fray. "You fucking bunch of American fucking psychopaths are going to sit your asses down and listen to me for the love of fucking God Almighty!"

The profanity mixed with the volume cut through the room and everyone sat. Conall was now quick with his words and harsh with his tone.

"I don't know what sort of family drama I've stumbled into but I was wrong. You are special because I've never seen a pack act as stupid as your lot. So I'm going to give you one more chance. You're going to sit, quietly, and let me lay out your situation. If you have questions, keep your fucking mouth shut until the end. If you have something you want to mutter that's

101

going to piss everyone off, keep your fucking mouth shut until the end. If you have anything to say at all, for any reason, keep your fucking mouth shut until the end. I'm trying to help you and you treat me like your fucking therapist. Christ almighty."

Conall tested the rules he had just put down by stalking around the room, staring at each person. Everyone got a wild-eyed stare from Conall, and when he got to Willie and didn't get any lip, he nodded.

"OK, then. Off we fucking go."

•••

As far back as the seventh century, art depicts man who could transform his features. Despite extensive study into the topic, no one is sure how this ability came about. Speculation is rampant, lore is detailed and abundant, but facts on this topic are very hard to come by. Complicating matters from a Paleolithic standpoint was the fact that most of those affected with this "gift" didn't share it. Getting lost in feudal times or the pre-electric age was not a difficult task.

Similarly, it's unknown when the first communities of the "gifted" began. It might have been much earlier, but the first record was in Ireland in the late twelfth century. This group employed the services of a brotherhood of monks to record the names of their family and the dates in which they "changed." These records indicate three vitally important details about these early people.

1) They exclusively changed their form into that of a wolf and were able to do so at will.
2) They were at war with other groups of "changelings" who opted for a variety of animal forms but most often a bear.
3) Both sides of this conflict were very careful not to alert the general population, as whispers of their abilities were already rumor and myth. They felt the revelation of their abilities would make them targets for religious punishment or fearful destruction by governing institutions.

The Bear Wars, as the monks wrote, were long and protracted and both sides saw casualties. But the bears were fewer in number and the wolves, who were fleet and never attacked alone, eventually won out. It was written that the last bear was brought to the camp of the wolves, fed a huge meal, poured the finest alcohol in the land and, only after they had cheered and toasted the last of his kind did the wolves kill him. The scene is written of warmly, the death and end of the last bear an afterthought.

The monks, who had taken vows of silence, were good stewards of these secrets. The invention of the printing press in the 1600s presented the "gifted," now calling themselves "The Warry Ones," with a difficult choice. They could be loyal to these men who had collected their history but who knew their secret, or they could kill them and begin the Age of the Written Word with all their history in their total control. No records exist of how the decision was made, but "The Warry Ones" silenced the monks through tooth and claw.

It wasn't until the 1600s that the histories show other groups with similar gifts beginning to make themselves known. Many had similar stories of battle with others of similar ability, with wolves always winning the battles and the wars. Stories also emerged of those who dared reveal themselves or who were discovered. They always ended with pitchforks or bonfires.

By 1800, wolves were living in secret in Ireland, Scotland, England, France, Germany, Russia, China, India and Japan. These groups would send ambassadors to the area and tell tales of their native lands to the delight of the others. Their numbers were small, by all accounts leaving a problem as to how to identify wolves when entering a new area. It was the Irish who came up with a code. The "Warry Ones" was shortened over the years to "Ware" and combined with "wolves" to form a nonsense word to those who didn't understand it. If you walked into a town in the 1600s and asked the bartender at the local tavern if he'd ever heard of "werewolves," he would give you a hearty "no" and go about his business. Within the next day, you would invariably find the group you were looking for.

So it went for many years, with groups finding each other, sharing knowledge about their gifts and forming communities. There were no records of wars among wolves with the exception of internal conflicts that had little to no bearing on the larger picture. A "governing body" was eventually formed based on the need to stay hidden, particularly from the Catholic Church. This group, referred to just as "The Council," met once every two years and their recommendations soon became best practices. Rules about how to best enjoy the transformation without rousing suspicion and how to deal with local authorities were soon adopted.

When the new world was discovered, The Council saw a unique opportunity to set up communities of only "werewolves" where land to run was plentiful and intrusion was minimal. That dream was never realized. The communities in Europe and Asia had heard rumors of many "gifted" among the Native population (with one rumor that a pack of "man bears" was responsible for the disappearance of the Roanoke colony in 1587) and contact was made. Indeed, there were many wolves, bears and even a few eagles, a phenomenon never before seen. A small community was established but the language barrier was an impediment. Soon, tensions flared and communication was suspended. The governments of England, France and eventually the United States would make sure the breadth of the Native community was never to be known and communication with the larger community was never reestablished.

There was not a mass migration to the "new world" as many in the werewolf community had set up very comfortable situations in their countries, but a few were established. The Northwest and northern part of the United States, as well as central and southern Canada had, and have, very robust communities living in basic secrecy. Based on the best practices set forth by The Council, success of these communities depends on their access to open, wooded land and a rural community where secrecy or acceptance is possible.

In their known history the most important "best practice" put forth by The Council was a strict census. Every pack had to be accounted for and when new wolves were born, The Council marked their date of birth and their first transformation. These records were exact and one member of each pack was responsible to The Council to provide this census. To this day, the census is taken very seriously by the community, but in the age before electricity with thousands of miles of ocean separating individual packs from their central governing body, there were gaps.

• • •

"That's where you all come in," Conall said. He had all their attention. The reality of their situation had sunk in. They were a rogue pack, a group that had been operating independently, doing their own thing and existing in a bubble for over a hundred years. That bubble had just popped.

"You always think you've got everyone accounted for, then, all of a sudden, two people are ripped apart by wolves in the span of a week and it makes the news and the floodgates open, don't they?"

There was a lot of murmuring and agreement. In retrospect it was obvious. Of course Byron killing Sandra and the pack killing Byron would draw attention. They just hadn't figured on what kind.

"Who is Mr. Stander?" Dave asked.

"Put two and two together please," Conall said. "I don't know you. I don't know your situation. But I've got a really, really good guess as to how he got here."

"So, what, he's not with you then?" Kenny Kirk blurted.

"No, he's not with me you idiot," Conall said. "I can imagine why he's looking for you, though. You a big fan of medical tests? Having your nuts cut open with a scalpel and examined? How about your blood and bone harvested while you're kept alive and kicking? You a big fan of that?"

Kenny Kirk looked at Dave, who became keenly aware that everyone was looking to him. Dilly looked like he was about to cry.

"OK, Conall. Two things right off the bat. I know you've got a temper and I know you're pissed at us, but we're going to do our very, very best to keep a civil tone and I ask the same from you. No more name calling from us, or from you. At least for tonight."

"OK," Conall said. "So long as you understand how fucking stupid you all are, I don't need to point it out."

Everyone looked at Conall.

"Fine, fine," he said. "It's out of my system."

"Second thing. You've found us at a very difficult time. We recently made a decision, as a pack, that is tearing us apart. I know this pack has existed for over two hundred years and with everything I know I can't remember a time when things have been this difficult. I know you're here to help . . . at least I hope you're here to help, and we want that help. But things are tense right now and if you could keep that in mind, we'll get a lot further than if you don't."

"Fair enough," Conall said. "Tell you what. We're all going to take about ten or fifteen minutes here. We're going to get some food if you're hungry, you're going to smoke if that's your thing and we're going to meet back here at 9:00 and we're going to talk this out. Be prepared for a long night and maybe think about calling in sick tomorrow to work. We've got a lot to go over and not that much time to go over it."

It took a solid beat, but eventually everyone got up and, with the exception of Josie and Dave who stayed in the house to make some food, headed outside.

•••

"Jesus Christ on a cracker with some Tropical Punch Kool-Aid," Kenny Kirk said as he, JoAnn, and Ron walked around the back of the Rhodes' house. "How in the hell, I mean, how in the *hell* did we not know about this? We sound like a bunch of amateurs, man. It's amateur hour over here. This guy comes in and if you believe Dave he can talk when he's wolfing out and we're over here unable to wipe our asses properly. Like we're a bunch of backwoods yokels, man."

"We are a bunch of backwoods yokels, Kenny," Ron said. "That's kind of our thing. We did that on purpose."

"I know that, man, but, I don't know. It's shitty when someone else says it."

"I've always wanted to go to France," JoAnn said. "This might be a good excuse to go travel a bit."

"There's a silver lining for you," Kenny Kirk said. "It's attached to a big dark cloud that might turn into a tornado and kill everyone in its path, but that is a hell of a silver lining."

Ron was tickled by the comment so much that his chuckle had turned into more of a solid laugh. Before long Kenny had picked it up, too.

"I could be an American werewolf in London," Ron said, his laugh picking up steam.

"I love French bread, man. I wolf it down," Kenny Kirk said, getting them both rolling. JoAnn was not nearly as amused, her dark hair framing a face that was not happy with the men in her life.

"You're a bunch of assholes," she said. "You all are just as sick of this place as I am. Don't pretend that you aren't."

"It's not that, darlin'," Kenny said. "This, here, I think is what you call 'gallows humor.' See, we are good and proper fucked right now if this guy can't help us. It looks like Byron may have screwed us worse than we initially thought."

"Yeah," Ron said. "Sorry, JoAnn. I didn't mean anything by it."

"That's OK," she said. "I get it. I get we're in trouble. I always was kind of jealous of you guys, going out there, running, having a good time. It's not the same for me or Josie. It sucks for us, you know? And now we get all of the bad shit and none of the good. You don't realize what you guys have. Or how much watching Dilly get out there has been hard for us."

Kenny Kirk put his arm around JoAnn as she stared into the dark behind the house. Ron, suddenly feeling as if he was imposing on a private moment, shut his mouth and let them have it. Losing a kid is something you never get over, he figured, but being reminded of how old that kid would have been had he survived, that was something else entirely. Suddenly Ron felt the passage of time acutely and focused for a second on his back, which had been giving him trouble lately. He was getting old and he felt it. He hoped, quietly, staring into the dark, that he had more fight left in him.

•••

Carl and Dilly immediately walked over to Conall as he smoked a cigarette.

"I wanted to say hi," Carl said. "I'm . . . um, I'm Carl and this is Dave Jr. and . . . um . . . we are really happy you are here."

107

"You need something?" Conall asked.

"Well, I wanted to let you know I had my first run yesterday," Dilly said. "I'm the newbie. Um ... it was great and I can't wait to ... learn more, I guess."

Conall, remembering his vow of civility, gave a weak smile to the kid, then blew a stream of smoke out the side of his mouth.

"Hell of a thing, isn't it?" he said. "How old are you, boy?"

"Just turned sixteen," Dilly said.

"You know, that's about right," Conall said. "There's been a push to go younger and younger, so kids can control it but I say let a kid get some time under his or her belt before having to deal with all this. Am I right?"

"Yeah," Carl said. "That seems right."

"You know, it amazes me," Conall continued. "You guys are cut off, completely. You're free range, yet here you are, making some of the right calls. It's impressive is what it is."

"Thank you," Carl said.

"That doesn't mean you haven't pulled some massive fucking boners out here, but we'll get you through that," Conall said, patting Dilly on the shoulder. "See you inside, then."

They watched him head back inside, his heavy boots crunching the gravel around their back door. He flicked the cigarette a good eight feet as only an experienced smoker can do and pulled out his cell phone. They could hear him talking but not make out what he was saying.

"It's weird how you can't understand what he's saying, but you still hear his accent," Dilly said.

"Yeah," Carl replied.

"He says 'fuck' a lot," Dilly said.

"Watch your mouth," Carl countered. "And yeah. He does."

"What do you think is going to happen?"

"I'm not your dad, Dilly," Carl said. "Go ask him those sorts of questions, OK. But if I were you, I'd stay close. I'm guessing something bad is going to happen soon."

•••

Willie sat on the back porch in a chair. No one spoke to him.

• • •

Dave and Josie spoke in short, whispered tones as they went about the ritual of preparing snacks. Over the seventeen years they had been married they knew subconsciously which way the other was going to go, especially in the kitchen. Dave would grab the chips and cut right to the counter, Josie would work the fridge and cut left to the table, they would both take a load to the living room before returning for drinks. This was the way they had done it literally thousands of times, but the ritual of preparing food gave no comfort from the panic both of them felt.

"Jesus, Dave, medical experiments? What are we going to do?"

"We're going to hear this guy out. I'm not sure I trust him one hundred percent but I've seen him change with my own two eyes. He's one of us, I promise."

"He is not one of us. He certainly doesn't talk like one of us. If we weren't all scared shitless I'd have kicked that guy out of my house by now."

"I get that," Dave said. "Hang on a little longer, OK?"

They both loaded up their hands and arms with food, made a trip to the living room and returned for drinks. For a moment, they worked in silence.

"Did you mean what you said back there?" Josie said. "About us being in the worst place we've ever been?"

"Not the time, Josie."

"Just a yes or no answer is all I need."

"As a pack, we're in a bad place and it's because of Willie. He's making this thing impossible."

"What about with us?"

"We've talked about this," Dave said. "Things are tense but OK, right?"

He put down his drinks and walked up to her, putting his hand on her back.

"Time will pass and the tension will go away and we'll be OK. I meant it when I said it back in January and I mean it now. Things are rough but I'm not going anywhere. Obviously."

"OK," she said. "Let's get through this."

Dave watched her walk out of the kitchen and grabbed the drinks.

●●●

"OK, welcome back," Conall said. "First thing's first. I've gotten the OK from The Council to share with you a couple of protocols. They wanted me to make sure that this pack is interested in meeting with other representatives from our group after you are out of harm's way. Is that accurate?"

"Yes," Dave said. "That's accurate."

"The hell it is," Willie said from across the room. "How do you know they're not going to make us pledge allegiance to some faggy goat God or something?"

"Willie, man, the time has long past come and gone for you to shut up," Kenny Kirk said, shooting Dave a quick glance as he finished talking.

" . . . meeting with other representatives from our group. We are not forcing you to do anything nor are we requiring membership. We will come and talk. That's the only commitment you're giving right now," Conall said. "Clear?"

The group nodded and murmured in agreement.

"Good. The next thing. The man who approached you, Dave, he works for one of three groups as near as we can figure. Two of them are bio medical companies who have been chasing us for years for research purposes. The other is a nasty group of religious zealots who feel we are of the devil and must be destroyed. I have to say, if it were those nut balls they would have come in guns blazing right away, so I don't think that's it."

There was a lot of looking across the room to gauge everyone's reaction. So far everyone was holding it together. Even Willie was holding his tongue.

"Second thing, these murders happened a few weeks ago, correct?"

Josie, who was always on top of scheduling, was on it.

"Sandra died just under two weeks ago. Byron the same night but they didn't find him until the day after."

"OK," Conall said. "So it took Mr. Stander about a week to find you which, to be honest, is quicker than I would have liked. We pride ourselves on having very advanced algorithms that track the sort of news stories and keywords that would point toward a group of your sort. What we didn't count on was that you'd be in a place so remote that you barely have media."

"The newspaper is a weekly," Carl added.

"And they don't have a fucking website . . . sorry, a website so you can't set keywords for content that isn't there. Anyway, they found you fast which means, if we're lucky, the second wave won't be here for another twelve hours or so now that he has confirmation of contact."

"Second wave?" Dave asked.

"They try to buy you and if that doesn't work they try to trap you. I got to you before you could consider the ridiculous amount of money he was going to offer you to come with him. Believe me, Dave, once you agreed and showed up at their facility, all his promises are worth fuck all."

"How much money?" Willie asked.

"Do you like having your nutsack cut open, old man?" Conall finally snapped. "I'm talking about this group harvesting your corneas. I've seen their plans myself and there's not enough money in the world for some of the shit they're going to do to ya if they get the chance."

"So what do we do?" Dave asked.

"Do you have a place that you go when you change? A place where you run? Are you catching my drift?"

"Yeah," Dilly said. "It's up by . . ."

"Don't tell me," Conall said. "I don't want to hear it but I want you all to think of it. If something goes bad or if you're attacked or if you feel like you're in danger, that's where you meet to regroup. Second thing, we need to get you all out of here."

"Out of here," Willie said. "That ain't happening."

"It's not permanent," Conall said. "In eight or twelve hours when the men with the guns show up . . ."

"I thought you said we have eight hours," Dave said over Conall. ". . . you will not want to be here. Once you're safe we'll figure out what to do."

"Can we call the police?" Josie asked.

"And tell them what, exactly?" Conall said. "Officer so and so, a group of biomedical researchers are coming with guns to try and capture my friends and family and harvest my eyeballs because I do this little parlor trick, you see . . ."

"Grey Allen couldn't do shit anyway," Willie added.

"Grey Allen isn't the sheriff anymore," Kenny Kirk said. "Keep up, man."

"I don't disagree with anything you've said," Ron piped up. "But you're asking us to put our lives in your hands and all we have is Dave's word that you're like us."

Conall took a moment to turn and look at Dave for a long beat.

"The word of your alpha isn't enough for you?"

No one said a word as the question made the air thick and every noise amplified. Carl shifted in his seat and the sound of denim on a fake leather was suddenly deafening.

"I kind of want to see a talking wolf," Dilly said.

The laugh started with Kenny Kirk and rolled around the room. Within ten seconds everyone was at least chuckling and Willie sat in the corner with a big grin on his face. Conall tapped Dilly on the shoulder.

"All right, then, boy."

Conall walked over to the two smaller windows in the living room and drew the shades. Then he arched his back into a hunched position, then pulled up hard, suddenly taller. He didn't scream or yell as the boys of Cherry sometimes did and when the hair sprouted it was thick and fast. Aside from the quick rustling of the transformation, the loudest sound was the stretch of the Irish Wolf's fingernails as they lengthened and cracked, eventually sharpening into claws. The man's clothing stretched with his changing body as it was designed to do.

The result was very similar in shape to what the pack from Cherry looked like, but the posture was different and the eyes sharper and brighter. He was more frightening than Dilly had expected because, he figured out later, he looked like a beast that would chase you. Also, the sight of a snarling creature in a domestic setting accentuated just how big he was and, somehow, how terrible.

"I ... speak," the Irish Wolf said in a growl so low and awful that everyone had to focus, hard, to understand him. "It's easier when I'm ... angry. Is this enough for you? Does this make you ... trust me?"

No one spoke, but they all nodded and the Irish Wolf, having sharp eyes, registered them all. Suddenly the wolf started twitching and banged his head against the wall in one smooth, violent motion.

"I must run," the Irish Wolf continued. "I will return ... be ready. We leave soon."

The living room in the Rhodes household was sunken from the kitchen and bedroom area, leaving the Irish Wolf with the difficult task of walking up the five stairs to the front door on padded feet bent at odd angles. He would have leapt up the stairs easily, Dave figured, but the ceiling was too low.

Dave tried to help but the Irish Wolf snapped at him, crawled his way up the stairs and turned back at the group, who were transfixed.

"Sorry ... about the ... door."

With that the beast gave a hard push off the carpeted floor and exploded through the Rhodes' front door, pieces raining and glass smashing and crunching. Dilly ran to the window only to catch a glimpse of the Irish Wolf's hindquarters as he ran down the street and disappeared into the woods to the south of town. Pieces of door were still falling from the sky when Kenny Kirk broke the seal.

"Holy shit, man," he said. "I cannot believe that. Can you believe that? I can't believe that. I can't believe he can chat looking like that, I can't believe he busted your door into a million pieces, I can't believe we need to run for our lives, man."

"We don't need to run," Willie said. "We just need to scratch. Let them take their shot. They'll end up dead in the woods somewhere."

"We need to think about this," Ron said.

"Yeah," Dave said. "Because no one will notice a paramilitary group prowling around the woods with guns and no one will notice eight or ten dead bodies in the damn woods. Use your brain, Willie."

"If you had used your brain, we wouldn't be in this mess," Willie said.

"I don't want to kill anyone," Dilly added.

"No one's going to make you kill anyone," Josie said. "We'd never do anything like that so don't worry."

"You should damn well worry about it," Willie said. "So, he can turn into a wolf. That doesn't mean anything he's said is true. All it means is that there are more of us out there. That is it."

"Why would he reveal himself like that?" Ron said. "Why would he save Dave from that guy in the bow tie?"

"I don't know," Willie said. "I'm following my instincts. It's all I got and something doesn't seem right about that Irish fella."

"I think he's telling the truth, Grandpa," Dilly said.

"Look, Dilly, you're smart, but I swear to you if we go with that guy nothing good is gonna come of it. I've got a bad feeling."

The group continued on for ten minutes about the pros and cons, some pacing the room, some staying put, afraid to move. Things got heated, but just when they started to calm down, three things happened in rapid succession.

The first thing was Josie feeling as if something was deeply wrong. It's the feeling she got sometimes when Dilly left the door open, only much stronger. One night in the house Dilly had come home after basketball practice and left the door open for an hour as snow poured in their front door, ruining part of their flooring. During that entire time when she was upstairs, she sensed something was wrong and couldn't put her finger on it. The part of her brain that told her "the door is open" suddenly caught fire.

The second thing was Willie started changing. He gasped a very human, terrified gasp that ended in a growl. His arms started lengthening, then his legs in a transformation that was unlike any the group had ever seen. Instead of a smooth, all at once sort of process, Willie's arms went first, then his legs, then his head in an uneven and awful sequence. His growl turned into a yelp and the White Wolf collapsed on the ground, whimpering in pain and unable to stand.

The third thing was the yelling. Three men in black tactical gear, complete with helmets, bulletproof vests and what looked like assault rifles, came tearing down the stairs ordering everyone on the ground. The sound of the guns being discharged filled the room, but they were not gunshots. They were darts shooting at the group and only the odd layout of the room and the limited space prevented anyone else from being hit.

When the first man came around the corner, Dave was struck by violent inspiration and kicked at the man's knee as hard as he could. His heavy boot struck its target and the man went down, adding another layer of screams to the noise. He grabbed at the man's gun but the man held on. Dave pulled on the weapon, the effect of which was to bring the intruder's entire body up just in time to catch three darts in the back. The man screamed and Dave could hear the scream devolve into wet gurgling behind the visor.

Josie had grabbed Dilly, Ron had run to Dave's side, and Carl and JoAnn were helping Willie, who was in rough shape. The men had taken up residence at the top of the stairs and started crafting their random yelling into instructions.

"GET OUT OF THERE," one man yelled.

"Come up the stairs and we won't make you transform," another yelled in a slightly more reasoned but still hostile tone.

Dave threw the man he was holding down and dead weight hit the floor. The only entrance to the living room (aside from the entrance through the laundry room) was blocked by the man's body. If the two men at the top tried to come down they would have to vault their fallen comrade, losing their tactical advantage. For the time being, there was a stalemate.

"You're in my house," Dave yelled. "Get out."

"Your friend there," one of the men yelled. "The furry one? He's not long for this world. You gotta get him help or he's going to die." The man's voice was gruff and he delivered the words like he meant them and had probably said them before.

Part of Dave thought "good" when they threatened Willie, but then he heard Dilly sniffle. He was now at his grandfather's side as the White Wolf labored to breathe. Seeing Willie, or anyone in his condition, on the ground

115

instead of on the hunt was odd in a specific way for Dave, especially since his father was a scrapper and fighter as a human and otherwise.

"You've got about half an hour before he's dead," the man upstairs yelled. The White Wolf's eyes shot open.

"You're just delaying it," the man continued. "Get up here and we won't make you transform. It's your only option."

The White Wolf growled.

Josie, who was now over by her son, looked at Dave, pleading with her eyes to make this end. JoAnn and Kenny were holding each other as she had started to sob, quietly, into Kenny's skinny shoulder.

The White Wolf looked at Dave.

Dave gave a small nod.

"Quit stall . . ." the man began.

In a fraction of a second, the White Wolf moved to put his paws underneath him and launched himself up the narrow stairway and right into one of the men. The other recoiled backward out of surprise and panic, tripped over his own feet and fell, hard. Everyone heard him fall and Carl made a move as if to capitalize, but Dave made a motion to hold him back.

"Not yet," Dave said. "Not until the screaming stops."

Upstairs, the powerful jaws of the White Wolf had bit through the hard plastic and metal of the first man's helmet, puncturing his head enough to cause bleeding, but not enough to do any major damage. Unfortunately for the man, he was unable to push the White Wolf off him as the beast was heavy but also hard to grab onto and it wasn't long until the helmet finally stuck to one of the powerful incisors of the beast and came tumbling off. Before the killing bite, the wolf paused for just a moment to survey his prey. He had done this dozens and dozens of times in the woods. Creatures who are about to die fight and fight until the life leaves them and the White Wolf savored that last bit of fight before they went limp.

The man did not disappoint. In this case he screamed and thrashed and kicked his feet but it wasn't anywhere near enough. The White Wolf got his entire jaws around the man's head and bit, ripping the flesh and crushing the skull. The screaming continued and the White Wolf tasted

116

all the blood he wanted, and then something more metallic and singular as the brain was exposed and gave way. A few bites later the fighting stopped, the kicking ceased and the White Wolf pulled up hard to see what had happened to the second man, and what he saw amused him, if such a thing was possible.

He was frozen in fear. The second man was still sitting, his hands desperately trying to load live ammunition in his gun, which was loaded with darts. The fear of the wolf was consuming him and the man's hands weren't working and he dropped bullets all over the floor. The man's eyes were wide and his whole body was shaking.

The White Wolf, with a grunt, turned his body toward the other man. Instead of screaming, like the first one, this man started pleading.

"Oh Jesus," the man said over and over again. "Please no, oh Jesus oh God no. I . . . I, no no NO!"

The man got louder the closer the White Wolf got, and in the end the great beast destroyed the man more to shut him up than anything. He would have liked to play around with him a bit, given the chance, but his whining was enough to annoy the White Wolf into granting a quick death. When he was done, having destroyed the second man in the same manner as the first, the wolf noticed the man had peed on the floor. *Not your territory anymore,* the wolf thought.

Slowly, the rest of the party emerged from the basement and were met with blood, bodies, and the smell of evacuated bowels. The White Wolf growled at them, but it was never in his mind to strike.

"What do we do now?" Ron asked.

As if to answer, the White Wolf collapsed again, the momentary blast of energy and vengeance having run out. The creature looked frail again as Dilly approached it.

"What's wrong with him?" Dilly asked. "How do we make him better?"

"What do we do with the bodies?" Josie asked.

"Where the hell is Conall?" Kenny Kirk wondered aloud.

"I don't know, the bodies aren't going anywhere and Conall can take care of himself," Dave said. "Ron, help me get Willie into your truck."

"Where are we going?"

"We're heading to the woods."

•••

Seven o'clock had come and gone and Stu sat, behind a tree, desperately wishing for something more substantial than sunflower seeds. He had picked up the habit when he had first rolled in to Cherry, having discovered ranch-flavored sunflower seeds at a gas station about ten miles away. He had never seen anything but regular, salted seeds in the various gas stations throughout his life and was confronted with a whole new world. On the spot he had bought ranch-, dill pickle- and bacon-flavored and proceeded to chow down during the day, so much so that he often skipped lunch, having filled up on seeds. Turned out, he thought as he leaned against the bark of a big cottonwood, that plan didn't work for dinner.

Still, there were worse ways to be spending an evening. The air was cool and pleasant, the air smelled wonderful, and the forest was blazing with fall colors. The yellows and reds of the season was something Stu had seen, but never been enveloped by. There was a girl on one of the dating sites that he had been messaging quite a bit and he decided, then and there, he was going to take the plunge and ask her to go for a hike with him through the woods.

Nah, he thought. That might seem a bit "murder-y."

He had been listening for the crunch of tires on the nearby gravel and was hoping to spy on Mr. Stander a bit before revealing himself. The best-case scenario, Stu figured, was to overhear a conversation that would shed light on who the hell this stranger was and how he knew about the two murders. But, as the sun set and the colors of the forest faded, Stu started to feel stupid. With the feeling came pieces of his "curse," and before long he was reliving dying children and remembering comments he would have been better not to have read.

"There goes my night," Stu said out loud. A loud *whoosh* answered him.

Stu had been listening for car tracks on the crunchy gravel but instead of car tracks, he heard something else. It was a quick yet thick sound of something moving very fast in such a way he couldn't tell where it was coming from. He heard the sound three times, each time thinking it was coming from somewhere different.

Then the sound of crunching gravel filled his ears, and he stood up and peered around the corner of the tree. It was hard to make out exactly what was happening, but he caught snippets of conversation.

"I don't see how this is going to help, even a little bit," a man was saying, running his mouth so fast he barely paused for breath. "We get him out to the woods and then what, man? The magic fairy nymphs take the poison or whatever the hell is in his system away and he lives for another decade?"

There was more mumbling followed by the motor mouth getting more upset. Stu was aware of three cars now pulling into the area. As far as he could tell in the low light, Mr. Stander wasn't among them.

"Tell me what you're thinking, man!" the motor mouth yelled. "Tell anyone what you're thinking? We're all confused as hell, here!"

People were piling out of cars and Stu lost count of how many there were. It was also hard to nail down faces in the dark, especially ones he was still committing to memory, but he did recognize Dave, the high school teacher. He was moving something with another man that was wrapped up in a sheet. It was far too long to be a human body, Dave thought.

The heavy *whoosh* returned and suddenly a different voice appeared from the other side of the campground.

"Aye!" the voice yelled, thick with what Stu identified as an Irish accent. "Good thinking. Bring him this way!"

"WHY!" the motor mouth yelled. "Are you a damn wolf doctor?"

Stu ventured a little farther past the trunk of the tree to take in the scene, but the scene had moved. The whole group was moving in a bunch, without any stragglers, into the woods and right past Stu. He repositioned himself and heard a few more words and phrases that made no sense to him as they passed. No one gave a glance backward, so he followed, being careful to make as little noise as possible.

The group was loud enough through their feverish and rapid

conversation to make following easy and about ten minutes later they stopped by the banks of a small stream. Careful to keep his distance, Stu listened and, because it was better to be safe than sorry, undid the strap that held his gun securely in its holster.

"... you're his son. You should be the one to do it."

"Does it matter that I don't want to?"

"Not in the least."

"But I can't control it. Not like you can."

"Look, I get it. I'm going to transform too and between me and your mates we'll be able to take what we need and keep everyone safe."

"If I lose it, my family is here."

None of this made any sense from a logical standpoint, but Stu was reasonably sure something bad was about to happen. He started thinking about when to reveal himself and what he would do when that happened. He was a decent shot but he was alone, in the dark woods with a bunch of strangers doing something bad. To turn around now would draw more attention. He suddenly, and rightfully, felt trapped.

"Dave," Stu heard the man with the accent say. "You have my word, my word, that I will keep your family safe. Trust me, I can destroy your ass if necessary."

There was a smattering of laughter among the group and suddenly Stu heard an odd howling sound that he couldn't identify. It warbled and faded into a sad moan and it chilled him, but for some reason, didn't scare him. The sound was coming from whatever was underneath the sheet, which rose and fell sharply as something twitched underneath it.

"OK," Stu heard Dave said. "OK. I'm ready. You go first."

It was dark and Stu was scared and behind a tree, but by the light left in the sky and from the sounds of crunching and muffled screams, he put together that something unnatural and terrifying was happening thirty feet or so from him and he was struck with a full body desire to run. It was almost impossible to overcome, his feet begging, screaming to move, but his brain applying all the brakes they possibly could.

If he moved he would be seen.

Conall had met them, in human form, the moment they arrived at the campsite. Dave was relieved to see him. The rest of the pack, not so much. But, they had worked through it and on their way into the woods Conall had told them the plan.

Packs were bonded, Conall told him, on a biological level. If you're near someone when they transform for a long period of time, you "get used to them" in a very ingrained way. Werewolves or whatever you call them were vulnerable during the change and that, mixed with others being vulnerable beside them, created a mix of sorts.

"The long story short is that you can heal each other," Conall said. "But only in the wolf form. We can't change . . . what's his name there?"

"Willie," Dave said. "He's my dad."

"OK, then. We can't change Willie back and if we did it could be a bad situation because I'm not sure what the bloody hell is wrong with him. Our best bet is to go out, have one of you transform and then . . ."

Conall paused, trying to come up with the words.

"Bleed a little, I guess."

"You need blood?" Dave said, incredulous.

"Look, I don't make the rules, Dave," Conall said. "I've seen it work and I'm telling you if you transform and we take some of your blood and give it to Willie, it'll fix everything from poison to losing an arm. It works. I've seen it."

Dave fell silent and Conall, in an act of European sensibilities, came close to Dave and put his weighty hands on his shoulders.

"You can save your father, Dave. You can do it."

So, off into the woods they went, all of them trudging across the suddenly cold plain of grass and leaves. Once they hit a clearing they worked it out—Conall would go first since he had more control. Dave would go second and the boys would work to try to keep him at bay. This was odd for several reasons, the biggest one being group transformation was the one and only way they had ever transformed. Going it alone was strictly forbidden for a number of very good reasons and here was Dave, about to break their cardinal rule.

Add to the situation the fact that Conall expected Dave to have some modicum of control after he transformed, and the whole thing seemed like a terrible idea to Dave. He pulled Josie aside and told her to take Dilly and leave, but Conall nixed it.

"Dave, you have my word, my word, that I will keep your family safe," Conall said loud enough for everyone to hear. Trust me, I can destroy your ass if necessary."

It was little comfort and Dave walked back to Josie and put his head over her left shoulder so they could whisper to each other.

"I'm worried about you," he said.

"I'm not the one bleeding," she pointed out.

"Willie's an asshole."

"No doubt. Willie's your father and Willie is Dilly's grandpa."

"What if something goes wrong?"

"Things have already gone wrong."

He took her meaning, macro and micro, and walked over to Conall.

"OK, I'm ready," Dave said. "You go first."

Conall kicked, fell and the group heard several loud pops and something akin to tearing. Less than thirty seconds later the Irish Wolf stood up, and immediately started sniffing the air.

"Someone's here," the wolf growled.

Quickly everyone started looking around until the Irish Wolf threw his nose, violently, in the direction of a bank of trees. Everyone took his meaning and began moving. JoAnn always carried a .38 in her purse and retrieved it.

"Just a second," Dave yelled when he saw the gun. Then Dave raised his voice and yelled at the trees. "Whoever you are, please come out. If you don't, I can't promise your safety."

Behind the tree, Stu had locked up for a second, but the sound of Dave's voice shook him loose. Without giving it much thought he quickly shifted his whole weight from one leg to another, moving clear of the protective cover. Stu didn't know what to say, so he said nothing.

"Shit," he heard Dave said.

"HE CAN'T BE HERE," the Irish Wolf yelled, almost howling. "LEAVE!"

Dave quickly came up on Stu and held his arms out to keep everyone back.

"Stu," Dave said. "This is . . . awkward. But I'm going to get you out of here if you let me."

Stu was getting his first, good look at the Irish Wolf and was doing the best he could to not shut down. The beast was large, but in the dark its eyes were the most prominent thing and they were full of murder. Stu was suddenly hyper aware of his body, his heart pounding very hard, his mouth producing more saliva than usual, his nose grabbing scents from the air, but he was almost oblivious to everything else. Dave might as well have promised him a lobster dinner and no funny business afterward.

"STU!" Dave yelled, snapping his fingers. "You gotta stay with me, buddy."

Stu came around to consciousness but still felt nothing but fear.

"Do you see the nice guy over there next to the woman with the gun?" Dave asked. "He's going to come and walk you back to the clearing, and you're going to wait there. He's going to make sure you wait right there. Then we're going to talk. Is that OK?"

Wet mouth but dry throat, eyes stinging from how wide they were open, Stu managed a nod. Words were not coming anytime soon.

"OK," Dave said. "Kenny, take him to your truck, please. Keep him there."

"I heard you," Kenny said. "JoAnn's coming with me."

"We might need her gun."

"Then give it to someone else, she ain't staying here when this shit goes down."

"Excuse me, who said I'm not?" JoAnn said. "Just take him, Kenny. I'll be fine. You're in more danger than I am."

"GO!" the Irish Wolf screamed, clearly struggling to not tear the intruder to shreds.

Kenny took the cue and put both hands on Stu's shoulders, whipped him around and started marching him through the woods. If Stu was beyond words, Kenny had enough for both of them.

"This is the biggest goddamn mess I've ever seen, man. Irish dudes and cops and a fucking SWAT team and Irish dudes and Willie on his way out. This is not how I wanted to spend my evening, man. I had plans."

"We don't have a SWAT team," Stu said, half under his breath, not sure what else to say.

"No, you don't have a SWAT team, man. This was a different thing. We're going to get you sat down in my truck and we'll talk. Although, to be honest with you, I don't have a real good grasp on this whole thing, man. I know about, like, seventy percent of what's going on. Maybe less. Maybe sixty but that sounds like I don't know anything."

Stu was happy for the distraction and was led, happily, into the passenger seat of Stu's truck.

A couple hundred yards away the Irish Wolf continued yelling.

"YOU BECOME WOLF!" it yelled, deep and guttural and pissed off. "NOW!"

Not unlike Stu, Dave had limited experience looking at a wolf when he wasn't one himself, and the Irish Wolf's screams were not putting him in a contemplative head space. He had a go-to thought for when he scratched involving pain—an injury when he was a kid where he busted his leg open. The panic of the bloody mess staining his socks and shoes got him started and the memory of digging deep and pulling himself home dragging one dead leg behind him usually got him over the falls and into the transformation. Conall had asked him to be both passionate and controlled as possible. Well, Dave thought, he was going to get one of those things.

The moment he made the decision to give up on control his brain flooded with thoughts he had pushed down. The confusion and pain of the past few hours melted and Dave suddenly remembered how he had found out about Josie's infidelity, the moment he put the pieces together, the little clues that added up to one big hole that ate his heart, brain, and soul. He remembered when she tried to play it off, to call him paranoid and jealous. He remembered the lies he eventually trapped her in. He remembered how the most fundamental thing in his life was undone by something as trivial as sex, how the rock where his life had been built had split wide and dumped him into the foggy, cold, unforgiving sea.

He remembered almost losing his son.

He hadn't forgiven her. He hadn't forgotten. He hadn't put his family before himself, he hadn't done the good Christian act of forgiveness, he hadn't let bygones be bygones and he sure as hell hadn't gotten this out of his system. He had put a cap on it is all. He had suffered in silence and the Irish Wolf, that intruder, was going to know what it meant when that suffering exploded all over these woods and the state and the fucking world for all Dave cared.

Without even realizing it, Dave let out a scream, which was not his normal ritual, then collapsed, twitched and kept screaming all the way through the transformation. Dilly instinctively walked behind his mom and she reached out and took his hand. From under the tarp, the White Wolf let out a long whine.

It took ninety seconds or more of loud, violent thrashing and noise but the Lead Wolf eventually rose from the dirty, leaf-strewn ground. Steam rose off him and he turned to face the Irish Wolf.

Dave Rhodes was forty-two. He had first scratched at fifteen. The Lead Wolf had only been lead for a little over two years. It had been a hard, ugly fight but he had won and now, when he rose, he was as hungry as he'd ever been. Hungry for flesh. Hungry for battle. Hungry as fuck. He turned to face the Irish Wolf and if the stranger could have smirked, he would have. The lead wolf growled and wrestled the sound as if it caught in his throat and croaked out a word.

"Blood," the Lead Wolf growled. Then, much louder, "BLOOOOOOD!" The two wolves leapt, hurtling toward each other with ferocious speed, claws out, teeth bared, intent unsheathed. Everyone ran for cover yelling and crouching as they went and as the wolves collided high in the air, lit by the moon, the force of their impact could be felt all the way back at an old rusted truck with the most confused and scared cop in the world in the passenger side, begging to be delivered from this new, fresh hell.

A Sermon by the Rev. Thomas Rhodes

March 7, 1958

I t's a difficult thing to love your neighbor.

Sometimes your neighbor is petulant. Sometimes he is brash and braggadocian, engaging in all manner of prideful thoughts and actions. I know of one man who wooed and bedded his neighbor's wife. Ask that husband if it's easy to love your neighbor. I bet you, brothers and sisters, will all get the same answer. It is not easy.

Your family, that's supposed to be another story. Your father and your mother, they are the ones who bring you into this world, that nurture you, that raise you up right in the word of God in a Godly household and if you stray, they are the ones who feel God's spirit moving through you and put you back in line. Your brothers and your sisters – your actual brothers and sisters, not what we call each other every Sunday – your brothers and sisters are your first friends, your allies and your co-conspirators. [laughter]

If you'll allow me, you know my brother and sister, Willie and Cindy. There they are, fourth pew from the back, like they always are. We grew up with a harsh father, Rev. Kane as you all knew him. He was a good man in his heart and from the pulpit but he could be a cruel man when his temper got the better of him, and because of that, Willie and Cindy, they looked up to me to protect them. I can see Willie smiling from here. I remember once we were playing in the living room and we knocked over the radio and broke it. This was the most expensive item in our modest house. A radio that brought the outside world into our home. We begged and begged mother for it and she talked good old Rev. Kane into it, even though it "could be used by the devil."

We broke that radio. On accident, as children do sometimes. And when my father, the Reverend, came home he asked who had done it. I told him it was me and he took after me with a vengeance, yes he did. Willie . . . Willie even tried to talk some sense into my father and he regretted it. But, it was all over soon enough. We had dinner that night, as a family if I recall, me with an ice pack on my eye.

My point, brothers and sisters, is not to ask for your pity for me but to illustrate, in a real and substantial way, that loving your family can be just as hard as loving your neighbor. It can be a brutal affair, family and Jesus, he knew it. And he knew why. Family can hurt you like no one else can hurt you because family are the ones who are your own flesh and your own blood and are supposed to be your own soul. Family are part of you that can betray you as no one else can – not a wife, not a friend, not an old Army buddy or the newest of lovers can hurt you like a family can hurt you.

But it can go the other way, too, can't it? You know it can, brothers and sisters, you *know* it can. Because just as I stepped in front of a flurry of fists from the good Reverend for Willie and for Cindy, I know they would step in front of an oncoming bus for me if I needed them to. I know that the three of us have a bond so strong that my wife, the person with whom I choose to share my life, she'll never equal it. Family is hard. But family is, sometimes, the only thing that can save us.

With that, consider today's reading. Luke 14:26 "If anyone comes to Me, and does not hate his own father and mother and wife and children and brothers and sisters, yes, and even his own he cannot be My disciple."

Think on that, ponder on that, brothers and sisters. Think of what Jesus is saying because this isn't a verse with hidden meaning. This isn't a puzzler. This is black and white, people of God. This is clear as clear can be and as plain and plain can be out of the mouth of Jesus himself. If you are to be my disciple, Jesus says, you must hate . . . hate your family. You must take that which is closest to you, that which feeds you and nourishes you, that which you value and you understand better than anything else on this Earth and you need to throw it away. Discard it. Leave it. Hate it. Jesus is saying compared to the best Earth can give you, compared to the most perfect and amazing love a human can offer, it is nothing, it is contemptible, it is rubbish compared to what being a disciple of Jesus can be.

Family is hard. Loving your neighbor is hard. But I look at you, my neighbors, and I look at Willie and at Cindy and I tell you with a swelling heart and tears in my eyes that it is worth it. It is worth every heartbreak and every betrayal and every wrong turn and every misstep to be your neighbor and to be your brother and to be your sister. It is worth it. It is worth it.

Being a disciple of Jesus, that's more than a man can hope to accomplish in one, small, meager lifetime, but the reward, brothers and sisters, is eternal life on the other side. Eternal glory and a seat at the heavenly banquet. What more can man ask for?

Amen.

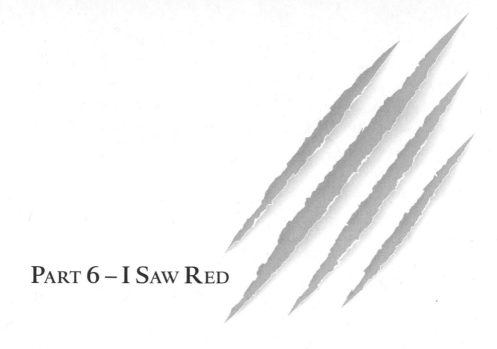

Part 6 – I Saw Red

"Bar" was still open. That was good.

That was about all for the "good" column.

Dave's shirt was gone. That was the first thing a bystander might notice. He was the lone shirtless guy sitting in the back, part of a group of a dozen or so people occupying the rear of the bar. They had pushed a bunch of tables together and, one bare-chested dude aside, they wouldn't be too conspicuous on first glance.

But if you spent a few seconds you might notice the blood. The shirtless guy was bleeding, more than a little. He was holding a bag of ice to a nasty gash on his chest and the red blood had seeped around the bag even though the man was holding it tightly. Closer inspection would reveal another man with his hand wrapped with blood-stains sprouting up in random intervals along the white fabric. Then, if you kept looking, you would notice how rough everyone else looked. There was an old man, white hair and beard, who had flecks of leaves and dirt visible and looked like he had just been hit by a truck. There was a young man, next to him, with visible tear marks down his cheeks. A group of three clustered in one corner, not talking or drinking.

And there was a woman at the end of the table who, in direct contrast to everyone else, could not keep still.

Finally, if you'd taken all that in, you might have noticed the Barter County Sheriff, sitting away from the group, staring at a wall.

But no one else was there. Even Chuck had stayed in the back, coming only when called.

Josie took turns between being uncomfortable sitting and being uncomfortable standing. She had never been this frightened in her life. She finally walked over to Dave.

"You have to talk to him," she said. "He saw."

"I know he saw."

"Then you have to talk to him."

"I know."

"Would you go over there and talk to him then?"

Dave looked up at her and gave her a bleary look. He was just about done.

"If you don't go over there now," Josie said. "Think about what happens next."

He would call other cops, of course. Or would he? Dave thought. What would he tell them? He would definitely lock Dave up, or maybe not. Come to think of it, Dave had no idea what would happen next.

"Nothing good happens next," Josie said, reading the look on his face. "He could arrest us, he could detain us, he could decide to shoot us. I hate to say this, but you gotta win him over. We can't leave here enemies."

Dave pulled himself up with a groan, careful to keep the ice pack hard against his chest and staggered over to the bar, yelling for Chuck. He whispered something, disappearing into the back, and soon Chuck came out with a shirt, a pitcher of beer, and two glasses. Dave patted Chuck on the shoulder, then put on the shirt, wincing through the process. The cut Conall had given him was deep and would require medical care at some point but as his wife had said, there was something else he had to attend to.

Slowly, Dave took the long walk from the bar to Stu's table. Stu had been dutiful and had stayed in the truck back at the campground, only to be rewarded by getting a close-up look at the fight between the Lead Wolf and the Irish Wolf. The blast radius of their fight had taken them deep into the woods, then toward the road and finally, after The Irish Wolf tried to change the direction of the fight, back to the truck. The Lead Wolf had been beaten, knocked unconscious after the Irish Wolf ran him, full force, into the truck's grill. The howl of the Irish Wolf's victory had drowned out the screams from the sheriff and the headlights had given him a good, long, detailed look at exactly what he was dealing with.

Stu had not said a word since that scream.

On his way to the table, Conall grabbed Dave's arm.

"Have you thought through this course of action, there?" he asked. "This could go very wrong very fast."

"I know you're trying to help us but with all due respect, I think I'm done taking advice from you for tonight," Dave said.

Conall went back to staring at his beer as Dave sat down with Stu, letting the two glasses clank loudly on the old, wooden table. He set the pitcher of beer down more gingerly. All of his angry energy was basically gone, but his internal rebellion was still calling the shots. He was going to handle it his way. If anyone had a problem with it, they could take a shot at being Alpha.

"Sheriff," Dave said. "Tough night."

Stu didn't say anything.

"I don't want to sound pushy, all right, but this is what's going to happen. There's this pitcher of beer and there are two glasses. I'm going to start drinking here in a second and I'm going to pour you a drink and you're going to drink with me. I insist."

Stu didn't say anything.

"As long as there is beer in this pitcher, there is no question I'm not going to answer. Ask me anything about what you've seen tonight. I will not lie to you and I will not hide the truth. If I don't know something, I'll tell you that. As long as there's beer in that pitcher, ask me anything."

Stu didn't say anything.

"When the beer is gone, I'm done answering questions and hopefully I'll have talked you into letting me and my family live in peace. If you decide you're not thirsty or talkative, I'm going to drink this pitcher by myself and you'll never have this chance again. Ever."

Stu didn't say anything.

"I'm going to need some sort of sign that you understand what I'm saying to you."

Flashes of teeth, fur, and blood filled Stu's brain, and he batted them away. The memories of his past trauma, his "curse," had given him training in this regard. There were so many times in public where he had zoned out, completely lost in the fog of his trauma. He had imaginary conversations with the boy who had shot himself, run the scenario a million times and, he had learned, there were times when you shoved those memories to the side and got some damn work done. This was different, obviously. But the process was the same.

In a moment, Stu snapped his working brain back into place and grabbed his cup.

"Pour the beer," he said.

"Thank you," Dave said and used the side of the pitcher instead of the spout, something he had done many times throughout the years, to pull a wide stream of beer into the glass, filling it in less than two seconds. The head rose and formed a bubble shape around the top of the glass. Just when it looked like spillage was imminent, the head held and started to slowly, slowly roll back.

"I guess my first question is why shouldn't I shoot you right now."

"In front of my family? I don't think I have you pegged that wrong."

"Fine then. Let me shoot your Irish friend over there and I'll take him to the nearest city with a university and they can figure this out."

Conall heard his name and turned around, raising his glass.

"Try it, mate!" he yelled.

"Don't look at him," Dave said. "Look at me. Conall, let the Sheriff and I talk, please."

Conall gave a slight shrug and turned back around. Both Dave and Stu were aware that everyone could hear them. Hell, Chuck could probably hear them in the back. It was just as well. This was a private conversation about a public truth.

"You shouldn't shoot me because we haven't done anything wrong."

"Excuse me," Stu said.

"If you exclude the little party trick you saw there, what did we do?"

"OK," Stu said, speaking rapidly and ticking his points off on his fingers. "Assault, destruction of property, attempted murder . . ."

"No one was trying to kill you, Stu."

"Disorderly conduct, disturbing the peace . . . no license for your animal, I don't fucking know. The point is that little 'party trick' . . . I don't even know. What the hell . . ."

Stu was starting to lose it again and Dave saw his opening.

"What you saw, Sheriff, was something that's been happening around here for, literally, hundreds of years. There are groups all over the world that do this, if you believe Conall over there. What I know and what I can tell you for certain is I've been doing this for over twenty years and I have never . . . I've never been a danger to anyone."

Dave was going to say he had never hurt anyone, but everyone in the bar knew that was a lie. By now, Stu had certainly put together that the two unsolved murders in his county were a result of the local pack and it was still the rawest of nerves among the group.

"Two bodies," Dave said. "That one blonde girl and that dude . . . Matzen. You and your people killed them."

Both men took a long drink of their beer.

"Truth is, Sheriff, you're half right. I told you I wouldn't lie to you and I'm not going to, so I'm about to tell you something really personal that's hard to talk about. I have no reason to lie . . ."

"Out with it," Stu said. "Don't tell me you're telling the truth. Liars tend to do that."

"Fair enough. Byron was part of our pack. He was a friend of mine and he's an ex-boyfriend of my wife, Josie, over there."

She looked up and gave a nod. It didn't register with Stu that the entire bar was listening to them.

"We all loved Byron," Dave continued. "But he got himself in some trouble. This thing, that we do, it's a high. It makes you feel incredible but we have rules in place because it's gotta be regulated. If it was one guy who could do this, they'd hurt somebody, they'd lose control. That's why we're a group. So we can help each other keep control."

The mood in the back of the bar immediately changed and softened. The group never talked about this part of the process. It was understood and refined by years of "scratches" and everything that went with it—the breaking bread, the absolute honesty. After you've seen someone turn into a wolf, how much more intimate can you get? But words about the process, spoken aloud, hit Ron and Carl and Willie and Josie.

"Are you a hunter, Sheriff?"

"No. I grew up in the city. Never got the chance."

"There's this teacher I work with, Mr. Shank, and Mr. Shank and his wife had a kid and one of the first things he said when that kid was born was 'I can't wait to take him hunting.' I asked him why and he said he remembered the first time his dad put a rifle in his hands. How careful he had to be and how closely he had to listen and then his dad took him out and showed him how to attract a deer and how to flush it out and they were outside and bonding. It was an experience he associated most closely with family."

"This thing we do, it's like that only a million times more potent," Dave continued. "My dad did it. His dad did it. I just . . . I just showed my son how this works," Dave said and stopped. He had started to choke up but quickly pulled himself together. "This is why we're here. This is as much who we are as anything on this planet. This is sacred to us. Those woods, that's our sanctuary. We have rituals we go through and we do it to keep the folks in this town safe."

"And Mr. Matzen?" Stu asked. "He wasn't safe."

"He did that to himself," Dave said. "The scratch wasn't enough for him, so he started messing around with drugs. Got himself addicted and then he did what an addict does."

"He was going to sell you out, wasn't he," Stu said.

"He was."

"What was he going to do?"

Dave took another large swallow of beer.

"Byron always was an attention whore," Dave said, letting it fly a little more. "If he wasn't getting attention when he wanted it, he would do anything to make sure he got it. He'd sing karaoke every week and if that didn't do it he'd go down to the school and play the pianos and sing to the kids. They all thought he was the best. If he was feeling low he'd get on the Internet and talk shit and message ex-girlfriends and anything he could to get that attention. He was an asshole."

Across the bar, Josie winced a bit.

"What was he going to do?" Stu repeated.

"He was with that girl, Sandra Riedel? They were together because of course they were. Fucker could charm the pants off anyone he wanted. So one night, Sandra comes to Ron over there and asks him if he can set up a secure webcam and make sure that no one else around could hack their signal. He asks why and it comes out that he's become a wolf in front of Sandra and now he's going to do it on webcam because he's a giant attention whore."

"I thought you said he was on drugs?" Stu asked.

"That was part of it, turns out," Dave said. "Ron, he goes along with it and finds out from Sandra that they've both been doing meth for a few months. She says that she can't keep up with him and that he does it almost every other day. So Ron digs a little more and it turns out he's not just cam whoring, he's trying to win something. Ever heard of the JREF prize?"

"No," Stu said.

"The James Randi Educational Foundation has promised one million dollars for whoever can prove existence of the supernatural. Byron was going to take him up on it. Apparently he was going to webcam with someone from their group and then go in and do it in person. Then he was out of here."

"What happened?"

"Ron got all this out of Sandra and then we all went and confronted him about it. He denied the whole thing and the next morning, Sandra was dead."

135

"What happened, Dave?"

"Sandra double-crossed him. She was going to take the money for herself and hang Byron out to dry. That's what he told us and I believe him. And we have rules and rituals for one reason and one reason only."

"To maintain control," Stu said.

"Exactly," Dave said, running his fingers through his hair and draining his beer glass. "If he can kill a member of this community and get away with it ain't nobody safe here. And we will never make our neighbors feel unsafe. Never."

That sat for a while. Dave poured two more glasses and Willie, who was in the corner, held his tongue. The phrase "there's more to it than that" was raging in his brain, but given how he felt and the current state of things, he fought the urge and kept it to himself.

"Did you kill him?" Stu asked.

"It was a group thing," Dave replied. "In full honesty, we all came at him at once."

"As wolves?"

"Yeah," Dave said. "As wolves."

By now the two men were drinking at fairly regular intervals and it was no longer a standoff, but a conversation. In that way, Dave had succeeded. His family and friends had gone from monsters back to people in the sheriff's mind, but the next step was going to be a lot harder.

"Shit," Stu said. "How do you do that?"

"What?"

"You know damn well what."

"I don't know if I can give you a good answer," Dave said. "I can tell you what it's like. I can tell you we've been doing it in this part of the country since pioneer days. I can tell you it hurts but you get used to it. I can tell you me and my family are in complete control over this thing and Byron's death, while tragic, was a rare thing."

"You'll understand if I'm having a bit of trouble believing you."

Dave sat back in his chair. The pitcher was more than half empty. Time to go for broke, he thought.

"Here's a question for you, Sheriff. How many people have you met on this job?"

"I don't know. A hundred or so."

"You've met Chuck there behind the bar. You've met the Meyers, the Chandlers, you've met Pastor Matt down at the church and Amy who manages the gas station?"

"Yeah," Stu said. "I've met all of them."

"So do you think that Chuck and the Meyers and the Chandlers and Pastor Matt and Amy and everyone else in this town would hesitate, even for a second, to tell the world there were werewolves living next door if they thought they were in any danger?"

Stu took a drink and leaned forward to meet Dave's gaze.

"You think this is the first time I've had this conversation, Sheriff?" Dave said. "You think most people around here don't know?"

Suddenly, a lot of things clicked into place for Stu, like every single time someone from the area asked him if they had met Dave yet or the multiple times he'd heard phrases like "you'll find some odd folks around here," or "this isn't your normal sort of town." Even Chuck, trying desperately to look like he wasn't listening, had made several out and out references to wolves that flew right over Stu's head. Of course, if he had known he was dealing with werewolves . . .

"The point," Dave continued, "is here's what we tell people."

Dave stood up for effect. The rest of the group behind him stood up as well and Conall, taking his cue about five seconds late, followed suit.

"I tell people that we are decent, hard-working folks who go to our jobs, pay our taxes, sing in the church choir and go out into the woods once or twice a month and do our thing. We're careful and we care. This here, this is our home. This is our refuge. If you're scared, we understand that, believe me. This is a scary thing. But give us a chance to prove ourselves. Get to know us. Don't be afraid because, if all goes well, you'll never have to encounter this thing that we do and if, by some chance, you do, we will do everything in our power to make it right."

"Plus, think of the absolute thunderstorm of bullshit that happens if you blow the whistle on us, man," Kenny Kirk chimed in from behind. "I mean, seriously, dark thunderclouds of thick, viscous shit coming down on this town in sheets."

"Vividly put," Ron snorted.

Dave sat back down and the rest of the group took the opportunity to start talking amongst themselves, and there was plenty to discuss. Josie started grilling Conall on the other packs in the United States and Europe, Kenny and JoAnn were talking quietly in a corner, and Carl tried to ignore Dilly's continued questions. No one spoke to Willie and he was fine with that.

"Nice speech," Stu said once Dave's butt hit the seat. "It doesn't change anything."

"I didn't expect it to," Dave said. "And, to be honest, we're in uncharted waters here. Usually when someone finds out about us it's because they've asked around and maybe are even trying to find us. You saw us at our worst. But here's what I'm asking—don't blow the whistle on us. At least not yet."

Dave refilled the glasses for the final time.

"I can solve two murders, here," Stu said. "Why shouldn't I do that right now?"

The correct answer to that question, Dave thought, was that they were not getting locked up tonight. There would be blood before that happened, especially given the circumstances, but he was also smart enough to know that would only put them on the run and make things a hundred times harder.

"Please don't," Dave said. "We were attacked tonight. I wish I could tell you the specifics of who attacked us and why but there's a really good chance it has to do with what Byron did. There are people after us, Sheriff. We're in danger and it might come down to the fact that we need your help."

"That's not my problem," Stu said. "I don't want to sound like a hard ass here, but—"

"YOU LEAVE THEM ALONE!"

All noise in the bar ceased and all heads swiveled to look at Chuck. He had slammed a thick glass mug down on the wooden bar which gave his yelling a nice, thud accent. This was "Bar" and Chuck had the floor.

"I've heard you, Sheriff Dietz. You go on and on about how you want folks to trust you. Well let me tell you, if you lock up Dave and you start screaming from the damn roof about werewolves, you ain't never getting anyone to trust you ever again."

No one in the bar could remember the last time Chuck had strung together that many words about anything other than Nebraska football or politics. Get him going about the coaching staff or what so and so was doing in office and he was worse than a radio announcer on Red Bull, but try to get him to talk about community or family or something important and it was like pulling teeth.

Not tonight, though.

"The Rhodes, they built this town. Hell, they built this county," the barkeep continued. "They've been pastors and businessmen and teachers and all of them have been wolves. They don't hurt nobody. What the hell, man?"

And with that, Chuck was back in the kitchen doing something else.

"That," Dave said, "was new."

"Not exactly a ringing endorsement," Kenny Kirk chimed in. "I'm not big on speeches from a guy who picks his nose as he serves your drink."

"One time, I saw him spit in the dishwater then use it to clean out a glass," Ron said.

"My friend at school found fingernail clippings in his burger once," Dilly added.

"That was only one time and you can all shut your damn mouths!" Chuck yelled from the kitchen.

It was Ron who started chuckling. Carl picked it up and within seconds, the table was laughing. A few seconds later, they were roaring and Dave, weary and beaten up and desperate for the safety of his family, couldn't help but be swept up in the wave. They laughed and laughed, Willie's big whooping guffaw raising above the rest.

The strange nature of the situation suddenly struck Stu in the face. A year ago he had been a cop in Detroit. Now, after time as a national punchline, he was in a dingy bar in the middle of nowhere, recovering from the trauma of watching supernatural beasts do battle. And now they were making fun of an old barkeep.

Life is weirder than you think it's going to be.

Almost against his will, Stu started laughing as well. The faces of the group were the opposite of threatening. They were not laughing for the same reasons, but when he started laughing, Stu found it hard to stop. Before long, they were all wiping tears from their eyes.

"Welcome to Cherry," Dave said through a few remaining chuckles. "You're one of us now that you've made fun of Chuck."

"You can all kiss my ass," Chuck yelled from the kitchen, setting off the entire group again.

The room sighed as the laughter died, an unspoken social sign the party was over and it was time for everyone to leave. Before that happened, Stu leaned across the table and motioned for Dave to do the same.

"I'm not going to arrest you right now," Stu almost whispered. "But you and your people have committed a crime and that will not stand."

"I get that," Dave countered. "But I'm going to protect the people I love at all costs. That's all I know how to do."

Stu gave a knowing smile and downed the last of his beer. Dave did the same and their eyes locked for a moment.

Dave's eyes said *"We never speak of this again."*

We'll see about that, Stu thought.

•••

Once Stu left, the pack met in front of "Bar" to plan out what happened next. No one had a good feeling about it.

"I don't think we can go back to our houses," Josie said. "Whoever attacked us obviously knows where we live."

"I'll do you one better, dearie," Conall said. "You've all got to get your asses out of town. Given your run-in with law enforcement, it makes all the sense in the world. Seriously, I thought you were all heading out of there in handcuffs."

"I'm gonna die running but I sure as shit ain't running away, if you get what I mean," Willie said.

"That's obvious from your substantial girth," Conall said. "But you're hurt and those men with rifles are coming back and they are coming back hard. Maybe think of it as regrouping."

"Or not standing in front of a truck coming right at you," Ron said.

"You didn't get shot and turned, asshole. That was me."

"Well at least you're back to your old self," Dave said. "I don't want to run either, but let's just hear Conall out. What are you thinking?"

It had started to drizzle and the cold was starting to get to the group. JoAnn was huddled into a ball and even the warm-blooded Dilly was rubbing his bare arms. Dave had borrowed a shirt from Chuck that was ill-fitting, thin, and smelled of God knows what.

"The first thing we do is get a few clicks down the road. Then I'll make some calls. Is there one of those god-awful shopping monstrosities you Americans have every few miles around here?"

"What, like a Walmart?" Kenny Kirk said.

"Yeah, something like that," Conall said. "I want to get some place public, some place warm, and somewhere we can buy some supplies. If there's a place we could all sit and talk, that would be stellar."

"The nearest place like that is in Kearney. That's forty-five minutes away or so," Josie said. "Kenny, you still got the van?"

"Yeah, it's by the shop."

"No," Conall said. "I know this sounds paranoid but any car you drive they might very well have a tracker in by now. I don't mean to frighten you, but there are very high stakes here for these people and anything licensed in your name is unsafe at this point. I've got a car that can take four. What else can we borrow?"

As various options started shooting around the group of whose car they could beg, borrow, or steal, the weight of what was happening came crashing down on Dave. Less than two days ago life was on the mend and back in a routine, his biggest problem being whether or not to bring his son into the fold. It had gone well and then Willie and then Conall and then everything else. Now his pack was being hunted and his family was in shambles. He was doing a hell of a job leading.

Whenever self-doubt crept in, Dave always felt the urge to act. It was a stereotypical male trait and one that annoyed Josie to no end, but the urge this time was too strong to stifle but strong enough to shake him out of his head and into the present.

"Let's take Chuck's Pathfinder. He has it out back that can carry seven of us if we pack in. With Conall's car, that's more than enough."

"Sold," Conall said. "We keep each other in sight the entire time. We can't lose each other. I don't think it will but if anything happens on the road, I'm in front and you follow my lead. Is that understood?"

The group nodded, even Willie.

"We meet in the parking lot of the shopping monstrosity in Kearney . . . where the hell am I going?"

"I'll ride with you," Josie said. "Me and Dilly."

"Fine," Conall said. "Who's driving the big van thingee?"

"I'll drive," Dave said.

"Of course you will," Conall said. "The rest of you, sleep if you can. You might not get another chance for a while."

Conall's car was out front and the three passengers piled in as the rest of the group walked to the back of "Bar."

"You gonna tell Chuck we're taking his Pathfinder?" Kenny Kirk asked.

"We'll leave him a note," Dave said. "I've already got a cop threatening us with murder charges. Borrowing a car I think we can get away with."

"Hope you're right," Kenny said. "Old Chuck holds a grudge like . . . like I don't know man. I can't think of anything funny to say. My brain is on autopilot."

"Yeah, I'm kind of running on adrenaline," Dave said.

"We'll stop and get you a Red Bull or something, man. You drink those things? They make you feel like you want to go out dancing or something. I never feel like going out but I drink one of those and I'm like 'what you all doing? Let's go do something.' It's crazy. JoAnn says I need to stop drinking them. "

"I think I'll be OK," Dave said. "Plenty on my mind."

• • •

The trip passed without incident, unless you count Willie complaining the entire way. Dave, Kenny, JoAnn, Ron and Carl were all too tired to give him any attention and after a while the dark and the humming of the highway knocked the old guy out. All of the passengers fell asleep, with the exception of Carl, who was in the front seat next to Dave, who was nostalgic.

"I remember the first time you scratched," Dave said. "You were younger than Dilly, weren't you?"

"Yeah," Carl said. "It wasn't my first time, but my first time with you guys, I was nervous."

"Really?" Dave said. "I didn't know that."

If you don't count Dilly, who had his spot in the pack predestined from birth, Carl was the newest member and Willie never let him forget it. Until several nights back Carl had been the target of Willie's barbs and for no reason other than his father, Jim. They used to run together, both literally and figuratively, or so Carl had heard. Then there was a falling out, some punches were thrown, some claws were unsheathed and when Carl was three years old his family moved away from Cherry.

They had settled in Kearney, a town far to the south of Nebraska along Interstate 80 and there Carl had gone to school, grown up, and eventually come out as gay. Jim had thrown a giant fit about that, even going so far as to say he regretted ever having a son if he was going to turn out that way. But Carl had been quietly strong, taking all the barbs his father had thrown at him, absorbing them and turning them inward. He had learned to hate himself and when his father died of a stroke six years ago, Carl had grieved and cried and, suddenly, turned into a wolf. It was quite a surprise.

After it happened, Carl started feverishly trying to figure out what he was and it was his mother, who sensed something had changed, that clued him in to Cherry. She had begged him not to go meet with Willie, the only contact she still had up there, but Carl didn't stay away long. The moment

143

his mother looked away he packed the car and headed up there. He had a long talk with Willie, who wasn't hard to track down. It did not go well.

"I turned one time in Kearney and then tracked down your father," Carl said to Dave. "He called me a 'faggot' within two minutes of meeting me."

"I would apologize for Willie but that's a full-time job," Dave said.

"But he introduced me to you guys," Carl said. "I'm thankful for that."

They drove in silence before Carl, uncharacteristically, started a conversation.

"Dilly is really confused," Carl said. "He's freaking out and he doesn't feel like you can help him."

The words hit Dave in the chest and the emotional wound bled down into his stomach and extremities. He knew this, of course, but to hear the soft-spoken Carl articulate it with such brevity somehow amplified the blow.

"He's been staying away from me," Dave said. "Josie's trying to get closer to him. I'm hoping she can pick up the slack."

"Some things he needs to hear from you," Carl said. "Especially about what we are."

"I'm not sure what we are," Dave said. "Forty-eight hours ago I thought I knew. I thought life was plugging along just fine, you know? But now maybe there's a lot more of us all across the world. I don't know how to feel about that."

"*You* don't know how to feel about that?" Carl said. "You? Your kid is terrified. I don't mean to be disrespectful, but pull your head out of your ass, man. Your family needs you."

With that, Carl shifted his weight and looked out the window at that special dark you only get when there's little to no light pollution. The Pathfinder, which smelled like ass, chugged on and Dave felt like the most selfish person on the planet.

• • •

They pulled in to the Walmart parking lot at around two in the morning. There are not too many places as sad at that time of night. There were only a few cars, belonging to employees, that littered the parking lot and the loudest noise by a country mile was the buzzing of the streetlights.

"I've never seen one up close," Conall said, getting out of his sports car and stretching. "It's even worse than I imagined."

"Walmarts ain't that bad, man," Kenny Kirk said as the group coalesced and began walking forward. "You can buy a pair of pants and some string cheese and an X-box and a deck of cards all in one place. Where else can you do that?"

"You already have an X-box," Dilly said.

"That's not the point, man," Kenny shot back. "Not even close."

The group trudged toward the automatic doors, their weariness evident, Conall the only one clearly energized by the experience.

"You ever hear about something like . . . like Bruce Springsteen. You hear forever and ever about Bruce Springsteen and how he's the best and you go 'yeah yeah yeah,' but then you hear 'Born to Run' and suddenly it all makes sense."

The harsh light from the sign illuminated Conall, making him look even more wild.

"It makes sense now."

"You said we're here to buy supplies," Dave said. "What did you have in mind?"

"Nothing special," Conall said. "Food, water, maybe a few changes of clothes."

"I thought you were talking about guns and bullets and shit," Kenny Kirk said.

"They sell guns here!" Conall said, and plowed headlong into the store without looking back.

Josie shot Dave a look that said "he won't get far" and grabbed a shopping cart. Like most retail establishments open twenty-four hours, this megastore took on a very different tone in the wee morning hours. The lack of customers and employees, with the exception of the one open lane, put an ominous sheen on the whole experience. A zombie shambling down the meat aisle would not seem out of place.

Dave tried to keep his eyes open but the combination of the home invasion, wolf fight, the confrontation with Stu, and the drive had put the zap on him. He was done. Like most Walmarts, there was a Subway in the front part of the store next to a phone shop and a salon. The sandwich shop was shuttered and dark.

"I'm going to pull up a booth and grab a quick nap," Dave told Josie. "You OK?"

She nodded and Dave noticed the lines in her face and the wideness of her eyes and knew she was worried, probably about him in part, but more so for Dilly. After worshipping her face while they dated and knowing her face and its idiosyncrasies and tics after years and years of loving that face, he knew when something was up. He clasped her shoulder to offer some semblance of reassurance and then made for the booth in the restaurant, thick with the smell of meat and some sort of sauce Dave couldn't identify, and promptly fell asleep.

While he was out, he had a dream. It was not uncommon for the first sleep after a scratch to feature a "wolf dream," a point of view experience where you were running, leaping, bounding and occasionally fighting. One odd part about "wolf dreams" was that while the actions in the dream were personalized, the dream was always set in the same place for everyone in the pack—a wide open grassy field under an intense blue sky. Also, they sometimes got weird.

This was one of the weird ones.

It started in the field. Normally he would pick up a scent and chase something, but not today. The air was still and even the wind carried no scent of living things beyond grass and clover, trees and plant rot. His head on a swivel, the Lead Wolf looked to the left and the right and saw nothing, but straight ahead of him was a large outcropping of stones. They were arranged in an odd way that was clearly not natural. The stones were in a crude ring with a pile in the center about two feet high.

On swift legs the wolf ran to the staged scene and stopped on the edge of the ring. Something told him not to go inside, but dream logic compelled him. Even as he stepped over the ring's edge the human voice inside his head, all but gone when in this state, was screaming to turn back and his stomach sank and bubbled in fear. But his path was set. The wolf stepped over the edge and to the center.

Several long sniffs revealed nothing. The wind had picked up but still carried no information. With hesitant claws, the wolf touched the stones and when he did, the world changed.

The wind was thick with scents of blood, the sky darkened an unnatural shade of blue with orange hues and the rocks started to melt into something resembling lava. The pile of rocks quickly descended into steaming goo and started rolling and changing, rising out of the ground five feet or so and began to morph and change. At first it was long and then round, then a face appeared in the lava. It was no one's face, the features smooth and indistinguishable, but the expression was one of rage. The face trembled and sputtered and the Lead Wolf, with his powerful legs and claws that could tear and rip could not make himself do anything other than stare at the face.

The bubbling goo got closer and closer until it blocked out all else—a fiery face of rage staring at the wolf. It exploded.

Dave woke up hard as Kenny was shaking his shoulder. He looked as white as a sheet.

"Dave, man, get up right now," he said. "Help me find everyone. You need to hear this right now, man."

Kenny's voice was low and panicked, all pretense of the fun-loving motor mouth gone. His heart beating so fast he feared for his health, Dave stood up, took a few deep breaths and steadied himself.

"What's going on?"

"There's a message on my phone," Kenny said. "It's from them."

• • •

Conall took the longest to find. He was near the Home and Garden center, staring at the fish.

"Why in the name of Mary do they sell fish?" he asked Kenny, who was racing around the store gathering everyone. "As pets? Are they a pet store too? What is this place?"

147

Kenny eventually got the Irishman removed from the pet aisle and they all gathered at two booths in the sandwich shop. No one was around and no one was in earshot. In the center of the table was Kenny's phone (Samsung S9 and he told anyone who asked) and he turned the speaker phone on, cycled through the options and played old messages.

"Hello, Mr. Rathman, this is Mr. Stander. You met my men earlier tonight. Your friend, Mr. Rhodes, doesn't seem to want to speak with me and I'm hoping you're a more reasonable fellow. We've created a website for you and I'm wondering if you'd give it a look. Please get a pen ready and write this down."

A URL that was a string of letters and numbers followed.

"Watching this video will give you a much better idea of who we are and, more importantly, where you stand. You can call me back at this number. Good-bye."

Silence hung heavy. Not only did they have Kenny's number and knew who he was, but someone had made a video? That meant resources, expertise, will. Any way you sliced it, this portended doom.

"If you watch the video, they'll know where you are," Conall said, plainly. "They'll be able to track the data signal at the very least. Don't be a fool."

"You're right," Ron said. "But we need to know what it says, don't we?"

"Can we watch it while driving?" Dilly suggested. "That might make it harder for them to find us."

"That won't work," Ron said. "But I think I might be able to rig something up. Come on."

Ron led the group through the sad, sad clothes aisles past the toy section and into the aisle where the laptop computers were on display. Some of them were on.

"If I can get into their wi-fi I might be able to mask our IP address so they don't see where we're coming from. At least not right away."

The clicks of Ron's fast fingers filled the aisles and after a minute or so, he started chuckling.

"Their wi-fi password is 'password,'" he said. "What else do you expect from Walmart?"

Before long he had worked his magic and turned to the group and heaved a sigh.

"You guys ready?"

"I've seen these before," Conall said. "They'll be some threats, some promises of monetary gain. Typically their first volley isn't full of blood and guts. Don't let it rattle you."

A few keystrokes later, which echoed in the empty aisle, a plain, white page with a video embedded on the screen. Ron hit play, cranked the volume and pulled up the full screen. It didn't seem like a video at first but more of a live stream with all the choppy skips and poor resolutions of something happening in the moment. From off camera someone yelled "Sir, they're on" and the camera shook wildly for a moment. Then it stabilized and focused on Mr. Stander, who was clearly outside.

"Don't worry," Ron said. "I turned off the webcam. They can't see or hear us."

"This is odd," Mr. Stander started. "I was hoping for more of a real conversation. You're also blocking your location, but you're probably in a Walmart somewhere. They're the only places open at this time of night."

His tone was far less formal than Dave had remembered. The man's bow tie stood out even more in the dead of night.

"I'll get right to it. We are very motivated to find you and I'm afraid the possibility of giving you generous compensation for your cooperation has passed. You proved that when you killed several of my men. That's not something I take lightly nor something my employers are going to forgive. So that's how it is."

The camera then moved from Stander to reveal their location. They were in front of Dave and Josie's house.

"I'll admit, we know less than we'd like at this point," Stander said. "But we do know a lot. We know about the Rhodes and their family. And where you live. We also know Mr. Rathman and his partner JoAnn are part of your group. There's a very good chance William Rhodes is also with you. From there, it's speculation."

The camera moved back to Stander.

"As for your Irish friend, I can be fairly certain he was sent by The Council. And that he knows how outmatched he is right now."

Everyone turned and looked at Conall who did not betray what he was thinking.

"I'm going to be frank with all of you. I'm not usually an emotional man but the way I've been treated has been absolutely beyond the pale. This town, this nowhere, I can see why no one's found you because who would come to such a place? It smells of cattle and desperation and I do not like it. But, I know, for some reason, that you do, so, hopefully, you understand what's about to happen."

The camera cut to a wide shot of the Rhodes household. "Oh God," Josie said, putting her hands to her mouth.

The smoke started slowly coming out of the doors but within thirty seconds the accelerants had ignited and the house started to burn. Fire was visible through the windows and through the open door and smoke ran along the roof, rolling over the shingles and flying up through the dark of the night sky.

Dilly started to cry and Josie joined him. Dave went over and encircled them both with his arms, his eyes never leaving the screen for a second. He saw into the living room where their television was melting and saw the fire had already spread down the hall, eating up their bedroom, Dilly's bedroom, Josie's work room with the scrapbooks. Mr. Stander stepped into the frame.

"We are going to go do the same to Mr. Kirk's garage here in a couple of hours, then his house. Then we're going to burn down that shithole bar and the church and the gas station and every other building that means anything to you until you turn yourselves in. I am not exaggerating nor am I bluffing. I am going to burn down your lives to the foundations unless you return. I'm going to give you until sunup and then the fires start. There might be a few deaths sprinkled here and there given that we are going to meet very little resistance from local law enforcement."

The fire had moved shockingly fast and Josie was sobbing, taking in giant gulps of air to feed the sound escaping her soul. Dilly was little better, but not by much as he watched the only home he'd ever lived in consumed. Dave's eyes never left the screen. His eyes were on the kitchen table where he and Josie and Dilly had sat just a few days before and decided to take him out to the woods. The table where Dave and Josie had almost ended their marriage. The table where they would have put their Thanksgiving turkey in a few weeks and have the entire pack over and eat and drink and watch football. The table from which all good things came was burning and would soon be gone.

"My entire job right now is to bring you pain, Mr. Rhodes," Mr. Stander continued. "My job requires me to wear many hats. This is one I enjoy putting on. It's time to come home and meet with me. The sooner you do so, the less pain I will inflict. This is non-negotiable. Good-bye."

The feed ended abruptly and Ron closed the page. The hum of the lights and Josie's echoing sobs were the only noise. At the end of the aisle, something moved.

"Do you folks need help finding anything?" a hard-looking woman in a Walmart smock asked.

"No," Ron said. "We're fine. Thanks."

"People come here to cry all the time," the woman said. "Usually they're alone."

"We're fine," Ron said again with a touch more force.

The woman vanished and Willie walked very slowly over to Dave, Josie, and Dilly who were clutching each other. His big arms suddenly closed in over Dave and Dilly, and soon Ron and Carl and JoAnn followed suit until the family was encircled. Conall stayed to the side, visibly uncomfortable.

"We'll get him," Willie whispered, though everyone could hear. "We'll get that son of a bitch. No one hurts my family like that. No one."

"No one but you," Dilly said through tears, and a few laughs echoed through the sobs and the unrelenting buzz of the lights echoing against stone walls.

A SELECTIVE HISTORY OF BARTER COUNTY, PART 4

In the 1970s, Cherry had seen its boom and was starting to see its regression. The age of Main Street had come and gone and while you could still find several small businesses in downtown Cherry—a Ben

Franklin, a small grocery store—none of them would survive any later than 1988. Throughout the 1970s, the decay that would lead to the abandonment of downtown was starting to peek through the cracks and make itself known.

The 1970s were also the first decade where the people of Cherry realized their young people were not going to stay. Generations of farmers saw their children leave for larger cities and population centers, even go to college. It was the sort of shift that left a generation rattled. Beyond that, however, the town was pretty much the same. Quiet, slow, full of people who valued their church, community, and privacy.

It was these three elements of community life that converged in 1978 to create an incident that was spoken of for years afterward. It involved the First Baptist Church in Cherry, overseen by the Rev. Thomas Rhodes. He decided, one Sunday, to try something he had heard about from his peers but had never been tried before in the town. This new innovation in worship was known as an "Altar Call" and consisted of the pastor or some other church leader offering public absolution and counsel for those with troubled souls.

Logistically that would mean the pastor saying something to the effect of "if you feel Jesus moving in your heart tonight, asking you to make a change, come to the altar and receive his forgiveness." The language varied from time to time and even though the nature of what brought them to the altar was kept private, the act of absolution, that you had *something* to confess or that needed changing in your life, was deliberately a public part of the process.

When Pastor Rhodes first tried an altar call, things went about as well as could be expected. During that time he was presiding over a fairly large congregation for the area and routinely saw over one hundred parishioners come to Sunday service. Some of those who attended the first altar call were no surprise—the woman who had well-known problems with money, the man who had been seen drinking too much in public, a child whose parents urged him to go. The second altar call drew an unexpected person—the pastor's own brother, William.

At that point William was known as a hard-working, solid individual.

He wasn't the pillar of the community that his brother was, but he was known and if not liked, tolerated. Some had seen his temper. None had seen him seek any sort of absolution.

But this Sunday he was seeking forgiveness, guidance and, if reports are to be believed, a handkerchief. The altar call came and William, tears flowing down his clean-shaven face, stumbled to the front of the church and threw himself prostrate near the altar. One of the aldermen came to help but Willie had descended into sobs.

Reports of the next few minutes vary, but the story that was told throughout the community involved William's tearful confession that his wife, Jessica, had left him. Details were confessed, loudly and publicly, as Rev. Thomas tried to console his brother. Finally, several volunteers from the congregation led William away through the side door, but not before he had confessed to ignoring his wife, not caring enough about her and, most embarrassingly, not being able to provide her with more than one child.

People in small towns have long memories and the whispers of that day followed William throughout his life in Cherry.

Rev. Thomas, a large man who famously enjoyed butter, pork and cig-arettes, died on January 4, 1981. His brother attended the funeral but did not cry. Several in the town wondered afterward what sort of man would blubber about the end of his marriage in front of the entire town, but would suppress his grief when confronted with the death of his brother. Some even more cruelly suggested maybe the wrong brother had died, or that something was wrong with William.

Of course, others in the town knew something else about Willie, as he started calling himself. That his dealings out in the woods had been met with mutiny and the group had split. Maybe the next generation would be better, some thought, but never said out loud. After all, that would be an invasion of privacy.

PART SEVEN - ALL THE COMFORTS OF HOME

Conall made his calls and went shopping while everyone got control of themselves. The huddle hadn't lasted long and when it broke everyone sort of wandered until they found themselves back in the dank-smelling Subway. By now it was almost 3 a.m.

Going through the check-out line Conall gave a quick whistle which made everyone look up. He held up a rifle that he had apparently just purchased and was grinning widely at the cashier. The look on his face was one of unbridled joy.

"Something's wrong with that guy," Dilly said.

"I always wanted to visit Ireland," Willie said. "That guy's making me rethink it."

"I would go," JoAnn said. "Looks like we might get the chance."

"Cart before horse, darlin'," Kenny said. "We've got a situation to deal with first. Right Dave?"

"Yeah, we do, but think I need some sleep and a shower first," Dave replied. Sleep was the last thing on Dave's mind but he was pretty sure he had miles to go, as it were, and would need any sleep he could get. Things were already a little fuzzy.

Before long, Conall was back, the rifle slung over his shoulder in a cloth cover.

"I do not believe this country, brother," he said to no one in particular. "Everyone and their mums have guns in Ireland but to go buy one in the middle of the night? Wow."

The eight pairs of bloodshot eyes staring up at him, unimpressed, gave Conall a pretty good hint to get on with it.

"Right," he said. "I've arranged safe lodging. What we're going to do is load back up and drive twenty miles south and there's a hotel that we can get some sleep. Tomorrow after breakfast or lunch or whatever, we'll lay out your options."

"You mean how I'm gonna go back to town and rip that stupid bow tie off Stander's neck with my teeth," Kenny said.

"We will go through all the options and you'll make a decision then. We need a bit of shut-eye, don't you think?"

No one argued and they piled back into the cars. Half an hour later they were checked in to a bare bones Day's Inn. Conversation was slim to none.

• • •

Surprisingly, Dave did get some sleep but his dreams wouldn't let him be. The same images of bubbling rage filled his head and he woke with a start after only a few hours. The sun was just coming up and Josie was out cold, next to him. Dilly was in the room's second twin bed, snoring.

Using skills he had acquired through years of staying in a hotel with his family, Dave dressed as quietly as he could and made his way out the front door, careful to lessen any loud sounds the door would make by moving slowly. He walked around to the back of the hotel where light was just starting to creep into the jet black sky, enough to give him a sense of where they were. The hotel was off the highway and, like so many others in the area, catered largely to truckers and those traveling east to west across the state. You could make it in about four hours, all told, but he'd heard that hotels did well in locations such as this. The miles and miles of corn and ranches tended to do in even the most stout of travelers.

Behind the hotel was a field, vast and undeveloped. Even with the little bit of light available to him, Dave could see the acres of grassland before him, even catching glimpses of the sharp October wind blowing through, creating waves, just like back home. Just like the home he'd likely never go back to.

"Figured you'd be up, brother."

Dave turned to see Conall sitting on a makeshift picnic area. There were two rusted iron chairs next to a tiny table, only big enough to set maybe two glasses. In the dim light, Dave could see the glow of something Conall was smoking and laying over the chair, his left leg up high over the armrest. How European, Dave thought.

"Come, sit, please," he said. "I need to address the alpha."

"Jesus," Dave said. "You make it sound so formal."

Plopping down in the chair, Dave was hit with the thick smoke of a cigar. The smell stuck to the inside of his nose and his body thought about coughing but retreated out of courtesy, catching it in his throat and swallowing it.

"You want one?" Conall said. "You Americans make the worst beer in the entire world but you're aces at cigars."

From his thin fingers, Conall held out a long, somewhat thin, cigar. Dave thought about defending American beer, especially some of the fine microbreweries that had popped up in the past few years, but he let it sit.

"I'm not sure how you do that," Dave said. "I smell triple what everyone else does. If I smoked one of those it would be stuck in my nose for days."

"That's sort of the point, isn't it?" Conall said. "Mark my words, you're going to want it. If not now, maybe in a couple of minutes."

The cigar continued hanging from Conall's fingers until Dave, after a few seconds, grabbed it. It felt lighter than he was anticipating with the paper wrapper thin. The smell was almost overpowering without the aid of fire and smoke.

"I haven't had one of these since . . . God, maybe since Dilly was born."

"Yeah, what is the boy's name?" Conall asked. "Surely you didn't doom the poor boy by naming him after a pickled vegetable."

"He's Dave Junior. We called him Dilly because he couldn't get 'Willie' right when he was a toddler."

"Fucking adorable," Conall said, bringing the cigar up to his mouth. He took a long drag and blew a smoke ring into the air that stayed long past the expiration date of a normal smoke ring. It rolled on and on before eventually expanding too far, the smoke giving up the shape and dissipating into the early morning sky.

"I need to level with you," Conall said. "You're in trouble."

Dave said nothing, letting the silence be his tacit endorsement of the statement.

"I'm not sure what you think about us, about The Council, but we are, in a sense, only human. We're in the middle of nowhere which means no cavalry is coming and even if it were, your group is not part of our group. You follow me?"

"I follow."

"Good. Then how about this—even if a plane full of wolves showed up in your town tomorrow and killed Stander and every single one of his men, you are now a known quantity. People who track this stuff know there are wolves in Cherry and those people tend to be highly motivated by one thing or another."

Conall's affect was flat, his tone even as he stared out into the field.

"Even if you got rid of this problem, things will never be the same for you and your pack ever again. You get that, right? That part has sunk in?"

"Yeah. I get that."

"Good. You want me to light that cigar now?"

As much as he hated to admit it, Conall was right. Dave wanted the cigar.

"Might as well," Dave said, leaning forward as Conall produced a lighter from his pocket and flicked it open with expert efficiency. The brightness of the flame highlighted how dark it still was, though Dave's eyes had adjusted and were far better than normal people. He put the tip to the flame and took three long puffs before turning over the end and looking at it to make sure the fire had taken. It had.

157

"There's so much you don't know," Conall continued. "I've been sitting here thinking of an analogy and you know the best I've come up with?"

"What?"

"You're like a kid's football club who's been thrown in against the pros."

"We're not amateurs at this thing."

"The fuck you're not," Conall said, his voice affecting for the first time since they sat down. "When you're a kid learning football, you learn how to pass and you learn the positions. You don't learn formations. You don't learn how to pick your matchups or any of the strategy that wins league matches. And your opponents, they aren't amateurs either. You're like a bunch of kids thrown into a match and you know the ball is round and that's about fucking all."

"You're saying we're going to lose," Dave said, the bitter taste of the cigar raging through his mouth and nose.

"I'm saying you're going to lose," Conall said. "But here's the thing. You don't have to stay amateurs. You've got talent on your squad, you've got youth. Hell, you've even got a leader who doesn't shit himself when confronted and can put up a decent fight. There's potential but you've got to get coached up. If you go out there, you're going to get murdered."

Conall tossed his leg from around the armrest and sat in a proper fashion, took a pull on his cigar and let it out, no ring this time.

"My inelegant analogy aside, Dave, your family is in trouble and if you don't come with me, they're going to die," Conall said. "I need to take you somewhere where you can learn. Somewhere you can train. Somewhere you can be a pack who can survive these sorts of attacks because they're coming at you for the rest of your lives and that's a fact."

On some level, this was inevitable. From the moment Conall had changed and spoken to him as the Irish Wolf, Dave knew life would never be the same, but he hadn't expected total destruction of his life in two days. The old feelings of failure and inadequacy started to creep into the back of his brain and the front of his stomach.

"Running feels like failure," Dave said.

"It is, on some level," Conall replied. "But nobody wins all the time."

"Do you have a family?"

"No," he said. "Nor am I going to. My line we . . . there's only so far we can go. That's for another time. Plus I travel around too much."

"Then you're going to have a hard time understanding how losing our home and our town and our lives as we know them feels like a colossal failure," Dave said, his voice raising. "I have two jobs on this planet. Provide for my family and keep them safe, and I am failing, miserably, at that last one."

"So your solution is to get them killed on your own terms?" Conall said, his voice also rising. "Pardon me, Dave, but that's really stupid."

The insult landed and all of a sudden Dave felt the hairs on his arms standing up and his nails starting to grow. He was transforming, almost against his will.

"Look at you!" Conall shouted. "You're at the end of your rope, brother. You can't even control the beast anymore. How in the hell are you going to fight Stander and his men?"

Gulping air and staring at the field now streaked with echoes of the big, impending sunrise, Dave tried to get his head under control. He thought of his son and his wife, but other ideas kept plowing through— the fight with the Irish Wolf, his miserable father, his unfaithful wife, his dead piece of shit friend . . .

Dave felt his leg start to stretch.

"Don't do it," Conall said. "I'll put you down. You know I will."

Confronted with his impending transformation and limited options, Dave thought fast. During the scratch, transformation was the point so feeling the change come was welcome and something not to be fought. Trying to turn back, that's something no one in the Rhodes tribe had ever had to deal with.

The enhanced senses that came with the change were already well upon Dave, and he smelled the smoke, heard the rustling wind and the animals in the woods, felt the fibers of his clothes and the heat in one leg. The cigar was burning through the jeans of Dave's right leg where he had set it moments earlier. Without thinking he grabbed the thin stogie and jammed it into his forearm, letting out a yelp not much louder than the hiss of fire on flesh.

Conall had risen from his seat but now watched Dave with fascination. Using pain to beat a transformation wasn't something many were capable of doing as it was a high-level move. But here he was, pulling it off.

The wind picked up as Dave got control over his brain. He swatted away a couple errant thoughts, focusing instead on the intense pain right below his wrist and the smell of his own skin, cooked and smoldering. The stretching stopped, the hair rolled back and he leaned back in his chair, panting.

"That was quite a thing," Conall said.

"That," Dave said, panting, "hurt."

The sun broke the seemingly endless Nebraska skyline and the dark reds and blacks and oranges bowed to the bright yellow. In his heightened state, Dave could hear the sunrise. It wasn't the sun itself or the heat, but the entire living infrastructure buzzed when the sun hit it from the grass to the trees to the men smoking in chairs outside a shitty hotel off the highway.

"I've never seen a sunrise like that," Conall said after a few minutes had passed. "Not on the hills or the moors. Never."

They watched and it was beautiful.

"What happens after we leave with you?" Dave said. "What happens to us and to our town?"

"The world will open to you and your family in ways you can't even imagine," Conall said. "And Stander will destroy your town, person by person, until it doesn't exist anymore."

"He'll kill people?" Dave asked.

"Yes, David. And if you go back he'll kill you. And if I let you go back, he'll capture you, torture you, perform medical experiments on you, learn all he can about how you work, then throw the spent husk of your body out in the back dumpster. No member of our group has ever been captured like that. And no one ever will."

They sat in silence until the sun started to burn their eyes, then went inside to catch the continental breakfast.

• • •

One advantage of being a wolf with experience is knowing how to avoid detection by other wolves. Lay in the ground, become one with the Earth, employ a few tricks of the trade to mask your breath and your sweat and if no one is looking for you, no one is going to find you.

The minute everyone ran to their rooms to grab as much sleep as they could, Willie had found himself some dirt and leaves, settled in and made himself as comfortable as his lumbago would allow. He nodded off a few times, weary from the transformation but the minute Conall lit up his cigar he was alert. He heard it all and made a decision on this spot.

The minute the men left for breakfast, he jimmied the lock on an Accord in the hotel parking lot, hot-wired the engine, and started driving back toward Cherry.

•••

Ron was having no luck trying to get his shirt clean.

When he was a kid, his mother had shown him laundry basics by hand but it had been years. He had gone to the University of Nebraska where there had been machines and he bought a used one and brought it with him when he moved back to Cherry. His setup now featured a top of the line Maytag and, being a single gentleman, he could play that machine like a fiddle. Now he was back to scrubbing and doing a pretty poor job of it when he was startled by a few sharp raps on the door.

He didn't have another shirt to reach for so whoever was knocking was going to get him in all his bare-chested glory. It was Carl, who immediately looked sheepish when he saw Ron's condition.

"Sorry I . . . uh, I saw your light on."

"Trying to get my shirt clean. Come on in."

The door creaked shut and Carl stood, for a second, and went to sit on the bed while Ron went back to working his shirt in the tiny sink. He listened for a second to the swishing of water and rub of damp fabric.

"Washing my shirt is not that interesting," Ron said. "What do you want?"

"I want to know what you think about going back."

While in the car on the way to the hotel, everyone had been too wiped out to talk, likewise when they fled Cherry for the friendly confines of a Walmart at three in the morning. Normally Carl and Ron dissected their scratches and would grab drinks. On rare occasion Ron would come over and help with the harvest.

"Jesus," Ron said. "We are like an old married couple."

"We fight less," Carl came back.

Throughout their friendship, Ron had divined that Carl was not the talkative type, but also could tell when he had something to say. Usually, he responded as opposed to volunteered conversation, so Ron let it rip.

"I believe Stander is going to kill a bunch of people," Ron said. "I don't think that new sheriff can do much by way of stopping it unless he calls in the National Guard and we're so isolated they might as well be on the moon. If we leave, we're condemning everyone we work with and hang out with to something rotten and maybe something worse. If it was just me taking my licks, I'd go back, but it's not just that. I think we could come up with a plan and make a good run at these assholes and I think that's what we should do."

"I figured that's where you'd land," Carl said.

"Are we about to have our first fight?"

"Yeah. I think so."

"So tell me, then, why should we run?"

"Easy. I'll give you two really good reasons. We can't win and I really, really want to."

Ron had figured this was coming as he knew Carl had larger aspirations. They had talked about it a few times and Carl would take time away from his job to travel and always came back with great stories and photos and an itch to go to the next place. Ron traveled too, particularly to Chicago and Las Vegas, but always felt much happier when he could return home.

While his position wasn't a surprise to Ron, that didn't mean he liked it.

"So you'd toss us all away for some new place, just like that?"

"That's not what I'm saying," Carl said, visibly uncomfortable.

"But it's what you'd be doing, isn't it?" Ron asked. "You'd be telling all of us to fuck off while you went and traveled the world and learned about being a wolf, is that about right?"

"We could all do it," Carl said, his voice rising. "We could all go our separate ways for a bit and come back. We could learn and grow and still be a pack. Just not in Cherry."

Backing off, Ron thought for a second. There was something else here, something Ron had vowed didn't matter and he didn't want to talk about. Still, it caused him to back off and try to put himself in Carl's shoes. He was scared, he was lonely, and he was confronted with the rest of his life being a desperate mission or a grand adventure. At his age he knew what he would have chosen.

"I see where you're coming from," Ron said, trying to even his voice. "Hell, it'd be fun to travel a bunch and even when this is over, things aren't going to be the same. But what about everyone in Cherry? What about that guy you like, that guy who works for Kenny Kirk at the garage, what's his name?"

"Nicholas," Carl said.

"Nicholas," Ron said. "If Nicholas was hurt and you were the only one who could help him, wouldn't you?"

"I suppose," Carl said.

Crossing the room, Ron put his hand on Carl's shoulder and stared him, cold, in the face.

"You would," Ron said. "You're one of the most generous guys I know. You'd help anyone you could and right now, people need your help."

"Yeah," Carl said.

"Besides," Ron finished, walking over to the door and opening it. "It's going to be a group decision."

"Last one of those we had didn't turn out so well," Carl said.

•••

Inside the hotel room, the steam from Josie's and Dilly's showers had created its own atmosphere. The humidity was a sharp, wet contrast to the

163

dry fall and Dave was glad to see Josie in a towel and Dilly nowhere to be found. A few days ago, he thought, his reasons would have been very different for finding his wife alone and nearly naked. Now, that was the furthest thing from his mind.

"Dilly getting breakfast?"

"Yeah, he and Willie are down there now. Where did you go?"

Suddenly feeling the pain in his legs and his forearm, Dave took a seat on the edge of the bed farthest from his wife. The bed gave a huge, disproportionate creak.

"Conall and I have been talking," Dave said. "He . . . he laid it all out for me."

"Laid what out?" Josie asked, drying her hair. She had turned from the mirror and was sitting on the bed, giving her full attention. "Have you been smoking?"

"Conall was," Dave said.

"No, you were. I can smell it."

"Yeah, fine," Dave said, trying to dismiss his lie. "The gist is we have to go with him. If we go home he thinks Stander and his men are going to kill us."

He let the phrase hang for a second, hoping it would hit hard. When Josie merely continued drying her hair, he continued.

"He also said he can't let us go back. That Stander wants to experiment on us and what he might learn is why he's so anxious to get us back to town. Apparently they've been trying to capture someone like us for a long time and finding a group not connected to Conall and his people is their best bet."

At this Josie stopped drying her hair and put her hand behind her neck and left it there. It was a posture she often struck when they were arguing or when she was in a particularly bad mood.

"So going back is not an option?"

"I don't see how."

"What happens to everyone in town?" she asked.

"Nothing good," Dave said. "Conall thinks Stander is going to do everything he can to get us back, so he'll hurt people and he'll burn down buildings. Just like he says he will."

The words echoed and bounced around the room long after Dave had said them. Neither of them spoke for what felt like a minute. The hand dropped from the back of Josie's neck and she rested her head on her hand. A few seconds later, Dave realized she was crying. Given her near nakedness and the sudden burst of emotion, Dave decided to not go over to the bed and comfort her. Turned out, that was the right decision.

"God damn you," she said.

"What?"

"I said god damn you. This is your fault you child. You fucking child. This is your fault and now all our friends are going to die and it's your fault."

Her voice did not raise and her fists did not clench but tears were now flowing down her cheeks. Dave had known this was coming for a while. After years of intense familiarity and intimacy, Dave knew she felt this way and that knowledge had been a bomb in the back of his head, waiting to go off. He knew she blamed him, knew he was the root of all the problems in her mind and now he had been proven right.

The night they had decided to "take care" of Byron for his many sins, they held a vote on what to do. It had to be unanimous, Dave said, because this decision was monumental. He had made a case, but had tried his best to make it clear any dissent in the ranks would mean finding another path. Josie had been the third person in line and the third "yes" vote.

"You voted with me to take care of Byron. Don't you put that decision on me," Dave said.

"What the hell was I supposed to do? Not support you? I already had them looking at me like I was some whore thanks to you. Willie was already openly mocking me and you weren't doing anything about it. What the hell was I supposed to do?"

"You were supposed to be honest," Dave said. "That's the core of all we do . . ."

"Don't give me that alpha shit," she said. "My husband decided to kill one of our closest friends and got everyone else to come along."

"That's right, Josie," Dave said. "Charming, funny, perfect Byron did nothing to bring that on himself. He didn't sell us out. He didn't kill that girl. He's perfectly innocent. He's a saint, if you think about it."

"We're not in high school anymore and look where your decision got us!" Josie shot back, letting the towel drop and running into the bathroom to grab a purple T-shirt that she flung on with vigorous speed. Even in the heat of battle, Dave couldn't help notice her nipples straining at the cheap material. "Our house is gone and all our friends are about to die because of you."

"Fine, what would you have done?" Dave said, bringing his tone back down. "Send him off with a wave and a smile to go find the nearest place he could sell us out and get someone else killed, send him off to find someone like Stander? Maybe give him one more good fuck for the road?"

"One, don't be gross," Josie spat back. "And two, you promised me, you promised me that had nothing to do with your decision. You said this was about the future, NOT the past."

"My decision wasn't about you sleeping with Byron," Dave said. "I've said this over and over again."

"Then how come I don't believe you?"

"Because you're sorry he's gone," Dave said, really seeing red now and keeping a close eye for signs of change in his trembling body. "Because you wish he was still here so you could get what you really want instead of what you're stuck with."

Josie's mouth hung open and her eyes narrowed as the tears came again. She sat hard on the hotel room's other bed which did not make weird creaks.

"You never wanted me and you prove that to me every day," Dave said, now staring at the floor. "You love the kid and I'm thankful for that and you are fine with your life but you aren't fine with me. You think I don't see that? You think I don't know you? I know you and I know you don't love me."

It hurt to say, more than Dave thought it would.

"I've said this a thousand times," Dave continued, "but Byron had decided to leave. He was out. He had betrayed us and he was going to betray us if he was left alive and that's the hard truth of the matter. Yes, I might have had a hand in driving him away and yes, I am not blameless and yes, I can be childish sometimes but letting him go gets us right here in this hotel room, just a few weeks earlier. Maybe worse people are after us. Maybe someone gets killed."

"Someone did get killed," Josie said. Dave ignored her.

"I appreciate your support and I'm going to need it a little longer, but once we're clear of this thing you're going to go your own way. I heard you and Conall talking and I think I know what you mean to do. The only question is 'is Dilly coming with you' and I guess that's a decision he's going to make."

The two sat, apart, not looking at each other. After a moment, Josie stood up and sat on the bed next to Dave. She sat, staring at her husband. He had aged well, she thought. His hair was still there, his body was still fairly lean save the love handles. He worked hard and they had years of history gluing them together and yet, he was right. She was mad and resentful and wasn't sure she loved him. He was good enough and now Conall had promised a world where she could travel, she could meet others beyond their town, she could be the person she always thought she would end up being. And Dave? What of him, she thought. This big bag of daddy issues would get along fine. In the end he'd be miserable with her or without her.

But in the back of her mind, she felt a twitch.

This did not happen often. The last time she had this twitch was four months ago and she had gone out, made the transformation and ran through the woods, feeling, thinking, running. The pain was excruciating, paralleled only by childbirth, but once she had done it the vast expanse of woods had been her playground. And she had taken Dilly out with her, talked to him, shown him the woods and what he would be doing when he was ready. She remembered her life as a mother and a wolf and as a member of the pack and as a woman whose house had just burned down.

Oh yeah, she thought. I'm really, really angry.

Sitting, staring at Dave, she wondered if this was the man who could keep her and Dilly safe. He would die for them, but so would every husband, so he says, and at the end of the day that's a bunch of bullshit. Would he fight for her, not in the romantic sense but in the practical sense? Was he smart enough to win? Would he lead them all to certain death and dismemberment in a lab?

She took a deep breath. Time to find out.

"We're not done yet," she said. "You and me. We have a lot to talk about and we're not done yet but if you think you know me and you think you know my heart, than what do I want to do right now, more than anything else on the planet?"

A jab about sleeping with Byron flickered across Dave's brain and prudently got caught in several filters.

"You're pissed about your work room," Dave said.

"I am *pissed* about my work room," she answered, a smile flickering on her lips. "And I need a guy who's going to make that right."

"You're behind me? For the time being?"

"I am behind you," she said.

"Good enough."

Dave stood up and opened the door to the hotel room, exposing the bright sun and activity out in the parking lot.

"You realize we're going to need to go to therapy after this, right?" Dave said.

"One problem at a time, please."

•••

Dave found Conall who asked him to knock on doors and get everyone down to the lobby. A few minutes later most everyone had gathered for a few stale bagels, pre-made pancakes, and rubbery sausage in the hotel's lobby. Whether they were eating was a different matter.

JoAnn had plowed through her food but Kenny Kirk hadn't eaten a thing and his face was drained.

"He's been calling me," Kenny said. "Leaving messages. Stander's got my number."

"He probably has all your numbers," Conall said, shoveling sausage into his mouth. "He's calling you for a reason. Probably thinks he can hurt you the most."

"Did you listen to any of them?" Ron asked between bites of biscuits and very suspect gravy.

"Yeah, man, I did," Kenny said. "Bastard says he's at my garage in town that's burning down. He sent a picture. It's hard to make out, but yeah. It's gone."

In a situation one quarter this exciting Kenny would be running his mouth as fast as he could, but not this morning. His words were exact. One by one everyone gathered around to see the photo on Kenny's phone and a few profanities and pats on the shoulder later, everyone was back in the seats more demoralized than before.

Everyone ate in silence for a moment until the real Kenny Kirk returned with a vengeance.

"What is this bullshit, man," he started. "What is this sitting around eating shitty food waiting for some Irish weirdo to tell us what to do? That asshole burned down my garage, burned down Dave and Josie's house, man. That was a nice house!"

"Your garage wasn't nice," Ron said, treading dangerous ground, praying he was on the right side of it. "All the oil on the ground it probably went up fast."

"See, now this is your problem, saying shit like that," Kenny said, a slight twinkle in his eye. "Your brain ain't got no filter on it, man, and you're missing my point. My point isn't whether he's burning down a garage full of oily rags . . ."

"You kept them in a big pile in the corner," Carl chimed in.

"OK, OK, let's all agree that my garage was full of oil and oily rags . . ."

"And you kept that nudie calendar on the wall," Josie chimed in.

"I kept asking him to take that down," JoAnn said and by then, any hope of a Braveheart-style speech was gone. Kenny waved his arms to get everyone's attention.

"MY POINT," he yelled over the chatter, regaining attention momentarily, "is that we need to go back."

Everyone fell silent.

"We need to go back and deal with this."

"The hell you do, there Kenneth," Conall said. "These bastards who

169

work for the biomedical companies, they're coming at you hard because they've never captured one of us before. If they got their hands on just one of you it would be terrible. They could start tracking people like us, profiling people like us. Hunting us if they wanted. I told Dave this earlier but I cannot, under any circumstances, let that happen."

"So Cherry burns," Ron asked.

"So Cherry burns," Conall answered. "I wish there was something I could do, sincerely. But it isn't the first town to burn, as you put it, and likely won't be the last."

"And if we try to go back, what you gonna do then, man?" Kenny said.

"Let's not go down that road, please," Conall said. "I don't mean to get all technical on the lot of you, but I've beaten your Alpha."

This was the first time it had occurred to anyone in the group that, yes, the Irish Wolf had kicked the Lead Wolf's ass, hard, the previous evening. While some of the rules were for the good of the pack, the line of leadership succession had been passed down from the very first pack of wolves in Cherry. The rule was the Alpha is the strongest and when someone beats the strongest wolf in the pack, they were the new Alpha. There had only been seven Alphas in the entire history of this pack. Now there were eight.

"So, yeah," Conall said, scooping some eggs onto a fork and wolfing them down.

"Well dammit!" Kenny Kirk said.

"Wait, Dad's not in charge anymore?" Dilly asked.

Everyone around the table braced for the inevitable comment from Willie about how his son had never really been in charge, but it didn't come. Willie wasn't there and this was the first time anyone had noticed.

"Where the hell is Willie?" Dave asked. "Was he staying with anyone?"

"Like anyone's going to share a room with Willie," JoAnn said.

Conall was riffling through his pockets looking for the receipts. He had paid for the rooms, generously, and was doing a quick count in his head.

"Oh fuck me," he said, recounting. " . . . two, three four . . . FUCK!" he slammed his hand down on the table. "I didn't even get him a fucking room. He could be in Mexico by now for all we know."

Murmurs spread around the group and Josie immediately went over to the front desk, which was in earshot of Conall's language and volume. Ron stood next to Conall, going over the receipts again. Dilly went over to his father, who gave him a hug, which was awkward since he was shorter than the boy. A few feet away, Kenny Kirk was letting out a stream of profanity himself. A few moments later, Josie came back.

"Someone stole a car from the parking lot early this morning," she said. "That girl at the front desk, she said it had been a crazy morning."

"All right, here's what's happening," Conall said. "I want you all to really think about Willie and use your noses. We have to track him down or at least get some sort of idea where he's headed."

"What if he's headed back to Cherry?" Carl asked, almost panicked.

"One problem at a time, brother," Conall said. "Everyone fan out. Track him if you can. Meet back here in five minutes. Go!"

Most of the group ran outside, Kenny with his nose literally in the air. Dilly went to his mother who came over, put her arm around Dave and led them down one of the narrow hallways of the hotel.

"Grandpa went back, didn't he?" Dilly said.

"Yes," Josie said. "He probably did."

"Are you guys going to go get him?"

It was one thing to be confronted with the possibility of harm to your family, but quite another to have your hand forced. The pit in Dave's stomach that had been building for the past couple days was roaring now and every bit of instinct he had was screaming not to put his family in harm's way, especially not for an asshole like Willie.

Back when Dave was getting ready for his first scratch, Willie had already made the turn from respected businessman toward town crank and had given Dave very little direction on what to do. When he turned sixteen he asked Willie, over and over, if it was time for him to go out on a run yet and after a few rounds, Willie had been so annoyed he shouted at Dave "if you want to be a man, make decisions like a man." In what was the boldest move in his life up until that point, Dave showed up the next time he knew Willie was going out and that was his first experience. He was embraced with open arms and still looked up on that victory as one of his greatest achievements. He knew he was ready and he showed up and proved it to everyone.

While he firmly believed his father had acted like an asshole, Dave now realized that his logic had been sound. This wasn't something that could be given to him. It was something he had to take.

"Dilly," Dave said. "The next few hours are going to be hard. Your mother and I are going to make our own decisions about what to do and I want you to listen to me. You are a part of this pack. In your heart, you know what's right. I believe that as much as I believe anything. It's going to be hard, but we're not going to tell you what to do. Consider the consequences of your actions and make your own choices. Think them over, make sure it's what your heart says is right and do it. You understand?"

Dilly's eyes were wide and his mouth open a bit. He had just been hit with a bomb and knew it. Josie lent her support.

"Your father and I are proud of the man you're becoming," she said. "These decisions are going to shape who you are. I know you'll make the right ones."

"OK," he said after a few seconds. "I'll do what I think is right but I'm going to follow your lead."

Patting his son's shoulder, Dave dared a quick glance at his wife. She had an excellent poker face.

"Good boy," he said. "Let's see if we can find your grandpa."

• • •

It didn't take long for Ron to find the note. He figured Willie had never checked in and immediately went to the outskirts of the hotel property and started sniffing around. He picked up Willie's pungent scent in short order and the path he followed led him to a clearing where he saw a waffle house in the distance. He jogged over and sure enough ,Willie had left a note. A couple minutes after they had split up, the pack was sitting in and around the lifted Pathfinder as Conall read the note, silently.

"Dammit man, out with it," Kenny said. "What'd he do?"

"He went back to your dumpy little town," Conall said, anger rising. "He went back knowing that you all would chase after him."

"Then let's go," Dilly said. "Let's go get him."

"No," Conall said, flatly. His tone was unwavering and had an air of finality to it.

"Wait a second," Dave started. "Let's talk this out a bit . . ."

"No," Conall cut him off. "They've already got one of us. I'm not giving him six."

"You don't think we can get him?" Ron asked.

"Are you joking with me?" Conall said. "You'll have to pardon me, sometimes American humor goes right over my head."

"I think we could get him," Ron said.

"And I know you're wrong, you idiot," Conall shot back. A few of the pack started to protest the breach of protocol but Conall was off to the races, running his mouth, venting his frustration into the bitter wind. "You have no training, you can barely control yourselves, you treat your women like shite, you've never been outside your black hole of a town and you've never killed anyone. You're up against men with guns . . . lots of them with training and armor. I feel like I've been over this. You're outmatched. You're outgunned and you're outsmarted. You have no chance of getting that bearded moron back and the sooner we can start the damage control on this giant cluster fuck the better off we're all going to be."

Silence was the only response Conall received to his rant which he had used all his limbs to articulate. He stared from person to person, partly begging for a challenge and partly begging for an idea, any idea, that would make this situation better.

"I've got to make some calls," Conall said and started walking off.

"We have home field advantage," Ron yelled as he started walking away.

"What are you on about?"

"You know that term? Home field advantage? It means that you're right. It means we've never left our black hole of a town but it also means we know every paved street, every access road. It means we know where the potholes are and how deep that historic marker is buried. We've lived

173

on those roads. It means that we might not be trained but if there's any-where we can fight it's in our town."

As he picked up steam Ron grinned at his own tenacity and the fact that he had a killer closing line.

"And we might not be killers, but I have a guess there are a few of us that wouldn't mind being killers by the end of the day."

"That's right. That's goddamn right," Kenny Kirk said, not one to miss out on a speech. "Home field advantage, man. Ron's probably got a plan in his head right now."

Ron nodded and Kenny walked up to stand next to him, shoulder to shoulder.

"And we don't treat our women like shit, which is how it's pronounced, by the way."

"Sometimes you do," JoAnn said, loud enough to be heard.

If the group expected Conall to come over to their side, they were very wrong. The Irishman's eyes, which were always a little sharp, were pierc-ing as he looked over Ron and Kenny. He couldn't hide his anger in pitch darkness.

"I've got calls to make," he spit.

"I think you should hear them out," Dave said, standing directly in Conall's path.

"And I think I've already kicked your ass," Conall said. "Move before I do it again."

"You should hear them out," Dave repeated. He crossed his arms in hopes it would hide his shaking hands.

Conall threw a long, arching shot with his right fist but Dave got his elbow up and it glanced off. As the shouting started Conall threw a quick left hand to Dave's stomach and caught him, forcing him to the ground gasping for air.

"I can beat you here or there," Conall said, glancing toward the woods behind the hotel. Dave took advantage of the momentary loss of eye con-tact by getting his legs under him and pushing off, hard, catching Conall with a shoulder to the lower chest and taking him down. The men started rolling on the ground, Dave more on the defensive than not.

"You . . . fucking . . . dirty fighter!" Conall yelled between blows. Dilly noticed his voice getting a little deeper and started to worry and the others gathered around, trying to figure out when and if they needed to jump in. Dilly backed away, slowly so his mother wouldn't notice, and started for the back of the hotel, never losing sight of his father, who was now on the end of an ass-kicking.

"Basketball, basketball, basketball," Dilly chanted to himself, trying not to hear his father gasp and yelp in pain.

Dilly wasn't entirely sure what he was doing and sure as hell hadn't given it much thought, but he knew what was about to happen. He knew he had to help and the only way to make any sort of difference, to help his dad, to save his grandpa, to be the man he wanted to be, was to do this. It only made sense, so much sense that thought would have only gotten into the way. The tall teenager, strapping and shaking and scared and tired, shut his eyes and tried to focus.

The second he got hold of the memory, of being hungry for the defeat of another and feeling the rush of wanting blood, the impact knocked him off his feet and onto his back. He had made it to the grass and he physically forced himself to a kneeling position and yelled the only word he could think to yell, the only word that would get the Irishman to stop beating his father and tearing apart his family.

"ALPHA!" he yelled. The deep, guttural sound that came out of Dilly's mouth sounded absolutely badass and only puffed the boy up a bit more.

Conall was already showing signs of transformation, though muted. His eyes had started to change and hair had begun to sprout but he was still a human, still kicking Dave in the legs and ribs. A gash had opened on one side of Dave's head and a long scratch mark on his neck was bleeding enough to stain his shirt.

"Dilly . . . Dilly." Josie realized what was happening and started running toward her son. He was just twenty yards away or so and was not moving, but by the time she turned around and had covered less than half the distance she felt a *whoosh* beside her as the Irish Wolf blew past her on his way to destroy her child.

The Young Wolf's transformation wasn't complete by the time the

Irish Wolf tackled him, taking him all the way from the mowed and tended lawn at the back of the hotel parking lot into the woods. The pack ran over and saw nothing but rustling leaves and the sound of snapping wood, brittle and dry in mid-fall weather. Soon those sounds were accompanied by chatter and sobbing and the anguished cry of a mother in a complete panic over her son.

Once they were out of sight the Irish Wolf, as was the way of his people, stood aside and let his opponent finish his transformation.

"This . . . is the only . . . mercy . . . you get," the Irish Wolf growled.

The part of Dilly's brain that would comprehend language was no longer functioning but as the Young Wolf found his footing and slowly rose to all fours, he understood. This was not a tussle or a row, a match or a contest. This was about blood and fangs.

And he was ready.

Immediately the Young Wolf bolted in the direction of some thick foliage, away from the road and the hotel and the crying mother. He had guessed, correctly, that speed would be his weapon and size would be his defense. The wolves were not evenly matched in terms of size with the Young Wolf standing taller than the Irish Wolf, but just barely. Not that it mattered. The Young Wolf felt stronger than his first time out and the fear, confusion, grief and rage he had inside him had informed his transformation, sharpening him, making him bloom into a bloody flower made of the guts of his enemies. He ran, sensing the Irish Wolf behind him but knowing he could run as long as he needed and avoid the fight. He was younger and he was faster and he could run and run and run. That was not what he wanted to do.

Remembering his failure when chasing the deer, the Young Wolf was able to pivot on his new paws and start leading his pursuer in a long, arching turn. He had no idea where he was going but knew water wasn't far and his instincts were telling him to get there. His conscious mind flashed, ever so briefly, on the image of his father telling him something while they were both in a pond and then rocketed back to the terrain in front of him. He dodged and evaded, he weaved and launched himself. The pleasure of the run was not lost on the Young Wolf, but he did not like being chased.

The stream quickly came up in front of him and at full speed the Young Wolf leapt over the water, turned his body around and caught himself in a crouching position on the other end of the bank. The Irish Wolf was not even a second behind him. In one fluid motion, the Young Wolf caught himself on the bank and launched himself in the air, meeting the Irish Wolf in air and landing with a thud and a snarl in the center of the stream.

The Young Wolf's instincts served him well, even if it only went so far. Initially, the shock of the water distracted the Irish Wolf, who spun around to take in his surroundings after they had landed, giving his opponent a chance to strike, biting deep into his shoulder. The Irish Wolf howled for a moment and swatted the Young Wolf, hard in the head, but he did not break the bite. Both creatures, moving at extreme speed, spun and shook and the Irish Wolf realized for a moment that he had underestimated the ability and tenacity of the creature latched on to his shoulder.

Not knowing much about the water underneath him, the Irish Wolf was desperate to get out of the stream and he ran full force into the bank forcing the Young Wolf to finally let go. He climbed out of the embankment and took a moment to examine his wound. It was deep and blood was escaping, but not so much that he would stop fighting. His intention was to scan for the Young Wolf but the instant he raised his head, his opponent crashed into him, throwing them both into the thick of the forest.

As they tumbled, a memory flashed through Conall's mind. He had been in fights (never two in twenty-four hours) and had enjoyed most of them. He was one of three boys, all of whom went through transformations, and when their dear mother had died they went out into the woods and had at each other. The pain and grief of their mother's death, so toxic in human form, had proven freeing in the woods. They were lighter and sharper, they fought harder and bled more, and he had never enjoyed a fight like that before or since.

With claws moving so fast the Alpha hardly had time to mount a defense, the Young Wolf slashed and snapped with the rage of youth. The Irish Wolf was able to get his paws up and absorb most of the blows with his flesh, finally punching upward into the Young Wolf's chest and stomach, knocking the wind out of him. Quickly getting to his feet, the Irish Wolf saw that his opponent could dish it out, but couldn't take it. The Young Wolf was down, taking giant gulps of air and trying to get to his feet.

The Irish Wolf reared up, hoping to inspire the youngster to action. It sort of worked as the Young Wolf did get to his feet and mount a weak attack of his own. The two locked front paws and while the Young Wolf was strong, he was still recovering and not nearly as strong as he needed to be to ward off an attack from an experienced, strong, and amused attacker. The Irish Wolf pushed the Young Wolf down and bit him in the same shoulder he had been wounded in earlier, partly out of spite. The Young Wolf howled long and hard, which echoed.

Standing atop his prize, the Irish Wolf gave up his bite, held the Young Wolf down and spoke to him again.

"Weak. Sad." It snarled. "Like . . . your . . . family."

He meant to scare the child. He meant to mark him. He had been challenged and he wanted others to know the victor. Slowly, the Irish Wolf brought his bloodstained claw up to the Young Wolf's face. He meant to tear part of his cheek off but the moment his intention was clear he was knocked off his feet and into the woods. He tumbled and tumbled for what seemed like a minute, each time thinking he would come to a stop on the forest floor only to be hit again and knocked farther into the woods. Somewhere in his mind, he knew one of his hind legs had broken.

Finally, finally, he stopped and was greeted to a gravely, leathery interpretation of a woman's voice.

"Get off him or I will kill you."

It was Josie, of course, but she had changed. When the Irish Wolf lifted his head and shook it to clear his senses he saw Josie, partially concealed in shadow. The part he could see was covered in coarse brown hair. The shirt she had been wearing was still on but she had lost her pants as her bottom half had grown and elongated. She sported powerful hind legs with muscles that bulged and flexed and visibly sharp, curved claws and was hunched in a way that resembled a feral cat. There was no mistaking the anger in her body language and when the Irish Wolf made it up to her face he saw nothing but dark eyes with darker intent staring back at him.

The Irish Wolf tried to stand but his left back leg couldn't support his wait and he crumpled, letting out a sharp yelp he immediately regretted. Realizing he was in no condition to fight, Josie stepped out of the shadows and toward him. He noticed she was holding a large rock in one hand.

"We can both speak," she said, her diction slightly clouded by her fangs. "I want to smash you with this rock until I see brains."

Threats were something the Irish Wolf could handle. The sight in front of him was far more interesting.

"How?" the Irish Wolf asked. "Others . . . cannot."

"WHY SHOULDN'T I KILL YOU?" Josie yelled with such force birds fled from treetops nearby.

"Without me . . . you . . . die," the Irish Wolf answered. The yelling had focused him, and all the memories of romping with his brothers were long gone. He didn't know what she was capable of but was pretty sure she was true to her word and looking for an excuse to kill him.

And yet, what an amazing creature. Conall's mind was starting to return and with it, the implication of what it was he was seeing. There were rumors but he had never seen a woman who could transform. This was, strictly, a male endeavor and he marveled both at this discovery and at the form. She wasn't nearly as stringy and skinny as her male counterparts but much more catlike but in a fiercer, deadlier way. Based on what she had done to him, she must have exceptional speed as well, he thought, and as he did so Josie walked, slowly, maintaining eye contact with the Irish Wolf, past his head and toward his broken leg. She then lifted the rock and slammed it onto his broken bone.

The first scream was punctuated by more howls and then whining pain ruled the Irish Wolf, blotting out all other influences. When his vision finally came back after nothing but white-hot agony clouding his vision, he saw Josie again with the rock over her head ready to strike.

"NO!" the Irish Wolf screamed. "NO! ANYTHING!"

"Change," Josie said in a measured tone. "Change back now."

"Trying . . ." the Irish Wolf pleaded. They both knew it was not that simple and some part of the process had to run its course. Rolling his head up at the sky, trying to get over the pain that still consumed his lower half, the Irish Wolf shut his eyes, hoping it would buy him some time.

Conall's mind came back almost at once, which was welcomed, and immediately started racing. He needed to call The Council directly, something he had never had cause to do. He needed to get the R&D team on this right away and he needed to make sure, above all, that this group was safe and sound. As the thoughts of his business intruded, his wolf mind started shrinking and shrinking, and soon, too, did Conall's body. The transformation back caused him to scream again as his broken leg settled into its human mold and by the time he was a recognizable human again, he was screaming and weeping in pain.

"I bet that hurt," Josie said through thick fangs.

"Yes," Conall said, panting. "It did."

She leaned close to the Irishman's face to give him a good look. Her eyes were even darker when he could see them and her features even more frightening. Her hair also stood up instead of falling around her neck giving, the illusion of armor or the back of a cape. She made a gesture toward the man's busted leg.

"That was for my son," she said.

"I'm sure you understand why . . ." Conall started.

"And this is for my husband," Josie said and threw the rock at Conall's broken leg, full force. He saw the rock fly through the air, heard the thud and passed out before the pain hit.

It was a good call.

SELECTIONS FROM THE BARTER COUNTY BUCK

November 11, 1995

Front Page
Headline: Cherry Man Opens Garage

Kenneth Rathman, 3404 Rural Road 6, has opened a garage in Cherry

Township and hopes to drum up businesses fixing cars, trucks and service vehicles.

The garage, located on Main Street in Cherry, will take over the old Chapman building and opened at the end of last week.

"I hate having to drive 30 miles to get my vehicles serviced," Rathman said. "It's crazy. There are more cars in this town than people, so I ought to do OK."

A graduate of Central Community College's Diesel Mechanics program, Rathman said he is willing to take a look at anything and that no one should feel shy about bringing in their vehicle.

"Chances are I can make it run," Rathman said. "I can at least give it a look."

March 4, 1997

Front Page
Headline: Lady Bucks Lose Class D Finals

The Consolidated High Lady Bucks almost made the most out of their trip to the Class D State Championships on Friday night in Lincoln, but fell just short of a title, losing to Pius X by a score of 61-59.

Leading for most of the game, the Lady Blue Knights made a comeback in the final quarter, outshooting Consolidated and drawing more fouls.

"I'm very proud of these girls," Coach Dave Rhodes said. "We lost our cool down the stretch but making it to State was always our goal."

"We'll get them next year," Rhodes added.

Consolidated's leading scorer, Janice Hogarth, scored 29 of the Lady Bucks 51 points and fouled out of the game in the fourth quarter.

March 11, 1997

Page 3
Cops and Courts Report

William "Willie" Rhodes, 50, of Cherry, was arrested on suspicion of driving under the influence on the evening of March 5. The report says Rhodes was driving from his son's house where he had ingested "a few beers" and was belligerent to the arresting officer Grey Allen. This is Rhodes' third drunk driving arrest and his license will be suspended for three months and he will be fined $2,000 plus court costs.

December 14, 1999

Front Page
Headline: Local Man Brings Laughs at Chamber Christmas Party

The Barter County Chamber of Commerce held their annual Holiday Gala on Friday night and while business was on the agenda, laughs were the highlight of the night.

Local Coop manager Byron Matzen was the host of the event and immediately had the crowd in stitches with his take on local and national politics. At one point Matzen sat at a piano and played a medley of pop songs as outgoing president Bill Clinton. His targets also included current Nebraska Football head coach Frank Solich, Chamber President Alan Cratch and Dave Rhodes, whose Lady Bucks basketball team failed to make it to State this year.

"We knew Byron was the man for the job," Alan Cratch, President of the Chamber, said. "He's always cracking people up. He did a great job."

"I've got performing in my blood," Matzen said. "Plus, everyone I was making fun of makes it easy."

The group discussed several agenda items including the importance of bringing in new business, maintaining funding through grants and working with farmers to create an attractive environment for their crops.

May 22, 1999

Front Page
Headline: Local Man Forms Motorcycle Club For A Good Cause

Ron Smith has always loved motorcycles, but never gave any thought to starting a club. His friend, Carl Eakes, spurred him on.

"Carl was always asking me why we didn't do poker runs and tours of the state and stuff like that," Smith, an IT specialist for the Greater Barter County Coop, said. "I never had a good answer for him."

This weekend the Barter Coyotes Wolves Motorcycle Club, founded by Smith, will host a poker run that spans 120 miles in northern Nebraska. All proceeds from the run will benefit the Barter County Community Hospital and the Red Cross. Those wishing to participate can contact Smith at the Coop.

"It will be fun," he said. "The weather's supposed to be great."

PART 8 – BAD LANGUAGE MAKES FOR BAD FEELINGS

For Stuart Dietz's eighth birthday, he and his friends went bowling. There was cake, there was pop (a rare treat in the household), there was Dana walking around like she owned the place. But the biggest take-away from the party wasn't the presents or the eighty-one he bowled or the caffeine buzz that kept him up late into the night. For a young Stuart, the highlight was a trip to the bathroom and a peek at another world.

Super Bowl-O-Rama was one part of a block-long entertainment complex outside of Detroit that included a skating rink and a five-screen movie theater located upstairs. Young Stuart had bugged his father to take him to movies, but the elder Kline hadn't budged. They had a TV at home, why pay to go to a movie? His mother, slightly more open-minded, took her kids to G-rated fare like the re-release of *Snow White*, *The Aristocats* and the like.

The bathroom at the Bowl-O-Rama was right next to the stairs leading up to the movie theater and when no one was looking, young Stuart took the stairs two at a time to catch a glimpse of the movie posters before he had to go back. That trip would change his life, though it would be embarrassing to admit it.

Hanging over the stairs was the biggest banner for a movie Stu had ever seen. It covered an entire side of one staircase and in Stu's line of sight was one big, metal foot connected to a metal leg attached to the meanest, sleekest creature imaginable. Wide-eyed, the young Stuart followed all the way up to the metal visor, the huge gun in one hand and finally drank the entire image into his consciousness. The creature was getting out of a car, gun ready for action, wearing a look of indestructability on the lower half of his face.

Before Stu knew much in this world, he knew he wanted to be RoboCop.

Of course, he begged his mom to take him to the movie and she, prudently, said no. It was rated R for a long list of reasons and that was a line not to be crossed. Such was his desire and mania for all things RoboCop, that Stu asked his sister to sneak him in to the movie theater. She promptly told on him and that was the end of that.

Over the years he saw several posters for more *RoboCop* movies come and go and his desire only grew until, at the tender age of thirteen, Stu committed his first crime. The Motor City Video Emporium was one of those VHS rental stores that made the crucial mistake early on of putting the physical videos in clear plastic behind the cases. If the tape wasn't there, it was checked out. Stu had his friend Ally cause a distraction by knocking over a candy display, and he grabbed the video and hightailed it out of there. She never told anyone and he had a stolen copy of *RoboCop* in his room, tucked under his mattress later that night.

Stu waited and waited for a time when everyone had left the house so he could watch and finally had to fake being sick from school so he could view his stolen treasure. He waited a long time to make sure parents and sisters hadn't forgotten anything (thought he was sure Dana was on to at least part of his plan) and after breakfast, he popped in the tape.

Regardless of what the movie turned out to be, RoboCop was already part of Stu's origin story, so the fact that the film was excessively violent and bloody, mean-spirited and ass-kicking, only added to the legend. An adult Stu knew the movie by heart and all of it, stealing the tape, getting his first blast of cinema and how much he loved that flick made him smile, ever so slightly, before another right hand landed to his cheekbone, sending him into increasingly more agony.

"I don't like having you beaten, Mr. Dietz, but at this point, what choice do I have?" Stander said. They were in Stu's office and had been for so long that Stu had lost track. It was light out so he knew it had been more than twelve hours, but beyond that he was at a loss. Getting the shit beaten out of you tends to suppress your appetite and make regular body functions less important, so he couldn't even use hunger or the need to pee as markers for the passage of time.

They had come in the middle of the knight, Stander and his men. After the events at "Bar" Stu had welcomed his bed, as his head was swimming with all manner of societal, sociological, scientific and religious questions. He had headed straight for his bed and what seemed like a few short moments later, was being manhandled and pulled up hard to his feet, slapped around, forced to dress and taken to his office. Stu hadn't had the wherewithal to put up a fight at the time and now he was hand-cuffed to a chair suffering his third round of fists to the face and stomach in . . . at least twelve hours. Maybe more.

"What you've told us just doesn't make sense," Stander said, walking a lazy circle around Stu's chair. "Think of it from our perspective. This man, Mr. Rhodes, tells you his family's deepest, darkest, most destructive secret and then lets you walk away? He doesn't protect himself? He trusts you, a stranger, with this secret? Tell me, Mr. Dietz, if I were a suspect and I came to you with such a story, would you believe me?"

That last punch was a weak one and Stu could tell that Stander's men weren't looking to hurt him in a lasting way, but they were loyal. They all seemed to hop to it whenever they were given an order and there were whispers of consequences that Stu hadn't been able to fully comprehend.

Just because they weren't looking to hurt him permanently didn't mean they wouldn't soon. Or that the punches didn't really sting on his already bruised and tender skin.

Stu spit and there was a bit of blood mixed in with his saliva. It looked tough, he figured.

"I don't know how to convince you that I'm not lying," Stu said. "If I were you, you know what I'd do?"

"Enlighten me," Stander said.

"I would look for inconsistencies in my story," Stu said. "It's one of the main tools used in interrogation. If a person is making up the story on the spot or even if they've made it up before getting in that room they are going to forget stuff. Little details, sequences of events, stuff like that."

"Mm hmmm," Stander said, his arms crossed.

"So I'll tell you what I know again and if it's different than what I've told you before, hit me with that. Because I'm going to tell you what I know and it's the same as the last two times, I promise you."

"No need," Stander said. "At this point I know your story, Mr. Dietz and I know it's consistent."

Stu started to get a sinking feeling in his guts, but wasn't sure why. Nothing had changed except for something in the air.

"What is surprising to me is you think you're getting out of that chair."

Stander knew enough to let his threat sit a second before continuing on. He pulled up his own chair from behind Stu's desk and straddled it so the two men's faces were inches from each other and Stander's anger suddenly started pouring out in quiet, punctuated bursts of speech.

"I can see it in your eyes, Mr. Dietz. You're trying to figure the magic words to get me to uncuff you and let you go but you must be so dense that you honestly don't realize what's going on here, so let me tell you. My men and I have already razed two buildings, committed three murders and are detaining upwards of twenty people. We have a plan in place to burn this blank spot on the map into nothingness, Mr. Dietz, even though it's basically there already. I will destroy each and every thing that Dave Rhodes and his compatriots hold dear until they come back here and when they get back I will tranquilize them and load them into trucks and ship them across the country where they will live the rest of their lives in Old Testament-style suffering."

The pit in Stu's stomach had already turned to full-blown panic that he was working hard to suppress.

"I don't mean to be vulgar with you, Mr. Dietz, but if it means getting one more, even one more nugget of information out of you that will lead me to these people, I will shoot your chest and fuck the wound until you bleed out. Do you understand?"

Stu managed a nod. Stander resumed his standing, arms-crossed position.

Somewhere, deep inside Stu's consciousness, something started to stir. It started logically—why was this man so hell-bent on finding Dave and his pack? Money didn't engender this sort of rage, so what was it? Dave was a good person, as far as Stu could tell, if a little wimpy at times. There must be more to this if Stander was starting to lose his cool now after several weeks of hunting.

Then, deeper in Stu's mind, he was thirteen, several weeks after watching *RoboCop* for the first time. His friend, Rick, had rented *RoboCop 2* while his parents were away for the weekend. The boys huddled in the basement and watched the sequel in a moment of joy so pure, its memory pierced the panic, fear and pain.

"Bad language makes for bad feelings," Stu said.

One of the henchmen punched him again. Stander's face was unchanged.

"I have a business call to make right now," Stander said. "Or else things would escalate. As it stands, you have probably around an hour before I come back and when I do you are going to deeply, deeply regret your insolence."

He walked away, his expensive shoes clattering on the linoleum. His men followed.

"Have a nice day," Stu said, and gave his cuffs a hard tug. The cuffs and the chair were solid.

• • •

Across the street from the Sheriff's office was a building that had recently been abandoned. While the fixtures had been pulled, the tile on the floor gave off the impression that the place had been a restaurant of some kind. Frankly, Stander couldn't have cared less. His eyes were glued to his watch, a high-end number he purchased for himself his third week on the job. He was to take a call at precisely 11:30 a.m. Central Time and for the people he was about to speak with, "precisely" meant something.

He watched the second hand click, heard the tick as there was no sound to distract from it, and pulled out his phone with ten seconds to spare. On the nose, the phone's simple, strong ringer went off.

"Stander speaking," he answered.

"Any progress?"

"Not yet."

"Any leads?"

"Several."

"Any need to remind you of the stakes involved?"

"No. I fully understand."

"You will take another call at 3:00 p.m. Central Time. Understood?"

"Understood."

The line went dead. As was his habit, Stander checked the length of time the call had taken. It had been fourteen seconds.

The company man let himself have a moment of humanity. His bosses would not have sent him if they didn't have faith he could accomplish the task at hand, but their support waned. Now it was time to deliver and receive the reward or fail and face the consequences.

He stared at the walls in the room where he stood. The patterns on the floor suggested tables and chairs had been there at some point and the northwestern corner showed signs that it had once been a kitchen. He let out a long sigh but before the breath had finished exiting his body, his phone rang again.

"Stander speaking."

"Sir, we have eyes on William Rhodes."

"You do? Where is he?"

"He's currently on Highway 11, four miles outside of Cherry."

Stander started to move his body before his mind had commanded it. His walk was slightly awkward as he wasn't in a full-blown run but certainly was moving about that fast.

"I want three units on him. Set up a roadblock on Main Street, I will be there to direct myself momentarily."

Stander was two blocks away and already saw movement down the street, which was pleasing. He moved as fast as he could, leaving Stu Dietz handcuffed to a chair behind him.

Willie smelled them first, the smell of plastic and gun oil and unfamiliar thread.

"Here we go," he said to himself and gripped the steering wheel a little more tightly, putting his foot further down on the accelerator, feeling the pressure and acceleration.

As far as plans go, Willie didn't have one. Not really. A good part of him wanted to go out in a blaze of glory but he figured that wouldn't accomplish much. They'd still have his body and something told him they wouldn't let Dave go, so his idea was to get captured. At the very least, it would force Dave to finally do something.

But as he got closer and smelled the strangers to his town, the thinking changed as his temper flared. Willie decided to make them work for it.

By the time he was rolling around toward Main Street, a car was behind him blaring its sirens and Willie was going seventy miles an hour. By the time he saw the checkpoint, he was going eighty.

"Suck on this, fuckers," Willie said to the empty car, pulling on his seat belt over his round belly.

The checkpoint didn't look like much—a few sawhorses and barrels, probably full of water. What Willie hadn't counted on were the spike strips that punctured all four of his tires a half mile away from the checkpoint, slowing him significantly. He started losing speed right as he neared the checkpoint as the weight of the burst rubber pulled and dragged the car. His "making them work for it" amounted to crashing into a few water-filled barrels at forty miles an hour or so, sending water spraying everywhere and knocking the wind out of the old man.

Before he knew it, the doors were open and men were pointing guns at him and screaming. He was foggy from the impact and tasted blood in his mouth, but knew he was basically OK. And he immediately regretted his decision.

"Shit," Willie muttered and spit blood before putting up his hands. One of the men in combat gear reached toward him with a knife and cut the seat belt. For a brief second, Willie contemplated biting him, but he wasn't sure all his teeth were still in his head.

The front of the car was smoking and before they pulled Willie from the car and pushed him, hard, onto the gravel road he was able to make out a man with a bow tie and a wide grin walking toward the car. A combination of his injuries from the crash and his sudden meeting with the ground caused him to black out.

•••

It hadn't hurt as bad this time.

As she watched Ron and Kenny Kirk move Conall (not nearly as gingerly as they could have, but still), the truth struck her and the implications burned through her mind.

It hadn't felt good, obviously, but Josie had only transformed twice in the past five years, and even then it was out of urging from the pack to make sure she could still do it. The transformations were immensely painful for her, rivaling childbirth but this time it had seemed like a more natural thing. It was less a ripping and more a deep, painful stretch, and once it was done she had been ready to kick ass.

She hadn't felt that way in a long time.

What happens now? Would it always be like this? Would she get the "hunger" her husband and his friends were always talking about? The possibilities were running ragged through her mind when Dave put a hand on her shoulder. She turned to face him noticing the deep bruises already forming along one cheek and eye socket and a few cuts visible from the beating he had taken at the hands of the Irishman.

"You OK?" he asked.

It was too simplistic a question, obviously.

"How do you mean?"

"I guess, for right now, are you OK physically?"

"Never better," Josie said. "I kicked his ass."

"Yes, you did."

"He kicked your ass then I kicked his ass. Does that make me the Alpha?"

She was half teasing but by the time the words were out of her mouth, she realized it was a serious question. Was she in the lead now? And if so, what the hell was she going to do with that?

"I think you're the Alpha if you want to be," Dave said, not reading her mind but sensing her unease. "But if I could give you a bit of advice, I think we're way past any sort of chain of command thing. I think this is a group deal."

She nodded, then got an idea.

"Can you cover for me for about fifteen minutes?"

"Yeah, what do you need?

"I need to go test something out. Get the guys together, take care of Conall and I'll be there soon, OK?"

Dave nodded and went off to do his job, leaving Josie on the edge of the woods, the wind starting to pick up, blowing a symphony of sound through the trees and grass. Her clothes were ruined. The T-shirt she had on was still basically sound but the jeans had ripped and torn in multiple places exposing her legs all the way up to her panties, which were also full of tears. She remembered when her mother did the laundry when Josie was a little girl, she called them "church underwear" because they were "hole-y."

Josie took her clothes off and folded them, placing the pile beside a tree, then took off running. Barefoot and naked, the run was initially awkward as she was used to having support in places that were now unencumbered, but she got the hang of it, until she was in tune with the sounds of her bare feet hitting the leaves. She gave intense focus to not stepping on roots and rocks and after a few hundred feet it became a natural state.

Then she turned to her memory.

Before, her memory was weak. It involved a time an ex-boyfriend had called her a cow and she had knocked him over, twisted his arm, gotten right in his face and said "moo." She had never felt so powerful as at that moment, and that feeling of anger-fueled power had given her the kick she needed to transform, but now something was different. When she had taken after Dilly and Conall, what brought about the transformation wasn't a thought, but a need. It was the urgency of needing to save her son, to keep him from danger that he was smack in the middle of.

Feet pumping and chest heaving, she tapped back into that feeling of primal urgency, of a mother protecting her son, and soon she was a wolf mother protecting her cub. The transformation was swift and while the pain was there, the running and the urgency helped push it away and her brain, focused on nothing but protection, stayed sharp and unaffected by the massive changes happening to the body. By the time Josie came to a stop, she had become the Mother Wolf without breaking stride, something that would have seemed impossible just a day earlier.

The Mother Wolf pivoted and began running, full speed, back the way she had come. The woods yielded to her movements creating a sleek, elegant harmony between wolf and trees, wolf and ground, wolf and stone. She glided with a never-before-felt sense of harmony and agility, mixed with the panic of her thoughts and the anger that fueled them all. By the time she reached the edge of the woods she could see her family and her pack gathered and, on a whim, decided to run up the side of a large pine tree and vault from the edge of the woods into view, landing with a gentle thud a few feet from where they were standing.

Kenny Kirk let out a "holy shit," when she landed and she could sense apprehension in everyone present.

"How's the Irishman?" she growled, her voice still feminine but many times more threatening.

"He's fine," Dave said, stepping up. "We laid him down in his hotel room. His leg is pretty messed up and he's not walking for a week or so . . ."

"His fault," the Mother Wolf interrupted. "Ron, you have a plan to get those fuckers out of our town?"

Dilly blushed after hearing his mother swear. She was the sort who let the occasional profanity out, but never an f-bomb and certainly not in his presence. She was different, Dilly figured, and after this was done, they all would be different too.

"Yeah," Ron said, sensing the urgency. "I know when and I think I know how if we can get to that garage of Kenny's a few miles outside of town."

"I think we can," Kenny said. "It's not on the books anywhere. I mean, JoAnn, you know about it . . ."

"You've taken me there once," she said. "Remember, when we were dating? What do you call it? Is it a Batman thing?"

"Superman, darling," Kenny said. "It's the Fortress of Solitude."

"Who gives a fuck?" the Mother Wolf swore. Her heart was still beating very fast and very hard and her desire to get something done was paramount. "If we get there, what do we do?"

Over the next half hour Ron laid out his plan to the group. It was a good one but a dangerous one on several levels. As his explanation went on it was tweaked and details were added and subtracted. Josie hardly noticed it, but she had begun to change back, realizing it only when the cold of the morning hardened her nipples, which were suddenly back where they usually were. She hopped off to find her clothes, hoping no one had noticed. By the time she got back, the plan had been set.

"I hate to be the one to bring this up," Dave said, "but before we do this we need to do something. I need everyone to think this through, really think about it, and decide if they're in or out. Some of you have a lot to live for, except Kenny."

Dave had planned that joke out before he started talking, knowing he'd get as good as he gave.

"Fuck you and your weird-ass wife, man," Kenny said, true to form.

"My point is if we do this, we all do this," Dave said. "We do it as a pack or not at all."

"I guess that means you're riding point?" Ron asked.

"Yeah, I'm riding point," Dave said. "I'm gonna insist on that."

"When was the last time you were on a motorcycle, Dad?" Dilly asked.

Well, Dave thought, at least he was acting as an equal part of the group.

"I got it, I promise," Dave said, half to Dilly and half to the group.

"How about this," Josie said. "I need to go talk to JoAnn and Dave needs to talk to Conall. If you're on board, meet out front in twenty minutes and we'll head for the Batcave or whatever."

"Fortress of Solitude. Jesus," Kenny said.

"If you're coming, do what you need to do. If you're not coming, don't show up. You won't have to face us. We'll make it easy for you. Sound good?"

Everyone nodded in agreement and the meeting started breaking up. Josie made a bee-line for JoAnn.

"Come here, darling," she said, making fun of Kenny's affectionate term. "I think I figured something out."

•••

Dave could hear, even before he got to the door, that Conall was on the phone and he was pissed. He waited outside the door to see what snippets of conversation he could hear.

"Come in, you asshole. I smelled you when you turned the corner," Conall yelled.

So much for that.

The Irishman was laying on the bed, his leg propped on several pillows, the legs of his pants cut open so some future medical care could be administered. Dave hadn't had a good look at the injury, but based on the coloring alone he knew something gnarly was going on under the skin. Conall caught him looking.

"Your psycho wife did a real number on me," he said.

"It'll heal," Dave said.

"That's not what I'm talking about, brother," Conall replied. "I find the clues, I come out to the middle of bumblefucky Nebraska and what do I find? One of the worst pack leaders I've ever met and his wife who can do something I've only read about on parchment. I mean, do you realize what this means? Do you have a clue?"

"There's a lot I don't know," Dave said. "But I know how special that woman is."

"I fucking doubt it," Conall said, shifting his weight and letting out a brief gasp of pain. "Because you've got your little slice of the world and that's all you know. If you knew what I know, you'd be freaking out right now and begging me for my protection."

"She looks like she can handle herself," Dave said, nodding at Conall's leg.

"Well, I'm glad you're so full of confidence," Conall said. "Because here's just a taste of what I know. I know that if Stander and his men get hold of her, she might very well be the key to figuring out what we are and weaponizing it. They could use her, most likely, to end our species or to turn soldiers into wolves or something worse. She is the missing link that we didn't know was out there, David, and on a global scale, this is a giant deal but let me make it personal for you. If you're captured, they are going to poke you and prod you and figure out everything they can and you and your friends will all suffer. But Josie? They will keep her alive until they figure it out. They will savage her like nothing you can imagine. If whatever your plan is doesn't work, you will all suffer but none will suffer as greatly as your wife."

For a moment, flashes of Josie on the table being cut up rushed into Dave's head, but he batted them away and attempted to change the subject.

"Who was that on the phone?"

"Did you hear what I just told you?"

"Yes," Dave said, leaning heavily on the word. "I heard you. And I get it. I get that this is stupid and I get there's no net and I get that you can't help us."

" . . . and that your family suffers and dies if you fail . . ."

"Right," Dave said.

" . . . and that you can leave Willie, get in the car and drive with me to places you've never been, where you can meet more of your kind and have your world opened in a way you can't imagine. You get all that."

"Do you even want to hear the plan?"

"NO!" Conall said, yelling hard enough to make him wince in pain. "Because I have zero confidence in you and your mate's ability to pull it off. Your father did something stupid, and that's unfortunate, but make the right decisions, goddammit and load up the car and come with me!"

It struck Dave, at that moment, that while his brain had weighed the options of going with Conall, his heart had not, and he gave in to his fantasy for a good, long moment. He pictured Dilly meeting a British wolf his own age, pictured Kenny running his mouth at the Tower of London, himself kissing Josie under the Eiffel Tower. And more than just travel, he imagined the freedom that would come from shaking Cherry off, starting clean, feeling the mass of possibility in front of him. He let the fantasy linger so long his heart began to ache and his pulse started to quicken.

Thoughts of Willie muscled their way in, some warm and some vile, then the vision of the old man on a table, being cut open and tortured. The excitement in his stomach turned, hard, and all the arguments came rushing back through his brain and out his mouth.

"Would you condemn your father to torture and death?"

"If it meant keeping my family safe, I believe I would."

"I don't believe you're that cruel."

"I am."

In truth, Conall had seen crack teams of wolves fly through the forest with speed and force. He had defeated enemies and beaten all comers in competition. He was an elite fighter in the world of wolves, but that woman had handily beaten him. Conall motioned for Dave to come closer.

"I've already failed at my mission, David," he said. "They already have a wolf. That's something they've never had before, so this situation is already fucked up beyond all reason and I can see your mind's already made up, so fuck it. And, if you breathe a word of this to anyone I will deny it and deny it until my final breath, but with Josie on your side, you might have a shot."

The two men spent the next half hour going over "the plan" and Dave left Conall with his foot up and an ever so slight smirk on his face.

• • •

Josie looked for her son in the room, by the edge of the forest and even behind cars and trucks in the hotel parking lot. His scent was strong but either he was moving or she was missing something. Kenny and JoAnn were jabbering in the parking lot with Ron and Carl, and just as Josie was

197

about to get really annoyed, she heard her son's deeper voice boom in laughter.

He was joking around with everyone.

" . . . so he's up on the bridge, right, and the rope is tied around his chest," Kenny Kirk was saying. "And we had added about ten feet of rope. He was going to swing down and we added the rope, right, and he took this running swing thinking the rope would catch and he'd go right back up and his stupid ass lands half in the water and the other half hits the bank—BAM! . . ."

Everyone was laughing and Kenny was rolling on the story. Dilly was between Ron and Carl and hadn't noticed her yet, so she watched him. He was tall, he was handsome, he was brave, he was loyal and while he still had a lot to learn, he was quite the kid, she decided. And he had saved his father. She couldn't bear to lose him, but maybe he was ready for something like this.

Just as Kenny was finishing his story, the boy noticed his mother and his smile faded. He gave a look around the circle.

"Well, go, man," Kenny said. "I'm not saying anything important here."

Dilly lumbered over, his head down.

"So, am I getting yelled at?" he asked, still a few huge steps away.

"A little," Josie said. "I'd certainly be in my rights to ask you what you were thinking, attacking a strange wolf who could have very easily killed you. But you held your own."

"A few more transformations and I think I've got him," Dilly said. "I'm faster than he is, Mom. If I can get the speed working with my attack, then . . ."

"You're not as fast as I am," she interrupted. "And you made your own decision. I'm proud of you for that. But my God, Dilly, he could have killed you."

"Like those guys in our house? Those guys who are hunting us right now?"

"Yes, like them, and what's your point?"

"My point is I'm already in danger," Dilly said. "And if we're going to go get Grandpa, I'm going to need all the practice I can get."

He was planning to take part and planning to fight, Josie thought. No other option had occurred to him.

"Listen to me," Josie started. "I want you to really give thought to not coming with us."

"I've given it thought and I've made my own decision," Dilly said. "Just like you and Dad told me to do, so instead of trying to protect me, start thinking about how you can use me, OK? This isn't me saying 'I'm not a kid anymore Mom!' This is me saying I'm part of this family and part of this pack and I'm going to go rescue my grandpa."

"Yeah," Kenny yelled from the circle a few feet away. "I mean, all hell, Josie, I mean yeah. He was talking loud and he's right and he was talking really loud."

Kenny shut up as Josie had given him an icy stare, the price for eavesdropping. Dilly had already turned around and was walking back toward the group.

"Dilly, come here," she shouted.

He reluctantly stopped in his tracks and started to trudge back. She met him halfway.

"Never run as fast as you can," she said. "If you're in a fight, you don't want your opponent to know how fast you can go. Save that until you absolutely need it."

She threw her arm around his waist and led him back to the circle where Kenny told him about what the claws were good for, Carl talked about the deceptively small spaces a wolf can fit into and Ron gave the young soon to be wolf advice on how best to use your jaws without doing any permanent damage.

• • •

It took Conall and Dave forty-five minutes to come out of the hotel room and when they did, Conall was on a makeshift crutch made out of the shower-curtain rod and a shampoo bottle. His non-crutch hand was around Dave, who was walking him toward his car.

"Leg's busted, huh?" Kenny said, smiling.

"Yeah, golly gee," Conall said, doing an impression of Kenny's twang. "Leg's busted."

"You blimey twat," Kenny shot back in a terrible brogue, smiling the whole time.

Conall steadied himself up against a wall and made a motion for everyone to gather round. Instinctively, they looked at Dave who gave a small nod and they all squeezed in making a suspicious-as-hell semicircle around the Irishman.

"Dave told me what you're going to do," he said. "So I want to give you a piece of information and a piece of advice. Then someone take me to my car and get me the hell back to civilization. Agreed?"

Everyone muttered in agreement or nodded their head.

"OK, then. I've made a few calls to my people and they are still too far out to help. The nearest group is about four hours away and Willie will be dead by then, I assure you. But my people are also tracking the company that has occupied your town. They are a group called Hartman Corp. and they are sending reinforcements and an extraction unit, most likely to collect the lot of you. My people aim to stop them."

No one said a word but the air shifted mightily around the circle. This was the first time in the past godforsaken week that there might be light at the end of the tunnel. They could fight and if they could win, out-side forces might win as well. Conall sensed the optimism and quickly squashed it.

"Don't think for a second this means all you have to do is kill Stander and his men," Conall said. "My people might not be able to stop the Hartman Corp. goons. A few might get through. Or, much more likely, you are all currently about to ride to your deaths."

"Thanks for the confidence, man," Kenny said. Conall ignored him.

"So go, fight for your town if you must. But I need you to know and understand down to your very soul that you are never safe there again. Others are going to come looking for you."

"About that," Ron said. "I think I might have an idea." He was met with Dave giving him a short head nod, as if to say "we'll deal with that in a bit."

"I can't tell you what to do anyway, which brings me to my piece of advice," Conall said. "My job is to go find people like you, but I've been places and I've done things. I've killed and while not pleasant, the impact of it doesn't hit you until you've become human again. You will be blood-thirsty and you will be vicious and I have no doubt that each and every one of you will kill if you must but when it's over . . ."

Conall tapped his makeshift crutch as if searching for the right phrase.

"When it's over remember this: There is more to come. You may feel like there's a hole, slowly eating you from the inside but there's more to come. It doesn't make sense now, but as someone who's been on the path you're about to walk, it will make sense."

He paused, raised his head, and took the time to meet the eyes of every-one in the half circle.

"There's more to come."

The wind chose that moment to blow, hard, tousling the hair and sting-ing the skin of the gathered and carrying with it the smells of the forest. The decay of the leaves mixed with the sunlight and undergrowth to form a sickly sweet aroma tinged with the earth, bark, and animal waste.

"One of you grisly bastards help me to my car, please."

Dave did the honors and Conall let out a short gasp of pain when start-ing off.

"Will we ever see you again?" JoAnn asked.

"Chances are you're riding to your deaths, so no."

They watched him in silence as Dave opened the door and helped him in and watched him lean over and whisper something. Dave seemed taken aback but before he had time to react Conall had shut the door, started the engine and put his car into gear. The engine chugged and kicked and before Dave could make it back to the group, all that was left of Conall was tail lights obscured by dust.

"What'd he say?" Kenny Kirk asked.

"I . . . I'm not sure it would make sense if I told you," Dave said. "I'm not trying to be an asshole but I'm not sure I get it."

Kenny kicked the dirt, like he had done a few days earlier in front of his shop. Was it still there? Was anything still there? The rest were similarly lost, wondering what had become of their town and it was Dilly who broke the silence.

"So," he said, in a clear, low tone. "What number y'all at?"

A Selective History of Barter County, Part 5

There is no consensus at all among those at the Barter County Historical Society about how the town of Cherry got its name. The several older ladies who make up the group had never considered the question nor given it serious study. Had they bothered, they would have found the following story in the book *Of Mountains and Plains: The Diary of a Mountain Man* by Rex Leschinsky.

In the book, Leschinksy attempts to interpret the writings of Elliot Goodchild, a "Mountain Man" who lived alone on the Nebraska plains and spent a number of years with the Native American tribes that had resettled there. From his book:

The diary entry on January 18 proves his relationship with the Chocktaw tribe was one of mutual curiosity, if not respect. Goodchild recounts being around the campfire and hearing a remarkable tale of forbidden love told around a crackling fire in the dead of winter. He writes "with a clear head, this story would never have been told. Bitter cold clouds the senses, if not loosens the tongue."

The story is of a spirit of the woods that guarded and protected the tribe. The spirit was ancient and when it saw a white woman, it fell in love. Having no form, the spirit chose that of a wolf and attempted to get close to the woman, but she ran for help and soon the wolf/spirit was being hunted by white men with guns. The spirit knew the woods and was wise and soon overpowered the men, killing them. The woman was so terrified by this that she found herself lost in the woods.

Any time the wolf/spirit tried to approach the woman she would scream and cry and so it went into the night and the next day. The woman was tired, hungry and exhausted so the wolf/spirit went to a very special part of the woods and harvested some chokecherries for the woman to eat, placing them gently in his mouth and depositing them a few yards away from her.

She was so hungry and desperate that she ate the cherries and upon doing so her mood improved. She still wouldn't get close to the wolf, so he brought her more and she ate them and he got closer still. Finally, after several trips to bring the woman chokecherries, she touched the wolf/spirit, who was more happy than he had ever been. She stroked his fur and hugged him, then offered him some of the cherries. The wolf/spirit ate them, not knowing they were deadly to animals. Soon, the wolf died and the woman was left alone.

The story, as told by the tribe, was meant to symbolize how changes to one's fundamental nature never end well. As Goodchild wrote in his diary, "the moral was to be hearty and do your job."

This story was a favorite of Nicholas Caspersen, a founding father of the town, so much so that he had part of the story inscribed on a historical marker just off the highway. The marker, made of solid granite and weighing well over a ton, marked your entry into the town and it made Caspersen immensely proud, partly because of the name he chose and helped foster. Instead of naming the new burg "Wolfwood" or something similarly silly, he opted for "Cherry," a simple, poignant reminder to the town of the fundamental nature of its founders.

Or it could have meant, as Mountain Man Goodchild so eloquently put it, "do your job."

PART 9 – THINGS THAT WILL BITE

It was not professional at all, the way Stander had forgotten about Stu, tied up in the Sheriff's office. The fact that he had allowed him to escape was nothing short of negligence. To be fair, operations had never been his strong suit. To be realistic, that didn't matter to those in charge.

Stander had started as a "number cruncher," which was a term he hated but wasn't at all apt. His job had very little to do with numbers and much more to do with computer coding and pattern recognition, both of which were vital to basic intelligence work. "Number cruncher" denoted he sat in an office all day pouring over budgets when, in actuality, he led a team of intelligent, diligent programmers whose job it was to search for patterns when they emerged from a wide variety of sources. No one but Stander had the full picture of what they were looking for, exactly, but his team was not dumb and had caught on. A week or so ago, when his team had put together enough data points to present to upper management, they had given him a silver bullet on a necklace as a "going away present." Everyone in the team had been awarded six-figure bonuses for interpreting the data so quickly in addition to their already-handsome salary, so champagne had been popped and backs had been slapped, which was a rare state of social affairs for a bunch of "number crunchers." He had been told multiple times to "stay safe out there," like he was going to some war torn nation. It had caused him to reflect on how he had gotten to where he was.

When Stander had been recruited from Wall Street where he had headed one of the R&D Departments at a large bank, the process of interviewing with HartmanCorp included much more than your usual Non Disclosure Agreement. It included a battery of psychological tests, a physical test and veiled talk stretching the law, if not breaking it.

Stander had gone along with it all and even embellished his bona fides because was bored. He was rich, his job was unfulfilling and an odd and exotic group promising adventure, if nothing else, had reached out to him. After agreeing to take a job analyzing data, he had been singled out for leadership, which meant learning more about the company, what it did and how it did it. The bottom line, Stander found out, was HartmanCorp was in the business of industrial espionage, among other services. If a company wanted something badly, like a sustained lobbying effort or a public information campaign, they could do that themselves. If they needed really nasty opposition research, there were places for that as well. If they wanted someone found, or lost, if a competitor was about to crush a company and they had no other option or if, say, a small town needed to shaken to its core in order to flush out a few special citizens, that was when you called HartmanCorp.

Sure enough, it had been fun. Stander had trained for a "leadership position" by tagging along on several paramilitary escapades disguised as "safety and protection" services. He had learned and knew the game, but was never able to shake the feeling that, while he was in a leadership position, that he was seen as nothing but a 'number cruncher". His affinity for bow ties and straight posture didn't help matters, so when the call came that he was under consideration to lead the Barter County operation, he lobbied, actively.

• • •

He had convinced his superiors he was "the man" and the minute the party with his department was over and all the backs had been slapped,

Stander had been whisked away to meet his Operations Team. In short order he determined he may have made a mistake as he was not his "intellectual safe space".

The problems started almost immediately with the "intel and prep" team. These men, who were a bit more physically intense than Stander was used to, were prepped and ready to invade the entirety of Barter County, knock on every door, beat every bush and get the information within 48 hours. Stander had said no. The operation could not, under any circumstances, draw undo attention unless there was no other option. He pared down the force and did a lot of the leg work himself, which prompted his first meeting with management.

The organizational chart at HartmanCorp was more or less a mystery. Employees knew who they reported to and who those superiors reported to but only a select few could go far up the ladder, so it was to Stander's dismay when a man calling himself Simmons called him on his company issued phone to discuss strategy.

"What department are you from, exactly," Stander had asked.

"Unimportant," Simmons said. "I'm talking to you because you are going against procedure and by going against procedure you are taking a risk, Mr. Stander. Either that risk pays off and you are rewarded or it does not pay off and you suffer consequences."

"I see," Stander said. He didn't know what it was, but the combination of the man's stern voice, his use of language which mimicked corporate speak within the company and his insistence on results convinced him that the man on the other end of the phone did work for his employer. And that his threats were backed up.

Over the course of five brief minutes, Stander explained his strategy and why he had broken protocol. "Simmons" offered no encouragement or excoriation, waiting until Stander stopped talking to respond.

"Your plan is acceptable for now," he said. "The less you talk to me the better your operation is going. Endeavor not to speak to me again."

The moment he hung up he received a text message from an unfamiliar number saying his phone was to stay on during the entirely of the operation. Failure to answer the phone when it rang was a failure to be met with "consequences."

He had been warned, of course. During the training his instructors had explained the importance of protocol but far more importantly, the importance of success. Each "operation" had parameters and those parameters were the be all and end all of his existence during the time he was operation leader. Failure was not acceptable in the field, he was told. Now he was being threatened via phone somewhere, but the threats were starting to creep up Stander's spine and were making way for his brain.

Before he received the bad news that Stu had escaped, Stander had already convinced himself that if he failed, it would be the last thing he ever did. When he got the news, his anger took over, which was an exceedingly rare thing. The last time he had given himself over to anger so completely was in high school when his girlfriend continued to deny his physical advances. He had called her every name he could think of and made her exit his car in the middle of a busy intersection with no ride home. He had paid consequences for that lapse in calm and had vowed never to do it again.

Vows were meant to be broken, apparently.

"Let me ask you," Stander said, speaking quietly and quickly, pacing around the room where an empty chair with a cut pair of zip tie hand cuffs on them were the central feature. "You've been trained by HartmanCorp, correct?"

"Yes," the man said. He was white, or possibly light skinned Latino, dressed in a Kevlar vest and other pieces of riot gear. Stander didn't care, but did note the man didn't address him as "sir," which was part of their paramilitary training.

"Forensic deconstruction is part of your training, is it not?"

"It is."

"Then tell me what happened here, please."

The man looked from the cut zip tie hand cuffs to Stander and back at the cuffs.

"How did he get out of them, you giant fucking idiot!" Stander screamed.

"This was the first outward sign of anger from Stander, but inside, he was already out of control. The man stammered and his body language reverted to that of a child in trouble.

"He . . .he cut them."

It took Stander significant restraint to not commit murder on the spot.

"How?" he asked, his voice again quiet and fast. "How did he cut them."

"Well," the man walked over to the cuffs and bent down, looking at them and the old chair they were on with a scientific eye. "It looks like he was able to rub them on something metal and cut them."

"So your answer is 'something metal?'"

The man in the riot gear looked up and gave a shrug.

"I guess so."

Stander walked over to the chair and bent over in the same position as the man. He studied the cuffs closely.

"What do you think it could have been?" he asked.

Before the man could answer, Stander put both hands on either side of his head and started pushing his eye toward the edge of the wooden chair. The man jerked, but the element of surprise was firmly in Stander's corner, and he quickly maneuvered the man's head until his right eye socket was pressing hard into the edge of the chair. The man attempted to overpower Stander, but any show of force was met with sudden and unrelenting pain as he pushed the edge of the chair further into the man's ocular cavity.

The scream of surprise heard outside the room turned into a shrieks of pain and Stander's anger took more and more control and the edge of the chair sank deeper and deeper, pushing the man's eye further and further back.

"Is there any reason . . ." Stander panted "that I shouldn't shove your eye all the way into your incompetent fucking brain? ANY REASON AT ALL?"

The answer was a pained scream as the pitch of the man's voice continued to rise, giving Stander all the fuel he needed to keep pushing. This man was the embodiment of apathy, the embodiment of arrogance, the embodiment of why he was failing and in a moment he wouldn't have thought possible a short few months ago, Stander punched the man in the back of his head, as hard as he could. There was a squish and a pop before the screaming started and the moment Stander released his grip the man bolted from the building, screaming and crying and carrying on.

"Piece of shit," Stander said under his breath. The other men in the room were actively trying to not react, which was a reaction in and of itself. He turned to one of them.

"Do we still have the Sheriff's sister in custody or are we too incompetent to detain a fat lesbian housewife?"

"She's at the town hall, sir," the man said. This was the first time Stander had ever been called "sir" by someone not in the service industry.

"Fetch her, please," he said. "I need her here and I need Mr. Rhodes here as well."

"Right away, sir," the man said. There was a hustle in his step as he started on his errand.

Outside, the first man was receiving medical attention. There was gauze being applied and even through the window, Stander could see a man off to the side, filling out a report. The man with the eye injury was describing how he got the wound, and there were a few glances back at Stander. When the man with the papers and the man applying first aid looked, it occurred to Stander to do something even more out of character, even more brash, in some ways, than physically assaulting one of his own men.

He smiled and waved. The crew quickly looked away.

• • •

The minute Conall had driven away, Kenny Kirk's mouth had started running and given his sheer word per minute output, there were bound to be some negative runs in there. By the time they pulled up on his storage unit, the whole pack was irritated.

"I remember the last time you rode a motorcycle it did not go well, man. It did not go well. I remember you wrecked that one time, you remember, it was a clear day and it had rained just a little and you ate it, hard, on one of those turns down by Rural Road 104. That was under the best conditions, man, so I don't know how you think you're going to pull this off, especially since you haven't been riding in, like, a year."

"I got it," Dave said. "If I don't got it, you have my permission to tell me 'I told you so' after you save my ass."

"Well that's just it. I don't want to tell you 'I told you so.' I want this to work and a big part of it working is you driving that motorcycle and not wrecking the damn thing if there's a puddle or a slight gust of wind or something."

Kenny and JoAnn had made a quick run to a friend who lived not far from the hotel and had borrowed a Suburban from his house. The seven of them in two cars were barreling down the highway, and Dave had done the chivalrous and honorable thing and volunteered to ride with Kenny.

"Let's worry about that in a minute," Dave said. "Right now let's just get the vehicles and go from there."

"I'm more concerned about your wife, if you don't mind me saying," Ron said from the shotgun seat. "I mean, she's bad ass, don't get me wrong, but she's got a lot to do and not a lot of time to do it."

"She knows," Dave said.

"That's not reassuring, man, not in the least," Kenny said. "I don't know how she's going to pull it off and I've been thinking about it. I mean, we don't even know if they're going to bite, much less how many guys they're going to bring. And then what? How is she going to . . ."

Dave cut Kenny off. He had been supremely patient up until this point but it was getting harder and harder to deal with the yammering.

"There are parts of this that are going to be rough," he said. "But let's get the bikes and go from there, please."

Kenny took the hint and they rode the last half mile in silence. The first part of the plan involved getting hold of two motorcycles and three cars, all of which were stored in Kenny's shed about eight miles outside of town. The shed was purposefully remote but off the highway, so they didn't know whether or not any of Stander's men would be staking it out. A quick glance of the road around the place showed that they weren't. There were no tracks in the dirt surrounding the shed.

"Looks good," Ron said.

"I don't know, what if they came in by helicopter or something," Kenny said. "I've heard of, like, really big companies having those helicopters with four propellers, one on each end, what do you call them?"

"Quadcopters," Ron said.

"Yeah, man, quadcopters. I've heard of those things equipped with guns and cameras and lasers and all sorts of shit," Kenny said. "If I hear a buzzing when I go in there I'm throwing one of you down and making for the truck."

"Why would you throw one of us down? It's in the sky, Kenny, it's not a bear," Ron said.

"I'll use the time they spend shooting you on the ground to get to the truck. Why is that so hard to understand?" Kenny said, unlocking the shed and pulling open the door. The contents inside were covered in dust, but they were there – one 58 Ford Mustang with a growl so loud the filter was just a formality, 82 Corvette that Kenny had spent years restoring and one big ass Harley Davidson motorcycle, twin cams and not enough to be garish.

The three vehicles were loud. That was the important thing.

"They got gas in them?" Ron asked.

"Gas and I put new tires on them not all that long ago," Kenny said. "They ought to work."

"They'll work, Dave said, and walked over to the Harley. He ran his fingers along the black leather seat, tracking a think line of clean in a cloud of dust. The bike had been Dave's and for years he loved riding it, giving it up only when Dilly had been born. He'd sold it to Kenny for a couple hundred dollars and though he never regretted it, seeing the bike in a minor state of disrepair was enough to hurt.

Dave took a second to let his mind drift on how it was kind of fitting he might go out sitting on top of his motorcycle. He had started riding when he and Josie had been newlyweds. She had no interest, but one Christmas had conspired with her family and friends to buy him a beaten up old bike, and he had spent time in the garage getting it up and running. By the time he sold it, he had spent more to restore the thing than a new motorcycle would have cost, but he knew every crack and shimmy the machine would dish out. At least he did. He didn't regret giving it up when the kid was born but he never felt quite as good as when he was riding it in those early days. Dave breathed a noticeable sigh at how complicated things had become.

"Hey, I took care of her," Kenny started. "It's just dusty is all. I've got some Armor All in the corner over there . . ."

"Keys," Dave said. "We've got to meet up with the others."

"I call the 'Vette," Ron said.

"You don't get to come in to a man's garage and start telling him what's what," Kenny said. "You'll ride out of her on my nephew's tricycle if you keep that shit up."

A few admonitions from Kenny later, and they were on the road. Dave had found a helmet that sort of fit, but had thrown it off when they started riding. The wind felt amazing in his hair and if he crashed and died before getting to where he was going, that would just have to be the way of things.

•••

The zip-tie holding Stu's hand had been cut by metal molding on Grey Allen's old desk. Stu had first noticed it after he had been worked over the first time, his whole face throbbing in pain and one of his eyes already starting to swell. The metal molding, sometimes seen on very, very old desks, looked worn and Stu had theorized there might be enough wear to create a couple of wicked sharp spots he could use to cut the cuffs.

He was right, but he had sustained a nasty cut along the palm of his right hand in the process, giving one final push so the plastic would give way. He had bandaged his hand the best he could with spare scraps of uniform, figuring the worst thing he could do is leave a bloody trail straight to wherever he decided to hide. A few minutes later, with his hand pulsing and stinging like crazy, Stu realized "hiding" was a relative term. He couldn't go out onto the street because most of Stander's men were that direction. The office had no "back way" leaving "up" as his only option.

Before he made his way to the roof, he grabbed a spare revolver he knew was in the desk. The occupiers hadn't thought to look through the desk, so in theory, Stu was armed. After making his way up on the roof, staying low and moving as quietly as he could, he tried testing out his firing hand only to find the cut was giving him a lot of trouble, throbbing and weak as it was. He could shoot, but it wouldn't be accurate, it would hurt like hell and he was not good enough with his left hand to make any sort of go of it. He had tried shooting left handed on a dare once at the shooting range in Detroit and was met with laughter and derision by his fellow officers, plus a sore shoulder the next morning to boot.

From his perch on the roof, Stu was able to listen and mark the moment they knew he was gone from the office. A few minutes later he heard screaming from down below and figured punishment had been meted out for his escape. No one thought to check the roof because, he reasoned, it was a stupid place to go – no escape, no utility, no real threat. He had even left the hatch to the roof partially open so he didn't get locked up there. Stu wasn't sure what he would do if they did check, but it was a cool day, he was armed, and the bleeding was under control. As far as murderous bands of cut throat occupiers went, things could be going a lot worse, plan or not.

As he sat and reflected on his relative good fortune, he realized the yelling from below had changed. It was higher now and as he focused, Stu realized the man had stopped screaming and a woman had started. And the screaming sounded familiar.

"You assholes!" the woman said between screams. "Damn it, you know I can't tell you . . ."

The words turned abruptly to a howl Stu recognized as Dana, his sister. His heart panicked while his brain reasoned that, of course they would go after Dana. He was lucky it had taken them this long. As her yelling sustained, the brain shut down and despair mixed with the panic as two extremely potent urges collided. He couldn't let them continue to hurt his sister, but there was nothing substantial he could do without getting recaptured and likely killed. The sounds of Dana's suffering did not abate.

"Damn you!" she had started chanting when words were possible between bouts of screaming. Over and over she said "damn you, damn you," until it started to sound like a prayer. After a while, she started crying, a high whimper Stu had only heard on rare occasions as a child and only then when extreme pain was involved. Dana had been in a car crash as a teen and had shattered a bone in her arm. The recovery was long and intense and she would whimper during the physical therapy that was part of "getting better". Now Stu heard it again and before his mind could tell him not to, he was on his feet.

He carefully lifted the hatch to the roof and eased his body down the ladder, painstakingly avoiding any sudden movements or unnecessary sound. The hatch was at the end of the back hallway of the Sheriff's Office with the bathroom and breakroom on either side. The corridor was long enough to conceal him from view, and as he crept closer, his movements hidden by the sound of torture, he gripped the pistol with both hands, down low, muzzle down like he had been taught as a young recruit.

The plan, as it was, was to grab a quick glance of the room and then come out blazing. He had seven shots with the pistol (he had checked the bullets while on the roof), and after he cleared the room, he would get Dana out of there. Past that, there was no plan. Dana could not keep suffering, Stu thought, even if the consequences were a bit hazy. Whatever they were doing to Dana was winding down as Stu peered around the corner, and the screams gave way to heavy breathing, which still masked the other sounds in the room well enough.

When he finally worked up the courage to look around the corner, Stu saw three men standing around his sister, two of which were very intently listening to the radio. The crackling, electronic tinged voice wasn't audible to Stu, in fact he hadn't heard it at all until his head was around the corner of the hallway wall, but whatever was being said had the men's full attention. Stu waited, getting a good sense of the room and hid back behind the wall.

"We gotta go," one of the men said. "You watch her, keep on her if you want to, but she stays here. Under no circumstances does she move from this chair. You get me?"

"Yeah," another man said. "I got it."

"If you lose her, we're both up shit creek, man," the first man said. "You saw what happened to Chris."

"Chris was an asshole," the first man said.

"You're an asshole," Dana said, weakly, followed by a spitting sound.

This brought a good chuckle from the three men, a few choice comments and a few seconds later Stu heard the bell on the door ding, meaning the door had opened and one or more men had left. This was a stroke of improbably luck, Stu thought, but then he remembered he had been attacked by a werewolf the day before. Probability was relative at this point.

Given his new found luck, Stu waited to see if he could determine how many men were now holding Dana. He figured two men had left, but he wanted to be sure. His answer came soon enough.

"How long you think they'll be gone?" Stu heard a man say.

"I want to light you on fire," Dana replied. Stu grinned despite himself.

"See, that's just it," the man said, taking a conversational tone. "You don't know how this thing works, lady. You think being tough is going to accomplish something. Torture always works. No one lasts forever, no matter how tough they are. We're going to hurt you until you tell us anything and everything about your piece of shit brother and then we'll be done with you. I don't know what happens to you then."

"I get to fuck your mother?" Dana shot back.

"No, probably not that," the man said. "I'm thinking they'll make you vanish, along with the rest of this town."

There was a creak as the man sat down in Stu's chair, an ancient rolling metal deal with a green cracked plastic seat covering. The first time Stu had sat in it, he had almost fallen out but hadn't replaced it as there was no furniture store for over 50 miles, but because of the squeak and noises that accompanied it, Stu suddenly knew exactly where the man was – on the side of the desk closest to the hallway, facing the door. And he wasn't paying attention.

"How about I cut you?" the man said. "I mean, have you ever been cut? A lot of people have accidentally cut themselves or had surgery or whatever but have you ever watched your own flesh get split with a knife, feel the blood? You kinky like that? That sound like fun?

"Untie me and give it a shot," Dana said.

"Or I could go get Robin, is that her name? I could go get her and bring her in here and cut into her while you watch. Maybe there's this moment, right . . ."

The chair squeaked as the man leaned forward, really getting in to his story. Stu crept very slowly from around the corner and raised the pistol.

" . . .I've cut into her a few times, arms or legs maybe and then I make a cut that won't heal. That won't get better. I cut a little too deep or a little too far and all of a sudden there's more blood than you know what to do this and you know she's not coming back from it. You know she's either going bleed to death or lose a limb or something.

Stu was clear of his cover and crept slowly toward the man, the pistol outstretched, awestruck by his luck. Dana had seen him and, to her credit, had kept the same look on her face. She didn't flinch or give up anything happening behind the man, whose rape fantasy was about at an end.

" . . .and she's bleeding and thrashing and the life is seeping out of her and there's blood pooling on the floor. She's dying, badly, and you have to watch and there's NOTHING you can do about it!"

The man suddenly bolted out of the chair and right in to Dana's face, his back still to Stu. The sudden movement sent a jolt through all of Stu's nervous system, that warm uncomfortable tingle that starts in the chest and goes all the way down, but he didn't jump or move, continuing his slow creep toward the man. Given his position, leaning right in to Dana, Stu wasn't sure how he could shoot the man and not hurt his sister as well.

"Do you suppose you'd talk after that?"

"I know where my brother is," Dana said, a wide grin spreading across her face.

The admission caused the man to stand up.

"You do? Then why in the . . ."

The pistol went off and the bullet clearing the man's head and lodging in the wood pancling of the wall near the window. It was a lucky shot that it didn't break the window, drawing even more attention than a gun going off. The man fell forward, but his smooth angle of descent was interrupted by his legs completely crumpling. From the back, his fall looked like a rubber mannequin had been thrown across the room, and there was nothing graceful or cinematic about the way he fell, or the way he twitched once he had hit the floor. After his face hit the ground, the man was able to turn part way on his side and begin kicking his top leg in a spasmic rhythm. Of course, his eyes were open and Stu immediately flashed back to the kid and the stains on his shirt and the screaming and the look on his face that said "I want to take it back."

Only, this man didn't look like that. There was no emotion in his face, just spasms in his muscles as the brain quit working because Stu had put a bullet where vital matter had once been. While part of Stu's brain flashed back and brought up all the old pain, there was a small part of him that thought "this is not as bad."The blood, the dead eyes, the sick dance . . .it wasn't that bad.

He held on to that, for what seemed like minutes, but in reality was just a second or two. He held on to the man's face not as a horror or a fault in himself but as just a moment, a terrible moment but one that was not part of him but part of his experience. It's a big difference, he would later think.

Plus, the guy was an asshole who had beaten and threatened his sister. So there was that.

While this psychodrama only took a second or so to play out in real time, it didn't take Dana nearly as long to react.

"THAT'S RIGHT!" she yelled. "DIE!"

Stu snapped to attention and gave his sister a quick hug.

"I'm sorry," he said as he grabbed on to her.

"Yeah, but you're a good shot," she said, quickly, stifling a quick sob. "Get me the hell out of here."

One quick snap of a utility knife later and Dana was right behind Stu as they headed toward the back. The gun shot hadn't appeared to draw much attention and no one had come storming in to the Sheriff's Office. The radio on the man's hip was silent, and Stu quickly snagged it, hoping it would come in handy later. Dana grabbed his gun. It struck Stu as lucky, and being lucky has an expiration date.

As they went down the hall toward the back, Dana attempted to grab Stu's right hand and he yelped in pain. Her hand came away bloody and Stu shook it as the pain came rushing in. After a few shakes, blood was dripping from the bandage.

"What'd you do?"

"Cut it escaping the first time," Stu said. "It hurts but it's OK."

"We are going to go out this door and to the left to the abandon tire store, you know the one?"

Stu shook his head as Dana disappeared into the break room for a second and came back with a first aid kit he hadn't known was there.

'Then I'm going to fix that hand and we'll figure out our next move."

"Where the hell . . ."

"You do the cop lookout thing. I'm behind you. Ready?"

" . . .where was it?"

"STU!" Dana said, snapping her fingers. "Head in the game, bud."

He held up the pistol and felt a stream of blood slide down his sleeve to his elbow.

"How are we getting in the abandoned tire shop?"

"Through the front door," Dana said. "Well, there used to be a front door. There's no door there but there are rooms and places to hide."

"OK," Stu said. "Dana for the win."

Luck held a little longer as they made it to the abandoned building and a few minutes later, Stu had a fresh bandage, a grateful sister, and absolutely no idea about what to do next.

•••

Stander had received another call.

This time there was progress to report. They had captured William Rhodes and while the others were in the wind, this result made the operation a rousing success of historic proportion. Hartman Corp had samples of blood and tissue, they had basic physiology, but it had all proved fruitless and frustrating. The goal was to discover what made transformation happen as the possible applications were astounding – tissue regeneration and transformation, instantaneous healing, weaponization. But all the samples they had added up to exactly nothing. Dead tissue went far, but not nearly far enough. They needed a live sample for the work to begin.

And they'd gotten close. There was the live subject who committed suicide in Helsinki, the live subject from Vladivostok who actually made it to the lab before succumbing to alcohol poisoning, the wolf who turned out to be something completely different all together. Then there was Byron Matzen.

It had all happened through deep, back channels through simple pharmaceutical reps. There wasn't a doctor's office in the nation that didn't deal with pharmaceutical reps and those reps were overseen by companies who had members of Hartman Corp. on their boards and in their administrative offices. Their network was vast and so when Mr. Matzen went only one step above the rep who dealt with the small clinic 45 miles East of town, the news made its way up the ranks quickly. The strategy had been to treat this contact, the first of its kind in the storied history of the organization, as a Faberge egg, the slightest sudden movement might send the entire thing shattering into pieces that could not be salvaged.

There were negotiations. Mr. Matzen was one of the "affected" but he would deliver other subjects. He would deliver one subject to them, he would be substantially rewarded and he and his friends and community were to be spared. The company was OK with this. The information had remained proprietary, the terms were generous and if things went wrong they had the firepower to erase this man and everyone he had ever met from the face of the planet.

Then, Byron Matzen was killed.

In the aftermath of this development, two camps within Hartman Corp had fiercely competed for their point of view to win the day. The first wanted to continue to handle things delicately. There were obviously "affected" in this small community that the larger groups of "affected" were unaware of their existence. They were also sure none of their competitors had this information and that none of the other various groups of interest were anywhere near this part of the world. They didn't have to hurry, the argument went. This could be handled.

The other school of thought wanted to go in with guns blazing. Yes, there was time, but that wouldn't last. They would go in with a paramilitary strike team, get the necessary intel and lay waste to anyone who could bear witness. There was no one in the vicinity to stop them (or even notice, as the argument went) so why not? Get the prize and get out.

It was Stander who had bridged the gap and won the position of lead on the operation. His argument had been to combine the two ideas – go in soft then go in hard but most importantly, do it quickly. Two weeks was the window of time, he had argued. The board, desperate for a compromise between warring factions, agreed. And they were on the phone.

"How soon will the subject be ready for transport?" the voice on the other end of the phone asked. It was not "Simmons" as before, but someone different.

"Two hours," Stander said. "I received word that the medical transport vehicle is on the road as we speak. We can't load him into the back of a truck in case there are any incidents during transport."

"Good," the voice said. "They are transporting him to our facility in Kansas City and from there he will be secure. What's the status of the town?"

"Taken care of," Stander said. "As soon as Mr. Rhodes is out of town, we will take care of the witnesses."

"Any word from the others?"

"No, sir."

"Be advised things are happening around you," the voice said.

Stander blinked.

"I'm sorry, I don't understand," he said.

"An outside group is working to block our resources and cut off routes for Mr. Rhodes to leave the area," the voice said. "We don't know who they are but they are quite effective. We are losing resources but all this is happening over 100 miles away. Continue to do your job."

"Yes, sir," Stander said.

"I will call ever hour for progress reports," the voice said. "Answer the phone."

"Yes, sir," Stander said. The line went dead.

The implications were huge – a group attacking the resources of Hartman Corp? That meant they had knowledge of the operations, had engaged in industrial espionage and, most importantly, were highly organized. It's one thing to learn there is an enemy you didn't know existed. It was another to know they were bad asses.

Stander's phone rang again.

"This is Stander," he said.

"This is Dave Rhodes."

It was a red letter day for surprising phone calls, Stander thought.

"Hello, Mr. Rhodes. I'm surprised to hear your voice."

"You have my father."

"I do."

"I would like to talk to you about a trade."

This had, of course, been a possibility the moment William Rhodes crashed his car into Stander's custody. Contingencies had been prepared and Stander knew where to take the conversation.

"What is your offer?" Stander asked.

"I would like to take his place."

"I see. And how do you propose to do that?"

"You will take my father to the corner of Rural Road 11 and the highway, near Beaver Creek. Do you know the place?"

"I do," Stander said.

"Take him there at precisely 3 p.m. I will be watching. Let him go and I will be along."

"So your proposal, as I understand it, is for me to let William go at a time and place you designate and then 'you'll be along?' You'll see how those terms might not be acceptable, Mr. Rhodes."

"You're not understanding me, Stander. That's where we go to . . ."

"Do you're little trick," Stander finished.

"Yes, that's our usual spot. If I'm not there at 3 pm you take Willie and leave. If I'm there, let him transform and head out into the woods. Either way, you'll have one of us to bring back."

"That seems almost too simple."

"Why make it complicated?"

"May I ask you a personal question, Mr. Rhodes?"

Dave caught the condescension in Mr. Stander's voice. He had him.

"Sure."

"Your father is awful, by all accounts. He's rude, churlish, he has hurt you quite a bit from what I hear?"

"Yes."

"And from the research we've done, it seems he's been difficult most of his life. I'm having trouble comprehending why you would change places with him. In fact, part of me thinks you've got something ulterior in mind."

"As to my father, yes, he's an asshole. But if there's someone from this family who has to bare this burden, it's not him. I'm the head of the pack and while I don't expect you to understand what that means within our group, I do expect you to take it as an answer. I'm the leader. End of story."

Dave deliberately waited a beat before moving on.

"As for an ulterior motive, you know about us. Do you think there are any circumstances where, even as wolves, we could make a dent in your security? We turn in to animals, Stander, not soldiers. Worry all you want, bring all the guys you want. This is a simple exchange. You have my word."

If things were going to fall apart, now is where it would happen and Stander took his damn sweet time responding. During that time, Dave tried, consciously, to control his breathing and modulate his voice as to project a heightened sense of calm.

"All right, Mr. Rhodes. You're right, I don't understand your . . .customs nor do I think what you're doing is particularly admirable. If you were to ask me I'd say your father deserves what's coming far more than you do, but at the end of the day I don't care. I'll leave you with this. If I get a sense that anything is amiss, if I feel threatened or if you fail to live up to your part of this exchange in any way, I will see you dead. Is that clear?"

"Yes."

"Good. My clock says 1:15 which gives you a little under two hours to get your ass to Beaver Creek. One minute late and your father goes to the lab minus his tongue."

Stander hung up. It felt good to be the one ending the call, he thought. He immediately got on the radio and called for all available personnel to come to the center of town to discuss the latest development. He didn't think for a second this was a clean exchange and he would have guns on hand and men by his side who know how to pull the trigger.

• • •

"We on?" Kenny asked. "We doin' this?"

"Yep, Dave said. We're doin' this. Let's get everyone together. Right now."

• • •

The sky does something strange when it's starting to get colder, Dilly noticed. The cloud cover hangs a bit different. In the winter, you can definitely see it because even though it might be sunny, the sky seems thicker, the blues less sharp. Now, when it was starting to get colder, the effect wasn't as pronounced but it was starting. The blues weren't the same color they were just a month ago and the trees around them were starting to get bare around the middle, a true sign of fall.

The young man had time to ponder as he and his mom were sitting on their car on a dirt road, nearly 15 miles away from Kenny's shed where he kept his cars. She was doing that thing some moms do when they want to talk – she would start talking about something else hoping to get things rolling and then steer the conversation. He was in a "yup" and "nope" mood, so he stared at the sky.

Finally, Josie came out with it.

"I saw you out there. You're different than your dad."

It was something he had felt, too. Every time Dave had talked to Dilly about being a wolf, it sounded to him what it must feel like to be the Incredible Hulk. He had pictured destructive power and little to no control, but in the two times he had transformed, that's not what he felt. The first time it was all about getting his bearings but when he had challenged Conall and taken off into the woods, it had been a night and day difference. He felt in control, focused and with more of his human brain working than he would have thought.

"I think I could have said something if I tried," Dilly said.

"Like Conall did?"

"Yeah, like Conall. There's more of me in the wolf than I thought there'd be."

Dilly was on the trunk of the car, his mom pacing the five to six steps on front, her arms folded like she was trying to solve a math problem.

"So you think you're more like me?"

"I think so."

"You want to try it out?"

"What?"

"It's not like you can only do it once, kid-o. We're out in the middle of nowhere. Why don't you try it? Transform and see what you can do."

At first, this seemed like a terrible idea for several reasons, one of the big ones being he'd have to get naked in front of his mom, but it didn't take Dilly long to figure out why she was pushing.

"You think I might be able to come with you?"

"Yes."

"To Beaver Creek to . . ."

"Yes."

"And with the . . ."

"Yes, Dilly. I want to see if you can do it. We've got about half an hour to figure this out. Come on already."

Dilly immediately tried to calm his mind a little bit as it was racing. Dad always said never to go out without the pack, that this was a group activity not a solitary thing. Now mom was giving him the opposite advice. It was a lot to process.

"Are you going to turn too?"

"I don't think so," she said. "It's harder for me. It hurts a lot."

"But when we get to Beaver Creek . . ."

"Don't worry about that now. Focus."

Instead of looking at his mother, Dilly turned around and looked back out at the fields and the sky when a thought occurred to him that had never taken root before, a nasty, evil little thought that seized his insides and thrilled him from his brain on down. He was the alpha. There wasn't a person, place or thing in this place that could stop him. His will was law, his whim was edict. He was stronger than his father and his friends and soon he would be stronger than his mother. Dilly shut his eyes and before he even willed it to happen, the transformation started.

"Dilly, your shirt," his mom said, but it was too late. The hair was sprouting, the bones were creaking, the teeth were returning to their rightful place and for the third time, the Young Wolf stretched toward the sky, pulling to the full length of its height and howling in the mid-day sun. The shirt was toast.

This was the second time Josie had seen her son like this and he was all the more impressive in the harsh light of the sun – tall and skinnier and sleeker than the others. She caught her breath and remembered their mission.

"Are you there, Dilly? Can you talk to me?"

The Young Wolf whipped its head around and sniffed hard at the woman. The scent caught in his nostrils and he took a few steps toward her.

"Yaaaaoooooooooessssss," the creature struggled. The words were growly but Dilly's unsure, strong voice was there if you really listened.

"You want to run, don't you?" she asked.

"Yeeessss," he hissed, a little more strongly.

"OK. You see that tree over there?"

She pointed at a tree, the first that led to an outcropping about 400 yards away. It was a solid tree, but not a big one that was the first step into the forest.

"Go take it down," she said. "Destroy it and come back to me."

The Young Wolf gave a snarl, resenting the instruction, but was on his way seconds later, taking giant bounds, leaving deep grooves in the earth, leaping 10 feet, 15 feet at a time. As he closed on the tree, the Young Wolf started thinking strategy. He couldn't just hit the tree with his shoulder as that would hurt him and likely not take the tree down. Instead, as impact became imminent, he pushed hard with his front paws, propelling himself through the air and sending his hind legs straight into one side of the tree's trunk.

The side of the tree exploded on impact with the sharp and hard paw of the wolf, and sent him barreling on his back, hard. He immediately flopped and squirmed to his feet and took another run at the tree, from a shorter distance, with his claws out. The hack and slash of the claws sent saw dust flying and sticking into his coarse, black fur. After a minute or so, he decided it was time to end it.

The Young Wolf took a running start and leapt as high as he could onto the tree, landing 10 feet up near the top of the tree and hearing the satisfying crack and waver that signified structural failure. The tree waved but the wolf pushed his weight against the trunk over and over until it cracked more and started to fall. As the tree gave way, the wolf rode it down, leaping away a second or so before it hit the cold but soft dirt below. He stopped to admire his work for a moment, then took off, panting hard, back to the car and the woman.

Seconds later he was back and he stood, proud, slightly bruised and pulsing with energy and anger. He had destroyed the tree in less far less time than Josie thought he would, if he was able to do it at all.

"THERE!" he yelled. "DONE!"

Even with this creeky nature of the speech and the struggle the Young Wolf had to put out, the annoyance in his voice was clear and for the first time, Josie felt a twinge of fear. She would not be able to transform in time if he decided to lay into her. He needed to be calmed.

"You did great," Josie said. "You're using your brain but you're angry, aren't you?"

"YES!" the creature yelled, the sound louder than before and echoing off the vast space.

"Good!" Josie said, speaking quickly but trying to keep the panic out of her voice. "I need you angry and you'll have your chance."

He started to twitch and move his head in agitation, unable to keep still. In a strange, melancholy moment, Josie recognized the movement in both her son as a child and her husband as a wolf. The Young Wolf reared up to his full height, spread his arms as wide as they would go and let loose with a howl that sent vibrations through the ground and filled the sky with frightened birds. The fear Josie had felt before spread through her body and as she bent her knees and her arms went up to shield herself, her brain went through every time she had scolded him or fought with him. If the current of emotion grabbed him too hard, he could tear the animal in front of him to shreds, mother or not.

The howl ended and echoed. Josie kept her eyes on the wolf's face and was able to see his reaction when he tilted his head downward and saw his cowering mother. The wolf immediately shrank, going down on all fours and changing his expression to one of deference and concern.

"Mom," the wolf said, the voice more like Dilly than ever before. "Mom. It's OK."

To her surprise, the howl had sent Josie into a shaking fit, part from the cold and fatigue but mostly in fear. The situation had turned so quickly her body had reacted and she was shaking almost uncontrollably.

The Young Wolf nuzzled her with his large, shaggy head. The harsh fur, not soft but more like nettles, irritated Josie's skin and helped her grab on to something in her fight through her fear and back in to her thinking self. Reflexively her hand went out to stroke the head of the wolf, and he whimpered, softly at her tough.

"You're so strong," Josie said, feeling the sting of tears on her face but not remembering the act of crying. "How'd you get so strong."

"Strong . . . mom," the wolf said.

The wolf stayed still and the woman stroked its head for a few minutes until they heard the rumble of cars in the distance.

●●●

At some point, Stu got it in his head that he needed to get back to his house and get his phone. He could pretend to be Robocop all he wanted, but it was time to call in the cavalry. Carol Cryer's guest house was about four blocks away, but those blocks were covered with dozens of men with guns. It was unlikely they'd get there, but the alternative was to sit.

"I don't think I can do anything but sit," Dana said. "That fucker busted up my already bad leg. A big girl limping around is probably going to draw some attention."

"I'd prefer you hide," Stu said. "I'm going to take a shot. My odds are better if I'm by myself."

Stu was staring out the hole in the wall that used to be a window, trying to discern any sort of pattern to who was walking by and when. There was no pattern to be found and very little activity to draw from. The radio was another story. Every two minutes or so it crackled to life and provided a lot of information. Being a private enterprise, the lingo they used was not indecipherable, and in their 20 minutes or so sitting in the abandoned tire shop, Stu had learned some things.

There was something important happening at 3 p.m., and it was all hands on deck. With the exception of a few men who were "holding down the fort," everyone would be down by Beaver Creek to provide "operational support." Again, not hard to decipher. There had also been talk of "clearing the town" at the end of the day, which had sent worried looks between the Dietz siblings, especially since Dana had no idea where Robin was. Stu would have liked to think that with a clock ticking toward the death of most everyone in his town, he would have come up with a better plan than "get to a phone." But here they were.

"You've only got about an hour before three," Dana said. "And even if you make it, how do you know your phone will be where you left it?"

"It's not a perfect plan," Stu said. "But maybe there's a phone in Carol's house or something. If I don't try . . ."

"Yeah, I know," Dana finished. "I know this is the best idea we've got but I don't want you to go out there."

Dana did not cry easily, if at all, but the pain cocktail she was on had cracked the code. Tears flowed liberally down her cheeks and dripped onto her T-shirt, leaving dark, temporary stains. Stu went over, careful not to expose his position out the window, and put his hand on her shoulder.

"I'm not going to lie and say 'I'll be fine,' but I will be careful. And strong. And brave, if I can be. You're the only one who believed I was any of those things."

They hugged and Stu couldn't help notice Dana trying to pull the tears back, even now.

"I know you're a tough son of a bitch," she said. "I beat on you for years. Go get 'em."

Making a quick calculation and turning the radio off (he had been holding it to his ear and keeping the volume low), Stu gave his sister one last glance back and headed out.

No one had yet to notice the body in the Sheriff's Department, so the idea was to keep low, use alleys when possible and go slow. With his pulse high and his head pounding from the day's earlier beating, Stu was having a hard time with that last part. He wanted to sprint, wanted to shoot, but both of those things meant torture and death so he concentrated on his breathing and took it as slow as he possibly could.

His first challenge was crossing the main street in town, which was oddly wide given the complete lack of traffic. There was parking on both sides and even a stoplight in the center of town that had blinked yellow as long as Stu had been there. His strategy was to head south to "Bar" which seemed to have little to no activity around it, make the crossover there and head to his guest house apartment. The plan was a solid one and hopping from alley to house proved an effective method. No one was looking out for him and everyone seemed otherwise occupied.

When he got to "Bar" it was empty, but unlocked and, on a whim, he went inside. In a flash of inspiration, he grabbed a bottle of vodka off the shelf and poured it on his hand, something he had seen in a movie once, hoping there would be some disinfectant value. Based on the stinging and throbbing that accompanied the vodka, it was working. He thought briefly of starting a fire to draw attention away, but just as he was pondering it, he heard yelling from the north.

Clicking on his radio, he was instantly met with yelling.

"...*gun and radio are gone. Repeat, man down, the Sheriff and his sister are on the loose and they are armed. They are armed. Everyone proceed with caution.*"

"*Do we need parties to start sweeping buildings?*"

Stu held his breath but heard Stander on the radio next.

"*No parties. Everyone keep an eye out but stick to the plan. Shoot first and shoot often. We don't need them anymore. I expect everyone to be near Beaver Creek in 20 minutes.*"

The radio was filled with chatter of reports from various locations. Stu exhaled deeply, happy that Dana would be somewhat safe if she stayed put. His apartment, on the other hand, might as well have been on the mythical land of Asgaard. Breathing slowly, shutting his eyes for a moment, it came to Stu in a flash—if he could get to his cruiser, he could use the radio to call other law enforcement. This, of course, was what he should have been doing all along but it hadn't occurred to him between the beatings and the werewolves and the town under siege and the werewolves and the tortured sibling and the bleeding hand and the werewolves.

Unfortunately, he had put himself several blocks farther away from his goal than when he started and the town was full of armed men looking for him, so he would have to make another run for it. With the adrenaline flowing and nowhere to direct his energy, Stu started riffling through the contents of "Bar" looking for anything that might be able to help him. He went in the back, thinking there would be knives or maybe another gun (and along with that thought, a brief, John Woo-style fantasy of firing two guns while jumping through the air) when he saw it.

A land line.

Tentatively, as if by providence, Stu walked over to the phone on the wall, picked it up, held it to his ear and heard a dial tone.

"No fucking way," he muttered, and dialed 9-1-1. He knew, by course of being on the job for a few weeks, that the 9-1-1 call center was 26 miles away in another county, as was the nearest ambulance service. It occurred to him as the phone picked up on the other end that he didn't have the slightest idea how to explain the situation.

"911, please state the nature of your emergency".

"OK, this is Sheriff Dietz in Barter County and I'm going to need you to keep an open mind as I tell you what's going on here." Stu was trying to keep his voice steady and slow but everything was coming out fast and warbly.

"OK, Stuart, we're here. Where are you right now?"

Alarm bells went off in Stu's head. He hadn't told them his first name, he sure as hell wasn't on a first name basis with anyone at the emergency management center a county away. Plus, the question didn't seem like any 911 call he'd ever heard, so he decided to play it safe.

"I'm in a house . . .I don't know who it belongs to but there are men in Cherry with guns. Lots of them."

"Can you describe the house," the voice on the other end said. "The color? The street?"

Damn.

"Do me a favor, Stu," the voice on the other end continued. "Don't run."

Stu tossed the phone back into the cradle and moved away from it like it was radioactive. Of course they'd tap the land lines. Cell lines, too.

"But they wouldn't be able to block the law enforcement radio," Stu said to himself, his voice sounding small in the big, empty bar. "Not without raising suspicion."

He decided to set his watch for five minutes, then leave "Bar" just in case there were eyes on the place or they expected him to run screaming into the street. Then he would head back toward the station and (unfortunately) Dana, and he spent that time rummaging around "Bar." He was opening cabinet doors behind the bar when his hand brushed against something long and metal that instantly felt familiar. His hands came back from the doors with a Remington Model 870 pistol grip shotgun.

"Oh, Chuck. I hope you have a permit for this."

Even though he was already armed, the gun's considerable heft gave him a shot of confidence he had been lacking. Who needed a plan when you had this sort of fire power? He rummaged around a bit more and found shells in the cabinet, loaded them and stuffed his pockets with more. After checking his watch (5 minutes 32 seconds), he peeked out the window and everything looked relatively clear. Plus, folks were a lot less likely to pick on a guy with a shotgun.

•••

Stander was on the phone.

"Did you expect to hear from the others?" the voice asked. It was different this time but still prickly and masculine.

"No, we did not."

"And you did nothing to facilitate this?"

"Nothing."

"How do you plan to proceed?"

"I'm going to go ahead with the exchange," Stander said. "If anything unexpected happens we're going to kill them all."

"Except for Mr. Rhodes."

"You will receive a live sample on schedule. I understand the consequences if I don't."

Stander couldn't help but notice how the dynamics had changed. He was used to being threatened and second-guessed. This new person was grasping, trying to grab more information. If he had to guess, things were not going well over at corporate.

"Good, good," the voice said. "And you've received no outside interference? This has been a successful black box operation? No recording equipment, no leaks?"

"We've dealt with the locals, they are all detained and there will be no one to bear witness . . ."

When he thought of it later, Stander wouldn't say he "snapped" at that moment. He simply ran out of patience for going over and over the same set of expectations. The voice had shown signs of weakness. It was time for him to show signs of strength.

" . . . and if I could add some of the personnel I've been provided are substandard. They're not seasoned or trained properly, they're not pre-pared to make any sort of decision and I've had to make an example or two."

The voice didn't respond.

"Despite piss poor staffing and doing all the prep and intelligence work myself, I've managed to get this done. And I'm going to continue until you have your sample and at that point I believe we need to talk about substantial compensation for my contributions up until this point. Am I clear?"

"Yes," the voice said.

"Good. I will be waiting in an hour with an update. Make sure to call on time."

It felt particularly good to be the one to end the conversation and Stander couldn't help let a slight smirk creep on to his face. For the first time since taking this assignment, the idea of shopping Willie around to another company crossed his mind. He batted it away, and then brought it back. He had been treated poorly during this operation, he had been second-guessed at every turn and he was no longer interested in dealing with this bullshit. Maybe he would become indescribably rich, stick it to his company and live out the rest of his life . . .

The rest of that sentence had no finish. He was a company man, a man who was lost without a goal to strive for. He would deliver Willie, he would receive his increased compensation and he would move on to the next thing the company wanted to do. And he'd do it with a smile, know-ing he was the competent one, the reasonable one, the best one.

He put his phone in his pocket and actually struck up a whistle as he strolled around the camp that had been set up around Beaver Creek. There were 22 men, all armed, with hand guns, all semi-well trained and all with eyes on either side of the road, where Dave Rhodes would likely appear in 22 minutes. They had orders to wait until he reached a certain point and then open fire. It didn't matter who they brought in or how they brought them in or, for that matter, who they shot and killed in the process.

He walked the length of his forces, everyone snapping to attention when he walked by. The message had spread—he's in charge and not to be messed with. To a person postures were straight and when anyone spoke it was all business.

Except for one.

"Got 'em whipped, don't ya, asshole?" Willie said through a blood and bile speckled beard, his body tied to a chair in the center of the group.

"God, I can't wait to get out of this place," Stander said with a heavy sigh, the wind catching the leaves of the trees behind him.

• • •

With twenty minutes to go before 3:00, Dave saw no reason to do anything differently.

Step one, you break bread. Even if there was nothing to eat.

"Anybody want a mint?" Dave asked. He usually carried them around after Josie had told him his breath got a little gamey by the time he got home from work. Everyone lined up and took one, more or less understanding the ritual.

"My breath is like a minty meadow," Kenny said. "I'm only taking cause you offered."

"That isn't true and you know it," JoAnn said. It was the first words she'd spoken in a while and of all the moving parts of this particular operation, she was, by far, the squeakiest. "Your breath smells like vinegar most of the time."

"Damn, girl, not nice," Kenny said, twirling the keys to the Mustang. The car was red, though it had been blue originally, and had more metal in it than the storage unit it was taken from. Kenny would drive the 'Stang, Ron in the 'Vette, Carl was driving the Suburban swiped from a neighbor and JoAnn would follow in the Pathfinder taken from "Bar." Dave was on the Harley and Josie was going a different direction.

JoAnn, who was a great bookkeeper and a "hell of a cook," according to her favorite apron, was not much of a driver. And she was nervous about it. Her part in the operation was simple and she could do it, but she had been clinging closer to Kenny than usual and the group had felt her anxiety. It gave Dave an idea.

"Everyone," he said, a bit louder than his normal speaking voice, giving his words some formality. "Come out to the field with me please."

The crunching of shoes and boots on gravel gave way to a softer clunk and squish as they left the road and ventured into the field. The prairie grass had been high this year but was starting to roll back and once they got 40 feet out or so, it was like a different world. There were still bugs, though most had gone back to the hell that spawned them, and there were plants with spikes and bright purple flowers, loose strife prairie flowers and so much more. In the midst of the death that comes with mid-fall the field was still teaming with life.

Dave stopped, and grabbed Josie's hand. She grabbed Dilly and on down the line until the group was in a circle.

"Ashes, ashes, we all fall down," Dave said, and dropped to the earth. Everyone followed, staring at the bright, blue and whispy white of the big Nebraska sky. When someone spoke, the words floated as if on the breeze, not connected to a face or an expression, devoid and free of body language. Dave hadn't planned this, but it couldn't have been more perfect.

"I'm gonna miss you guys," Kenny started.

"Where am I going?" Ron said. There were a few murmurs of agreement.

"Paris or Rome or some shit," Kenny said. "If we get through this, and I think we're gonna, every single one of you is going to shake the dust of Cherry off your sandles. Even if it's just for a little while."

"Things change," Josie said. "Can't change that."

"But this never did," Kenny continued. His voice was slower, more modulated and free of the "like"s and "man"s that peppered most of his conversations. It was a voice he didn't use much outside of the house.

"This was what I could count on. No matter what happened I knew I could depend on all of you. And you could count on me and it felt . . ."

The motormouth's voice cracked.

"Special," Dave finished.

"Yeah, special," Kenny said.

"Things were different before Stander showed up," Dave said. "Things were different because of Byron. And because of me."

Dave tried to feel any shift in the way his wife was holding his hand. She didn't react.

"I thought, for so long, that I made the right call for all of us. I was wrong. The truth is I had two impossible choices to make and I made the one I thought was best."

"Best for us?" Ron said.

"I don't know," Dave said. "I've thought about it and thought about it and there were things I could have done better. Lots of things. But I don't know I'd ever come to a different decision."

"Rock and a hard place," JoAnn said.

"Between a boulder and a boner," Carl said.

"Between a stone and a stiffee," Kenny said.

The laugh started slow and rolled and this time Dave felt Josie's hand squeeze and release as her chest heaved with laughter. He snuck a peek at her as she laughed and remembered how beautiful he still found her. The laughter lasted long and died slow.

"Do you think we're doing the right thing now?" Dilly asked after quiet settled back in. "I mean, we're going to . . ."

"Dilly, I know you're of a tender age, but fuck those guys."

Everyone was a little shocked to hear Carl speak up, much less show any aggression or drop the "f" bomb. But here they were.

"These people came in to our town and want to capture us, detain us, experiment on us, eventually kill us, terrorize everyone in town and take our lives completely away in every sense I can think of. They think we're morons and beneath them because of where we live. They think they can come and destroy a small town and get away with it. I'm sure some of them are only in it for a paycheck and that's their bad luck, but the people they came to Cherry to find the monsters. I say they found 'em."

"Yeah," Dave said.

"YEAH!" Kenny said.

"Fuck yeah!" Dilly yelled, His mother did nothing but squeeze his hand tighter.

"It's almost three o'clock. Everyone ready to do this?"

There was a round of whoops and hollers as everyone stood and started embracing. These weren't timid hugs or the kind of hugs exchanged daily, but the hugs of family who were fired up, an aggressive tenderness if such a thing exists. They were holding on tightly to the only thing that could get them through this. They were grabbing, desperately, to the only thing that could get them home.

When Dave came to Dilly, he already had tears in his eyes. He tried to remember the last time his son had seen him cry and couldn't come up with a time. They grabbed each other, Dilly taller than his father.

"Dad," he whispered. 'I'm going with mom. I'm going to fight."

"I know," Dave said. "You stay safe, son. You are precious to me."

He heard his son gasp for air as the tears racked his chest. They held on a long time and as he kept going, it was clear Josie was going to be last. When he finally got to her, he grabbed the small of her back and pulled upward, popping her back in a way he used to do when they were younger. It was that perfect moment of affection, something no one else can see you do that holds resonance for the person you're doing it to.

"He's coming with," Josie said.

"I know," Dave said.

She was crying, too.

"Your life is in our hands, you know?" she said, half laughing half crying.

"There's nowhere else I'd rather put it."

"We aren't done yet," she whispered into his ear. He felt the hot splash of her tears on his jaw as she leaned up.

"We aren't done yet," he said back. And meant it.

"It's almost 3!" Kenny was yelling "Giddyap!"

As they walked to their cars, Carl caught up with Dave.

"Can I make a phone call?"

"I don't see any reason why not," Dave said. "This is about over, they know we're coming. Doesn't much matter that they know where we are."

"Cool."

Carl swiped, dialed and smiled as he did.

"Hey, Steve," Carl said. "I'd like to request a song. This is a real special case. Any chance I could talk you in to playing it in the next little bit?"

At no point in the history of luck had anyone been this lucky. A gambler hitting on 00 while fucking a cocktail waitress while missing his flight that crashes over the ocean wasn't this lucky.

Stu had managed to make it back down the street from "Bar," check on Dana ("you're doubling back? Are you a genius or an idiot?") and get back in to the Sheriff's Department office where the body had been removed but the keys to his patrol car had not. He had run in to one member of the occupying forces who would have seen him had he not gotten a call over the radio and high tailed it back the way he came. And now, as he gingerly approached the car, parked on a gravel road behind the Sheriff's office, there was no one in sight. Not a soul.

"I am the luckiest son of a bitch . . ." Stu said to himself as he got in the driver's side. Then, as quickly and fiercely as it had arrived, his luck ran out.

The first bit of bad luck was the radio was gone. Whoever had removed it had done a thorough, if rough job by seemingly ripping the entire console out. Wires were hanging and when he started the car, a spark shot from one of side of the gap where the radio had been.

The second bit of bad luck was that whoever had ripped out the radio had also turned the lights and sirens on. Stu should have checked but was caught up in the moment and, to be honest, the feeling of confidence that came with being so lucky for so long. The second he turned the key in the ignition the cherries shot to life and the sirens screamed and everyone in a three mile radius knew exactly what was happening and why.

The third bit of bad luck came when he actually tried to start the car and it didn't turn over. Upon hearing the sirens he shot in to action and tried to start the car, his blood immediately racing faster and his face flushing with embarrassment at being so goddamn stupid.

"Oh hell," Stu said to the sputtering engine. "No, no, no, turn over . . ."

But, luck is fickle and it smiled one more time and did as he asked.

"Yeah!" Stu yelled in the shortest lived triumph of the day as seconds after the engine started, bullets hit the passenger side, shattering the window and making an unmistakable "thunk" against the door. Three men were running toward the car, eager to take responsibility.

Stu laid on the gas, catching gravel and shooting it behind the car as he sputtered to make a fast getaway. The tires caught and he took off but not before losing another window and hearing the whiz of a bullet flying past his head. His plan was to get in the car and use the radio to call for help. His reality was driving a car with sirens going through a town barricaded off from the outside world. In other words, he was going to have to bust through at least one road block to get out.

At least they wouldn't be looking for Dana, he thought.

The whizzing and thunking stopped, at least for the moment, as Stu put distance between himself and the gunmen and barreled down the street toward "Bar". He hadn't grown up around here but he knew enough to know the roads in the direction he was going ended soon and his cruiser was not equipped for off-roading on gravel, so he whipped a hard right and headed toward the first barricade, the one that had caught Willie a few hours earlier.

Stu had seen the barricade, but from a distance, so he wasn't sure what sort of chance he had. At normal speed, would have probably been able to figure out the barrels were likely filled with water and that leaving out Main Street was a nonstarter, but as he rocketed forward, his decisions already blunted by fatigue and pain and fear, he crashed headlong into the barrels, splaying the hood straight up and sending Stu into an air bag, knocking him unconscious.

"That was a swing and a miss," one of the men said, running up on the car and the unconscious law man.

"That is one unlucky dude," a second said.

"Stander wants him down at the encampment. Can the car drive?"

"Block looks in tact," the second man answered. "Car looks fine. Driver, not so much."

The men didn't bother to move Stu from the seat, instead putting the car in neutral and giving it a quick push the two blocks toward Beaver Creek, joking all the way.

The seat of the Harley felt exactly like Dave remembered. He had an "uncle" who had once driven up on a loud motorcycle, hopped off and talked to an 11-year-old Dave extensively about the bike, the experience, the culture.

"Every single person who rides one of these things has a little bit of outlaw in him," the family friend had told him. "It may be way down deep, but it's there. Reasonable people, they drive a car. The troublemakers . . ."

He gestured at the bike and as soon as Dave could drive, he had started begging, begging for a motorcycle. Willie hadn't been a big fan, nor had his mother, but in the end he got a job and bought one himself. Then he started racing them and by the time he had a wife and family, he was a regular at the race track 70 miles to the South. He always relished that ride to and from the race, his mind blank, melding with the machine that was moving him down the road like the little troublemaker he was.

Then, one day, he lost the taste for it. The death of his "biker" self was not gradual. One day, he didn't feel like riding and he didn't feel like fighting Josie over the bike anymore. Kenny gladly took it off his hands and he never looked back and seldom missed it. That is, until he got back on.

"You remember what you're doing?" Kenny said. "I can do it. I won't like it but I know I can do it."

Dave didn't say anything, instead spending his time relishing the moment, the feel of the seat beneath his ass and the stance he had to strike to grab both handles. He put the keys in the ignition and looked toward the road.

"Dilly and Josie?"

"They ought to be about where we need 'em," Kenny said. "You got this?" Fixing a hard stare on the road ahead, Dave didn't move a muscle. He was in front with five cars piloted by five of the most important people in his life sat, engines off, waiting to follow his lead. Behind him, Carl gave a small "whoop" noise and turned the radio way up in the Suburban so everyone could hear.

"We don't usually do this," the DJ was saying, "but I've got a good friend who's about to do something stupid and he's made a request. You all oughtta know this one. Be careful, fellas."

Jason Newstead's full, confident bass filled the speakers as Metallica began their Sisyphussian climb that was "Enter Sandman." No one acknowledged the radio shout out. All eyes were on Dave who was still atop his motorcycle. The bass started driving, Lars started his equally full pedal work and by the time the first, big chord thundered through the speakers of the Suburban courtesy of Kirk Hammett's 1987 ESP KH-2, Dave had fired up the Harley and revved it as loud as it would go. The engine thundered and was followed by the unmuffled roar of the Mustang, the higher but bad ass squeal of the Vet and the other vehicles, all hitting a crescendo in time with the music.

As Metallica began their final run before the chorus, Dave hit the gas having never once looked behind him, trusting in his crew, his boys, his pack and his faith was rewarded with squealing tires and screaming engines. He heard Kenny and Ron scream out the open windows of their cars, a war whoop if there ever was one, but Dave betrayed none of the fire in his guts that were burning intense and violent. The Harley would it for him and James Hetfield singing along wouldn't hurt a goddamn thing.

They rode toward town, in a straight line toward Beaver Creek.

•••

Stander's watch beeped. It was 3:00.

"Not very punctual," Stander said to the man next to him.

"Go fuck yourself!" Willie yelled from his position a few yards back, toward the forest.

The men, all dressed in similar blue paramilitary style uniforms, each carrying assault rifles, waited for an order. Or failing that, a cue. Instead, the man in charge stood, silently watching the road, his radio up to his ear in case any news were to come across, leaving his men to ponder his final instruction.

"If you see anything that resembles a wolf, shoot it until it stops moving."

241

Part of the plan was to be loud. To that end, the operation was a complete success.

Dave led the pack down the Highway, not languishing, but not rushing either. Still, at 45 mph or so, the five vehicles sounded like a natural disaster, some swirling, kicking accident of nature come to fuck up your house and kill your livestock. That's how they sounded. That's how they felt.

The sound was so much it drown out the radios, which were cranked in all the cars (except JoAnne's, who was far too sensible for loud music). Dave didn't hear Hetfield invite everyone to "exit light." It didn't matter if he had. They were coming up on Beaver Creek and everyone needed to focus.

•••

"Here they come."

Stander was annoyed anyway, but particularly annoyed at Willie. If the old man wasn't his ace in the hole, his insurance policy and his ultimate victory, he would have shot the old coot cold between the eyes and shut that stupid mouth of his.

That being said, he had a point.

"What are they doing, sir?" one of his underlings asked.

"I'm not sure," Stander said. "But it doesn't change anything. Follow your orders."

In his brain, Stander was running possibilities as fast as he could. What were they doing? He didn't know and not knowing was starting to put a pit in his stomach. Even though the temperature was in the low 50s, a bead of sweat formed on the man's brow and glistened in the sun.

•••

Josie heard the cars and their deliberate, deafening approach. The young wolf was with her and he was starting to get antsy.

"Nnnnow?" he growled, the drool hanging from one side of his mouth in a thick, viscous rope.

"No," Josie said. "Wait."

The Young Wolf continued to shift and dance, threatening to make noise in what had otherwise been a silent approach.

"Please," Josie said, turning to face him. "Follow me."

"Yes," the Young Wolf said. He crouched, a coiled mass of energy waiting, and was as silent as possible.

"Good boy," Josie said, mainly to herself.

The noise from the engines were getting louder and Josie realized she had overestimated her ability to gauge how far away everyone was. Timing was important. Going too early meant bad things. Going to late meant equally bad things. She needed to use her brain, but her animal brain was screaming for blood, screaming for vengeance. Moments started flashing in her mind of their house burning down, the small kitchen in that house where she had cooked Thanksgiving dinner aflame, the entry way where they had set their son after bringing him home from the hospital, split and blackened. She couldn't take it, whipping around and making contact with the powerful animal behind her.

"Now."

• • •

The first two disappeared quickly, pulled behind the trees. With all eyes on the road and all ears on the radio, no one saw and no one heard, even when the two unfortunate HartmanCorp employees were thrown against a tree trunk and their throats ripped out. The tearing and gurgling were no match for the roar of classic care engines and a bad ass outlaw motorcycle. Not even close.

Two more, lined up against the trees, vanished next. This time one person heard and one person saw. Willie's nose had been twitching but what it told him made no sense – that Dilly was in the woods with someone he didn't recognize. It wasn't that piece of shit Irishman, it was sharper and sweeter. It was someone else, so he kept his eyes sharp and tried to track any movement. He didn't see who pulled the next two guards into the woods, but he saw their bodies snap as if pulled by an invisible string tied to the bumper of a big invisible truck.

Willie wanted to cheer, wanted to cry out, but thought better of it. Instead, he took a quick survey of what was around him even as his nose caught the first strong whiff of blood that was splattering a few feet into the woods. There were a dozen men, all with their fingers on the triggers of some nasty looking, well-oiled and sleek assault rifles. Most of them were in front of him, watching the road but two more were hanging back, facing the same direction. They were also quickly pulled behind the trees and this time Willie saw the Young Wolf, pulling each grown man into the woods with one hand. They locked eyes for a an instant before the creature vanished back into the thicket.

"Damn," Willie said under his breath. "Strong kid."

The engines were now roaring as the convoy was in sight, Dave in front astride his Harley. Six men down, about, 10 or so to go, plus that asshole Stander, all facing the road. This had to be part of the plan.

Pretty quickly, Willie put it together. The Young Wolf was going to snipe as many of the soldiers of fortune as he could, giving his pack a fighting chance.

The old man couldn't have been more wrong.

• • •

"What the hell are they doing, sir?" one of the men asked Stander, who had donned his sunglasses to counteract the harsh glare coming off the road.

"Doesn't matter," Stander said. "You have your orders."

"But they're driving right in to our fire. Doesn't that concern you?"

"Not in the least. Now kindly shut up and do your job."

The man complied, staring at the horizon and the approaching vehicles, right up until he heard the screams behind him.

• • •

244

"Be fast," Josie growled. "Be clean. Guns first, then blood. Do you understand."

"Yes . . .mm.mmom," the Young Wolf growled. The rope of saliva was gone and he was already breathing heavy from the exertion of pulling six men into the forest and helping dispatch them.

"Follow me. Be fast," Josie said again. She needed that part to get through.

She stared at the backs of the men with guns at the ready. She could get to them and take out at least two before they knew what happened. Dilly could probably do the same and then it was six on two with the six armed to the teeth. Fear drove her heart rate up in a weak sort of beat that made her legs feel weak.

Those men, she thought, trying to refocus, broke in to my house. Those men burned my home. Those men shot my father-in-law, which might not be such a bad thing. She grinned, then thought that those men would kill her and her son and everyone she loved if there was money in it. They would destroy her if she stood in the comfort of the woods. They crossed a line and if there was one thing being a wolf meant, it meant being dangerous. Being a wolf had hurt her marriage and hurt her child and brought these men.

Time for her to bring the hurt for once.

• • •

Willie smelled the blood before he saw the wolves burst out of the forest. He had learned to identify some emotions by scent, bloodlust being the most obvious. The smell poured from the woods and when he saw The Young Wolf and his daughter-in-law (THAT was the smell!) burst from the woods at a full run, descending upon throng of rent-a-guns with the force of a demon bent on destroying the world.

The Young Wolf, good to his word, almost split one of the men in half with his right hand, and half punching/half shoving a second man so hard that his neck made a sick, moist crunching sound as cartilage and bone rubbed and snapped in unnatural ways. The men didn't have time to scream, just bleed and fall and die. Josie was almost as lucky, slashing one man's chest as he screamed and fell and punching a second so hard that her fist got stuck in the gory mess that used to be his head.

The scream woke the remaining men (10 down, six or so to go) and Willie got the distinct pleasure of seeing Stander's eyes get big, his face register panic and his constitution totally fail him as he involuntarily vomited while trying to scream. Willie took a second to register the sound and take immense pleasure from it.

A third man on the Young Wolf's side went down quickly after having his arms torn off his body, his screams loud, then quieter as gallons of blood left his body on either side. Dilly was so fast and so strong, faster and stronger than any wolf Willie had ever seen and Willie felt a twinge in his guts as his transformation started. The shooting also started and the Young Wolf held the armless, screaming man in front of him as the five men turned and started shooting in the same direction out of instinct.

Panic is a hell of a thing, Willie thought, as one of the men shot another in the melee, plugging him square in the back of the head causing blood and brain to splatter on the man in front of him. By this time, Josie had retreated, pulled her hand clear of the bloody head from where it had stuck and charged again taking another man down by biting his neck in a pose that might have been two lovers, if not for the screaming and splatter.

The bullets were mainly hitting the center mass of the man without arms, but a few of them hit the Young Wolf in the shoulders, causing him to howl in pain. That howl, coupled with the site of his grandson's wounds was enough to put Willie over the edge and he sprouted and stretched and screamed as the White Wolf pulled free of his bonds and threw the chair he had been on directly at one of the men. The chair hit him square and sent him completely off balance, his gun flying from his hands. The White Wolf began running at the man only to draw the fire of two remaining soldiers.

The shots whizzed by the White Wolf's ear and he felt one hit his shoulder and another penetrate, deeply, into the meat of his left leg before he made his final leap. In the air, he was grazed in the side and hit square in the chest but landed on the man in the uniform and sank his teeth deep into his cranium, biting hard and hearing the cracks of skull and squish of brains. Out of the corner of his eye, the White Wolf saw the Young Wolf tearing the last man apart in a bloody decoupage, blood and shit spraying across the dirt and into the road.

Inspired, the White Wolf tore the soldier's head from his body and threw it toward the Young Wolf who howled, screaming at the sky. The White Wolf joined him in a powerful, tearing roar high pitched enough to rise above the roaring engines but low enough to rattle the dirt beneath their feet in one, unified, powerful message.

DO NOT FUCK WITH US!

•••

Josie had not taken any hits but had seen Dilly's arms and noticed the blood. When Willie broke free and drew all their fire, she had batted clean up, making sure everything else went to plan. Her son hurt but was going to be OK. That was the important part.

Stander had bolted toward the only shelter open to him – Stu's banged up police cruiser with Stu in the backand she thought she had seen one of the men get in as well. They had switched places so Stander wasn't driving when Josie jumped on the roof and started dragging her nails along the ceiling. As expected, gun fire came from inside the car, with Josie rolling out of the way and the car taking off, spitting gravel fishtailing a bit.

Moments later, the convoy blew by and took their positions around the town car.

"All yours," Josie said, smiling to herself.

•••

"What the fuck just happened!" Stander screamed. The man behind the wheel, a muscular, tattooed sort named Antonio, was in just as much shock. The gunshots toward the ceiling were stilling ringing, loud and long and unbroken in Stander's ears. Part of him was in full panic mode

247

while part of his brain was trying, desperately, to process what it was that had happened. He glanced in the rear view mirror, hoping to not see any carnage or a small convoy of country hicks in loud cars bearing down on him.

He saw both.

"What do you want me to do, sir?" Antonio asked.

"Drive, DRIVE" Stander screamed through clenched teeth. "How the FUCK did that happen? Are you all fucking stupid!?"

The cruiser was OK after the earlier crash and the duo were thrown back as Antonio hit the gas, then thrown forward and he slammed the break, missing the back of Carl's Suburban by centimeters.

"Go around him!" Stander yelled, and Antonio jerked the wheel until he heard metal grinding. Kenny was in the Mustang and the Mustang had more metal in it than most newly constructed houses. It wasn't going anywhere and when JoAnn pulled up behind them in the pathfinder, it was obvious they weren't going backward either. The passenger side of the car hovered along the shoulder, veering close to an off road of nothing but dirt, plants and other material unhospitable to the town car.

Through the rolled up windows, both men could hear the roar of the engines and something higher pitched with a distinct melodic quality. Antonio narrowed his eyes.

"Is that a guitar solo?"

"Who gives a fuck?" Stander yelled, throwing all décor out the window as he started rummaging in the back seat for one of the assault rifles. All he found was the semi-conscious body of Sheriff Stuart Dietz.

"Why is he still back here?" Stander asked as the Pathfinder plowed into them from behind. JoAnn was starting to have fun.

"We had no place else to put him, sir," Antonio said, panic clinging to his voice. "We weren't supposed to kill him yet."

"DAMMIT!" Stander yelled. He was down to one guy, one car and no guns and he had lost the upper hand in about a minute and a half. He swung his eyes from window to window, his brain running through every scenario he could think of, every option and tool at his disposal. He could see no way out and could see nothing but the Suburban, the Pathfinder,

248

the Mustang and the shoulder, whizzing by them as the convoy pushed the cruiser faster and faster.

"Sir!" Antonio yelled. "The van is . . .signaling."

Sure enough, the Suburban's left turn signal was blinking a fluorescent red, made all the harsher by proximity.

"He's not going to turn," Stander said, leaning forward in his seat. "What the hell is he doing?"

Slowly, and as if merging politely into traffic, the Suburban started changing lanes but before Antonio or his boss could see an inch of daylight, the motorcycle who was leading the pack roared to take its place. The motorcycle rider didn't turn around, confident in his bearings and in that moment Stander no longer cared about what the hell they were doing. There was sky in front of him and Stander wanted to seize it.

"HIT HIM!"

•••

The switch was as smooth as if they had practiced it. Carl swerved, Dave got in front and the second he heard the cruiser's engine rev, he accelerated, his eyes hard and focused in front of him. He had driven this road literally thousands of times and knew every slight turn, every crack in the pavement.

Every historical marker made of granite and weighing well over a ton and buried deep.

Dave also knew, all too well, that when the sun was starting its descent, it was sometimes hard to see. He had almost hit the damn thing dozens of times. Now his life depended on a stranger making the same mistake.

The granite marker came up fast, faster than Dave had anticipated. The plan was to stay on his wheels as long as he could, but to lay the bike down in the soft Earth off the road if that wasn't possible. Everything happened so fast that Dave immediately knew he'd have to lay the bike down, and slammed on the break for as one of the longest seconds of his life, then turned hard away from the marker. The bike immediately went down, sliding along the Earth that was now decidedly not so soft, and

Dave slide for a few meters before going in to a roll. He spun and spun, his arms up next to his head.

•••

If anyone had a great view of the action, it was Ron. He was the support car and his job was to "play the invariables." If anyone got hurt, his job was to help. If gunfire were needed, he and his revolver riding in the passenger seat (shotgun! Ha!), could handle that as well. As it stood, he saw Dave come up on the marker, saw him lay the bike down and tumble, and saw Stander and crew plow, head long and at a speed of roughly 45 miles an hour, square in to the thing. The car hit the marker on its driver's side, crushing the headlight and hood and sending it spinning across the other lanes. The ditch was a little higher on that part of the road, so when the cruiser spun at high speed into the ditch, the car tipped over on its side. Momentum continued carrying them over on the hood and come to a rest, wheels spinning, engine smoking and a dank smell of oil coming up from the scene.

For the monument's part, the car took a big chunk out of one side. Other than that, it wasn't going anywhere.

Ron checked on Dave first and was surprised to see him already up and walking toward the road. He pulled over along the side.

"You OK?"

"That was . . .a ride," Dave said.

"Bleeding or anything?"

"I'm sure I am somewhere," he said, knowing full well his chest wound from earlier had torn open and was bleeding badly. "Let's move. Nobody's getting away today."

Ron suppressed a smile as he hopped out of his car and followed. The other cars had pulled around by this point and were making their way back to the wreck. On the way, JoAnn drove up and rolled down the window.

"Everyone OK?"

"Yeah," Ron said. "You might as well drive off. You're not going to want to see this."

The windows on all sides of the cruiser had shattered from the impact, and Stander had already exited the car and was crawling, fist over fist, through the wet dirt and grass that had survived the cold of the season. One leg was at a terrible angle, obviously broken and the other seemed fine, but Ron wasn't about to ask why he wasn't using it. Kenny pulled up next, followed by Carl who had the windows down and the radio cranked. That was fine, Ron thought. Covering up the screams was probably a better idea than not. Besides, he had always loved this song, even the creepy kid prayer at the end.

If I die before I wake, I pray the Lord my soul to take . . .

Stander never stopped crawling, even when Dave and Ron and Carl and Kenny made their way down in to the ditch, but crawling is a slow way to move and the men, wearing big smiles and removing their shirts, caught up to him in a few steps. The company man was grunting with exertion and pain, his face caked in blood and dirt. His bow tie was nowhere to be seen.

From inside the car, Stu had awoken with a jolt to find himself in a crunched and leaking car and staring out the window at the naked backs of four men. And hearing Metallica for some reason.

Hush little baby, don't say a word

He felt the presence of the men behind him and even sensed that they had begun to change but the company man on the ground continued to claw big fistfuls of mud in an attempt to pull himself somewhere, anywhere other than where he was. He knew something very bad had happened to his leg, but didn't want to see. Tears came to his eyes, partly from pain and partly because he didn't even want this, didn't want this job or this life. He wasn't a killer, not a bad guy. He had a temper, sure . . .

. . . and never mind that noise you heard

Inside the car, Stu's memories flooded back and while he couldn't yet put two and two together, he remembered the danger, the sneaking around, the torture, his sister and all the rest. He also saw the man in the driver's seat start to mess with his door.

It's just the beasts under your bed . . .

For most of their lives, the pack had to draw on very specific memories in order to transform. That was not the case anymore. There was prey, wounded and supine in front of them, bleeding and desperate. They transformed quickly and without pain.

In your closet, in your head . . .

Stu saw the wolves lunge in one, fluid motion at whatever was on the ground. One of them threw what looked like a body, hard, against a nearby telephone pole while another grabbed the body in its jaws and threw it back toward the car. Then they all descended, mouths open, latching on to arms, legs, shoulders, thighs and any center mass they could find to tear skin away and feast on the blood that gushed forth. Every part of the body was covered in fur and teeth, except the head. Stu was able to see Stander's face as he was torn apart by the wolves, as chunks flew off he was able to make a last, fleeting eye contact with Stu and convey one final message.

It was something Stu had seen once before.

"I want to take this back." That was the understatement of the decade.

A sharp sound drew Stu's attention away from the carnage as Antonio, the driver, was making a break for it, managing to shimmy out through the broken window. The driver was limping, badly but was moving quietly, trying not to draw the attention of the wolves who were currently feasting on their boss.

Stu looked at the door, tried it and saw found that it was undamaged and opened easily. He was even more surprised when he realized a shotgun, which must have belonged to one of Stander's men, was among the debris inside the car.

. . .grain of sand . . .

Testing his tender and sore joints and muscles, Stu rolled onto the pavement, gingerly stood up, aimed his weapon and shot Antonio in the back as he fled. The man went down and a split second later, one of the wolves had left the snarling mass in the ditch and was investigating the noise. The beast, large and lean and savage, poked at the body before grabbing it in its jaws and tossing it, easily 20 feet, to the rest of the pack.

Stu got his first long, full lit look at the wolf. The creature was tall, easily over seven feet, but hunched and ready to leap or run. There was blood across its snout and his claws were covered in viscera, but the eyes were another story. The eyes weren't desperate or murderous.

They were proud. Most likely, it was Dave, Stu thought.

The wolf gave Stu a quick snort and joined the rest in giving Antonio the same treatment they had given Stander just moments before. The "wolf who was probably Dave" gave a loud, long howl as "Enter Sandman" faded into nothing and the wolves took off across the field at a high rate of speed, back toward Beaver Creek. There were two bloody spots in the road, a couple of cars pulled off the Highway, and an overturned cruiser that Stu had no idea how he was going to deal with.

"Hope that went well, fellas," the radio DJ was saying. "Either way, we're back after the break with some Rush and maybe some Van Halen if you're lucky."

•••

The Lead Wolf ran at a full clip toward his mate and his child and found them cradling the White Wolf. He was bleeding badly.

The Thin Wolf slightly whimpered. The Young Wolf, also bleeding, held his grandfather in his wounded arms that were still strong despite being torn up. Josie noted that some of the Young Wolf's bullet hole injuries had already stopped bleeding and were starting to heal.

Josie had been trying to fix this, trying to figure out what to do, but there were so few options and she didn't do her best thinking as a wolf. Every time the problem solving part of her brain would engage, she would smell something or hear something and any serious thought fluttered away. She had tried to transform back, but too much adrenaline was coursing through her. She was stuck, and so was Willie, who let out a yelp of pain every so often.

The Young Wolf looked at his mother.

"Help," he said. "Mmmom, help."

The other wolves started lightly howling as well, trying to speak but unable.

"He needs to change back," Josie said, surprised by the tightness in her

253

chest that was making it hard to speak. "If we changed back, I could get him to a hospital."

At the word "hospital" the White Wolf's eyes shot open and he stretched his neck so he could see who had said the word. Josie ran through the pack to get in his line of sight.

"No," the White Wolf said. He attempted to raise his paw, failing at first then summoning more strength so he could gesture at the ground.

"Here," he said.

His meaning was clear but it caused the Young Wolf to throw his grandfather to the ground and scream.

"NO! NO! NOT HERE! NOT HERE!"

Thrashing, his long limbs pawing at the ground, the Young Wolf clawed and slashed at the air in his grief. The Lead Wolf rose up, just as high as his son, taller than he'd stood in a long time, and roared back at him. The Young Wolf howled but complied and fell to all fours as the rest of the pack gathered around and pressed their noses and bodies to his fur.

"Not here," he said, the "here" trailing into a howl.

His breath starting to rattle, the White Wolf got to his feet. The fall had knocked the air out of him and he was lucky to have gotten it back, but he was on his feet. Josie could see his hind legs drag and his front legs quiver.

He fixed the Young Wolf with a stare and the howling stopped. It was as if exerting some control gave him strength and his legs stopped shaking.

"A wolf dies . . . running," he said. "We die running."

The voice that came out was as much William Rhodes as it was the White Wolf, the growl modulated to a higher timber. It was the voice of a man speaking on his own terms and a wolf being gentle with those he loved. He whispered something else in a different language that the Young Wolf didn't understand but carried with it ancient meaning, a benediction with meaning only to him.

"Taimid bas ag rith."

Without warning, the White Wolf ran in to the woods, stumbling ever step or so but with a speed the pack hadn't seen out of him in years.

He was 20 yards away before they followed, tearing through branches, leaves, spitting dirt and mud behind them. They all caught up and kept pace, the seven of them in almost a line broken only by terrain or tree. They ran until the White Wolf started to fall away. They heard the gurgles of fluid in his breath and the beating of his paws start to slow until they finally heard the thud of his body as it hit the earth.

The pack kept running, at a trot. The Young Wolf started the howl, followed by Josie, then the Thin Wolf, the Straight Wolf, the Large Wolf and finally the Lead Wolf howled and ran sending a cloud of sound past the tree line and into the sky. They howled because they were no longer what they had been. They howled for loss and for the change and for the blood they had to shed. But mostly, they howled out of pain. It all hurt and howling was the only thing that made any sense.

They ran until they collapsed, exhausted, by a stream where they stopped howling and turned into humans once again.

THE LAST WILL AND TESTAMENT OF WILLIAM RHODES
CREATED AND CO-SIGNED JANUARY *11, 2011*

I, William James Rhodes, presiding at 104 Rural Route 118, Cherry, Nebraska, declare this to be my Will and I revoke any and all wills and codicils I previously made.

Article 1 – Burial
I couldn't care less. Bury me in a pine box or leave me to rot. Don't give a shit.

Article 2 – Distribution of assets
Lacy gets the house and the car and all that. She can give what she wants to anyone she wants except for my asshole brother. I leave him sole possession of my diddly squat and he's lucky he's getting that.

Signed and notarized.

Part 10 – Son of a Bitch

The people of Cherry were pretty accommodating, considering their town had been taken over and by men with guns.

Phrases like "something like this was bound to happen" or "we knew you boys would handle it" or even the odd "well, that's all over with now," were bandied about the usual gathering places. Chuck had run interference with a lot of his regular customers at "Bar" and possibly spun a tall tale or two in the process. Not that the actual story wasn't exciting enough.

"All those bodies, they had been ripped apart and their guts laid end to end to spell "Stay Out," Chuck had told Stu over a hamburger lunch. "I swear that's what I heard."

This was the fullest and most complete sentence Stu had ever heard Chuck utter, and he smiled.

"I don't doubt it for a second," Stu said. "I'm sure a drone or something picked up the message."

"Damn right it did," Chuck said. "Those things are everywhere."

In reality, Stu had limped back to Dana, gotten her and Robin home safe and then slept for a good 12 hours in their guest room, waking only to receive medical attention from Robin. Diligent, tender Robin with a great bedside manner and the kind of eyes that would make a man work hard to get better. Of course, she was not interested in him "that way," nor he in her (not really, as the consequences would be more than several humans could handle), but it had been a long time since he had any sort of female companionship in his life and he was starting to feel it. Plus the whole "fearing for your life, surviving torture and being pushed hard enough to shoot a man in the back" thing really made him wish he had someone to share the experience with.

But, for now, all he had was Chuck and the hamburger. It would have to do.

"The drones, they can be tiny. They can be in your car and you wouldn't know it," Chuck was droning on. "They know everything you're doing and if you don't believe that, you're an idiot."

"I don't know," Stu said between mouthfuls. "I still think there are places where you can keep a low profile if you want to."

He got three-fourths of the way through his burger before Dave walked in and saddled up next to him.

"Got time for a beer, Sheriff?"

"I'm on the clock, but meet me after? Six-ish work for you?"

"If it's OK with the bartender."

Chuck gave them a look and walked back to the kitchen without saying a word.

"Six o'clock, then," Dave said.

Stu pulled himself off his bar stool with a grunt. It had been two weeks since the torture and car wreck and other car wreck and he was beginning to think the soreness was going to stick around forever like an unwanted cousin sleeping on your couch.

"I won't have any trouble staying busy till then," Stu said and it was the truth. He had made the decision, with the blessing of his sister and his sister's beautiful partner, to pretend the last week had never happened, to clean up as much as he could and to go around to the community and talk with everyone he could to make sure things were cool. But not using the word "cool." The phrase he had come up with was "are you OK after the recent nastiness last week" and go from there.

So far, everyone he had spoken to had been "OK" and everyone had an opinion on why the town had been overrun, ranging from "it was the government coming for our guns" to "it was the United Nations coming from our guns" to "wanna see my guns?" Stu would have felt terror at the future of his country had each person not been friendly, hearty and understanding. No one threatened to use said guns and no one seemed overly afraid of something as monumental as a siege happening again. No one blamed the Rhodes and their friends.

One conversation in particular had stuck with him. Sidney Layton, who lived next to Kenny's repair shop, had seen Stu coming and waved him off.

"I don't need you stopping by," he said. "I heard all about it, you sneaking around, trying to get help. You did good. Don't worry about it."

Stu slowed his approach but he still wanted to talk a bit and Sidney let him up on the porch of his shabby home. The older man threw himself on an old rocking chair that creaked and shifted under his weight but held.

"I'm making sure everyone is OK after last week," Stu said, going in to his stump speech.

"Got roughed up a bit," Sidney said. "So I'm not asking questions about where everyone went. Figured I'd find some bodies if I went looking for 'em. I ain't looking."

"That's good," Stu said. "I want you to know we're working to make sure nothing like this ever happens again."

"Save it. If it happens, it happens."

"Even if . . ." Stu said, asking a leading question.

"Kenny Kirk once drove six miles in a blizzard to come save my ass when I got stuck. Ron, he set up the wifi in the house. Didn't charge me. That smaller fella, he mows the lawn at the church. Nobody asked him to. He just does it plus he gives me a big bag of cucumbers every August. He heard somewhere I like cucumbers and I do. Love em. Put them in a bowl with vinegar, water and a pinch of sugar and it's the one snack by doctor says I can still eat."

A chilly wind blew across the porch. October had given way to November and November in Nebraska means the slight nip in the air turns serious. Sidney rubbed his arms.

"Truth is when you're in the middle of nowhere you don't get to pick your neighbors. But that doesn't make them any less your neighbors."

With that, Sidney stood up and walked back in to the house without saying another word. Stu still had a couple dozen houses left to visit at that point, but he had a feeling Sidney had summed it up. Something also felt a little dirty about hearing it said out loud. Of course no one was going to run to the press or the government or the United Nations or whoever because sometime, someday soon, they would need their neighbor's help.

Stu saved the hardest conversation for last, which was why he was in "Bar" eating a so so hamburger. Dave walked in around five minutes late with a backpack slung over his shoulder and sat next to Stu at the bar.

"Sheriff," he said.

"You want another pitcher of beer?" Stu asked.

"No, not today. But we can definitely head to that booth in the back."

Chuck made a slight guttural sound to express his disapproval as Stu grabbed his plate and headed to the other end of the building. Dave plopped down and ran his fingers through his facial hair, which he had started growing out since Willie's death.

"We probably need to get some things straight."

"OK. Shoot."

"Well, if I were a pessimist, here's how I would sum up last week. I would think that local law enforcement knew a secret about me and my family and that I had no assurances that he would be keeping that secret. I'd also think that he saw, first hand, a lot of death and violence that we might have been responsible for. And, if I were a real pessimist, I would worry that he would blame me, personally, for the takeover of his town and all the pain and suffering that it brought."

Stu finished up his fries and Dave laid it out.

"Good thing I'm not a pessimist."

The heavy glass plate made a loud noise as Stu shoved it aside and put his elbows on the table, meeting Dave's gaze. Eye contact had never been his strong suit but Stu held this time. He felt it was important.

"I've spent the last couple weeks talking to people about what happened. A lot of people have vouched for you."

"That's good."

"I don't know if you know how I ended up here, but something very bad happened to me where I used to work."

"I heard about that."

"I had a real rough go of things and got a lot of advice but there was only one thing that anybody said that helped me out. A therapist told me that being in pain and constantly feeling like shit was a good thing. He said it was proof that I cared about the people I had hurt and if I cared about the people I had hurt, I couldn't be a bad person. Bad people hurt others and don't care or don't even remember it. Good people care."

"I think that's right," Dave said.

"I don't know you or your folks very well, but I've heard from a lot of people that you care."

"Again, that's good."

"I also heard why folks think this happened and it goes back to those first two murders. Those assholes coming to town, shutting everything down, kidnapping and beating people, all of that, nobody blames you for that and I guess I don't either. But one of your own killing some local girl and then you guys taking the law into your own hands? You can see where that might be a problem moving forward."

"Sure."

"Plus those two killings put you on Stander's radar, didn't it? Even if people don't blame you, it's not a huge leap."

"Not a huge leap at all."

"So you can see my problem."

"Yes, I can."

Stu kept unbroken eye contact while Dave got a stupid grin on his face.

"Something funny?" Stu asked.

"I'm just sitting here thinking," Dave said. "I'm thinking of all the guys like me who have sat across the table from guys like you. How this is such a complicated thing but it's been done, dozens of times for hundreds of years. I've never had to have this conversation and you've never had to have this conversation but what we're doing, it ain't new. Not even a little."

Dave reached into his backpack and pulled out a worn, leather bound book, the pages dry and flaky. It hit the table with a light thud and Dave started opening pages.

"I found this when we were going through Willie's things. It's a history of sorts. I never knew it existed until a few days ago and I've been reading over it."

As he watched the pages flip, Stu could see a variety of different handwritings on the yellow pages, all of which were incomprehensible upside down.

"Sometimes there were bribes involved. Sometimes, and it says this here, the police were 'bound by the constraints of polite society.' That's an A+ phrase, right there. Sometimes the local law enforcement were relatives, sometimes there were some other type of quid pro quo . . ."

"What are you getting at?" Stu said.

"Nobody ever threatened anyone," Dave said. "I've looked and looked and at no point has anyone like me said 'keep this secret or we'll hurt you.' Never. And this book goes back a ways."

"Were you thinking of threatening me?"

"No, I wasn't, but I think there's a bigger point here. I think what this means is our thing and . . .your thing, it can coexist in this place. I don't think that's true everywhere but in Cherry, I don't know. It works."

"It just works?"

"I think so."

Stu let his brain wander for a second to what would have happened in Detroit or Minneapolis or Sterling or Tallahassee or Burbank if one of their law enforcement had set upon a seven-foot-tall wolf creature. Someone would have been there with a camera phone or a dash cam. Someone would have uploaded a video and it would have broken the Internet. Someone would have made a meme about werewolves and it would have turned into a joke before the actual event could be processed.

Here, it just worked.

"Of course," Dave continued, "you came to us at a rough time. This book shows that there have been other times when we had to police ourselves, so to speak. What we're dealing with is not uncommon, but we have to worry about things my ancestors never had to. I would love to give you my word that our town is safe and you won't have to worry about us anymore, but it's looking less and less likely that I can do that."

"Then let me police things for you," Stu said, moderately shocked that the words had come out of his mouth. "If I'm your neighbor than that's not a half way thing. If you need help, even with your werewolf whatever-the-hell-you-call-yourselves problems, come to me. Or at least keep me in the loop."

The stupid grin returned to Dave's face.

"I can give you my word on that, Sheriff."

Stu smiled too.

"Thank you, citizen."

They left with a handshake and a promise to have Robin cook for the lot of them sometime in the spring. Dave said he had somewhere to be and beat it after a few more minutes of bullshitting and Stu was on the way out before Chuck gave him a quick whistle.

"Sheriff," Chuck said. "You didn't pay for your burger."

"Sorry, sorry," Stu said, fishing out his wallet.

"I'm not running a charity, here,"

"Of course not," Stu said, smiling before adding one more word.

"Neighbor."

•••

Dilly had taken his grandfather's death hard. Josie could tell because it lit a fire under his ass.

He had never been a lazy kid but after "the incident" (a term that the group had once used to describe what happened to Byron and now used for the occupation of the town), he started working around the clock as if he were going to war. They were homeless, of course, and had no worldly possessions to their name, so the first 48 hours were spent gathering up donations from neighbors and getting the basics in place. Willie's place was now vacant and even though it was the last place they wanted to stay, given the circumstances, it was by far the most convenient.

After a day or two's worth of grieving and depression that came with having committed several murders and losing your grandfather, Josie found her son up early one morning doing reps on a set of dumbbells that had either been donated or abandoned by Willie.

"Hitting the weights a little early?" she had asked.

"It's the only time I have," he said. "I've got school, practice and then the other practice with dad later."

"You guys are going out?"

"I told him we need to. All of us. We need to get back to doing it for ourselves, you know?"

Josie did know. Since "the incident" things had changed significantly for her, as well. Her transformations had once been excruciating and traumatizing; now she was mildly looking forward to the next one. There was also a sense, growing every day in her mind, that Dilly was something special in the wolf world and she wanted to explore that and work with him but had decided at this point not to press the issue too hard.

"If you want, we can go out together without dragging everyone else in to it."

"I'll talk to dad and let you know," he said between grunts as he started a set of arm curls. "But that sounds good."

"I'm stronger than them, you know," he said just as Josie was leaving the room.

"I know. They know it too. But it doesn't mean you get to stop listening to them," she replied, dead serious, and was met with grunts and the clanking of metal.

Willie's death had the same impact on Dave, but in a different way. He was motivated but it was out of anger, not preparation, youthful drive, hormones or whatever else Dilly was on. Dave had lost the chance to reconcile with his father and that meant short fuses and cold shoulders. It also meant they had yet to really discuss what came next. They had never needed to have a discussion more but they kept putting it off.

Dave was spending a lot of time over at Willie's house going through his mountains of stuff and when he found the unmarked diary detailing the history of wolves in Cherry, he immersed himself in it. He would spend long nights at the kitchen table making notes, trying to figure out who had made particular entries, what codes meant and going over every line like it was some sort of code. They hadn't gone to sleep at the same time since the night Willie died, where they had held each other tightly in the guest bedroom, both wracked with equal parts gratitude and depression. Since that night it had spent most of his time at the table and on phone calls he didn't want Josie to know he was having.

It was Dave who eventually came to her, two weeks or so into their stay at casa de Willie, as Josie was getting ready for bed.

"I've been going over this book."

"Yes you have."

"Know what I haven't found?"

She put down her book and rolled on her side to face him.

"What?"

"Anything like you."

"What are you talking about?"

Dave stepped inside the door frame and sat on the bed.

"It's stupid, but I always figured Kenny's mom and Ron's mom and all these families who do what we do, I always figured they were male wolves and female wolves, right? I mean, my mom, I knew she could change but Willie never let her run with us and she died so suddenly I never got to talk to her about it."

"Right."

"And when you started to change after Dilly was born, I figured that's how it worked. I remember asking Willie once and he told me that's how it worked and I took it for granted. But I've been over this book twice and I think I understand what I'm reading and there's no mention of female wolves in there. None at all."

"That kind of makes sense," Josie said. "Women weren't always equal, right? Maybe they were just omitted."

"I thought that too, but look . . ."

He crossed over and carefully opened the book. Even with ginger handling, a few pieces of the old pages broke off the edges as he sat.

"There's a census in here, a list of all our people starting all the way back in pioneer days, like the 1860s or so. Apparently when a man took a wife and started a family, sometimes the male heirs would be able to make the transformation and others wouldn't. They would mark it, here . . ."

He leaned forward and pointed at the one piece of scribbled writing.

" . . .that symbol, see it? That means they could make the transformation. Even if they didn't do it very often, they got the mark. There's one section . . ."

Dave flipped through the pages, concentrating hard.

" . . .here. Some of us who could make the transformation moved away and they had to make a promise they'd never transform again. There's a whole section on it, the oath they had to take and everything. But they still got the mark next to their name."

"And no women ever had that mark?"

"None."

Josie was suddenly very aware of her heartbeat. Willie was the only one who had access to this information and hadn't shared it with his pack. It's anyone's guess if he wanted the information out at all. The fact that he had been trying to keep this from her for unclear purposes sent waves of anxiety crashing in her mind.

"So I did something," Dave said.

"What did you do?"

"I called Connall."

Conall had not contacted anyone in the group since driving away with a busted leg, but his presence had been felt. There had been strange text messages that had come to all their phones from unknown numbers offering vague words of encouragement. One read "Thanks for handling things on your end" and another "Way to kick ass, green horns". Two days before, a cryptic message reading "whenever you're ready, there's a whole world out here" was delivered, and everyone was waiting for Dave to call a meeting and discuss how to respond.

"Is he still pissed about the leg?"

"He's still pissed about a lot of things," Dave said.

"Don't attack my kid."

"No argument here, but I went ahead and asked him about female wolves. Turns out, you're special."

"Really?"

"Really special," Dave said. "So special Conall said he needs to see us, in Ireland as soon as we can get there. He doesn't want to put pressure on us, which is why he's kept his distance, but he wants you, me and Dilly on a plane."

"We don't have a house. How are we going to afford plane tickets to Ireland?"

"He and his group are paying."

"OK."

"He's willing to pay for more than just a plane trip. He said he'll 'set us up' somewhere. If we want, we can pick somewhere else to live and Conall and his group will set us up with housing, cars, jobs. Whatever we want."

"Really?"

"Yeah."

"Does that offer stand for everyone?"

"I didn't ask."

"Why can't he 'set us up' here?"

"Because he said this place is compromised. The company that sent Stander and all of them, they know we're here and so do other groups."

"What other groups?"

"He didn't specify, but he said there are other groups that would want to track us down and he didn't know how well he'd be able to protect us if we stay."

For the first half of her life, Josie couldn't wait to get out of Cherry, out of the State, maybe further. Her parents had once told her they didn't care where she lived as long as it was close to an airport and she had big dreams of living abroad, getting to know exotic locales intimately and finding a man from outside her culture. These were dreams she'd often revisited, particularly in her youth. Then Dave and Dilly kept her in Cherry and while her fantasies never left, she accepted that they were fantasies and would never be reality.

But around the time she hit her early 30s, her mood started to shift. She loved her job. She loved her family. Her situation was unique and while she hated driving 30 miles for basics like food, her roots were deep and set. Every time she visited a city, the crowds and traffic drove her nuts and slowly but surely, the worldly woman she had envisioned had turned into the comfortable Nebraskan she had become.

Byron had been her last shot at the fantasy, the attractive, charismatic man who could whisk her away to different places and different experiences, at least, that's what he had promised. Part of her had wanted that so intensely she considered leaving her child and abandoning her husband to torture and death to attain it. But in the end she hadn't. She had said "yes" to running away with Byron and changed her mind almost immediately. He didn't take the rejection well, as most charismatic people don't. Later she learned he was already in over his head and if she had gone with him, it would have come with a cost that would have consumed her.

She took a second to look at Dave. He was a little fat, a little homely and while he was often in a good mood, the heat he gave off would never be enough for her. She would never want him. She loved who he was but would never love him. But Dave had come up with the plan to stop Stander, Dave had pulled it off, Dave had stepped up and while he was never going to be a good leader, he might be the guy who could lead everyone well enough to get the job done.

Maybe that was close enough to love for the time being.

"Let's go to Ireland," she said. "But tell him we're all coming. We'll hear what he has to say and then come back to Cherry."

"That's what I was thinking."

"Good. Tell him."

"What about us," Dave said. "What about you and me?"

"We'll come back to Cherry," Josie said. "We'll figure it out."

Dave left the room and in a flash, Josie followed, spun him around, wrapped her arms around him and kissed him. Her mouth opened to Dave's surprise and their tongues touched, then came into full contact as the kisses got deeper. They made love in the guest room of Willie's house, the future uncertain but for a few moments feeling like they were home with each other.

A long time ago, Dave loved his job. Before last week, he sort of tolerated it, a victim of routine. After Willie's death going to work seemed like a completely necessary and wholly honorable waste of his time. The kids annoyed him more, the paperwork drove him nuts and he couldn't keep some of the images from the siege – the dead bodies, the gore in his living room, the smell of gun powder and radiator fluid and blood from flooding his nostrils.

It was those memories that led Dave to keep his phone in his pocket instead of his desk, just in case something went wrong and he needed to leave. He didn't have to wait long. During third period on his third day back, the phone rang and the number had one or two too many numbers in it. He was in the middle of class so it went to voicemail, but the same number called again and again and again until he finally excused himself and stepped into the hall.

"Conall?" he said, taking a very educated guess.

"So I was in my ceremonial robes, I hate the ceremonial attire. It's green and uncomfortable and itches like hell. So I'm talking to the Council, right, in the main hall and all these arsholes are staring at me . . ."

"I'm kind of busy right now."

"Teaching? You're blowing me off for your job? Fuck you, man."

"Just . . ." Dave floundered around, trying to not make things worse. "Move it along, man."

"Right," Conall said. "Wouldn't want to get you in trouble with your boss. You might rip his throat out and have a good gargle with his O negative."

"Conall . . ."

"Right, so I'm in these hideous green felt robe that's got some sort of significance and the council calls me forward and you know what I do?"

"Does it involve the 'F' word?" Dave asked.

"Strangely, yes, but not the one you think. I fart really loud, just lay it all out there. Kaboom, you know. Everyone starts making a stink, as it were, and even those thick green robes can't hide the smell.

Dave pictured a huge, Catholic style cathedral complete with the smell of smoke and oil and thick tapestries hanging from the balcony of the hall. The juxtaposition of the setting and the action made a smile tug at the edges of his mouth.

"Why did you do that?"

"The call of nature, as it were."

"What'd they say?" Dave asked.

"The leader was all 'for God's sake, boy, show some decorum.'"

They both chuckled, Conall's laugh still full of brogue. Dave was happy for the break and to hear from his friend.

"They've got the wrong guy if decorum is what they're looking for," Dave said.

"Fuckin' a. You know why I was there? Talking to the Council?"

"I'm guessing it was about us."

"Two for two, sort of," Conall said. "I was there talking to them about your wife."

For a moment, Dave flashed back to the previous night where Josie had been all over him, her hands constantly moving and grasping as if he was about to disappear.

"What about her?"

"Well, you know that little trick she can do? The one where she grows hair all over her body and totally kicks my ass? That one?"

"Yeah," Dave said. "She's pretty special."

"I'm not sure you realize just how special," Conall said. "I'm pretty plugged in over her and I've only heard whispers of women that can do what your Josie can do and I had never seen it with my own eyes until she kicked my ass and busted my leg."

Putting two and two together, Dave's heart started to race.

"So you went to talk to The Council?"

"I went to talk to The Council."

"And what did they say?"

"Dave, my friend," Conall said. "I'd like to tell you about the legend of the Alpha Prime."

ACKNOWLEDGMENTS

First and foremost, thank you to Talos Press, particularly my wonderful editor Alexandra Hess who has to be sick of me saying "more blood on the cover" by now and yet, continues to work with me. It's a genuine pleasure and I hope we can do it again. I also want to thank my agent Steve Schwartz of Sarah Jane Freymann Literary for the consistent guidance, good council and saving myself from my own worst instincts on several fronts in several instances.

I also want to sincerely thank everyone who got as excited as I did about this book including Chad Plambeck, Steph Romanski, Katie Robinson, George Ayoub and crew and so many others who have made this project a delight. Finally, Sarah, Emaline and Tessa, the loves of my life, may none of this reflect poorly on you.